Weeks in May

A Novel

I G Cummings

Prologue

"Come out, Shonda. It's time!" Jo Ann shouted. "Aunt Tiffany wants to say goodbye."

Jo Ann Davis stood in the driveway of her red brick, two-story home in northwest Houston on a cul-de-sac amidst small trees and similar houses with well-tended shrubs and manicured lawns. Warm April sun accented a cloudless blue sky. Jo Ann's son, Tony, and his wife, Kristin, put bags into their white Chevy Suburban for the drive home to Denver. They'd spent three days catching up with Tony's high school football teammates and other friends and celebrating Jo Ann's birthday.

Shonda bounded out the front door. She wore a green velvet sweat suit and pulled her red roller bag, "I'm ready!" she shouted. "Where's Aunt Tiffany?" At age five, her brown eyes sparkled and she exuded energy.

"I'm here," Tiffany Boyd replied. She walked from her green, mid-sized Mazda she'd parked on the street. "I couldn't miss seeing off my Shonda." Tiffany wasn't Shonda's aunt, but she was part of Jo Ann's circle – four black Houston area women connected by dreams, shared experiences, and social media.

"Hey, Miss Tiffany," Tony said. He closed the Suburban's back door. "Thanks for stopping by before we left."

Tony walked around the car and leaned on the hood. Tiffany said, "I have what you said you'd sign."

"Oh, yeah," he replied. He took the paper from her and pulled a pen from his shirt pocket. "Gotta make your quota, right?" Jo Ann heard him and wondered what those words meant. Tony, at 27, was Jo Ann's oldest child. He shared her dark skin and flat nose. He shaved his head now. His body differed little from his high school and college linebacker days

-- broad shoulders, narrow waist, and powerful legs toned by running and weightlifting. He carried 225 pounds easily on his six-feet, two-inches frame.

His scribbling done, Tony looked over his shoulder at his mother, then gave Tiffany the paper. "Yeah, Shonda," he said, "we're visiting your other 'MawMaw' on the way home. Know where she lives?"

"W-Wi-Wic—"

"Wichita," chimed in Kristin, from the front seat. She and Tony met at New Mexico State University and married after dating eight months. Shonda arrived 11 months later. "Your other grandmother lives in Wichita. We'll see her tonight. Now get in the car, so your daddy can buckle you in."

"Wait," Tony said, putting Shonda's bag in the back seat. "We forgot something. What did we forget, Shonda?"

Jo Ann backpedaled and stopped at her front door. She knew what they'd forgotten.

Kristin, who wore her jet-black hair tightly braided, got out of the car. Tony came around to her side and stood between Tiffany and Shonda. He looked at his mother, who leaned against the front door. He frowned before grasping hands with Shonda and Tiffany, whose skin tone matched Tony's. Everyone in the circle bowed their head.

When they finished, Tony helped Shonda into the car, waved at his mother, walked around to the driver's side, opened the door, buckled himself in, and backed out of the driveway. Jo Ann knew her boycott of the prayer cost her goodbye hugs from Tony's family.

As the car disappeared, Tiffany approached Jo Ann. "Nice they came for your birthday."

"It was. I adore Shonda. Regina and Melissa may not have children. They're caught up in careers. Doctors say Kristin shouldn't have any more. Shonda may be it for me for grandchildren."

"You never know. The Lord works in mysterious ways."

Jo Ann scratched beneath her left ear. "What was Tony signing?"

"Just something from church."

Jo Ann didn't ask more, but she had a bad feeling about whatever it was.

Part 1
TWO WEEKS IN MAY

Chapter 1

In the night club, Jo Ann nursed a glass of wine. An old school rhythm and blues band finished Al Green's "Let's Stay Together" and took a break. Her date stood up and said, "I'm going to the restroom."

Soon Jo Ann shifted in her chair and wondered where he was. She noticed him standing at a table across the room, carrying on an animated conversation with two women. His fingers snaked their way up one woman's arm. The firm grasp of the other's hand produced a smile that said he was enjoying himself.

Jo Ann long ago tired of black men's wandering ways. She hated thinking of it in racial terms, but she only dated black men, and so many behaved that way, that's how she saw it.

She'd had high hopes for Frank Wilson, a tall, brown skinned, medium-build man with short hair and a round face. A 48-year-old bank lawyer, he claimed he worked all the time and went out sparingly. She saw through that story after he put her off or stood her up three times.

"Who were you talking to?" Jo Ann asked when he returned. "You said you didn't know anybody here."

Wilson sat down and crossed his arms over his chest. For a second, he said nothing. He seemed flustered by Jo Ann's directness. Finally, he stammered, "I don't, baby. I was just being friendly."

Jo Ann sneered. "That wasn't being friendly. You were hitting on those two."

Wilson flinched and swallowed. "I just said hello."

"Your hands were all over them," she replied. "At least have enough class not to hit on somebody else – two somebody else's, in fact – when you're out with me."

Now, he spoke sharply. "We're not a thing. I can be friendly with anybody I damn well please. You don't own me --"

Jo Ann held up her hand and gritted her teeth. "You were going to call me a bitch, weren't you? That's what men like you call any woman who dares call out their low-life behavior."

He cracked the knuckles on his large hands. "Quit acting a fool, Jo Ann."

"I'm tired of being made a fool." She shook her fist. "I need a man who at least pretends he respects me. That was insulting."

"I've had –"

"Take me home. You're not staying over. I'm not seeing you anymore." Her eyes went cold, and she glared at him.

He sat up. "Fine. I don't need this. I don't care if you are a big-time corporate executive with a six-figure salary. I didn't do anything except talk to a few folks here at the place."

Her voice rising, Jo Ann said, "You did more than that. And you've told me lie after lie about where you were, like the time you claimed you were playing tennis with your buddies, but my girlfriends saw you with some woman at a sports bar."

He put down his drink. "The woman at the sports bar was an old school friend."

"Why lie about it?"

"My tennis match was later that day."

Inside, Jo Ann felt dirty being near Frank Wilson. "Once upon a time I would've put up with your shit," she told him. "Not now. I'm done with you."

∞ ∞ ∞

The next day, Jo Ann and her friend Betty Martin ate dinner at an Italian place near Betty's house in southwest Houston. The setting sun provided a comforting backdrop as they sat on the restaurant patio. The roar of nearby freeway traffic blended with the clatter of plates and the hum of casual conversation.

"Did you go out with Frank last night?" Betty asked toward the end of the meal. "You've been seeing him for two months now? Must be something to it." A thin, brown-skinned woman of 50, Betty's bright eyes and ready smile hid the pain of family life troubled by a wayward son who kept getting into trouble.

Jo Ann wore a blue top with long sleeves and white slacks. She put down her fork and leaned forward. "I'm done with him."

Betty jerked her head back. "What?"

Jo Ann looked more intently at her friend. "He's like the other black men I've dated. If it has tits and indoor plumbing, he gets on its tail."

"What'd he do?"

Jo Ann tugged at her left ear and wrinkled her nose. "He hit on two women at a table across from us on his way back from the restroom. It was blatant."

"You couldn't hear him, could you?"

"No, but I saw." Jo Ann pushed up her sleeves. "It wasn't the first thing he's done that showed me what he's like. Kendra and Tiffany saw him with some woman when he'd told me he was playing tennis with friends. He got phone calls he'd hang up on when he realized I was listening. It was as bad as with James."

"James was bad." Betty said, chuckling at the mention of Jo Ann's ex-husband. "I'd just met you. You'd call and tell me about his philandering."

Jo Ann pressed her lips together. "I'm not doing that again."

Betty sighed. "There must be a good brother out there somewhere. I found one."

"Charles is a good man. You've been great for each other."

Betty nodded. "Our marriage has been good," she acknowledged, but shifted the conversation back to Jo Ann's latest love life fiasco. "What're you gonna do now that this one's over?"

"Hope the next guy is different, that he wants something real, that he wants more than adding to his conquest list."

Betty leaned closer. In a low voice, she said, "You have friends."

"I do. I'll hang out with you and Kendra and Tiffany." Jo Ann stopped and grinned. "My vibrator will get more work. That's the one thing I'll miss about Frank. He may be a no good s.o.b. but he can use his dick. It's long and thick. He must be on Viagra or something. I think he could stay hard that four hours they talk about in the commercials."

Betty giggled and dropped her lips. Jo Ann sometimes said things like that, having fun at her friend's expense. Betty was kind and compassionate, but her prudish streak set her up for embarrassment when Jo Ann flaunted her own, more open attitudes about sex. "I don't need it as much as you," Betty said. "Once every few weeks is enough."

Jo Ann frowned. "I need more than that, but I'm not staying with a shit just so I can get laid."

"You'll find someone." She stopped for a moment and scratched her cheek. "Maybe not where you expect him, but you'll find him."

"I hope so. I'm tired, tired, tired of being alone. Did I

mention I'm tired of being alone?"

"You did." Betty picked up the check.

Jo Ann reached for it. "Let me get that. I cried on your shoulder. At least I can buy dinner."

Betty wouldn't let the check go. "You reminded me how good my life is compared with what it could be. Buying dinner is a small price for knowing how good I have it."

∞∞∞

When Robert Hart woke up, he felt lost. He rubbed his eyes. Red numbers on the end table clock said 8:33 p.m. As he ran his hands through his brown hair and noticed the contrast between his tanned arms and the pale of his wrist where he wore his watch, Robert realized the big screen television across the room was on.

Fifth inning said the corner box. Didn't the game just start?

Robert stretched his arms. He blinked. "The Astros are playing the Mets," he said aloud. "It's eight thirty. I fell asleep." He stood up, walked to the window, and looked into the darkness of the warm May evening.

When he turned from the window, Robert moved to the desk in the corner, and reached for the land line phone. He had a Smartphone with all the bells and whistles. There wasn't much it couldn't do. Neither the youngsters at work nor his adult children outdid him on technology. He kept the land line, though, because of the feeling of familiarity it gave him.

After four rings, he heard the familiar voice say, "This is Terry. Leave a message. I'll call you back." Robert thought about calling Jon Weinstein, one of his few guy friends who was single, but remembered he was busy with a client meeting.

As he put down the phone, Robert heard the flap of the

utility room dog door being pushed open. Moments later, Rufus, his nine-year old golden lab, ambled into the family room. Rufus stood just inside the doorway that led from the kitchen. He wore his feed me expression.

"It's coming," Robert said, starting toward the cabinet where he kept the dog food. "It's you and me again, big guy. We watch the game together."

Rufus whimpered and turned his head upward, emphasizing that eating meant more than baseball. Robert retrieved the food, filled the dog's bowl, and watched him eat for a few moments before going back into the family room and sitting down.

Tonight felt like eight years ago, right after Darla died. Watch a game for a short while, fall asleep, wake up after a couple of hours, the television blaring, go to bed when the game ended, lie awake for an hour, play around on the computer until 2:30 a.m. or so, crawl back into bed, and fall into fitful sleep until seven o'clock.

Being single in the couples world Robert and Darla inhabited made things hard. At first, friends like Joyce and Terry Peters and Harry and Jeri Morris regularly invited him over for dinner, card games, or watching television. Their hospitality helped but couldn't continue indefinitely. Robert felt himself wearing out his welcome, even if they insisted he wasn't. Soon he spent most nights at home with Rufus.

Two years after Darla died, things started getting better. Still, every once in a while, the restless nights returned. Friends offered advice he resisted or only sort of took. A doctor prescribed sleeping pills. Robert, fearful of getting hooked, balked at taking them, but briefly relented. They worked for a while but left him feeling hollowed out. He stopped taking them.

Good friends, after what they called the "decent interlude" of two years, suggested he work at getting laid. Even now, with

Darla gone eight years, Robert had problems with pursuing another woman. Her memory burned so brightly he couldn't think about sharing a bed, much less his life, with someone else. Here he was again, watching a baseball game with Rufus curled up beside him, wondering if he again must endure sleepless nights, drowsy days, and the blah feelings that went with being alone.

When the game ended, Robert turned off the television and invited Rufus outside for his evening romp around the yard. The dog comfortably in for the night, Robert headed for bed, knowing that in the wee hours he'd likely end up at his computer, surfing internet sport sites.

Chapter 2

Robert arrived at his JAX Oil Company office assuming he had the place to himself. It was 4:35 p.m. Friday, May 24. It appeared everyone had cleared out for the Memorial Day weekend.

As he walked down the eighth-floor executive suite hallway, he heard a muffled voice. He couldn't make out the words, but he sensed distress. He heard a phone receiver slammed into its cradle, then sobs. The sounds came from Jo Ann Davis's office.

Robert barely knew her. Her job involved data gathering and other research. When he needed a fact or figure, he sought her help. They'd attended a few meetings together and smiled at each other in the hall.

The door ajar, he looked into her office. He saw a black woman with dark, medium length hair and a small scar on her chin. She appeared upset, working at holding back tears and not succeeding. Her chair faced sideways. Robert noticed mascara streaks on her face. She turned and shifted her reddened eyes in his direction.

"I'm sorry, Jo Ann. I didn't mean to intrude. I just .."

"Robert! I should have closed the door before I took that call."

He studied her. He saw round, brown eyes, long lashes, thick eyebrows, a flat nose, and full lips. She wore a green and blue scarf over a tan sweater top. A blue suit jacket hung in the corner. "Is everything all right?"

"I could claim I'm fine," she said, as she looked up at him. "But you can tell that'd be a lie. I'm sorry. Can I help you with something?"

"I was headed for my office and heard you. I felt I should look in and see if you were okay. I heard someone in pain."

She forced a smile. "You got that right."

"I'm intruding here," Robert said and backed away.

"I wish you'd stay. Being alone isn't what I need right now. Sit down. Let's talk for a few minutes."

She motioned him to a chair in the corner. He sat down, hands clasped between his legs. He wore dress khaki slacks and a blue polo shirt.

"I heard you sobbing," he said. "You seem like a strong person. You wouldn't be crying in your office unless something was wrong. If you're up for telling me about it, I'll listen."

"That's very kind. I'm not sure I want to talk about it. But I'd like to talk with you. I'd like knowing who you are."

He tilted his head sideways. "What can I tell you?"

"Whatever you'd like."

"I'm 63 years old. I retired from JeVon Oil last year after 39 years in the industry. When I retired, my old friend, David Marks, asked me if I'd work for him. I said no. He begged. We finally agreed on this consulting arrangement."

She squeezed her eyes shut. "I didn't know all that. I looked around one day, and you were here."

"I work on strategic planning, people management, things of that nature. I set my schedule. They pay me well."

With parted lips, she asked, "Do you have a family?"

Robert took a long, slow breath. "Three children – two sons and a daughter. My wife died eight years ago. The kids are grown, so I live alone except for Rufus, my nine-year old golden lab. And no, I don't have a girlfriend." He wasn't sure where the last line came from.

Jo Ann sat up. "How tall are you?"

"The years have cut me down. I'm 6-7, but in college I was 6-9. And yes, I played basketball, at Drury, a small college in Springfield, Missouri."

"That's always the next question, isn't it?"

He leaned on the armrest of his chair and propped his chin on his fist. "I expect it."

Her sniffling had stopped. "Where did you grow up?"

"Suburban Kansas City. I was a 6-6 high school center who was too small for major college basketball. I picked Drury partly because of its church affiliation. Before starting college, I grew three inches. Coaches at schools like Missouri and Iowa State who'd ignored me, started calling. I told them they could go to hell."

"Were you good in college?"

A satisfied smile spread across his face. "I made small-college All-America twice. My junior year we lost by three points in the finals of the national tournament. I was tournament MVP, but not winning that championship still galls me. My senior year, two of our other top players got hurt. We lost in the semi-finals."

"Did you have a chance at the pros?"

He answered in a quiet voice. "At only 200 pounds, I couldn't play center in the NBA. I didn't have the outside shot for playing forward when I got out of college. I've wondered what might have happened if I'd played in Europe a few years like guys do now. Could I have developed that? I don't know."

"So what did you do?"

"MBA at Harvard."

"I got one too, finally. Nothing so elegant as Harvard. Night school at the University of Houston."

"Don't knock it. It seems you do your job well."

"Thank you. Being appreciated is nice. Tell me about your wife."

He took a deep breath. "We met at Gulf Oil, my first job after school. She worked in marketing, like most women in big corporations did then. We got married three years later and stayed married 28 years, until she died. She was kind, smart, and dedicated to the kids and to me."

Jo Ann leaned forward. He thought her calm now. "Your kids?"

Before responding, he looked around her office, noticing pictures of her with children at sporting events. "We had two boys, Bill and Al, and a daughter, Sandra. The boys attended Stanford, then got MBAs from other, different schools. They work for big companies. Sandy graduated from Central Missouri State."

"Grandchildren?"

"Bill and Marcia have a four-year-old daughter."

"Where do they live?"

"Cleveland. Al and Deena in Memphis. Sandy stayed in Florida, after she divorced her husband who grew up there."

"I have a granddaughter too," Jo Ann said, looking out the window, before turning back toward Robert. "She's five and delightful. Her name is Shonda, my son's child. They live in Denver." Robert felt her pause and wondered why she turned the conversation as she did next. "Let me ask you, why no girlfriend? I can't fathom such a handsome gentleman wanting for female company."

He grinned. "Thanks. I still can't imagine being with anybody but Darla."

Jo Ann's eyes widened, and she shook her head. "I get that,

but eight years is a long time."

"Seems like it, sometimes. Other times it seems like yesterday."

"Do you still grieve her?"

"I guess I do."

"It's great you had her in your life. It doesn't happen for everyone."

"I guess not. But wait," he added after a pause. "Why are we talking about me? You were the one crying."

Her face lightened. "I was crying because I'm so lonely. The woman who called works in accounting. I've tried cultivating a friendship with her, expanding my circle. We planned a Fourth of July trip to San Diego. She backed out. She's going to Las Vegas with other people."

"Sounds like she's just rude, mean as my older son's wife would say."

"And as my youngest daughter would say," Jo Ann added with a chuckle.

"She wouldn't be much of a friend," Robert continued. "How long was the trip planned?"

"Two months."

"I take it you weren't invited on her trip?"

"I wasn't."

Robert turned calm and made a rare, impulsive suggestion. "I doubt you feel like working anymore. What I came in for can wait. We could have a drink, maybe eat something at one of the places nearby. You can tell me about yourself. I'll buy."

"Deal," Jo Ann replied. She stood up and retrieved her jacket from the coat tree in the corner.

∞ ∞ ∞

At Daisy's Grill they ordered drinks and dinner. Robert raised a delicate issue. "I shouldn't ask but, how old are you?"

She sipped red wine. "I'm not offended. I turned 51 April 11."

"I would've guessed 43. Your face and skin are so smooth and healthy looking. No wrinkles."

"I'm lucky on the face and skin. I am 10 pounds too heavy."

He lifted his glass. "Me thinks the lady dost protest too much."

She grinned. "Point taken."

Once the food arrived, Robert asked, "Why did your co-worker back out of the trip?"

Jo Ann kept her hands under the table, considering her response, he thought. "Do you want the diplomatic, politically correct answer, or my gut feeling?"

"I'll take either, or both."

"Because of these few minutes we've had talking, for some reason, I think I can tell you what I really think without you going nuts. It's because when she got the chance to take a trip with people she was more comfortable with, white people I'm sure, she took it."

Robert squinted and wrinkled his nose. "I'm curious why you believe you can say what you think without my going nut's, as you put it?"

She sighed. "I don't know that. Maybe, it's because you reached out to me when you heard me crying. Maybe, I just see you as kind and understanding."

"You have good instincts. I don't know enough to say one way or the other. I don't know the woman. Much of what I know about you I've learned in the last hour. Maybe it was about color and maybe it wasn't."

He studied her again. The mascara streaks cured by a

touch-up in the restroom, she had regained the soft, easy appearance he remembered from attending meetings with her. Her curled, jet-black hair framed a thin face, punctuated by inviting eyes. Robert hadn't thought much about what made a black woman attractive but, in those moments, he understood he knew it when he saw it.

He thought it best if he changed the subject. "I still want to know more about you."

"You know how old I am. I grew up in New Orleans as Jo Ann Jackson. I did well in high school. That got me out of the projects and a scholarship at Southern University, an HBCU in Baton Rouge –"

"HBCU?"

"Historically Black College or University."

Robert's face lightened and he sat up straighter, startled by memories of rebounds and hook shots. "We squeaked by them in the national tournament. They were small and quick, with no big man. Good shooters. I had 31 points and 13 or 14 rebounds."

She offered a smirk, then a bemused smile. "Do you remember that, or are you making it up so you can impress me?"

"I remember most of my games, especially the losses."

"Anyway," she continued, lifting a fork of grilled salmon, "I got a math degree from Southern. I moved to Houston and worked for Texaco. I met a *Houston Post* sportswriter named James Davis. We dated for a year and married. We had three kids. I discovered he was cheating on me. I left him. I've been single since.

"I got an MBA at UH. JAX hired me I've been there 11 years. I made assistant vice president after three years. I became Vice President for Data Services two years ago."

"How long were you married?"

"Fourteen years. I married when I was 22. I worked at Texaco for two years and Texas Commerce Bank for two. We started having the kids. After the second one, I stayed home."

His jaw dropped and his eyes widened. "You stayed home and lived on a sportswriter's salary?"

"While I was working, I saved everything I made. Raising my kids at home in their early years was important. I did without a lot, but it was worth it."

He remembered the office photos. "Tell me about them."

"Tony, the one who has my granddaughter, is 27. He played football at New Mexico State and graduated with honors. He got a master's degree in public health from the University of Colorado and works as a hospital administrator in Denver."

"That was him in the football uniform in the pictures in your office?"

"Yes."

"Handsome young man. The others?"

"Melissa is 25. She ran track at Kansas. She almost made the 2012 Olympic team. She now spends summers in Europe, earning a decent living as a hurdler and sprinter. She needs 20 hours for her degree. She promised she'll finish when she's done with track, but it remains her dream. I won't stand in the way."

He sucked in a quick breath, "Two top notch athletes in the family. Do they get their genes from you?"

"I'm an okay athlete, nothing special. I can play a little tennis. Their dad was an outstanding baseball player."

"How about your other child?"

"Regina is 23. Despite how good her siblings were at sports; she never gave a hoot about any game. She finished high school a year early, graduated magna cum laude from Austin College in Sherman, and went to law school at Texas. She made law review and is clerking for a federal appellate judge in North Carolina."

"Wow!"

Jo Ann clenched her jaw. "Are you surprised a black single mother could raise such accomplished children?"

"I'm surprised any parent could raise such accomplished children."

She slumped in her chair. "Fair enough. I shouldn't have made it about race."

"I haven't walked in your shoes," he said. "A single woman of any color who's done what you have should be proud. Hell, the wife of a Wall Street financier should be proud of all that."

She gave him a small nod. "I appreciate that. I wouldn't have mentioned race if people didn't assume that because I'm black I must be a deadbeat and my kids are thugs."

They talked through the meal, dessert, and after-dinner drinks. He told her how much he liked sports and the outdoors and disliked long-winded banquet speakers. She told him she loved watching football, attending track meets and the outdoors. She said how much she disliked long-winded banquet speakers.

They finished the evening with a handshake and a promise they'd talk again. As they left, Robert began plotting how he could make that happen soon.

Chapter 3

J o Ann awakened Saturday craving waffles. She decided she'd skip her morning workout and spend the day indulging herself without her friends. Things that consumed the three women she hung out with sometimes exasperated her. Today, she couldn't stomach hearing about Betty's kid and his drug problems, Tiffany's battles with the white boys at work, or Kendra's man troubles.

As she moved around her bedroom, Jo Ann noticed her naked body in the full-length mirror on the wall. At five-feet, ten-inches, she was taller than many women. She was heavier than she wanted, though not 10 pounds. Robert had been right about that. There were attractive things about her body, like slim, muscular legs, toned arms, and C cup breasts she fitted into a pale blue bra that matched lace front hipster panties.

As she dressed a question bubbled up. How would she feel about Robert Hart fondling and nibbling at her breasts? She smiled at her answer. She'd love every minute of it!

Fantasizing about Robert that morning and the possibility of his hands roaming her body made Jo Ann reflect on who she was and where her life stood at 51. The last few years had been good, and they'd been miserable.

The good came from what she'd accomplished

professionally and the progress of her children. As she'd told Robert, her kids excelled, and she took great pride in them.

She found Tony's religiosity overbearing at times but, Jo Ann thought, maybe she should cut him some slack. So far, he hadn't hurt anybody. She relished her warm feelings for Shonda. Tony gave her a great gift in that little girl. Thinking about Shonda made Jo Ann sing inside.

As much happiness as her education, her job, and her children brought Jo Ann, loneliness darkened her life. The frustration that went with being a professionally successful, middle-aged black woman who couldn't find a man grated on her. The things in which she took so much pride got in the way when it came to men.

Some black men called her *stuck up* and *snotty* when she talked about her work and her children. A few months ago, one said, "I guess you ain't got time for a brother like me from the streets with all your schooling and hanging out with the white boys in that oil company you work for."

Jo Ann sometimes felt like giving up hope of finding either real love or true friendship with a man. She had little in common with the poorly educated, professionally inept men she attracted. Accomplished men like Frank Wilson offered love and companionship to too many others.

Over time, Jo Ann convinced herself she shouldn't settle. She wouldn't take whoever came along just for having someone she could go out with and quench her ample sexual thirst. Having given the children so much, she needed nurturing herself. It wasn't happening and the resulting sadness now ruled her life.

Was Robert Hart her answer? She sure liked how he talked, what he said, even the sound of his voice. His insight into things made her wonder what unpeeling the layers of his mind and heart would reveal. Something drew her to him, something that made her crave being around him.

He was white. How much did that matter? Maybe a lot, maybe not much. As she got ready for her day of self-indulgence, she recognized the fact that if Robert was the answer, she'd face a decision about whether she'd let color stand in the way.

∞∞∞

After putting on jeans and a KU track t-shirt, Jo Ann headed for her favorite breakfast place, the cozy Toast 'N Jam near the office. She adored the earth-toned wall coverings, paintings of forest scenes, and subdued lighting. The host seated her in a booth near the back where she lingered over her waffle and the newspaper.

On her way out, she noticed a flyer posted on the community bulletin board that said,

COME CELEBRATE LOVING DAY.

JUNE 12. HERMANN PARK PAVILLION

– The Coalition for Intercultural Families.

Jo Ann didn't know what "Loving Day" was, but the name "Loving" triggered something she knew she'd heard about. She fished her phone from her bag as she walked toward her late model Lexus. Regina's sleepy voice answered after three rings.

"Mom? It's a holiday weekend. I was asleep."

"You can sleep after you answer a question for me."

"Okay. What?"

"Have you ever heard of Loving Day?"

"Loving Day?"

"Yes, Loving Day. I saw a flyer where I had just had breakfast. It said, 'Come Celebrate Loving Day June 12.' It was sponsored by a group called The Coalition for Intercultural

Families."

"I imagine it's about *Loving v. Virginia*, the 1967 U.S. Supreme Court case that invalidated laws against interracial marriage. I read it in law school."

Jo Ann stood at her car, scanning the parking lot and absorbing the still-fresh morning air. "Did you talk about it when you came home after your first year, when you told us about all the cases you'd read?"

"I might have. I did a lot of that. It got on everyone's nerves. Why do you ask?"

Regina wouldn't believe a story about a "friend" inquiring about mixed marriages. She would immediately suspect her mother of at least contemplating an interracial romance. Jo Ann decided she'd tell no lies but leave out some things.

"It was the flyer. I wondered about the connection between Loving Day and a group called The Coalition for Intercultural Families, that and wondering where I might have heard the name."

Regina still sounded sleepy, but less irritated. "I think that's what it's about."

"Baby, go back to sleep." Jo Ann hung up, unsure if her daughter bought her story.

Chapter 4

J o Ann's phone rang at 8:30 a.m. on Sunday. This time she recognized the number. "Robert! Good morning. Don't tell me something's come up. I'm looking forward to some baseball today."

"Nothing like that," he said, cheer punctuating his voice. "Games usually start at 1:10 p.m. Sundays. They moved today's to 3:05 p.m. for national television. I didn't mention that last night. How about lunch before the game?"

"Where?"

"Southwest Grill on Texas is near the stadium. We could meet there."

"I went there with friends once after a game. I'll meet you there at one-thirty."

"That's perfect. Now I can take my time after church. See you then."

Jo Ann hung up with a new concern, Robert's comment about church. Hadn't he said he attended college where he did because of the school's church affiliation? Were race and religion issues with this man?

Thinking about religion distracted Jo Ann as she sipped tea and nibbled on fresh fruit. She didn't like thinking about religion, but maybe he wasn't overbearing about it.

Jo Ann finally told herself she should wait and see if Robert's church going created a problem. She resumed scrolling through internet material about "Loving Day."

Robert arrived at Southwest Grill and waited for Jo Ann. He asked himself: Why am I doing this? I preferred being with her over others I could have asked, he thought.

The possibilities Robert saw terrified and thrilled him. Terror flowed from the idea of getting involved with somebody new after all these years and a black woman at that! Thrill flowed from the idea of getting involved with somebody new for the first time in forever and with a black woman at that! Since Darla died he'd resisted thinking about or pursuing other women. The sleepless nights reminded him of how much he missed her.

The sense of a void hadn't left. For all he knew, it never would. He still missed Darla's smile, her mischievousness, her gentle-at-times, ferocious-at-times lovemaking. He found ways of enjoying life, like pursing his hobbies, attending games, playing sports, and helping children, particularly Sandy, who'd had a tough time during and after her divorce. Something about Jo Ann told him those things were no longer enough. Maybe life held more for him.

Robert felt clueless about the race part. He grew up in the Midwest, separated from the ugly racism of the Old South. He played basketball with and against black guys in high school and college and got along well with them. Those friendships, though, remained superficial. Professionally, he worked around a few black people but, a career as an upper level oil company executive meant interacting mostly with white people.

Darla counted black women among her friends, but they never socialized with black couples. Robert didn't know much about black people or how race worked in America. Caution lights and red flags suggested stopping, but he also saw a "go" sign.

Jo Ann walked in, oozing a beguiling, calm maturity. Her smooth skin and brown eyes reminded him of a stunning black woman from college. Jo Ann's ample breasts made her athletic figure more enticing.

Robert thought about greeting her with a kiss, but resisted. Instead, they lingered over the handshake. The hostess seated them, which broke the tension. "You look lovely today," Robert allowed as they settled into their seats.

"Thank you. I guess you've never seen me out of uniform — power business suits or dresses, with pantyhose."

"Your ball game attire wears well," he said. She wore pressed khaki slacks, topped by an orange Astros team polo shirt and less makeup than Friday when tears streaked her mascara. Again, he found himself intrigued by her dark skin.

They ordered and the food arrived. For a while, chit chat overruled the desire Robert had for talking about things he'd turned over in his head since Friday. When he bit into his cheeseburger, he decided he'd chance it. "I wondered if you were curious about why I asked you to the game. You must know I could've asked one of my guy friends."

"That crossed my mind," she said, looking intently at him. "I figured it might mean you wanted some time with me. I wanted some time with you. I'll get the 300-pound gorilla out of the corner of the room. You and I see something in each other. I understood that when I woke up thinking about you the last two mornings. You must have seen it since you asked me to today's game.

"Let's see what happens. The good thing about being our age is that the need for hurrying has gone. I'm not seeing anybody. You're not seeing anybody. Let's figure out how we feel about seeing each other. If it doesn't work, what have we lost?"

Robert threw up his left hand and opened his palm. "I'm amazed. I was thinking the same thing."

She reached over and touched his arm. "I hoped you'd say that."

"Maybe I shouldn't ask this, but have you been out with a white guy before?"

She shook her head. "No. My girlfriends, the three I spend the most time with, can't stand the idea. In trying to broaden my circle, generally, I started cultivating friendships with white women like the one who backed out of the trip. Going out with white guys is new for me."

"Since you're here, I assume you see nothing wrong with giving it a try?"

"That's right." She paused. "Given that you haven't dated at all since your wife died, I guess you haven't gone out with black women?"

"I haven't."

"We'll have an adventure. It starts with watching baseball." They stood up and Jo Ann grabbed his arm as they left the restaurant.

∞∞∞

When the game ended, neither wanted to call it a day. Jo Ann suggested a postgame drink at Home Plate Bar & Grill across from the stadium. They bought drinks at the bar and found a booth in the back.

"I wonder," she asked over the chatter in the room, "why you haven't been with anybody since Darla died? Eight years is a long time."

He sipped beer from a mug. "It is," he said. Glasses clanged and the wait staff scurried around. "I was afraid."

She stared at him intently. "Of what?"

"Getting hurt."

"That you'd meet somebody, start caring for her, and she'd die? That seems far-fetched. If you'd been through a divorce, I could see that."

He wrapped his hands around his beer mug. Cold seeped into his fingers. "Darla's illness and death freaked me out. I thought I was invincible, bulletproof. Hell, I had been. Nothing bad ever happened to me. School, basketball, all of it came easily. I got my first job offer after two interviews. I always got promoted on time or ahead of time. I started getting offers from other companies after three years in my first job.

"Other parents complained about their kids getting into trouble or being difficult but, except for Sandy's ordinary academic performance, ours were flawless. We had a great marriage. Then, all of a sudden, Darla gets sick, and she's gone. Getting back on the bike is hard. I have no idea of what I should expect. Would another woman tolerate the fact I still think about Darla every day?"

"I wouldn't expect you'd forget her. You were with her 30 years and loved her all that time, right?"

"Yes."

She reached across the table and squeezed his hand. "I wouldn't forget."

He shook his head and closed his eyes. "Until this weekend, talking with women was hard for me outside business. I felt like I was a teenager again, afraid I'd say something dumb. I was always unsure of what I should say about Darla. Would that make a woman crazy?"

Jo Ann propped her elbow on the table and rested her head in her right hand. "I get that."

After a moment, he continued. "We talk effortlessly. When

I told you about Darla, you didn't bat an eye.   Something happened inside that made me think it was okay if I let myself explore."

"Were you afraid of talking with me?"

With his eyes still closed, he nodded.   "That's what was different. The fear went away."

"Even with a woman of color?"

"That didn't matter. What I felt was more important, and better than anything I'd felt in ages."

She reached across the table and slid her fingers up his arm. "I told you I woke up thinking about you both Saturday morning and this morning. That hasn't happened in a long, long time. You made me feel like I was a real person, like you cared what I said."

"Is that why you said yes to going to the baseball game?"

Jo Ann leaned forward. "That and your eyes. I love them. And it's not just that they're blue. Remember, I've never been with a blue-eyed man before. I see strength in your eyes, something that says you're real."

He moved to her side of the table. They grasped hands and enjoyed the warmth of their thighs touching. He walked her to her car and gave her a peck on the cheek before she got in. She lingered a moment, as if hoping he'd give her a real kiss, but he left things as they were. She rolled down her window and waved as she drove off into the warm May night. He walked the three blocks to his car with a spring in his step he hadn't had since before Darla got sick.

Chapter 5

A t home after her day with Robert, Jo Ann made tea and read some of *The Glass Castle*, the next weekend's book club selection. She found the story of a young girl's impoverished childhood interesting, but tonight it didn't hold her attention. She put the book down and headed for her computer.

She checked her e-mail. Monday, she'd have to respond to Kendra's frantic messages. Ignoring Tiffany any longer wouldn't work either. She thought about calling Betty, since she wouldn't require a play-by-play account of the weekend. Other needs, however, came first.

Jo Ann wanted a long, leisurely bath, not a shower. That meant using the upstairs bathroom. While she ran the water, as hot as she could stand it, she surveyed the photos of her children and granddaughter on the hallway walls. The pictures told the story of Tony's football years, Melissa's track career, and Regina's spelling bees and school plays, and Shonda's infancy.

The bathwater drawn, Jo Ann stripped and again stopped before a mirror so she could look at her body. She'd never been vain about her figure. She worked out for the health benefits and her own enjoyment. Now, two days in a row, she'd lingered over her naked body and wondered how it might strike others. No, she wondered how it would strike one person.

After 30 minutes in the tub, Jo Ann headed downstairs, brushed her teeth, and crawled into bed. She couldn't sleep. She tossed and turned for an hour before giving in. She got up and pulled her vibrator from the chest in the corner.

After the divorce, Jo Ann took the advice of a friend and learned about masturbating. The friend died of cancer a few years later, after teaching Jo Ann she could experience strong, satisfying orgasms by herself. Tonight, she used a vibrator with a rubber, bulb-like ball that massaged and stimulated the area around her clitoris. It had three settings, so she could ramp up the intensity in stages. As she worked the vibrating bulb just above her clitoris, a powerful sensation flowed through her loins. She kept her eyes closed most of the time, but when she opened them she saw how hard and extended her dark nipples had become and she massaged them with her free hand. Her breathing quickened and she tossed her head back and forth.

Jo Ann usually didn't fantasize when masturbating. She let the feelings overtake her and orgasm came easily. Tonight, however, as the vibrator drove her toward climax, an image seeped into her consciousness. Robert Hart appeared, all six feet, seven inches of him.

His blue eyes sparkled. She noticed his thin lips and wondered about kissing them. He had a scar, smaller than hers, on his chin and a tiny black mole on his left cheek. He appeared naked before her, his huge erection aimed straight at her center. She spread her trim, muscular thighs. Her tightly coiled pubic hair drew him to her opening. As he neared the bed, she climaxed, and his image faded. Her rapid breathing subsided, and she let the vibrator fall away. She slipped into a deep sleep from which she didn't wake for seven hours.

∞∞∞∞

The day after the baseball game, before leaving home to play golf, Robert made a call. In his home office filing cabinet, he found the number in a file marked *2001 Drury Team Reunion*. A graveled voice answered. "Hello."

"Is this Coach Ronnie Dawson?"

"This is Coach Dawson. Who's calling?'

"This is Robert Hart, your old ---"

"I know who you are. You played for me in the dark ages, back when I still recruited tall, slow white kids."

"I wasn't slow, coach."

"Maybe you weren't, but there were plenty of them around in those days."

"Coach, how are you?"

"Remarkably well for an old fellow, thank you."

"How old are you now, coach?"

"I turned 83 last week. You never thought I'd last that long, did you?"

"We thought you'd never die. Sometimes we hoped you'd keel over at practice."

"No such luck. I probably coached twenty years after you played for me."

"When did you retire?"

"1994."

"You made it 23 years after my time. My senior year was 1971."

Robert heard a shallow sigh on the other end. "That was the year we almost won it all, wasn't it? Or was it the year before?"

"The year before. My last year we had those injuries and lost in the national semi-finals."

"What's on your mind, Robert? I doubt you called just about old times."

"Do you know how I can reach Jackie McFadden?"

"Jackie runs a recreation center in Little Rock. Give me your e-mail address and I'll send you his contact information. Bet you figured an old codger like me wouldn't use e-mail, right?"

"I knew you'd keep up." Robert related his email address.

"I got it," the coach said. "I'm curious why you're trying to reach Jackie. Are some of you thinking about another team reunion?"

"Nothing like that. I have a question I think Jackie could help me with. Thanks again, coach."

"Come see me when you can, will you?"

"You bet. I go to Kansas City from time to time. One of those trips I'll route myself though Springfield."

∞∞∞

Robert prepared for a golf round by cleaning his clubs and polishing his golf shoes. When he finished, he checked his email, then dialed Jackie McFadden's number. He paced the room. Rufus curled up on the couch. A pleasant, recorded female voice identified Jackie's extension.

After four rings, Robert thought about hanging up, but before he could, a deep voice answered.

"This is Jackie. May I help you?"

"Jackie? Jackie McFadden? This is Robert Hart, your old teammate."

"Robert Hart? For real?"

"Yes, it's me. How are you?"

"I'm great! I haven't heard from you since that reunion, eleven to twelve years ago."

"Our 30th in 2001."

"I was leaving and almost didn't answer the phone. We are closed for the holiday until this afternoon. I was here doing paperwork. It's good to hear from you."

Robert knew he should keep the chit chat brief. "I want to talk to you about something that's difficult, personal. If you're willing, we may not want to do this over the phone. It may be best I come see you."

"Where do you live?"

"Houston."

"I remember that. What's on your mind?"

Robert fiddled with his watch, "I need some advice. When I played with you and the other guys, the black guys on the team, I never got to know any of you. We joked around before and after practice and we hung around a little on campus. Mostly, the black guys went one way and the white guys another."

"I'd say you're right about that. Call us ships passing in the night."

That Jackie saw things that way too bucked up Robert's courage. "Life hasn't changed that much. My friends, business associates, nearly everybody I go to church with, is white. Now, something is happening that makes me feel I should learn more about black people and what their lives in America have been like. I realize -"

"What's happening?"

"I've met a woman I'm really interested in and -"

"And she's black, right?"

"Yes."

"You had a white wife when I saw you at the reunion, right?"

"That was Darla. We were together thirty-one years, married twenty-eight. She died eight years ago. We found out about her cancer a year after that reunion."

"I'm sorry for your loss."

"Thank you."

Jackie cleared his throat. "This black woman you've met -- how did that happen?"

Robert felt relieved that Jackie seemed interested in the details. If he was insulted, he hadn't shown it yet. "We work together. We had a strange moment recently. I'm just consulting for this company since I retired. She is a vice president. She's helped me on projects, but we never really knew each other. This moment that happened changed everything."

"How can I help you?"

"I'd like to talk with you about what life has been like for you as a black man in America who grew up when I did. My guess is your life has been different than mine and maybe like hers."

"It's interesting you'd think of me," Jackie replied. "Is she your age?"

"Fifty-one, so a little younger. Her kids are grown and she's told me she's not involved with anybody now."

"I imagine there's a lot you don't know. You are right about one thing. This is way too deep for just phone calls. You say you can come up here?"

"I set my own schedule. Other than catching up on things tomorrow, I can come anytime."

"Come up Wednesday. You could stay at my house, except we're remodeling and the upstairs is torn up."

"No problem. I'll let you know what hotel I get. I've been to Little Rock a few times. Things aren't spread out enough that where I stay makes much difference. I'll see you Wednesday."

Chapter 6

Jo Ann dreaded Monday and her calls with Kendra, Tiffany, and Betty. They left eight phone messages between them starting Saturday morning and sent as many e-mails and texts.

First, though, Jo Ann searched for something she needed for another call she decided she'd make.

In a home office file, she found the program for Irma Simpson's memorial service. Irma was the friend who told her she should masturbate and relieve the sexual tension that went with the man scarcity she experienced after the divorce. She read the obituary on the back and jotted down the name of Irma's law firm. Then she opened the program and scanned the speaker list. She came to the one who gave the talk "Irma as Friend" and wrote down the name Hanna Leslie.

Jo Ann called Kendra Watkins. "What do you have to say for yourself?" the tirade began. "I've been looking for you since Saturday morning."

From the kitchen window, Jo Ann gazed out on her manicured back yard. "Come off it. You knew I'd call. There's no reason for being nasty."

"I don't treat my friends that way. You could've called me back."

"I was busy." Jo Ann immediately regretted using that word.

"'Busy' with who?"

"You're not my mother. I had things to do. Leave it at that."

"Are you coming to the cookout? We've been slaving, getting everything ready. What are you contributing? Or did you get too 'busy' and forget our little event?"

Jo Ann sighed and turned from the window. Her mood lightened when she noticed the picture of Shonda on the counter beside the spice rack. "I'm bringing what I said I'd bring."

"Is that all you can say?"

"What do you want from me?"

"Don't be snooty. I just asked a question."

"I'll see you this afternoon. Goodbye."

Jo Ann arrived at Betty Martin's house at 3:30 p.m. In years past, she got there early and helped get things ready. Today, she could barely stomach going at all.

"Hi, Jo Ann!" Betty greeted her, accepting the large dish of beans and sausage Jo Ann handed over. "I've been waiting for these. You know how much everyone loves them."

Betty, Tiffany, Kendra, and Jo Ann started this Memorial Day cookout five years ago. Betty hosted because her house had the best outdoor amenities -- a spacious patio, a big, landscaped yard, and picnic tables. As she slipped into a patio chair, Jo Ann wondered if she'd be at this event next year.

She looked around. Every person there was black. It had always been that way at this gathering, but she never thought about it before. Could Robert fit with this crowd? Would he try? Wouldn't they both have to get used to being the only "other" at social events?

Jo Ann mingled while Betty, slim and dressed in khaki shorts and an I Love Michigan t-shirt, stayed busy with hostess duties. Her husband Charles, a short, wiry, brown-skinned man with closely cropped hair and a small moustache, assisted. Betty, Jo Ann's darker color, tied her long hair in a blue and red scarf. Only a childhood chickenpox scar marred her smooth face.

Tiffany Boyd, the oldest of the group at 52, cornered Jo Ann midway through the party. They'd talked on the phone earlier that day, when, like Kendra, she'd been hostile. "I just wanted to know what was going on," Tiffany said, leaning on the kitchen table. It seemed she'd calmed down. She reached for a potato chip. "I have your back, Kendra's, and Betty's. It's hard when we ignore each other."

Tiffany, unlike Kendra, Betty, and Jo Ann, didn't work out and it showed in her oversized rump and bulging waist. She wore little make up on a face that long ago passed the point of just being round.

"I needed time away," Jo Ann replied, after she'd finished a glass of wine.

"What did you do?" Tiffany asked. She adjusted a bra strap under her loose-fitting Grambling State University sweatshirt.

"Saturday, I indulged myself with breakfast, shopped a while, took in a play."

Tiffany grabbed a handful of chips and spooned up a helping of the beans and sausage. "What about Sunday? I know you didn't do something like go to church."

Tiffany often chastised Jo Ann about church. Live-and-let-live Betty didn't bug Jo Ann about it, but Tiffany did. She claimed Jo Ann's sporadic attendance guaranteed eternity in hell.

Kendra also attended church most Sundays. Though raised Baptist, she now attended the biggest, wealthiest black

Methodist church in Houston. Kendra sometimes invited Jo Ann there and she accepted occasionally in the name of harmony. Jo Ann believed Kendra mostly used church in searching for men.

"No," Jo Ann replied to Tiffany's question about Sunday, adding a little white lie. "I just chilled."

"How come you didn't answer your phone?" Tiffany asked, reaching for another potato chip.

"I needed time for myself."

"Oh, here's Kendra."

The youngest of the friends at 48, Kendra liked showing off her curly hair and curvy body. She had lighter skin, thinner lips, higher cheekbones, and a smaller nose than the other three.

Why Kendra had such trouble attracting men could have been a mystery -- until she opened her mouth. Her caustic personality and mean-spirited comments made keeping male or female friends difficult. Jo Ann, Tiffany, and Betty, however, accepted her, warts, and all.

Kendra held her fire as she approached Tiffany and Jo Ann at the kitchen table. Small talk about the coming work week flowed. The party went on until early evening, without more sniping between the friends.

After the crowd left, the three helped Betty clean up. Standing by the kitchen table, Kendra asked, "What's going on next week, girlfriends? Can we avoid a repeat of this weekend?"

"I have book club Saturday night," Jo Ann said. "I don't know otherwise." The last part privately acknowledged her hope of seeing Robert.

"You have lots of time other than Saturday night," Kendra said, raising her voice. With a sneer, she asked, "Or are you 'busy'?"

Jo Ann didn't take the bait. "We can do something. Let's see what happens."

"That's probably best," Betty said, playing peacemaker, as she often did.

"Let us know if you get 'busy' " Kendra said, looking directly at Jo Ann. "Maybe we'll all find somebody we can get 'busy' with, especially me and Tiffany." Jo Ann understood Kendra's reference to the other single woman in the group, but knew it meant nothing. Tiffany, with her deteriorating appearance, no longer spent much time looking for men. She even said once she knew her time had come and gone.

"I'm out of here," Jo Ann insisted. "I have a big day tomorrow. This is a short week and I need an early start. I'll be in touch."

∞ ∞ ∞

When she reached her car, Jo Ann noticed a missed call from Robert. She didn't like having involved phone conversations while driving. She found a shopping center, parked, and dialed his number.

"Hi," he answered. "I hoped you'd call me back."

"Of course, I'd call you back."

"Aside from just wanting to hear your voice, I need to tell you I'm going out of town for a few days this week."

"Oh?" she asked, disappointed. "Business?"

"It's about you and me."

Her voice rose in anticipation. "About us?"

"Our talk Sunday about what may be happening between us brought home the fact I have no experience with the race part of this. I'm attacking my ignorance."

"How?"

"By talking with an old basketball teammate, a black guy in Little Rock. I'm driving up. I leave tomorrow afternoon. I'll get back Saturday."

The idea of such a consultation intrigued her. She softened her tone in wonder. "What do you hope he can tell you?"

"I've lived all my life in a white world. I know nothing about being black in America. Here I am falling all over myself about a black woman. I'm afraid I'll suck at this."

"You won't suck at this. You won't suck at anything."

"Thanks for the vote of confidence. I doubt it's deserved. My friends, business associates, people at church – they're nearly all white. Darla had black women friends, but they weren't my friends."

"I live mostly in a black world," Jo Ann said. She remembered the cookout crowd. "I interact with white people in business. You've noticed I'm one of the few blacks in an executive position at JAX? As you learned Friday, I'm not doing so hot at getting white women friends."

"I think that woman is a jerk. Her not going on your trip might not be about race at all."

"Fair enough. But who's this guy you're seeing, and why him?"

"Jackie McFadden and -"

"A black last name!"

"Really?"

"You know any white people named McFadden?"

"No."

"I rest my case."

"Anyway, we played basketball together in college. We weren't close. Hardly any black players and white players were close. But, I always liked him. He seemed like a good person and very smart. I hope he can tell me about his life and what he's dealt with. I owe us that before we start down this road."

She still wasn't quite sure how she should react. This idea took her by surprise. Finally she said, "I don't know exactly what you'll learn, but the fact you're doing it makes me think more of you. A man who'll challenge himself is worth knowing."

"Thank you."

"Do you know how he'll react to the idea of you being with a black woman? Some black men don't approve of black woman/white man couples."

"He didn't say much one way or the other. It seemed he found it interesting."

"You might talk with him about that."

"I will."

Their conversation continued until she got antsy about being alone in a rapidly emptying parking lot. They signed off with a promise they'd stay in touch during his time away. While she drove home, Jo Ann felt her loneliness lift because Robert's willingness to take a risk impressed her. That he was doing it in the interest of their potential relationship touched her in a place she had forgotten existed.

Chapter 7

When Jo Ann arrived at work Tuesday, she resisted the temptation to run to Robert's office and say she hoped she could see him before he left town. She heard him tell someone in the hall he'd been there since 5:30 a.m. preparing for getting away a few days. That she caused this spur-of-the-moment trip pleased her.

An e-mail popped up from Robert's secretary asking that Jo Ann attend a 10:30 a.m. meeting about an old project he was reviving. She arrived early, but several others were already there, preventing a private conversation. At the end of the meeting, he noted his upcoming absence, so he wouldn't expect progress reports until the following week. As the group broke up, Jo Ann stole glances at him and talked with his secretary while he finished a call. Finally, everyone else left, leaving them alone.

"Can we see each other before you go?" she whispered.

He spoke as softly as she had. "Meet me on the corner of San Felipe and Post Oak Boulevard in half an hour. There's a Panera Bread and a Five Guys there."

At the meeting spot, Robert waved her over to his silver BMW 325i. She noticed his neatly trimmed brown hair, parted on the left, the mole, the scar, and his blue eyes. Jo Ann slipped into the passenger seat and kissed him on the cheek.

She said, "I wanted to say goodbye. In just a few days I've gotten used to seeing and talking with you. Then you're leaving town and I'm depressed."

"I have a good reason for going," he responded. "I'll miss you too, but I hope this trip helps make things work between us. We've fought wars over race in this country. I must understand the struggles, and then, maybe, I can see the big picture."

She leaned against the window and looked at him. She reached over, touched his arm, and asked, "You have feelings for me?"

"I do. I don't want this race business getting in the way."

He'd pulled into the traffic. She asked, "Where are we going?"

"For a short ride," he said.

After several turns, he guided the car into a cove of trees in the picnic area of a park. Obscured from traffic by thick branches and the car's tinted windows, Robert reached over and wrapped his arms around Jo Ann. She leaned into him as he kissed her, softly at first, then hard. A shudder ran through her body. She closed her eyes and felt herself floating, as if on a calm sea. They were in one of America's busiest urban areas, but she might as well have been alone with him in the middle of the Pacific Ocean. She pressed her tongue into his mouth. Their lips locked in place and they battled over who could hold the other tighter.

As Robert ran his hand across her back, Jo Ann felt herself getting wet under the skirt of her navy blue suit, pantyhose, and bikini panties. Beneath her jacket, blouse, and bra her nipples burned with desire. The idea of stripping and giving herself to him right there ran through her mind. Mercifully for them both, she refrained from reaching for the erection she knew raged inside his slacks.

Slowly, Robert drew back from her. They later named the moment *The Kiss*. He drove back to her car. He never said a word but gripped her hand the entire way.

"To be continued," he whispered when she got out. She blew him a kiss and repeated his words. At her car, to the world she undoubtedly looked like any other professionally dressed, middle-aged black woman completing an errand and heading for her next task. Actually, Jo Ann Davis's life had been rearranged.

∞ ∞ ∞

She returned to a nearly empty office. Four hours of work remained before she could feel call it a day. First, though, she made that call she planned Monday.

"Simpson and Wilkins," the male voice answered.

"May I speak to Rod Wilkins, please?" Jo Ann asked.

"This is he. May I help you?"

"This is Jo Ann Davis. I was a friend of Irma. How are you?"

"I'm okay, thank you." After a pause, he said, "I remember you. Weren't you at Irma's memorial service? You're in the oil business, right?"

"I was there and I work for an oil company."

"Irma spoke highly of you. She wanted me to get to know you, but it never happened, for whatever reason. What can I do for you?"

"I'm trying to reach Hanna Leslie, the woman who spoke at the service about Irma as a friend."

"Hanna was Irma's best friend. She's in a writing group with me. I'll get you her number."

"She made a really good talk."

"Hanna did what I asked. All the speakers did."

"Your son was great. I was amazed a college kid could have such poise."

"I'm really proud of Kevin, I'm proud of all my kids."

"How many do you have?"

"Five. Irma and I had three, Kevin, Margaret and Karen, all in college at the time. Kevin is out now. Samantha and Kendall, my children from a prior marriage, were also there."

He gave her Hanna's number. "She's out of town, but should be back for our Wednesday meeting."

"I won't hold you," Jo Ann said. "I appreciate your help."

"Hanna will like hearing from you. She loves talking with people Irma knew. It's a way of keeping her spirit alive."

Jo Ann resumed her work. Periodically she relived *The Kiss*. When she left the office, though famished, the wetness remaining between her legs made getting home to her vibrator a higher priority than food.

Chapter 8

At the beginning of Robert's drive up U.S. 59, he couldn't get *The Kiss* out of his mind. He found the fact odd, but it made him think of Darla. During her illness, their physical relationship dwindled to nothing. Since she'd been gone eight years, it had been ten years since he'd experienced passion with a woman. He'd feared no one could ever bring him the joy she did. *The Kiss* told him he'd been wrong, or that at least he was no longer right.

So, what came next? Sex? What did that look like? Did they date and sleep together from time to time? Did he and Jo Ann spend every night together? Who slept at whose house? How did they present themselves to the world and at JAX? Did they come out in the open or keep this hidden?

As he neared Texarkana, his overnight rest stop, Robert thought about the trip. He remembered Jackie as a tenacious, savvy player who knew when he should gamble and when he should play safe. He recalled him as reserved, but not shy, serious, not dour. Jackie had a sense of humor, but never pulled pranks. He conformed when necessary, but possessed an independent streak.

Robert didn't know much about what had happened with him since their playing days. Other than Monday's call, 20 minutes of chit chat at the 2001 reunion represented the sum of their interaction in 42 years.

In college, he and Jackie talked occasionally on road trips and after practice. It seemed Jackie understood and appreciated life's nuances. Robert saw himself as good at evaluating individual strengths and weaknesses. His instincts told him Jackie knew a lot about the things on his mind.

Jo Ann's concern about how Jackie might view his involvement with a black woman gave Robert pause as he drove through the night. Jackie's reaction on the phone had been polite but non-committal. Was he just being nice to an old teammate? The athletic brotherhood ran deep and didn't shatter easily. This visit should reveal his true feelings.

∞∞∞

Wednesday morning in Texarkana, Robert ran three miles, ate a light breakfast, and left for Little Rock. He arrived at 11:35 a.m, checked into a hotel on the city's west side, touched base with the office, and returned messages.

Did he dare call Jo Ann's office phone? Someone else might answer. He tried her mobile number, not knowing if she'd pick up during the day. "I hoped you'd call," she said breathlessly.

"Are you in your office?" he asked.

Through the phone, he sensed excitement. "I closed my door."

"How are you?"

"Not bad for a woman missing this man she can't get out of her head, who gives her *The Kiss*, and leaves her sopping wet between her legs."

He took a deep breath, savoring the memory. "It was amazing. We have to do that some more."

She giggled. "We have to do more than that."

"I agree but, as a famous philosopher once said, 'All things in time.'"

"That famous philosopher didn't know what getting left high and dry in a parking lot with no relief in sight for days is like."

"Yesterday was tough for me, too. I had a hard time not taking you to my house and screwing your brains out, though it sounds like you might have led the way."

"This will work out fine, just fine. Now I have to go. If I leave my door closed and we keep talking like this, I'll be writhing on the floor. Can we talk tonight?"

"Jackie and I are having dinner. I imagine we'll be a while. But, I'll call after we're done."

"I'll be waiting."

∞∞∞

That afternoon, Jo Ann's mobile phone rang again. She'd just talked with Robert. Her friends used the office line during work hours. The number looked familiar, but she couldn't place it. "This is Jo Ann," she answered.

"Jo Ann, this is Hanna Leslie, returning your call."

"Oh! Hanna! Thanks for calling back. I didn't recognize your number at first."

"What can I do for you? Your message said you were a friend of Irma Simpson."

"Irma and I knew each other twelve years. I heard you speak at her memorial service. Something's come up that reminded me of what a great person she was. I wondered if we could talk so I can get insight into things about her I don't know."

"I'm glad to. I'm busy the next couple of weeks. I leave Thursday for a retreat in California, exactly the kind of thing Irma would have loved."

"I'm happy to see you whenever I can. I hoped it could be soon."

Hanna and Jo Ann agreed they'd meet at 5:30 p.m. that afternoon at a place called Jo's in Hanna's suburb. Jo Ann arrived first, at a mostly empty dining room. She appreciated the simple décor of bare walls and plain wooden tables and chairs. When Hanna appeared, Jo Ann rose and extended her hand. "I'm Jo Ann Davis. Thanks for coming. I ordered a bottle of Merlot."

"I like that," Hanna said. "Tell me what I can do for you. You said something has come up that made you think of Irma."

"I'll tell you about that," Jo Ann said. She measured her tablemate who had short, blonde hair and wore large, round glasses that helped hide crow's feet around her blue eyes. A few facial wrinkles suggested she was about 65. A white, V-necked top accentuated ample, but not oversized, breasts by revealing a bit of cleavage.

Jo Ann continued. "What flabbergasted me about the memorial service was the crowd. That church bulged at the seams."

"It was the best attended event in the church's history. I've been going there since the 1980s. Nothing else comes close."

Jo Ann looked around, then spoke in a low voice. "The racial composition of the crowd amazed me. Other than family, I was one of a handful of black people there. How does a straight black woman have so many white friends, many of them gay?"

"Irma was an outlier," Hanna responded, as she sipped wine. "She marched to the beat of her own drummer."

"I mostly live in a black world. I grew up in a segregated housing project in New Orleans, attended an all-black high school, a black college, and married a black man. I don't know my white neighbors. I socialize with black people from other parts of town.

"If I get run over by a bus tonight, at my memorial service, other than a few white co-workers and my book club friends, there won't be anybody there except black people."

Hanna looked at Jo Ann quizzically. "Is something different now?"

"I've met this man. He's white. If it works out, my world will change dramatically. I saw Irma's life and I want to know how she did it."

Hanna looked up. "You're aware Irma's first husband was white?"

A dazed look hit Jo Ann's face. "I wasn't."

"His name was –is – Charles. He was at the service. Nice man. They divorced because he got skittish about having mixed race children. I think he felt like experimenting. They married at 19."

Jo Ann nodded. "I see."

"Things worked out," Hanna continued. "Irma decided she'd at least date black men. I don't think she set out to marry one. It just happened that Rod is black. Irma and Rod made a great team, partly because he's open to all kinds of people."

Jo Ann rested her elbows on the table. "I guess that helps."

"Irma didn't put people in boxes. She saw people as people. That resulted from how she grew up."

Jo Ann rubbed the back of her neck. "Which was?"

"Her dad was career Air Force. They lived all over the world, including places without many black people. She had her hardest time when they moved to Fort Worth near the end of high school and, for the first time, confronted blacks and whites staying with their own. She thought that was silly. Her crowd became the white theater kids, many of them gay."

Jo Ann listened intensely. "Her openness came from her

upbringing?"

"That," Hanna said, nodding, "and her time at the University of Texas. She enrolled in 1972, the heyday of counterculture Austin."

With a frown Jo Ann said, "Irma lived in a different world. My black friends are suspicious of most white people they meet. I'm tired of that, but my efforts at making white friends haven't gone so well." She told the cancelled trip story.

"I'm not sure about that," Hanna responded. "You may have just run into a jerk."

Through a chuckle, Jo Ann replied, "That's what Robert says."

"He's your new man prospect?"

"Yes."

"Where are you with the idea of getting involved with a white man?"

Jo Ann leaned back in her chair before drinking more wine. "It's new, that's for sure."

"Tell me about him?"

Jo Ann offered a thumbnail sketch, but acknowledged she still had lots to learn about Robert Hart.

"How does he view getting involved with a black woman?" Hanna asked.

"Apprehensive, unsure, intrigued. Like I see getting involved with a white man. We've both lived in racially isolated worlds."

"Irma believed people should do what makes them happy. If you want Robert, the fact he's white isn't a reason not to be with him, she'd say."

Hanna finished her wine and looked at her watch. "My writing group meeting starts in 15 minutes. I'll see Rod there and tell him we had this talk. Even though he has a girlfriend now, he still worships Irma."

"He said you'd enjoy talking about her."

"Let's talk again. I hope you and Robert find out if you can have something together. Rod and their kids always ask WWID. That's a good rule for you."

"WWID?"

"What Would Irma Do?"

"I get it," Jo Ann said to Hanna as she left, then again to herself as got into her car.

Chapter 9

The receptionist at the Jordan-Bussey Recreation Center told Robert, "Mr. McFadden will see you in a few moments." Soon, Jackie emerged through a wooden door, talking with a gangly black teenager. Jackie's trim, athletic frame looked like it had in college, though the closely cropped hair, jet black then, was now speckled with gray. He wore a thin moustache. Robert remembered the brown skin and large hands, hands that made steals and rebounds easier during their playing days.

As he'd waited, Robert recalled their roles on the Drury basketball team. The offense through Robert because of his height and shooting touch. Jackie provided an additional scoring option as a sharp shooting guard. He stood only five-feet, ten-inches in those days but his quickness, and those hands, made him effective in Coach Dawson's full court press. Just seeing Jackie made Robert wistful for his playing days.

When Jackie finished with the young man, he turned and exclaimed, "Robert Hart! My man! Welcome to Little Rock!"

They embraced. "It's been a long time," Robert said.

"Yes, it has." Jackie agreed. He led them down a hallway and into his spacious, sparsely furnished corner office. Outside, Robert noticed a row of basketball goals and manicured, lush green soccer and baseball fields.

"Ever go out and shoot a few, Jackie?" Robert asked.

"I play. My knees don't let me get up and down the court like I once did, but I can still put the ball in the hole. How about you? Still bang the boards?"

"I mostly play golf and tennis now. I played basketball with my kids while they were in school. Bill played at Stanford. Well, he was on the team. My other boy, Al, played in high school, but gave it up after that. My daughter played through junior high."

"You keep up with any of the guys?" Jackie asked.

"John Timmons lives in Houston, so I see him some. Rick Roberts lives in Kansas City. We've done business together, so I see him every once in a while. And you?"

Jackie leaned back in his chair. "I see Joe Witherspoon regularly. He lives in Oklahoma City. He was an assistant basketball coach at a high school there until he retired two years ago. Willie Bradley lives in St. Louis. We talk occasionally."

"The pattern held, hasn't it?

"That you've kept up with the white guys and I've kept up with black guys?"

"Yes. Maybe you and I will change that."

The conversation turned to their lives since college. "You know I didn't graduate from Drury?"

"I didn't know that," Robert replied, sitting up. "You finished college. There's a degree on the wall, two in fact."

"Look closer. The bachelor's degree is from The University of Texas at San Antonio and the master's degree is from the University of Arkansas."

"What happened?"

Jackie balled his hands into fists. "When my senior season was over, I dropped out of Drury. What only a few people at Drury knew was that I'd gotten a girl pregnant at Christmas. I went home and got married. Her father gave me no choice. That's what happened then."

"What was next?"

"We lived in my hometown, Prescott, Arkansas."

"I drove by it on the way up here."

"It's off I-30, 90 miles southwest."

"What did you do for a living?"

"Farm work, cutting timber, manual labor."

Robert's mouth slackened. "You were, what, 20 to 30 hours from a degree? Couldn't you find anything else?"

Jackie crossed his arms over his chest. "Not as a black man in Prescott. If I'd had my degree I could've taught and coached, but there were no professional jobs for a black person."

"I hate that."

With a hard, cold expression, Jackie said, "I had a white high school teammate who played two years up the road at Henderson State in Arkadelphia before he flunked out. He came back to Prescott. His daddy's friends got him a job as a teller at the local bank. The next thing I know, he's a vice president, wearing a suit and tie to work every day, making loans. He ended up being president of that bank. That's the way it was."

"You didn't keep doing those menial jobs, did you?"

"I changed women, not immediately, but I got rid of my first wife. We divorced after three years, and I joined the U.S. Army in 1975."

"And the baby?"

Jackie's face lit up as he talked about his son. "Jimmy stayed with his mother until he was 14, then lived with me. I'd remarried by then and had two other children. I was an officer, stationed at Ft. Hood near Temple, Texas. Jimmy did well in school and played basketball at Lamar in Beaumont. Now, he's a high school girls coach in Atlanta, Texas. They almost won a state championship this year."

Robert clasped his hands together between his legs as he sat on the edge of a chair. "Tell me about the military."

"I saw no future at home. I wanted my degree. Because I had as many hours as I did, I could join up, finish college, and get into officer's candidate school if I'd stay in a certain length of time."

"What job did you do?"

"Artillery. It's a wonder I can hear anything, but I survived. I retired as a Major after twenty years. I might have stayed in and made, maybe Light Colonel. After Desert Storm, I'd had enough."

"And afterwards?"

"I used my GI benefits at Arkansas for a graduate degree in recreation."

"Then here?"

He shook his head. "I first spent three years in Tulsa as assistant director of a center."

"So, you've been here for 13 years. How long will you stay at it?"

"At least three more years. At 62, I'm in good health. I love working with kids. I'm doing some good. With my military retirement, this job, and Linda's pension, we do fine financially. My kids are grown and doing well. We have everything we want. Life is good."

"Sounds like it."

Jackie leaned back in his chair. He flashed the white teeth Robert remembered. "Fill me in on this sister you're hot and bothered about."

Robert smiled, then described his chance encounter with Jo Ann and their interaction since, including *The Kiss*. He related her dedication to her children and explained their accomplishments. He repeated his concern about the all-white world in which he'd lived and his fears about what that could mean for a relationship with a black woman.

When he finished, Jackie said, "You need a history lesson about how black people have been treated in America. Before you leave, we'll meet with a lawyer friend of mine who also can help."

"Maybe lunch tomorrow?" Robert asked, pulling up the calendar on his phone.

"I'll call him and e-mail you."

∞∞∞

Jackie took them to dinner at a barbecue place in the west central part of town. Reminders of Bill Clinton's presidency filled the walls, including an autographed photo of Clinton arriving in Little Rock on Air Force One. More than half the people who came into the restaurant during their two hours there knew Jackie. He introduced Robert as the college teammate he always fed the ball and who scored the points. After ordering, they began the history lesson.

"How much do you know about what slavery was like?" Jackie asked as they sat at a corner table.

"Not much, what we read in high school American History class."

"No college courses?"

"Somehow I got out of taking American history, so no."

"What about the Jim Crow South, after Reconstruction?"

"I know nothing about that."

Jackie's disappointment with Robert's lack of knowledge showed through. He swallowed hard. "I'm going to tell you one story that you need to know and understand. Does the name Emmitt Till mean anything to you?"

"No." Robert said, shaking his head.

Jackie's eyes took on a cold, dead appearance. "Emmitt Till was a black teenager from Chicago, who visited relatives in Mississippi in the summer of 1955. One day he and some friends were at a drug store and this white woman walked by. She claimed he whistled at her. He probably didn't, but even if he did, he shouldn't have been killed for it."

Robert's mouth dropped open in disbelief and he leaned forward. "He was killed?"

"That night, a group of white men dragged him out of bed, took him to an isolated spot, beat and tortured him, and threw him into a river. His body was recovered several days later."

"What happened to the people who did it?"

"Nothing. Eventually two guys were charged, tried, and acquitted. They later bragged that they did it."

A shudder went through Robert's body. He thought of Jo Ann. "I can't imagine that."

"It hurts that so many white people don't know that story. They don't understand why blacks feel they've been treated unfairly in the criminal justice system. Most black people know the story, especially people our age. I bet your lady knows it."

As Jackie told America's racial history, Robert realized he knew as little as he feared. He'd never heard of Sojourner Truth, Carter G. Woodson, W.E.B. Dubois, or Booker T. Washington. When Jackie got to more recent times, the names – Thurgood Marshall, Marian Anderson, Martin Luther King, Jr. – became more familiar, but Robert still needed details of their accomplishments.

Finally, Jackie described the 1957 Little Rock school desegregation crisis. He included an emotional account of becoming friends with one of the nine black students who braved taunts and physical attacks by angry whites when they integrated Central High School.

Before getting into his car for the return to the hotel, Robert asked Jackie why he'd never talked about these things during their playing days.

"Some of it I didn't know myself, at least not the details," he admitted as a gentle breeze blew over them. "I was a kid playing basketball. As a history major though, I worked at learning what had happened with my people. I matured and had children. I felt responsible for passing them that history.

"I didn't think they should wallow in it. I hoped they wouldn't use it as a reason for hating white people. I'm a religious man and the God I worship makes a hate a sin. But, my children, and white America, must know the truth."

As they stood in the warmth of that spring night, Robert said, "You have done something great for me. You've helped me, my old friend, understand things I knew little or nothing about. Whether this romance with Jo Ann works or not, you've done that and I won't forget it." They embraced and parted for the night.

∞ ∞ ∞

Robert felt a surge of hope as he dialed Jo Ann's number. She answered on the first ring and said, "I told you I'd be waiting."

"I owe you so much. But for you, I wouldn't have made this trip and I wouldn't have had the experience I had tonight."

"Tell me about it, my love."

He took a deep breath. "I understand, better than ever, the words in that old hymn, 'I once was blind, but now I see.' Tonight, I began understanding what black people have experienced and why they might see the world differently than my white friends at the country club."

She also breathed deeply. "How did that happen?"

"Jackie took me through the entire history of slavery, Reconstruction, Jim Crow, the civil rights era, the whole nine yards. Did you know the Emmitt Till story? I didn't."

"Yes, I know it," she said quietly.

"Jackie explained the lack of opportunity he had in his life." Robert related the bank president story.

Jo Ann just listened.

"I heard about at least a little of this in school, of course," Robert explained. "Jackie's telling of it made it real, personal."

He heard her fighting back tears. "You're a remarkable man. How many people, of any color, have the courage to look at the world through other eyes?"

"I'm trying."

Jo Ann turned the conversation in a more intimate direction. "I've been thinking about you. When I see you, will you kiss me again like you did Tuesday?"

"Yes and do some other things."

"I'm especially interested in those 'other' things."

"Be patient. I have two more days here. I want all I can get out of this."

They talked for over an hour. She told him more about her children and asked about his life with Darla before she got sick. He opened up on things he never talked about, especially how he'd had trouble connecting with his daughter, Sandy, after her mother's death. Neither wanted to hang up, but Robert finally reminded her she had work the next day.

∞∞∞

Just before noon Thursday, Robert parked across the street

from a downtown Little Rock restaurant called the Copper Grill. He walked in and noticed Jackie at a corner table, accompanied by a distinguished looking man with very dark skin and a trimmed, graying beard. He had short, salt and pepper hair and wore a starched white shirt and red tie. An expensive looking suit jacket hung on his chair. Jackie, casually dressed in slacks, a blue polo shirt, and a tan jacket, waved Robert to the table.

"Robert, my man, meet Henry Walker, attorney-at-law and businessman supreme."

Walker, tall but perhaps five inches short of Robert's six feet, seven inches, stood and greeted him with a firm handshake. Robert noticed his huge brown eyes. "It's a pleasure, Mr. Walker," Robert said. They sat down.

"I am delighted to meet you, Mr. Hart. Please, call me Henry."

"Call me Robert."

"Robert it is."

Jackie began the conversation after they ordered lunch. "Henry, Robert is an old college basketball teammate. He lives in Houston. He was a year ahead of me at Drury. Henry is a big basketball fan and perhaps the two of you can talk basketball later. Today, Robert is here about the dynamics of race in America. He has his reasons, as he'll tell you."

Jackie explained that Henry led the student body at the historically black Arkansas AM&N College before it became the University of Arkansas - Pine Bluff. He attended law school at Wisconsin, started a law practice upon his return, and achieved a number of milestones. They included prestigious political appointments and election as the first black Arkansas Bar Association President.

Henry took a deep breath. "Allow me a disclaimer. I did those things Jackie describes. I no longer practice law. I spend my time on real estate and video production. I always delight in helping a white brother understand the struggle of African-Americans."

Robert wondered if Henry's precise, formal language and upright manner were genuine or contrived. "Thank you for talking with me. Jackie speaks highly of you. I'm sure you can give me great insight into this topic, though I've learned a lot from him already."

Henry crossed his arms and said, "Tell me about Robert Hart."

"I grew up in the Kansas City suburbs. You know about college and basketball at Drury. I got an MBA from Harvard and started work in the oil business in Houston in 1973. I've done well enough professionally and financially. My family life has been good, though my wife of 28 years died of cancer eight years ago. Our three children are grown and doing well."

"I'm sorry for your loss."

"Thank you. That's very kind."

"What interaction have you had with African-Americans?"

"Minimal, I'd say. I got along with the five or six black guys on the Drury basketball team. I didn't know any of them well, including Jackie. I've learned more about him in the last 24 hours than in the three years we played together.

"There were a handful of black students at Harvard Business School. I didn't meaningfully interact with them. At Gulf Oil there were no blacks in my section. In the '70s and '80s, you began seeing black faces in executive positions in oil companies.

"The companies I worked for tried recruiting minorities in the '90s. We partially succeeded, but there never was a critical mass of blacks such that I had a lot of interaction."

Robert sensed real engagement and sincerity on the other side of the table. "What about socially?" Henry asked.

"I might play in a charity golf tournament and end up in a foursome with a black guy who worked for a vendor. My wife had black women friends, but I didn't know them well."

Walker bit his lip. "Do you have a political view about what's happened in America concerning civil rights?"

"As Jackie showed me last night, I didn't know much about race in America, including the Civil Rights Movement of the 1960s. I've been indifferent."

"Why was that?"

Robert bowed his head. "Disinterest in anything except my own world, I'm sorry to say. I follow the news for how events impact business. I generally felt that since I'm not black, race didn't matter in my life."

"What's different now?"

Robert cleared his throat. "I- well, what often changes a man -- a woman. The woman is black. I feel ill-equipped for understanding her life and culture because I've lived in a white world."

Henry offered a soothing tone. "You are wise for considering what larger racial issues might mean in the context of a romantic involvement with an African American woman. Do you have particular fears?"

Robert gazed downward. "That I'll say and do really stupid things."

Henry looked at Robert, before glancing at Jackie. "Racial nuances certainly exist, but civility and human decency represent beginning points for avoiding, as you put it, saying and doing 'really stupid things.'"

"Meaning?"

"Meaning one must first treat one's significant other with respect for her humanity, then worry about the racial issues."

"Fair enough and point taken," Robert said.

Food arrived and Henry probed for Robert's attitudes about terms like "law and order," "welfare cheats," and "freeloaders." Robert acknowledged some of his friends used those terms as code for hostility toward blacks.

As they ate, Henry asked a question Robert hadn't anticipated. "What are your politics?"

He hesitated. "I'm mostly a Republican. I voted for Bill Clinton the second time because of the good economy. I admit I voted for George W. Bush in 2000 because of my disgust about Monica Lewinsky and in 2004 out of patriotism generated by September 11. I regret both votes. I didn't like McCain or Obama in 2008. I thought McCain was wishy-washy on that fall's economic meltdown, but I didn't think Obama had any better ideas. I held my nose and voted for McCain. In 2012, I voted for Obama because I found Mitt Romney's 47% comment insulting."

"You are actually an independent?" Henry asked, laughing.

Robert smiled. "Based on the record, maybe I am."

"What are your lady's politics?"

"Everything she's said makes me believe she's a Democrat."

Henry propped his elbows on the table and rubbed his large hands together. "I do not have a formula for you. Today, I have asked questions and listened. You are doing what a sensitive, thoughtful person does. You've examined your behavior and challenged the way you've always thought and approached life. Those are traits of a grown up.

"I assume you'd like to broaden your horizons. I propose you read Taylor Branch's three volume series about the Civil Rights Movement called *America in the King Years*. I also suggest *Master of the Senate*, volume III of Robert Caro's series about Lyndon Johnson. It describes the political and legislative side of the early civil rights struggle. Give me a business card and I will e-mail you the publication information."

When Henry stood to leave, Robert rose and thanked him. Walker held up his hand. "This has been good for me. It reminded me things are never as clear cut as they seem, seldom, pardon the expression, black or white. We must not put people in boxes."

Robert accepted Jackie's invitation for dinner at his home Friday night, paid the check, and relished Saturday' trek home.

Chapter 10

Robert played golf Friday morning at Rebsamen Park, a public layout along the Arkansas River Jackie recommended. He walked the round alone and pleased himself with a two over par 74 on a course he'd never seen before.

After eating a salad and soup lunch, he stopped by a Barnes & Noble. He retrieved the message from Henry Walker about the books and bought them before calling Jo Ann. "Where are you?" he asked.

"In the office, with my door open," she said.

"Can you call me from a place where you can talk? We should discuss some things."

"Give me ten minutes."

Back at the hotel, Jo Ann's number flashed as he arrived in his room. "I can talk now," she said. "What's up?"

He closed his eyes and sighed. "I know what we both want tomorrow. I remind you that this time last week we barely knew each other. Friday night was a spur-of-the moment, impulse thing. We've had one planned date - the baseball game."

In a bubbly, loud tone, she said, "Makes no difference to me. I count Friday night. Given *The Kiss*, how much we've talked, and how I feel, I don't need a few movies and dinners with you before I jump your bones."

He laughed. "Let the record reflect that I raised the point."

"You sound like my lawyer daughter."

He lowered his voice. "Let's talk about how tomorrow will work."

"My book club meets tomorrow night. I could not go."

"You should go. That's an important part of your life. What time is it?"

"Seven o'clock."

"How long does it last?"

"Three, three-and-a-half hours. We have a gathering period, then dinner, then dessert. The book gets discussed in there somewhere."

He held his breath. "I'll leave here tomorrow at 5:30 a.m. That gets me back about 2:00 p.m. I'll make a reservation in your name at the J.W. Marriott in the Galleria. I'll meet you there as close to two o'clock as I can. We can do a lot with five hours, don't you think?"

She giggled. "Yes. I can come back after book club, right?"

"You can!"

"There's another thing we should talk about, given where we're heading tomorrow."

"What's that?"

She cleared her throat. "Whether either of us has diseases the other should know about."

"I don't," Robert said. "Darla and I were faithful. I haven't been with anybody since she died. I've had lots of medical exams and blood tests since then. Nothing ever showed up."

"Since my divorce, I've had brief relationships with several men. I've insisted they use condoms. I've also had blood tests. I don't have anything. I can show you my papers."

"I trust you."

"And I haven't had a period in months. I'm done with that."

"We're good to go?"

"We are."

They hung up and Robert made the hotel reservation. He spent the afternoon returning calls and finishing a report. When he left for dinner, life seemed better than it had been in ten years.

∞∞∞∞

Robert rang the doorbell at Jackie and Linda McFadden's house setting off loud barking inside. A small, casually dressed, brown-skinned woman with a short Afro hairstyle and wire rimmed glasses answered. She demanded that the black lab who'd announced Robert's arrival "calm down." She flashed a smile, but her erect posture suggested a dedication to order.

"He's harmless," she assured Robert, inviting him into a spacious living area. She extended a slim hand with long, pink fingernails. "I'm Linda. You must be Robert."

"I am. It's great to meet you. After my time with Jackie, I feel I know you."

"I'm sure he told many lies."

"He didn't, at least in the looks department. Jackie chose well."

"You're too nice. Come into the kitchen. I'm finishing dinner. I sent Jackie for some things at the store. He'll be back in 15 to 20 minutes."

Robert sat on a bar stool on one side of the kitchen while Linda worked at an island facing him. When she looked up, she had a full view of his blue eyes, brown hair, and angular features.

"I'm intrigued by your trip up here," she said. "Jackie has told me all about your conversations. I'm impressed."

He tugged on his shirt. "I was apprehensive about what

you both might think. Jo Ann warned me black men and black women can get agitated about interracial couples. Neither Jackie nor his friend, Henry Walker, seemed fazed at all."

"For Henry, this is an intellectual exercise. He's intrigued by your thought process. Jackie told you, I'm sure, his God, our God, doesn't permit hate. We respect that people love who they love and, yes, that includes gay people. A white woman taking a black man off the market upsets some black women."

Linda's words put Robert at ease. "So I've heard. There is, apparently, also some hostility toward black woman/white man couples."

She put a tray of carrots on the bar, well within his reach. Before speaking she twisted a ring on her right hand. "There's a shortage of black men for educated black women. That shuts some black women out of the marriage market unless they consider white men. Some black men don't like that."

"I didn't know that until Jo Ann told me."

"I imagine she mentioned the statistics about black men in jail, etc. I don't need the statistics. I saw it every day before I retired."

"From what?"

"I was a cop."

Robert's fingers touched his lips. "You were a cop?"

"I don't look it, given my size, but I was, for 30 years as a civilian and five years in the U.S. military. Jackie and I met when I was a M.P. on his base. I retired two years ago at age 60. I had a desk job at the end, but I spent 25 years in a squad car.

"I carted a lot of potentially good young black men off to jail. I went down to Cummings, one of the Arkansas state prisons, from time to time and watched them there, their lives draining away.

"When I gave talks in high schools and colleges I saw these eager black girls, sitting on the front row, absorbing everything said. They graduated and got good jobs. I wondered who they were going to marry."

"So white men aren't a threat?"

Linda dumped the vegetables she'd been cutting into a bowl and shook her head. "I don't see it that way. Black men have plenty of black women they can choose from."

Robert munched on a carrot stick. "You and Jackie found each other."

"We married 30 years ago, when things were different. I'm not sure I could compete for him now. Jackie would have smart, educated, attractive black women after him and white women too. When we met, he had his college degree and was a military officer. Look at what he's done since he got out -- master's degree from a good university and he's taken this little rec center from a budget of $500,000 a year to almost two million."

They continued talking until Jackie arrived with the last items for dinner. Robert liked Linda. He found her funny, irreverent, and insightful about the issues he and Jo Ann might face as a couple.

During dinner, she asked "I bet you're worried about what your friends will think, right?"

"That crossed my mind," Robert replied. He bit into the grilled salmon.

"I doubt that's much of a problem. One or two may say tacky things. Your bigger problem will be her friends."

"Really?"

"Some will talk about how she should support her black brothers. Some will be jealous that Jo Ann snagged an attractive, successful gentleman, while they didn't. Her married friends will be less offended by you being with her than her single friends. This won't just be about color. The basic man/woman rules don't all change because of race."

Robert relaxed. Jackie and Linda made him comfortable. "I see what you mean. But what makes you think my friends won't be a problem? They're mostly well-to-do, Republican white guys."

"I worked around white men all my years as a cop. Many are intrigued by black women. Some of that is titillation, the idea of forbidden fruit. Some of it is attraction to power. Black women have power in their society, something like what white men have in theirs. If there's one thing I learned about white men it was how power attracts them."

Jackie took a back seat in the dinner conversation and that which followed over white wine and cheesecake. As Robert's departure time neared, Jackie said he regretted they hadn't talked more about old times.

Robert reminded him, "This week, we created memories that could mean more than anything that happened back in the day." At the door he added, "We didn't give ourselves a chance at knowing each other when we played basketball. Our challenge now is staying connected. I'll make a real effort. Will you?"

"I will, my man. Yes, I will."

Robert embraced Jackie and Linda and headed for the hotel. He slept as well as he had in ages. When the alarm went off at 4:45 a.m., he felt entirely ready for his future.

Part 2

A SUMMER

Chapter 11

J o Ann bounded out of bed Saturday morning and curled her hair. She covered her lingerie with a blue polo shirt and gray shorts, then slipped on sandals, drank a glass of juice, brushed her teeth, grabbed the suitcase she packed Friday night, and hurried out the door. She worked three hours in her office and, at 9:05 a.m., headed for Toast 'N Jam and the breakfast Betty arranged for the four friends.

Betty and Tiffany beat her there. She joined them in a booth near the back. Kendra showed up five minutes later, in a short skirt and a plunging top that, if she moved just so, allowed a glimpse of her turquoise bra. "Nice to see you, girls," Kendra said, as she slipped in beside Tiffany.

"Bacon sure smells good, doesn't it?" Tiffany asked.

Betty, dressed in brown shorts and a white top, sat next to Jo Ann across from Tiffany and Kendra. "You aren't going to spoil today, like you did last week, are you?" Kendra asked Jo Ann.

"What are you talking about? I'm here for breakfast with my friends, and yes, Tiffany, that bacon smells great."

Kendra curled her lip. "Don't change the subject. What else did you plan today? Will you get 'busy' and abandon us again?"

Jo Ann swallowed. "I'm free this morning. I don't have anything until afternoon."

"What's this afternoon?" Kendra asked. "We could do something then."

With a pained expression, Jo Ann said, "I have the morning.

This group doesn't run my life. I love you all, but I'm not letting anybody here 'pull the reins in on me,' as the old Linda Ronstadt song says."

"You're always quoting some tired-ass white singer," Tiffany sneered.

"I take wisdom where I find it," Jo Ann replied.

"You're changing the subject again," Kendra said. "I thought we'd have the day together."

Jo Ann pulled back her shoulders and said, "I have the morning, so let's enjoy it. Can we eat?" A waitress arrived and took their orders.

They talked about the week since the cookout and their latest forays into social media. Kendra brought up a topic that tied a knot in Jo Ann's stomach. "Did you hear Brenda Watts is dating a white boy?"

Tiffany gasped. "Get outta town! That can't be true!"

"It is," Kendra said, nodding. "Somebody who knows told me."

"Who?" Betty asked.

"Rhonda Johnson," Kendra replied.

"She would know," Betty affirmed. "Rhonda and Brenda are tight."

"I can't believe Brenda would do that," Tiffany said. She rubbed her bare forearms. "Why?"

Kendra whispered, "Rhonda said Brenda got tired of brothers who don't measure up intellectually. Sisters shouldn't talk about their black brothers like that."

"That's disrespectful," Tiffany added. She pressed her hands just above her breasts.

Jo Ann had said nothing, so Kendra asked, "What's your opinion, Miss Big Time Corporate Executive? You probably think that's okay."

Jo Ann didn't want a tussle on this topic. But she wouldn't silently accept an assault on a woman probably doing what she saw herself doing, grasping for happiness wherever she could find it. "Brenda is almost forty, has never been married, and is accomplished in her profession. She has a doctorate in biochemistry, for crying out loud. I don't know what her love life has been like and neither do you."

"When did you get so high and mighty?" Kendra asked with a smirk. "I don't care what's going on with her. She shouldn't be with a white boy."

"She could find a black man if she wasn't so picky," Tiffany said.

"We shouldn't judge," Jo Ann concluded. "It's Brenda's life. She can do what she wants."

Kendra wouldn't let go. She asked Betty, "What do you think?"

After crossing her arms over her chest, Betty said, "It's better if sisters date brothers but sometimes it doesn't work out. I found a good black man. Not everybody can, so I don't know."

After the food arrived, Jo Ann shifted the conversation to the day. "Like I said, I only have the morning. Who's up for visiting an antique shop in the Rice Villages? We have just enough time."

"I'll go," Betty said.

"I'm game," Tiffany added.

Kendra snickered, "I still want to know what's so important this afternoon?"

"It's the principle of the thing," Jo Ann answered. "Also, I'm not quite ready for book club tonight." That was true, but the library, where she was headed, first and foremost, would serve as a holding tank while she waited for Robert.

At the cashier's stand, Jo Ann again noticed the "Loving

Day" flyer that drew her attention last week. Now, she understood what that name might mean in her life.

∞∞∞

Visiting the antique shop lightened the mood. With Kendra's haggling on hold, Jo Ann remembered why she enjoyed these women. Betty's innocent delight at things new, Tiffany's humorous irreverence, and even Kendra's smart-aleck, in-your-face personality each had their charm. For a moment, she regretted not having more time with them today, but just for a moment.

"Gotta go, girls," she shouted, when she moved toward her car. "I'll be in touch."

Knowing Kendra might follow her, Jo Ann took an out-of-the way route to the University of Houston. While a graduate student, she used the law library for total isolation. She parked, grabbed her copy of *The Glass Castle*, and found a spot deep in the stacks. She reviewed and outlined the book and clock watched. Finally, at 1:30 p.m., she left for the hotel.

∞∞∞

Robert's drive let him reflect on his time in Little Rock. Half way home, he called the family member he most expected would lend a sympathetic ear about Jo Ann.

"This is Marcia," she answered.

"It's Robert."

"How's the world's greatest granddad? Tricia will hate that she missed you."

"Where's my little angel?"

"She and Bill are at a play group outing. He said I'd earned some time away from our four-year old. I have an hour before he can't handle her and brings her back."

"Can I have 15 minutes of your free hour? I hoped we could talk when Bill wasn't there."

"You can have the whole hour if you need it. What's up?"

"I found a woman I'm interested in."

"Say that again."

"I found a woman I'm interested in."

"I've been praying that would happen. I can only say, amen!"

Robert, using his phone's hands free feature, scanned the highway as he talked. "It's complicated," he said.

"What's the complication?"

"Jo Ann is black."

"What's the complication?"

"I never imagined that would happen."

"Maybe you didn't, but I ask you again, what's the complication?"

In a soft, shaky voice he asked, "You don't see that as being an issue?"

"Why should it be an issue? I assume you like her or you wouldn't be telling me this, right?"

He answered loudly, "I like her a lot."

"Is she a good person?"

"She's wonderful. We're still learning about each other, but we've talked for hours about so many things. I haven't felt this way since Darla died."

Robert heard a sharpness in Marcia's voice. "Then whoever has a problem with her being black has the problem, not you."

"Is that how it works?"

"Robert," Marcia asked, with a heavy sigh, "who are the people who love you?"

"You and Bill, Tricia, Al and Deena, Sandy, my brother Tim and Candace, their kids."

Marcia groaned. "Do you think any of us will stop loving you because you love a black woman?"

"I wonder about Deena but, really, no. What about my friends?"

"I don't know your friends that well. Except for meeting some of them at weddings and Darla's funeral, everything I know about them is what you've told me. If somebody has a problem, how much of a friend are they?"

"What about work? She works at my company."

Marcia replied politely, but firmly. "It's not your company, not like the places you worked before you retired. You don't need the money. If they hassle you, leave. I bet there are plenty of other opportunities if you look."

"Okay," Robert said, noticing the tall pines start giving way to shorter oak trees.

"You should learn some things about black people, since you know almost nothing, based on what I've seen."

"I've already started." He told her about his Little Rock trip.

"Doing that was neat. I bet Jo Ann appreciates it."

"She does, Marcia. She does."

"Tell me about her."

As he wound through small towns and forest land, Robert related Jo Ann's story and an abbreviated version of their time together. He left out their afternoon plans.

Marcia concluded by saying, "If you want Jo Ann, don't let color stand in the way."

At 1:35 p.m., he hit the outskirts of Houston. It wouldn't be long now. He wondered if Jo Ann had reached the hotel.

Chapter 12

J o Ann swiped the card key to open the door of her room at the J.W. Marriott at 1:55 p.m. She hung her outfits on one side of the closet and put her folded lingerie in a dresser drawer. She refreshed her makeup and sat on the bed.

She switched on an ESPNU preview of the NCAA Track & Field Championships. A few years ago, she'd have been getting ready to go to that event and cheer for Melissa. Today her mind raced to where she was and why, so she switched off the television.

A week ago, Robert Hart had just been a man she passed in the hallways at work. In a few minutes, they would make love. Or, she asked herself, will we just fuck? She wasn't sure. Jo Ann yearned for real love making, that she would feel more than the rush from consuming Robert's hot flesh, more than the excitement of his hardness thrusting inside her.

The talks on the phone, the longing she felt at the sound of his voice, and what she'd experienced during *The Kiss* gave her hope this might turn into something special. Despite herself, she crossed her fingers.

Kendra and Tiffany's anger with Brenda Watts for dating a white man invaded her thoughts. How would she choose between them and Robert?

Her phone rang. It was him. "That's good timing," she said. "It's 2:12p.m. I got here 17 minutes ago."

"What room?"

She told him the number.

"Let's see how fast I can get there."

"I'll time you."

Jo Ann looked around the room at paintings on the wall of green, open spaces. The knock came three minutes later. She opened the door. "What took you so long?" she asked. He gave no answer and she never expected one.

Her long, lean legs, narrow waist, rounded butt, up lifted breasts, yearning brown eyes, and curled, jet black hair dominated the room. They stood just inside the door which, together, they pushed shut. He put down his bag and reached for her.

They embraced. Leaving their arms around their waists, they pulled back and looked at each other. No words passed between them. They resumed *The Kiss*. As tongues probed mouths, they held each other even tighter than on Tuesday.

He bent his knees, since he was nine inches taller. Jo Ann ground her hips into Robert's groin. Her hands clutched and rubbed his back and shoulders. The hint of wetness she sensed seeping out of her while she waited for him became a river.

Today, Jo Ann had every reason for exploring Robert's slacks for the erection she knew she'd find there. When she rubbed it through the fabric, she gasped at its firmness and length. If this is just a fuck, it could be one hell of a fuck, she thought. He swung her around and guided them to the bed.

Robert stepped out of his loafers during the trip from the door. Jo Ann let her sandals fall off as they sank on to the bed. She started undoing the buttons on her shirt, but he stopped her.

He toyed with the top button, and several times slipped it into and out of its hole. He did the same with the remaining buttons. He provoked a gasp when he snaked a hand into the black lace of her bra and stroked her nipple. Her lips brushed his and they kissed again.

He reached behind her and lifted the shirt. He rubbed her bare back before running his hand into her shorts and under her panties. He kneaded her buttocks. Jo Ann relished the strength in his grip. Soon, he moved up her back again and unsnapped the bra. She began unbuckling his belt.

Robert pulled the shirt over her head. He swept it away, along with the unhooked bra. He stared at her bare breasts and their black areole and nipples. Soon, though, watching wasn't enough. He dropped his lips to one nipple and began nibbling and suckling. She threw her head back and moaned. The nipple hardened.

His nibbling and suckling encouraged Jo Ann's furious work on his belt. She pulled it out of the loops on his pants, slid down his zipper, and reached inside his briefs. He returned the moan as she grasped his erection. Robert pulled his shirt over his head. The belt gone, Jo Ann pushed off his pants and briefs. She noticed he wore no socks and wondered if he'd driven home like that, with the aim of making this easier.

With all Robert's clothes off, Jo Ann savored the long, naked man before her. A shudder ran through her as she scanned his body and stroked his erection. She burned inside.

Robert leaned back and stared at her dark, round breasts. He undid the button on her shorts. She relaxed, so he could unzip and push them off her. He lingered there for a second. She lifted her hips as he grasped the waistband of her black bikini panties, the ones she would tell him later she picked out for this moment. He pulled them off her and tossed them away.

Now naked, Jo Ann thrashed about on the fresh sheets. Robert kissed her hard again and held her tightly. She ground her mouth into his and her hips undulated wildly. Gradually, she worked her way under him.

Jo Ann grasped his erection, curious about the fact he wasn't circumcised. She wondered if that would make any difference in their lovemaking. She pulled his hardness into her aching center and closed her eyes. She wanted to speak, to say how wonderful this felt. She dared not.

The fever of their foreplay receded into an easy rhythm. Jo Ann wrapped her strong legs around Robert's thighs as he thrust into her. They kissed, rubbed, and nibbled on each other. Robert played with her nipples as she moved easily beneath him. Her mind cleared. This felt so right! Whether it was just an afternoon tryst or the start of something special, this was where she wanted to be, with him inside her.

She built toward an orgasm. She desperately hoped he could hold on until she made it. She pushed harder and harder into him. Soon a climax shook her body. She assumed he would soon finish. Instead, he slowed briefly, but picked up speed again. Urgency returned. Their moans filled the room though no words passed between them.

In an instant, Robert changed the rhythm. The smooth, even strokes that followed their coupling became the driving thrusts of a piston-like machine. Again, she expected his finish. She tightened her arms and legs around him, determined she wouldn't let go until their passion brought them to a thunderous crescendo.

Just as she felt him throb within her, announcing his explosion, another orgasm shook her. She'd never had this happen – her climax and her man's at the same time. Her arms, legs, and her sex squeezed him. With eyes closed, she savored the moment's warmth.

Inevitably, they slept. Finally, Jo Ann woke to the sight of the clock radio. Red numbers said 5:47 p.m. Book club beckoned.

Jo Ann looked at the man beside her. She compared

his white skin to hers. She found the difference amusing, interesting, and titillating, as she'd heard happened with interracial couplings.

Jo Ann threw her legs off the bed and headed for the bathroom. After a toilet stop, she picked up her scattered clothing, showered, and retrieved her evening outfit from the closet. When she stepped toward the dresser, she noticed Robert had shifted onto his back.

She dressed in light slacks and a blue, V-necked top, then finished her makeup in the bathroom. When she stepped into her open-toed sandals, she found Robert awake and looking over her.

He sat up. "My, don't you look great!"

"I thought you liked me better without clothes."

"If you insist on wearing clothes, those are nice."

"Thank you."

"We could talk about what we did this afternoon, but there's nothing I can say except let's do it again as soon as you get back."

She strapped on her watch, walked to the bed, leaned down, and kissed him. "I second that motion."

"What's the deal on the book club?" he asked as their lips separated and she stepped back. "You haven't told me anything about it."

"I only have a few minutes." She looked at her watch and sat down in a chair. "What can I tell you?"

"Who's in it? How long have you been in it? How does it work? Stuff like that."

"Margie Scott started it ten years ago with six people, three couples. Margie split up with her boyfriend, leaving only five, so they invited me along with Bonnie Walton, a woman my age who worked at JAX. She's now marketing director at a non-profit. Bonnie later married John Brooks, an HR guy at a big bank. That made eight."

Robert laid on his side, his head propped on one elbow. "So, three couples and two single people?"

"We rotate selections. Each person picks a book every eighth meeting. We meet once a quarter for dinner at a couple's house. Margie and I, as the singles, are paired for purposes of meeting location. Margie moved to Austin a few years ago, so when our turn comes up, one time we meet at my house and one time we meet in Austin."

"Who are the other couples, the other original members?"

"James and Della Bryant are in their mid-50s. He sells heavy equipment and she's assistant director of the Houston Public Library. Devin Allen and Connie Cross, who are in their early 40s, are the other married couple. He's an in-house lawyer for an auto distributor and she's my gynecologist."

"I guess she'll find out about us when you go for a checkup after we've spent a night together and you're full of me."

"I'll keep you away before I go see her."

He sat up on the bed. "Are all these people black?"

She shook her head. "No. What makes you ask that?"

"You told me that, other than work, your world is mostly black. I figured this was too."

"Because the three women I hang out with are so race conscious, perhaps it feels my world is blacker than it is. Five people in the club are white. Three are black."

"Who are the other two black people?"

"Connie and Devin. Devin grew up in Houston, did college at Missouri and law school at Texas. Connie is from Florida. She attended college and medical school at Duke, came here for a residency, and stayed."

A slow smile spread across his face. "Is that strange – being friends with your doctor?"

Jo Ann stopped for a moment. "It could be, but Connie is so caring, so down to earth, it doesn't matter. Except at checkups, I don't think of her as my doctor. If she weren't so busy, I'd hang out with her a lot more – and less with Kendra and Tiffany."

"Do Connie and Devin have kids?"

"Two girls, 13 and 14."

Robert listened for clues about Jo Ann's life in the stories of her friends. "What about the rest of the group?"

"James and Della's kids are grown and gone. John and Bonnie don't have kids together, but both have grown children from prior marriages. Margie is 53 and has a six-year-old daughter and a 33-year old son."

"How'd that happen?"

Jo Ann stared at her hands on her lap. "She had a son at age 20. Her husband died in a light plane crash. She raised that kid on her own. She put herself through the University of Illinois, moved down here, and made a good life for them. Her son graduated with honors from A&M."

"What's the deal on the daughter?"

"At 46, Margie got involved with a younger man, got careless, and turned up pregnant. She loved him, but he couldn't handle a kid. He disappeared. She agonized over whether she should have the baby, give it up for adoption, or keep it. I spent a lot of time talking with her about it. She finally decided she'd keep the little girl and raise her herself."

"Will I get to meet these people?" he asked, clasping his hands behind his head as he leaned back against the bed's headboard.

She stood up, grabbing her keys and the book. "How about in September? I can make it a tryout for whether the group will take us in as a couple."

Nothing else she could have said would have made him feel as good. She was bringing him into her world. She leaned over the bed, kissed him again, and walked out the door.

∞ ∞ ∞

After Jo Ann left, Robert got up and threw on a pair of shorts and a Harvard Business School t-shirt. He picked up a snack in the lobby and began reading Robert Caro's *The Years of Lyndon Johnson: Master of the Senate*. In no time, it was 10:45 p.m. and Jo Ann returned, seeming giddy as she brushed her teeth, washed her face, and undressed.

"I wish you could have been there," she whispered, slipping off her panties and sliding into bed. "I wanted to show you off."

Robert said nothing. He reached for her, and they made passionate love for the second time that day. Afterwards, they snuggled and chatted about the book club meeting. When she returned from a bathroom trip, she pressed him for a confession.

"You faked being asleep this afternoon and watched me dress, didn't you?"

"How'd you know?"

"You couldn't keep that grin off your face, or your eyes closed."

"You weren't offended?"

She wriggled her eyebrows. "I'd have been offended only if you hadn't watched."

He said, "There are two things – undressing my lover and watching her dress – I enjoy about an intimate relationship that I've really missed these eight years."

"What do you like about watching your lover dress?"

"Gradual covering of flesh and imagining baring that flesh

later. It's the process, the order in which she puts things on. Does she put on the bra first or the panties, the top first or the skirt or slacks first?"

"What did you learn today?"

"You put your panties on first, then tuck your breasts into the bra, then you put on your slacks before the top."

"When you watch me dress for work, you'll see something different."

"What's that?"

"I put on my pantyhose over the panties, then the bra."

"I've noticed you're one of the few women at the office who still wears hose every day."

"My legs look better and I look more professional in hose."

"Your legs look great, hose or no hose."

With that, she reached for him and again guided him into her. Afterward, they fell into a deep sleep, wrapped tightly around each other.

Chapter 13

Though Robert's 63 years dictated two bathroom trips during the night, they otherwise remained asleep and entwined until 7:30 Sunday morning when intense hunger awakened him. Jo Ann stirred. He begged off her advances, warning that if he didn't eat soon and replenish his energy, she'd find sex a major disappointment.

He started to order room service, but she stopped him. "We should eat downstairs. Let's see the world for a while."

He hesitated. "I guess so. We can do that if you want."

She sat beside him on the bed and patted his thigh as he put down the phone. "Sooner or later," she said, "people will see us and know we're together. It's okay."

"I – well --," he stammered.

"I'm ready for whatever happens. Well, I'm not ready for Tiffany, Kendra, and Betty knowing about us, but that's not a problem this morning. Still, people will see us together.

"We can't have what we had yesterday and last night unless we have a total relationship. I'm not hiding from the world. I don't want to be with you if that's what you're planning. Whatever people say, they say."

"You're right," he said, rubbing his palms together. "I'm not embarrassed about being seen with you."

"I didn't say that. You're afraid of explaining why, after years alone, you're with somebody who looks like me. You've never done anything that wasn't conventional. Being with me isn't what anybody expects from you. We'll help each other through it. You mean a lot to me already. I'm not letting you get away over that. Now get dressed!"

This woman was special. "You do take charge, don't you?"

"I know what I want. I want a relationship with you. I've never hidden who I'm with from the world and I'm not starting now."

"I get it," he said, pulling on his shirt.

∞∞∞

In the elevator, Robert told Jo Ann he'd extended their stay through Sunday night. He said he'd forego church so they could do anything with the day they liked.

At breakfast they laughed and touched each other across the table. Her gaze alternated between the mole on his nose and his blue eyes. He closed them from time to time and remembered her dark nipples and areole.

Not long after the food arrived, a stocky, middle-aged white man approached their table. He wore a dark blue suit, white shirt, and red tie. He looked like a man on a mission. Robert jumped up once he realized the man's presence.

"Jimmy Hundley! I didn't expect I'd see you here," Robert said, extending his hand. He towered over the man, who stood about five-feet, seven-inches tall. He smiled and greeted Robert in return. He had a ruddy complexion, hazel eyes, and a receding hairline.

"I could say the same thing." Looking at Jo Ann, he added, "I didn't mean to interrupt. I just thought I'd say hello."

"You aren't interrupting. Let me introduce Jo Ann Davis. Jo Ann, my old friend Jimmy Hundley."

"It's nice to meet you, Jo Ann. I'll just take a moment. Robert, how've you been?"

"I'm great. What are you doing these days?"

"Putting deals together. This morning, I'm meeting guys who claim they have production I could get a piece of." Hundley paused for a second. "Are you still consulting at JAX?" he asked. When Robert nodded, he continued, "I think you should look at doing what I do. I can set you up. Together, we might do some great stuff."

Robert recalled his conversation with Marcia. "You know, I might consider that. Why don't we get together sometime?"

"Take my card," Hundley said, pulling one from the pocket of his starched white shirt. "Call me. I should let you folks get on with breakfast. Jo Ann, it was nice to meet you."

They shook hands, Hundley left, and Robert sat down.

She grasped his hand. "I'm so glad that happened," she said. "It's not such a big deal. He was nice, whether he meant it or not. I imagine he said the same things about business he would have said if I had the blondest hair in Houston. Anybody who shuns you because of me, you don't need."

Robert squeezed her hand in return. "Thank you, my love. Thank you."

They planned the day as they ate. Back in the room, they made love again, this time slowly, without Saturday's urgency.

Just after 11 o'clock Robert and Jo Ann stepped out of the hotel lobby and walked toward the parking lot across the street. They both wore shorts and athletic shoes. She held his hand because she wanted to hold it and so the world could see them as a couple.

Jo Ann had never attended a car show, events Robert went to regularly. They headed for Reliant Stadium, today hosting a major show with over a thousand vehicles. She marveled at the care the exhibitors and owners put into their cars. Robert, who owned a vintage 1966 Pontiac Firebird, enjoyed explaining the exhibitions they saw and the pleasure it appeared she took from this adventure.

As they left the stadium parking lot, Jo Ann got quiet. Finally she said, "There is something that may divide us as much or more than race. We have time now. It's been on my mind."

"What's that?" he asked.

"Religion."

Robert jerked his head back. "Why would religion divide us?"

"Because you're a really religious person and I'm not."

He raised his hand, then rubbed his throat. "That's a broad stroke. You don't know how I see religion. You know I go to church and attended a church-affiliated college. That's all you know."

"I hardly go to church at all," she said, as he swung the car onto the freeway.

He leaned toward her. "Let's start with your religious history. Everybody has one."

"I attended a Baptist church near the project where we lived," she began. As she continued, her tone deepened and he noticed her eyes turned cold. "I hated the mean things I heard about hell and what could happen if I did the smallest thing wrong."

He chuckled and asked, "You got a lot of Old Testament, and not much New, right?"

"I barely know the difference."

"Not unusual. Go on."

"In my teen years, my mother quit making me go. Later,

some school friends took me to a Methodist Church, which I found friendlier. In college, I stopped going at all."

"What happened when you married and had kids?"

"James took them to his Baptist church. After the divorce, I let them decide. Tony went. Guys on his high school football team were big into the – "

"Fellowship of Christian Athletes?"

"That's it. Anyway, he went, but the girls didn't."

"What do you do now?"

She shrugged. "A couple of times a year I tolerate attending a Methodist church with my friend Kendra in the name of keeping peace. I doubt Kendra is much of a believer. She goes to be seen."

"I understand why you might be bummed about church."

In a soft voice, she asked, "Where do you go to church?"

"First Congreational United Church of Christ Church on Bienhorn. I've attended UCC churches all my life. A lot of people in the helping professions attend UCC churches. You wouldn't find a lot of hardcore business people in most, but its where I feel most comfortable."

"Can I go to church with you sometime? I sense there's a lot I don't know?"

"Of course. I also have books you should consider reading."

She took a pen and pad from her purse. "What are they?"

"Write down *Meeting Jesus Again for the First Time*, by Marcus Borg -- B-o-r-g -- and *The Historical Jesus for Beginners*, by William Linden – L-i-n-d-e-n. He was a really smart tax lawyer at the biggest firm in Houston. He died last November. I met him when he did some work for my company. He retired and went into full time theological study. He sent me an autographed copy of his book."

She looked at him and squinted. "We each have books we

should read about race and religion. We make quite a pair, don't we?"

$$\infty \infty \infty$$

Robert parked the car near Mercer Arboretum in the northeastern part of town. They walked the nature trail, held hands, and stopped for kisses. In the late spring air, Jo Ann snapped photos of them amidst the trees and Robert pointed out the names of plants. A romantic dinner followed at a candle-lit restaurant.

Back at the hotel, they cleaned up. Exhausted from the walking and the excitement of the weekend, they fell into bed and slept. Deep in the night, they reached for each other and made love again.

Monday morning, Jo Ann awakened first, but Robert soon stirred. She put on the dressing show she'd promised. He said before showing up at the office he needed to retrieve Rufus from the kennel, then check things at home since he'd been away almost a week. Jo Ann gave him a long, sensuous kiss and left for work. Only when she swung her car onto the street did she realize she hadn't thought for a moment what she'd say about what she had done with herself, except book club, since one o'clock Saturday afternoon.

Chapter 14

T uesday Jo Ann found herself longing to gaze into Robert's eyes, run her hands through his hair, and hear his voice. She felt a need for his touch on her naked body and for his hardness inside her.

Meetings consumed her morning and he didn't show up until mid-afternoon. When she left for the day, she noticed his door closed.

At home, his number flashed on her phone. "I wondered when we'd talk," she told him. "I never caught up with you today."

"Two finance people held me hostage. I stopped by your office when I got free, but you'd left."

"You wanted to see me, too?"

She heard desire in his voice. "I did."

"What are we doing about our mutual angst?"

"I love that word," he said. "I would have called it lust."

She laughed. "That's right too."

"How do I get to your place?"

She gave him directions.

"I'll be there – soon! I'll bring food."

"Bringing food is nice, but bringing yourself is plenty."

By the time Robert arrived carrying Chinese dinners, Jo Ann had shed her work clothes and showered. She greeted him wearing green shorts and a white New Mexico State football t-shirt. They embraced and lingered over a kiss just inside her front door. She led him to the kitchen table where she'd left two wine glasses and a bottle of Merlot.

After the meal, she took him to her bedroom. They kissed again and she asked that he "wait a second." When she returned, she found him sitting naked on the bed, his clothes discarded on a corner chair.

Jo Ann stood in the doorway between her bed and the bathroom, wearing a white bra and matching bikini panties. The contrast between her dark skin and the white lingerie lit up the room. She undid the front clasp of the bra and watched it fall away. She hooked her thumbs into the waist band of the panties. His eyes widened as she lowered them from her hips, down her legs, and into a pile on the floor with the bra. She watched his eyes dart back and forth between the dark triangle between her legs and her smiling face as she fell to the bed.

Afterwards, they cuddled silently, her back to him as he held her in his arms. Eventually, she turned around and propped her chin in one hand. "This was even better than the weekend," she said.

"Why do you think that?"

"I know now I want to be with you. Since I want to be with you, the lovemaking gets better and better."

"I like that," he said. "Did you have doubts before Saturday?"

She frowned and bit her lip. "I couldn't be sure. I know how much we talked and how confident I was we were ready to make love."

"You said you didn't need dinners or movies before you 'jumped my bones.'"

"I said that, but I remember sitting in the hotel room before you got there wondering if we were just going to fuck or really make love. I would have been okay with just fucking. I liked being around you. I thought we could have a good time together, even if we just became buddies who got together and blew off steam in bed from time to time. I discovered Saturday and Sunday I want way more than that from being with you."

He leaned over and kissed her. "Who knows where this'll go. Let's not worry about that. But I'm with you. I want more than just getting in your pants from time to time."

"I may not keep them on very much when I'm around you."

"Then I want you again. Now!"

Jo Ann turned over and pulled him into her from behind. She rolled up in a ball, her back to him as he plowed into her. The deep penetration brought her more intense pleasure than she'd known in years. He threw his leg over her and she grabbed his ankle, anchoring him for his thrusts. Their cries and grunts filled the room. Both hurtled toward orgasm. Finally, he emptied himself into her and they slept.

In a few weeks, people at JAX knew about them. One night a female executive walked by as they embraced in the parking garage. Jo Ann heard two secretaries comparing notes after both saw them leave together late one day, then noticed Jo Ann's car parked in the same remote spot at 6:30 a.m. the next day. A middle level manager who worked closely with Jo Ann saw them together at lunch two days in a row.

"It's not a problem for me," Robert said as they sat at her kitchen table one night in late June, after the salmon and rice dinner she cooked for them. "I can leave anytime I want. But I worry about you."

"Why? I haven't violated company policy. If we were married, that might create a nepotism issue and maybe somebody could say something."

He tapped a finger on the table. "People might make life uncomfortable for you."

"I've worked there 11 years. There've been office romances. The talk fades. The difference is that this romance is between a white man and a black woman. Well, so what?"

"Maybe I should offer David Marks my resignation."

"Do you want to leave?"

"Not now. Finishing my projects before I move on would be nice. I've thought about taking Jimmy Hundley up on getting involved in his business."

"Do it if that's what you want. But don't leave JAX because of whispers about us."

They cleaned the kitchen together. When they finished, without saying a word, she took his hand and led him to her bedroom. He leaned down and kissed her, unbuttoned her shirt, and unsnapped her pink, front close bra. She lowered her shorts, let him slip off hipster panties that matched her bra. Together, they removed his clothes and fell into her bed, where they stayed until the next morning.

Robert kept working on his JAX projects and they continued seeing each other as they had all summer. Neither spent time in the other's office except for business. They lunched together occasionally and still left together from time to time but curtailed the garage necking sessions. The rumors swirled a while longer but, as Jo Ann predicted, they died down by late July.

$$\infty\infty\infty$$

As the summer wore on, they worked at finding out the big things and little things, important things and trivial things, about each other. He learned she keenly followed current events and politics. She learned that he was largely apolitical. His reading of the books Henry Walker, Jackie McFadden's friend, suggested opened for him a new window on the world. Jo Ann appreciated the intensity with which he attacked the huge volumes. He finished them by early August.

Robert followed football, basketball, and baseball from high school level up and played golf and tennis two or three times a week each. Besides Saturday mornings with his regular foursome, he often snuck away one weekday afternoon for a round of golf with a friend or by himself. He played tennis nights and Sundays, competed in a men's league, attended clinics, and took private lessons.

Jo Ann didn't play golf and wasn't interested in learning. She liked tennis so, despite some trepidation, Robert began taking her to play at the club. She wasn't an accomplished player but, given her athleticism and physical conditioning, she improved quickly by working with Robert and taking lessons.

In mid-July, they began playing mixed doubles matches against other club members. Initially, they got some disapproving looks from adjoining courts but soon, Jo Ann became just another female guest at Starling Country Club.

Both cherished being outdoors and looked for trails they could hike. They talked for hours on car trips. Only love making excited them as much as their conversations. Robert detailed his hobbies like wood working, sports, and cars. She told him of the joy she took in reading – novels, political works, history, and self-help books. Their common interests – plays, music, and movies – became clearer.

For the Fourth of July, Jo Ann talked him into joining her on the ruined San Diego trip. He balked at first, given his distaste for flying. Ultimately, he decided the benefits of soothing her feelings, playing golf at Torrey Pines, and time in bed with her outweighed his disdain for the TSA.

Since the Fourth fell on Thursday, they left Wednesday night from Houston's Hobby Airport. Walks on the beach, an afternoon at the San Diego Zoo, delicious food, and scintillating sex made the weekend a memorable holiday.

One weird thing happened. Once on the plane, Jo Ann told Robert she felt watched in the airport terminal. She didn't see anything unusual, but something spooked her.

Right before the San Diego trip, Robert called Jimmy Hundley who enthusiastically greeted Robert's potential interest in his ventures. Hundley had an international trip scheduled, so they couldn't meet until late July. Robert continued researching Hundley's holdings and investment history. He grew excited about the idea of moving in a different direction.

Chapter 15

After San Diego, Jo Ann sensed her three friends backing away. The next weekend Betty and Charles visited family in Michigan. The following weekend Tiffany, claiming a work emergency, begged off an art gallery excursion. When nothing came together for the last weekend of the month, Jo Ann suspected something was amiss. Early one weekday evening, her phone rang as she left home for a tennis date with Robert.

"Wonder why you haven't heard from me?" Kendra fumed.

"I assumed you'd call. I don't know what you've had going on," Jo Ann responded.

"It's what you've had going on," Kendra snapped. "You know what I'm talking about."

"I don't."

"You do!"

"I don't enjoy this game, Kendra."

"San Diego!"

"What about San Diego? You knew about that."

"You didn't say you were going with your white boy lover."

Jo Ann recalled that strange feeling at the airport. "Say again?"

"You acted like teenagers," Kendra sneered, "slobbering all over each other. It was disgusting."

Jo Ann clenched her jaw. "Why were you spying on me?"

"I wasn't spying. My flight arrived at the gate next to yours. I got off my plane and there you were. I can't believe you didn't see me."

"I didn't. Not that it would have changed anything."

"That's even more disgusting."

Jo Ann lowered her voice. "My relationship with Robert is my business. I'm sorry you found out this way. I assumed we'd discuss it at some point. Now is not the time. We can talk later, but right now I have an appointment."

"I'm sure he's the appointment. We don't need to talk. I'm done with you, as is Tiffany. We understood we had to support the race. You don't support the race by sleeping with white boys!" The phone clicked.

Jo Ann knew Kendra wasn't bluffing. She would cut Jo Ann out of her life. Tiffany would follow her lead. Jo Ann called Betty. "Can you talk?" Jo Ann asked.

Betty's usually strong voice sounded distant, far off. "Kendra and Tiffany don't want me talking to you."

"I assumed that. You're my friend. Please let me keep being your friend."

Betty sighed. "This is hard. I don't like what you're doing either, but it's your life. I said that when we heard about Brenda Watts dating a white guy."

"Do you remember saying then you understood that sometimes things don't work out so we can all find a good black man?"

"I said that," Betty stammered. "I never thought this would happen in our group." She then asked, "We've been friends 14 or 15 years, right?"

"Yes, since right before my divorce."

"Given us being friends that long, tell me why you'd do this?"

Jo Ann took a deep breath. "You know how lonely I've been. You said yourself I might not find love where I expected it. You know about the black men I've dated, like Frank Wilson, who hit on every woman they see. I tried finding a black man. I'm happy now. Kendra and Tiffany don't care about that. I hoped you'd be happy for me."

Betty's voice waned. "I want you to be happy. I found a good black man. Couldn't you find one, too?"

"It's harder now. We both know why. At some point, your own happiness becomes more important than protecting the race."

"Did this white guy fall for you or did you fall for him?"

"We fell for each other. We both saw there was something between us. It's been a hell of a ride."

Betty offered a suggestion. "For now, let's just talk on the phone and not meet. We should let things cool off. Kendra and Tiffany don't know what to do with this. The best thing now is to just stay out of each other's way."

Jo Ann pulled into the club, parked, grabbed her bag, and got out of the car. Robert, blue eyes sparkling, waited beside the tennis center entrance. His warm embrace eased her sadness from the phone calls.

A few days after Kendra's tirade, Robert asked Jo Ann about how her friends felt about them being together. "You haven't said much about them," he told her as they finished dinner one night at his house, Rufus parked under the table looking for scraps.

"Two of them have decided I'm persona non grata. Tiffany and Kendra say they'll never speak to me again."

"They can't mean that."

"Kendra means it and Tiffany won't dare cross Kendra."

"What about your other friend, Betty?"

"She wants it both ways. She talks to me behind the backs of the others, but won't stand up to them. That's her personality. I haven't given up on her."

"Two won't speak to you just because I'm white?"

"They think I'm betraying the race, being disrespectful to black men."

"Are you?"

"No! You can't say that!"

He lifted their plates from the table and moved toward the dishwasher. "I wouldn't have asked that before that week in Little Rock and reading the books. I now know something about how black people have been hurt."

Seeming to him on the verge of tears, she said, "I love you. I spent many years putting the race first, not bringing home a white boy, buying into that stuff about supporting my black brothers.

"What I got was long nights by myself or, when I was with someone, wondering who he'd been with the night before and who he'd be with the next night."

"I get that," he said, feeding Rufus a piece of bread.

"Don't worry about what my friends think. We'll have challenges and hard times. I want to be with you and if I have to do without some people, I'll do without them."

He took her hand when they finished cleaning the kitchen. They stopped in the hallway and embraced, then walked the remaining steps to the bedroom they now shared most nights.

They grappled with each other's clothes. Down to her lingerie, she looked up at him. "I need you," she said. "Don't let go of me."

"I won't, my love. Don't doubt me."

"I don't. Just know how I feel inside."

Her clothes gone, she opened her legs and he plunged into her. They grunted, laughed, moaned, and giggled for the next 30 minutes before he emptied himself into her. He enveloped her with his long body and they slept.

Chapter 16

Robert thought it inevitable some of his 25-30 close friends and business associates would disapprove of his involvement with a black woman. Many grew up and lived in the same lily-white world he had, attending schools with little black presence and moving into similar business and social worlds. Only a handful had more than a superficial understanding of America's racial history.

While Robert hadn't seen much overt racism, he had observed the subtle variety. He hadn't ever considered the effects of stereotyping and profiling on the black psyche. One night, for example, when Jo Ann left to retrieve some things from her house, she said, "Wish me luck and hope I don't get stopped for DWB." The blank look on his face required that she explain *Driving While Black*.

After looking up the statistics on the difference in police stops of blacks and whites in his neighborhood, he understood. Some of his white friends saw nothing wrong with that gap. At the club, on the rare occasion someone said something about blacks, it usually wasn't supportive.

As his involvement with Jo Ann became obvious, Robert knew one particular shoe would soon drop. It did in late July, in the club grill after the Saturday golf round. As Robert poured beer from a pitcher, Jerry Blanks leaned over and inquired, "Robert, my boy, how's that black tail you've been getting?"

Tommy Smith, the group member Robert most expected would hassle him, asked with a scowl, "What's up with that? I saw you leaving here one night with some colored woman. The two of you were getting real friendly." Tommy, 56 and a little chubby at five-feet, nine-inches, had a square jaw, and large blue eyes. He constantly chewed gum.

"Hey, guys," Robert began, "that's private."

"You haven't been private about it," Jerry said, rubbing the back of his neck. He was 60 and, at six-feet, four inches, the only one of the group anywhere near Robert's height. "I've seen you out here playing tennis with her. I first thought she was a friend of some woman club member. Then I saw you with her again, and again, and again after that."

"Is it true?" Tommy asked. "Are you really banging a colored woman? This is just chasing some tail, isn't it?" The youngest of the group, Tommy still had the hair from his youth, though it had turned from flaming red to a dull rust color.

"I like getting laid too, but I can't believe you'd fall for some ghetto babe," Jerry said, taking a sip of beer and squinting his brown eyes. A smirk crossed his thin face as he uttered the words 'ghetto babe.' "I know you're lonely. You haven't been with anybody since Darla died, too long, if you ask me. But why this? There are plenty of good white women out there."

Terry Peters, Robert's closest friend among the group, had remained silent. A broad-shouldered man of 61 with longish hair, wire framed glasses over blue eyes, and perfect teeth, he'd been a hot tight end prospect in high school until he tore up a knee. Except for a family tragedy, he'd lived life simply and worked uneventfully as a suburban real estate lawyer. He revered Joyce, his wife of 33 years. She and Darla had been close and Robert never heard either Terry or Joyce utter an unkind word about anyone.

"You guys aren't fair," Terry said. "First, Robert told you it was private, so maybe he isn't interested in talking about it. Second, even if he was, you won't let him get a word in edgewise. Third, Robert's got a right to be with who he wants to be with. It is a free country, and he is a grown man."

Jerry looked at Robert. "You want to tell us about her?"

"I don't if this is about making fun of someone I cherish. I don't if it's about adolescent, locker room bullying. You guys have been my friends a long time, but I'm not letting you disrespect somebody who's special to me."

"Hey," Jerry said. "I was just b.s.-ing you. I didn't mean any harm." Despite his crass side, Robert knew Jerry's capacity for kindness.

Tommy was another matter, and he was giving only a little. "We should hear what you have to say for yourself." Robert took that not as an olive branch, but only as a tip of Tommy's cap to Terry's dignified stance.

"It's not what I can say for myself," Robert said. "I suppose it shocks you I found somebody who has black skin. I wasn't looking for that. I wasn't looking for anyone. It just happened. She's not a piece of tail and I'm not with her just so I can get laid.

"You guys talk about people taking personal responsibility. She put herself through college, got an MBA at night, and worked her way up to a corporate vice presidency in an almost all-white environment. None of you have any idea what that might be like for a black person. She raised three accomplished children largely by herself. Don't talk to me about a 'ghetto babe!'" He looked straight at Jerry.

Jerry lifted his hands, then let them fall. "Man, I'm sorry. I didn't know."

"You still haven't told us why you're doing it," Tommy sneered.

Before Robert could respond, Terry spoke up. "Sounds like he's doing it for the same reasons you're doing it with Jessica."

Tommy married his second wife less than a year after a messy divorce.

"That's different," Tommy protested, shaking his head.

"How?" Terry asked.

"Jessica and I have a life together," Tommy stammered.

"Are you saying a man can't have a life with a woman who's a different color?" Terry asked.

"It's not supposed to be like that," Tommy countered.

Robert's face lightened for the first time since Jerry and Tommy attacked. "Many things happen differently than they're supposed to happen. Tommy, you and Kelly weren't supposed to get a divorce. Terry's son wasn't supposed to get killed in that car wreck. Jerry, you weren't supposed to have your company tank and you have to rebuild at age 48. Darla wasn't supposed to die at 53."

Jerry stood up. "I shouldn't have said what I did. Does she have a name? I want to meet her sometime."

"It's Jo Ann, Jo Ann Davis."

Kendra and Tiffany kept giving Jo Ann the silent treatment. Betty called Jo Ann occasionally and they exchanged e-mails. In late July, Jo Ann convinced Betty she should have lunch with her and Robert. They met for hamburgers at the Five Guys near JAX.

"You know how much I love this place," Betty said as they waited for Robert. Her brown skin glistened with sweat from the day's brutal sun. She had her hair pulled back and wore little makeup. "I eat here only once in a blue moon. Otherwise, I'd look like Tiffany."

"You wouldn't," Jo Ann replied. "You don't gain weight. But

I get it about Tiffany. She's let herself go, hasn't she?"

Betty smoothed down her floral print summer dress. "I heard Tiffany was a looker once upon a time. Kept herself in great shape. It seems life has beat her up."

Jo Ann slung a purse over her shoulder. "I wonder if Tiffany is carrying around a deep, dark secret."

"Maybe. I wonder what it could be."

"Oh, here's Robert," Jo Ann said, eyeing her man's long frame as he strode across the parking lot. He spotted them when he opened the door. Jo Ann relished his embrace, especially the fact his hand lingered on her back, at the clasp of her bra.

"Hello, my love," he said. "Am I late?"

"You're not late," Jo Ann assured him. "Robert, this is Betty, Betty Martin."

He stepped back, shook Betty's hand, and said, "I'm Robert." He wore gray slacks, a red and white striped dress shirt, red tie, and a blue blazer. He towered over both women, though more over Betty who was three inches shorter than Jo Ann's five-feet, ten-inches.

"Let's eat," Robert said, pointing toward the ordering line. Jo Ann and Betty picked small burgers and diet drinks. Robert showed no such restraint. He told the man behind the counter, "I'll have a half-pound cheeseburger, fries, and a large Coke." As they made their way to a table, he said, "I need my cholesterol fix for the week.".

"That'll do you for a month," Jo Ann sneered.

He jabbed back. "You didn't order fries but you'll poach mine."

"That's possible," Jo Ann admitted. "This way I don't feel guilty."

While waiting for their order, Robert asked, "Betty, tell me about yourself. I've heard Jo Ann's version. I'd like the Betty Martin story from Betty Martin."

"There's not much to tell. I grew up in Flint, Michigan. I went to college at Eastern Michigan."

"Ah yes, Ipsilanti. I spent a week there one night," he said, drawing a smile from Betty and a smirk from Jo Ann. "After college you moved here, worked for a bank, and ended up where you are now – assistant admissions director at Houston Community College. I know all that. What are you really like?"

"I'm about family," Betty said. "My husband of 25 years – Charles – is a dentist. We have two children. Our son, as Jo Ann may have told you, has had problems. He's been in and out of the juvenile justice system since he was 13. The usual teenage stuff – drugs, drinking, petty theft. He's 17 now, so his next mess-up will put him in the adult system, which terrifies me.

"Our daughter, who's 14, has been great – honor student, athlete, musician. All the things you hope for. Sometimes I feel I'm neglecting her because Robbie – our son –takes the air out of everything."

"Must be hard," Robert said. "Any sense he's figuring it out?" They got a call for their food before she could answer.

"A little," Betty allowed as they returned to their table. "Robbie hasn't been in trouble for a year. I still worry about the crowd he runs around with."

"How've you coped?"

"Good friends, like Jo Ann."

"What about Tiffany and Kendra, the two who're giving Jo Ann the silent treatment because of me?"

Jo Ann looked for discomfort in Betty's face. She wasn't sure Betty could talk with Robert about Kendra and Tiffany.

"They've been okay – not like Jo Ann – but okay. Neither has children, so maybe they have a harder time relating."

Robert took a bite of his cheeseburger and a sip from his drink and leaned back in his chair, then forward as he spoke. "I don't have an axe to grind with you because of Tiffany and Kendra. I think what they're doing goes way too far, but I hope you and I can be friends. I know how much you mean to Jo Ann, which is important to me."

"I appreciate that," Betty said as her eyes turned soft, with a bright glow. "I know Jo Ann cares deeply for you. I can't stand in the way of Jo Ann finding happiness."

Robert changed the subject and lightened the mood when he asked, "Your husband is a dentist, right?"

"Charles is a dentist and a good one. He's been practicing 22 years."

"Does he make you brush and floss every day?"

Betty laughed. "He's a fanatic about it. Gets on my nerves."

Jo Ann squeezed Robert's thigh under the table. He turned and kissed her.

"Jo Ann told me you were like that," Betty said.

"Like what?" Robert asked, looking startled.

"Very affectionate, including in public. Charles won't kiss me in public anymore. I love him dearly, but I wish he was different about that. Maybe he can learn from you."

Robert turned away for a moment, then looked directly into Betty's brown eyes. "It was that way with Darla and me. Darla was my wife who died. I imagine Jo Ann has told you about her." Betty nodded.

Robert and Jo Ann exchanged smiles and squeezed each other's hands under the table. He continued, "Showing affection was important in keeping our relationship young and alive. Besides, if I don't kiss Jo Ann in daylight, she won't kiss me at night or do other things with me I want."

Betty squirmed and let out a nervous giggle. "I've heard

about those other things. She says you're good at them."

He laughed. "Only half as good as she is."

They finished eating. When Robert stood up to leave, he said, "I hope I'll see you again. Meeting you was nice." Then, Betty rose and he hugged her.

∞∞∞

Later on the phone, Betty told Jo Ann, "Robert's a good man. I see why you care for him so much. He adores you. I'll tell Tiffany and Kendra that."

"They have to get there themselves," Jo Ann replied. "I hope they can see this is right for me. The fact I'm happy is what's important."

Nothing changed, however, despite the lunch. Word came back from Betty that Kendra and Tiffany didn't want, as part of their circle, "a sister who betrays her black brothers."

Jo Ann resigned herself to their loss. She missed them, but her life was good without them. She had her children and grandchild. Her relationship with Robert washed away the smothering loneliness she'd lived with so long. Weekend trips, walks, wide ranging conversations, and lovemaking left her fulfilled and at ease. Often, she reminded herself the good life she now enjoyed began with sobs on a Friday afternoon in May.

Chapter 17

Tennis became a major part of Robert and Jo Ann's life together. They played three or four times a week, including doubles contests with couples like Harry and Jeri Morris.

Harry, a corporate lawyer in a downtown Houston firm, displayed exceptional quickness for a man of 59. Jeri, a tenacious player despite not being a gifted athlete, resumed her advertising career after raising three children. They welcomed Jo Ann as Robert's new regular mixed doubles partner.

"You should've seen the battles we had," Jeri said of their matches when Darla was Robert's partner. "Both being athletes in school, they were insanely competitive. We almost stopped playing with them."

"I didn't know Darla played sports in school," Jo Ann replied. It was a Sunday and the two women waited outside the club pro shop while Robert and Harry changed. "Robert never told me that."

"She played soccer and tennis in high school, but focused on tennis in college. Aside from being in the band, she won intramural tennis tournaments at Texas. She was as nice as could be off the court, but she'd rip you apart once a match started. You know how Robert is. Together, they could be brutal."

"Harry – and you – seem competitive, but not overly so."

"We matured and changed. Harry and I, who weren't that competitive by nature, ramped it up. We couldn't enjoy playing with Robert and Darla if we didn't get more aggressive. They mellowed with age. By the time she got sick, we'd found a happy medium."

"I'm in the middle," Jo Ann said. She stood up and began stretching. "Two of my kids played school sports. Some of that rubbed off on me. It's still just a game, at least at the level I play."

"Don't sell yourself short," Jeri said, as she started her own stretching routine. She wore a white tennis dress that stopped upper thigh. A thin woman with dirty blonde hair pulled back in a ponytail, her deep tan suggested plenty of time in the sun. "You don't give up on points. I can see you don't like losing."

"What are you two jabbering about?" Harry asked as he and Robert emerged from the locker room. Harry, six-feet, one-inch tall, with sandy hair and brown eyes, wore a blue visor, dark, thigh length tennis shorts, and a maroon Texas A & M polo shirt.

"I could have called off today when he put on that shirt," Robert told Jo Ann as they warmed up. "It will make kicking his butt more fun." Robert took on Darla's University of Texas loyalty when they married and it remained stronger than ever, as his orange polo shirt with the Longhorn logo attested.

Starling offered clay, concrete, and grass outdoor courts. No one in the group except Robert cared much for grass, a surface that rewarded his big serve. For the sake of fairness, they alternated surfaces. Today, it was grass and Robert salivated.

"I'll take it easy on Jeri, but I'm giving you nothing, Bubba," Robert said, looking at Harry as they took their starting places. He'd won the toss and would serve first.

"We'll see," said Harry, settling into receiving position. He had good reason for confidence, Jo Ann thought. Robert admitted, privately, Harry was the best return-of-serve player he knew.

Robert aced his first two serves and produced a service winner on his third. That put him and Jo Ann up, 40-love. Harry punched back a return-of-service winner before Robert delivered an ace past Jeri to win the first game.

As they changed ends, Jeri told Robert, "I'm ready for that take-it-easy-on-the-woman business. That was nasty."

Harry held serve in game two, setting up Jo Ann's first service effort. That remained the weakest part of her game and both Harry and Jeri easily returned her offerings. At deuce, however, she chased down Harry's cross court forehand and laced a winner down the line. Robert's hard volley on the next point meant they held service.

In game four, with Jeri serving, Jo Ann had a chance for a winner at the net and a break point. She netted the shot, however, and Jeri held serve.

At the next changeover, Jeri asked, of no one in particular, "When did we start playing together?"

"Five or six weeks ago," Harry replied, wiping his brow. "Late June."

Jeri added, "Jo Ann, you've come so far in that time. When we started, I wasn't sure you'd ever played before."

"I never took it seriously," Jo Ann said, drying the grip on her racket. "You can't be with Robert and not work at a sport you play. He won't play with you otherwise. I worked on fundamentals. The conditioning part, I had. The game is fun now because I have some idea of what I'm doing."

"You sure do," Harry said as he skipped back onto the court."

Neither team broke service in the first set, so they played a tie breaker Harry and Jeri won, 7-5. The match continued through the second set, as it had in the first, with both teams holding serve. Robert dominated from behind the service line and Jo Ann placed her serves so the returns, especially from Jeri, came back in Robert's wheelhouse.

At the changeover before the 12th game of the second set, Harry told Jo Ann, "I've never seen two people bond together on the court as fast as you two have. You and Robert seem like you know each other as well as he and Darla did."

Jo Ann, sweat dripping from her face, said, "Robert and I carry the bond we share in life to the tennis court. We've both been lonely a long time. Now that we've found each other, we want all we can get out of being together. Tennis is just part of that."

"I admire you," Harry said. "I really admire you for that."

In that 12th game, Robert delivered four straight aces, evening the set and forcing another tie breaker. This time, he and Jo Ann won.

They started the third set on Jeri's serve, which she held. At the love-one changeover, instead of bantering with Harry and Jeri, Robert took Jo Ann aside for some coaching. "Try getting your toss on serve higher," he whispered.

"I'm trying. It's hard."

She leaned on her racket as they stood in the corner at the fence on one end of the court. Sweat poured from her face and her dark skin glistened.

He leaned down and kissed her, meaning he could taste the salt of her perspiration. She wrapped an arm around him and said, "I'm so glad I'm here with you."

"I wouldn't want to be anywhere else," he said. "Now, let's close the deal."

After Robert held serve, tying the set at a game each, Jo Ann decided she should inch forward when receiving Harry's serve. She had progressed enough at return of serve she could force the action.

She thought through the block technique she'd learned in her lessons. Sure enough, one step forward let her hit the ball back deeper. During that third game in set three, Harry twice netted shots off Jo Ann's service returns. Robert and Jo Ann had a break point. When Jeri hit a high, floating shot to Robert's side of the court, he smashed an overhead neither Jeri nor Harry could reach.

"Nice job, partner!" Robert shouted as they changed ends. "You 'da man!"

Everybody laughed, including Jo Ann. Inside, warmth spread through her. Robert used that guy expression sparingly, only when someone did something special, something he respected. That she'd earned it marked another milestone for them. She belonged to his world in a way she hadn't before.

Service breaks in the fifth and seventh games of the third set closed out Jo Ann and Robert's 6-7, 7-6, 6-1 victory.

Cooling off in the club grill, Jo Ann looked around at the crowd. She was the only person of color in the room, except one light-skinned black man dressed in golf clothes who shared a table with three other people. His female companion was white.

Jo Ann asked herself, 'How did I ever end up here?' She looked at Robert and admired his blue eyes and tousled hair. How she got here didn't matter. She was here with him. That's what made her life better than it had ever been before.

Chapter 18

A week before Labor Day Jo Ann prepared for a business conference in Washington. Before her Sunday departure, she and Robert played another hard, three set tennis match against Harry and Jeri Morris, winning 6-4, 5-7, 6-3. Jo Ann rushed off for a shower and a change of clothes. As Robert waited in the club grill, Jerry Blanks approached his table.

"It's been a month since we jumped you about your girlfriend, hasn't it?" Jerry asked as he sat down. At 60, what little of his blonde hair Jerry had left had turned gray. His broad shoulders and 220 pounds spread over a six-feet, four-inch frame kept him looking like the small college defensive lineman he'd once been.

Robert looked directly at Jerry. "About that. Why do you ask?"

"I realized I never apologized. I said some stupid things."

"You kind of did that day, at the end of the conversation, but I appreciate this more."

Jerry tilted his head forward. "So is this the real thing?"

Robert shrugged his shoulders. "Who the hell knows? We're letting whatever happens, happen."

Jerry leaned across the table. "We told Tommy he should look at it like that, but he couldn't wait so that marriage happened faster than it should have."

"It seems they're doing well. What works for some people, doesn't work for others. What happens with Jo Ann and me, time will tell."

"What do your friends say, other than what you heard from us?"

"Not much. I was worried. Most people take it in stride. When we've socialized with them, they don't make anything of it. We've played tennis with Harry and Jeri Morris eight or nine times now. Neither has said anything about Jo Ann's color."

"Nasty stares?"

"A few. Mostly, people ignore us. I'll tell you one thing."

"What?"

"It's like buying a red car, or a blue car. You never saw one before, but now they're all over. I never noticed mixed couples. I see them everywhere now."

Jerry opened his palms. "I see young black guys with white girls. I don't see that many white guy, black woman couples."

"You asked how my friends reacted, but not about hers."

Jerry seemed startled. "There's a problem?"

"Two women friends of 10 to 15 years won't speak to her because of me."

"What?"

"They want her available for a black man. She's a traitor who betrayed the race."

"Huh?"

"They oppose her being with a white man."

Jerry's posture stiffened. "What does Jo Ann think?"

Robert looked around. "She doesn't view herself as a traitor, but she understands why they see it that way."

"Are you worried she won't stay with you because of them?"

"Not now. I once did. She's decided being happy with me is more important. For years, Jo Ann tried finding a black man. It never worked out. When she found she was happy with me, she quit worrying about it anymore."

"I told you, I want to meet her."

"You're going to get to – right now."

Jo Ann emerged from the locker room, carrying her tennis bag in one hand with a small purse slung over the opposite shoulder. She looked at ease in open- toed sandals, pressed gray slacks, and a pale blue knit top that showed a hint of cleavage. Her lightly made-up face and athletic body completed a picture of mature grace.

"Jo Ann!" Robert greeted her. He rose and kissed her on the lips. "Meet my friend and golf buddy, Jerry Blanks."

Jerry bounced up and extended a hand. "Meeting you is a pleasure. I've heard wonderful things about you."

"He lies a lot," she teased, looking at Robert while returning Jerry's handshake. "You've been playing golf with him for years. You know that. I'm pleased to meet you." Robert had told Jo Ann about the July attack, but sanitized it. He didn't hide from her the fact Jerry didn't immediately embrace his romance with a black woman.

The three chatted briefly before Jo Ann reminded Robert they should leave for the airport. "I'm not messing up this trip. I'm staying on schedule so I can see my baby girl," she said. She grabbed her bag and stood up.

Robert explained, "Jo Ann's daughter, Regina, is a University of Texas law grad who clerks for a federal judge in North Carolina. Jo Ann will stop there on her way home from a meeting in Washington."

"I hope I see you again," Jerry said with what Robert thought might have been a little too much politeness. At least he's trying, Robert told himself as they walked out.

Part 3

THE OCTOBER SURPRISE

Chapter 19

Jo Ann arrived at Dulles Airport Sunday night and took a taxi to the conference hotel in Arlington, Virginia. She followed a light dinner with a 45-minute conversation with Robert that left her longing for him, but reassured he missed her as much.

She found the Monday seminar on using statistical analysis in corporate policy making interesting, but her mind wandered. She thought about the upcoming book club meeting at which she would ask that the group include Robert.

After the seminar, Jo Ann ate dinner at an airport restaurant and reached her gate an hour before departure. She settled into the waiting area and began reviewing office memos.

She looked at her watch. It said 7:32 p.m, meaning 5:32 p.m. in Denver. She dialed Tony's number, hoping for a few words with Shonda.

"She's out playing," Tony said. "I just got home from work and Kristin took her and one of the neighborhood girls to the park."

"How are you?" Jo Ann asked.

"I'm good. Work is crazy."

"I won't hold you. I had a meeting in Washington today. I'm at Dulles Airport, headed for North Carolina. I'll see Regina."

"I'll tell Shonda you called."

When she hung up, Jo Ann felt a twinge in her abdomen. On her last bathroom trip before boarding, she noticed wetness between her legs. Some kind of post-menopausal discharge, she assumed. She barely looked at it as she fished an old pad from her bag and slipped it inside her panties.

Jo Ann hadn't seen Regina since March when she left for North Carolina. Regina graduated from law school in December, took the February Texas bar exam, and planned on beginning her clerkship in July. The clerk she was replacing resigned early and Regina's judge asked that she start work right after the bar exam.

In North Carolina, Regina collected Jo Ann in her still-new Toyota Corolla, a mother's law school graduation present. Regina's one-bedroom apartment wasn't suited for overnight guests, so Jo Ann had booked a hotel. She felt no more twinges. When she undressed and showered, everything seemed normal, though she found the pad slightly soiled.

Tuesday, Jo Ann met Regina's fellow clerks. Later the boss, United States Court of Appeals Judge Evelyn Moss herself, appeared outside Regina's cubicle. A short, trim woman with dark hair and blue eyes, she wore a flowing, dark blue, ankle-length dress. The judge announced she was taking her native-Texan clerk and the clerk's mother to lunch at the faculty club at Wake Forest University where she taught before taking the bench.

That evening Regina, having exchanged her work clothes for green shorts and a white top, picked up her mother for dinner.

"You seem happy. How do you like the job, Baby?" Jo Ann asked as they settled into a booth at a small café 15 minutes from the hotel. She studied her daughter across the table. Her curly, jet black hair, big, round eyes, thin lips, and light brown skin highlighted her face. Regina inherited her father's

Anglicized facial features and light complexion. Jo Ann liked thinking she gave Regina her brainpower and work ethic.

"It's a good job. I'm getting an education on practicing law because in the cases we work on I see what lawyers should and shouldn't do."

"You have a year left?"

"Ten months. My clerkship ends June 30."

"What comes next?"

"I have offers from firms in Austin, Houston, Dallas, and Washington, and teaching prospects."

"Where?"

"The University of Minnesota, and maybe here, at Wake Forest."

"Would you like that?" Jo Ann asked, sipping her wine.

"Judge Moss think I should pursue it. She taught there for nine years and knows the faculty situation well. It could be a good life."

Jo Ann's smile built slowly. "Speaking of life, how's your love life?"

"I'm actually dating a guy."

"Tell me more," Jo Ann said. Her face lit up.

"It's not much yet. He's a basketball coach, an assistant for the Wake Forest women's team."

Jo Ann sat up, startled. "A basketball coach? You're dating a basketball coach?"

Regina's eyes widened. "I wouldn't have believed it either. He's no dumb jock. Master's degree from Florida and he graduated from Northwestern, where he played basketball."

"How in the world did you meet him?"

"Through Judge Moss, who's a big fan of the Wake Forest women's team. She invited the clerks to a meet-the-new-coaches function. He and I struck up a conversation. He called me at the office a day or two later."

"How many times have you been out with him?"

"Four or five."

As Jo Ann mulled whether she should ask more, Regina turned the tables. "So, speaking of boyfriends, how are you and your white boyfriend doing?"

Jo Ann recoiled. "How do you know I have a boyfriend? And what makes you think he's white?"

"Give me some credit, Mom. When you asked me about *Loving v. Virginia*, and miscegenation laws, and you eagerly agreed you'd read the Ralph Richard Banks book about problems black women have in the marriage market, I could assume you either had or were thinking about having a white boyfriend."

"Well, I ---"

"Just one question– what's his name?"

Checkmate. "Robert. Robert Hart," Jo Ann answered, laughing.

For 30 minutes, as they ate, Jo Ann told Regina about her summer with Robert. She left out the sex details but didn't try hiding she relished their time in bed.

When dessert arrived, Regina asked how Jo Ann's friends reacted to her taking a white lover. "They aren't happy about it," Jo Ann hung her head.

"Are they being mean?"

"If 'mean' includes the silent treatment, yes."

"Who's doing that?"

"Kendra and Tiffany, Kendra, being the ringleader."

"How about Betty?"

"Betty says she doesn't care for me being with a white man,

but we still talk when the other two aren't around. She had lunch with Robert and me. By the end, it seemed like she liked him."

"What're you doing about Tiffany and Kendra?"

"Nothing. I miss them, but I can't let their small mindedness ruin my life. I'm having too good a time with Robert. I'm 51. I may not get many more chances."

"I'm glad you're looking at it like that. They'll come back."

"Maybe and maybe not. I won't beg."

They briefly discussed the Banks book. Jo Ann told Regina how much she looked forward to talking about it at her book club meeting. In the hotel parking lot, her daughter's embrace and the prospect of a passionate reunion with Robert Wednesday warmed Jo Ann inside.

Robert used Jo Ann's trip in advancing the Jimmy Hundley project. In late July they'd begun discussing how Robert could invest in Hundley's oil and gas properties and help run a new company that would manage them. On the Monday of Jo Ann's trip, they reached a handshake deal and put lawyers on drafting necessary documents.

That night Robert called his son Al about Jo Ann. He'd put it off because he dreaded the reaction of Al's wife, Deena.

If Marcia was the Hart family's house liberal, Deena was its resident right winger. A native of Holly Springs, Mississippi and an Ole Miss sorority girl, Deena was one of a kind at Hart family gatherings.

She spent much of her time watching FOX News and listening to conservative talk radio. Rabidly anti-abortion and aggressively Republican, Deena constantly baited Marcia about her progressive beliefs. Buoyed by Barack Obama's 2012 reelection, Marcia relished verbal combat with Deena. Last Christmas resembled an old *60 Minutes* Point-Counterpoint debate between Sheena Alexander and James J. Kilpatrick.

"Al, how are you?" Robert asked. "I have some news."

"What, Dad?"

"I have a girlfriend?"

"Bill told me, but said you swore him to secrecy. I don't know details."

"Did he tell you she's black?"

"No."

"Does that bother you?"

Robert thought Al seemed surprised by the question. "No. Why should it?"

"It will bother Deena, won't it?"

"No."

"Isn't she the champion right winger? I assumed she thought we never should've abolished slavery."

Al sighed. "You've totally misread my wife."

Robert pushed back. "On any political or social issue, she takes the most reactionary position possible. Why shouldn't I think she'd react negatively?"

"Deena is conservative, not racist."

"Meaning?"

"You're guilty of the same stereotyping that goes on about blacks and other minorities. You assume that because some conservatives are backwards about race, they all are."

Robert remained unconvinced. "Deena supports

candidates who favor suppressing the black vote and think racial profiling is okay."

"That's because of abortion. Other stuff comes with it. Marcia doesn't care for everything some of her candidates support, either. It's not about race with Deena."

"What makes you so sure?"

"We've talked about it?"

"This isn't what I expected."

"One of her sorority sisters at Ole Miss dated the star black running back. Deena won't have a problem with her father-in-law being with a black woman. She'll only ask one thing."

"Which is?"

"The same thing I ask. Does she make you happy?"

"Jo Ann and I are very happy. It's only been three months, but the best three months of my life since your mother died."

"That's great. When do we meet her?"

"As soon as I can figure it out. Very soon, I hope."

Though Robert feared Deena's reaction about Jo Ann, he never thought his daughter Sandy might have reservations. "Oh, Dad. Hi," she said when he called a few days after his talk with Al.

Robert didn't feel warmly greeted by a daughter he hadn't talked with in two months. He ignored the coolness. "I have news for you," he said.

"You do?"

"I'm seeing somebody."

Seconds of silence told Robert this might not be easy. "There are rumors," she finally replied. "I don't want to hear about this."

Robert pressed on, despite Sandy's reaction. "You didn't think I'd never see anybody again. Is that why you don't want to hear about it?"

"I don't know what I thought. Why did you call me about this?"

"I told your brothers. I felt I should tell you. It sounds like you already know. Did one of them tell you?"

"I have my sources."

"What's that supposed to mean?"

"You can't carry on in a place where as many people know us without somebody seeing something – and saying something about what they saw."

"I don't ---"

"Don't worry about how I found out. You have a thing going with some black woman. It's bad enough people see you all over town, and at the club, squeezing and kissing each other like 17-year olds. I suppose you're letting her stay at our house and sleep in Mom's bed."

Robert sat in his favorite TV room chair. He crossed his legs. "That's not fair, Sandy."

"It is if it's true."

"It's my bed too. Your mother isn't coming back."

If what he said stung, she didn't acknowledge it. "I really don't like hearing about this."

"What's wrong with it? Your mother's been dead for eight years."

"I know, but did you have to do this? It's weird."

Sandy's words hit Robert hard. This wasn't his right wing golf buddy spouting about a "ghetto babe." This was his daughter, his flesh and blood, telling him being with a black woman wasn't cool.

Recalling the Little Rock visit, he said, "We didn't teach you much about race, but we didn't teach you hate either."

"I don't hate her. I don't even know her. I don't hate anybody because of their color. I have friends from other races."

Robert resisted a sarcastic so some-of-your-best-friends-are-black retort. He opted for asking, "Why's my having a black girlfriend weird?"

"It's different, Dad."

"Why's it different?"

"It just is," she said. "It just is. It's weird. It's, I don't know, strange. Normal people don't do that."

Anger, frustration, and hurt built inside Robert. Some of that must have come through as he demanded, "What do you mean, normal people don't do that?"

"Normal people date their own color, people from their own tribe, their own kind."

Robert gasped. "When did you start thinking that way?"

"I've always thought that way."

"Weren't there black guys dating white girls when you were in high school and college? I see it all the time."

"There were, especially in high school. But we knew why the white girls were doing it. It was a phase, an experiment, just seeing what it was like."

"Do you mean what I think you mean?"

"The white girls I knew in high school who hooked up with black guys were checking on whether the stories were true and ---"

"You mean the stories about size?"

"Yes. Nobody planned on marrying some black guy. One or two did, but they were the class sluts. No white guy wanted them anyway."

The venom in Sandy's tone stunned Robert. He took a breath. This was painful and he wanted out of the conversation. "I had no idea you thought this way. Jo Ann is special. I don't know what will happen in the future. We're living day-to-day. We barely think past next week. We've become very important to each other. I don't know what else to say."

"Don't say anything else. Let's leave it at that. I have to go. I'm getting ready for a date – with a white guy."

Chapter 20

During dinner with Regina Tuesday night, Jo Ann turned off her phone. At the hotel, she noticed the message light on her room phone blinking. Who leaves messages with hotel operators these days? She checked her phone and found three texts and two voice mails.

JAX Senior Vice President Don Tipton left the messages. Tipton held the spot just above Jo Ann on the organizational chart. Though wary of him, she responded positively when he asked for something.

"I'm glad I found you," Tipton said when she called him.

"No problem, Don. What's up?"

Tipton's booming voice grated on her. "I need you to do something that's a pain, but is important for the company."

"What's that?"

"You're on the east coast, aren't you?"

"Yes. Winston-Salem, North Carolina."

"I need you to go to a trade association convention tomorrow in Miami. I've been scheduled there for months, but something came up today with a South American project. I'm taking a team down there. There isn't anybody else ranked high enough or anybody else we feel would make the right appearance at this thing."

Jo Ann dismissed Tipton's attempt at flattery. Plenty of others 'ranked high enough' and projected the 'right appearance.' They had enough clout they could decline. A detour would delay her reunion with Robert, but she couldn't say no. "I'll help if I can."

After Tipton explained the meeting and Jo Ann's assignment, she hung up and rearranged flights. Then she called Robert with the bad news. Given his long corporate experience, she assumed he'd endured this kind of thing before.

"I have," he said. "That doesn't make me any less unhappy."

"Getting home tomorrow was what I really wanted. Now, I ache and you can't stoke my fires until Saturday."

"I feel as bad about it as you do."

Jo Ann spoke softly. "You saying that makes me feel so warm inside."

"We crave being with each other. That's how it was for Darla and me. I finally found somebody else it can be like that with."

Jo Ann relished the reference to Darla. She accepted that no one would replace Darla for Robert, but it made her happy that he now, without guilt, could experience old joys with someone else.

"This makes Saturday morning hard," Jo Ann said, returning to the practical. "We planned that we'd leave at ten thirty for Austin for the UT-New Mexico State football game. The only flight I could get that makes that work leaves Miami at 6:30 a.m. and arrives in Houston at 8:15. I have to get to the airport at 5:30, so I'll need to get up at 4:30."

"Bummer isn't it?"

"It sure is. I thought I could have you tomorrow night."

They talked for 30 minutes before they accepted the reality of the long day ahead and signed off. Jo Ann stripped, brushed her teeth, showered, put up her hair, and climbed into bed. She used her fingers in bringing the orgasm that would have to suffice until Robert could give her what she really needed.

∞∞∞

Wednesday turned into the ordeal Jo Ann feared. Her plane left late, so she barely made her Atlanta connection. In Miami, she missed the hotel shuttle and waited 30 minutes for a cab. The briefing material, supposedly overnighted for morning delivery, arrived late afternoon. She didn't have enough clothes, meaning a shopping trip Thursday.

Things improved at the opening reception, thanks to two stimulating conversations. First, she met a woman from California who had the same job at her company. About 45, the woman wore her flaming red hair long and overdid the matching lipstick. She carried her tall, thin-as-a-rail frame uneasily.

Jo Ann chuckled at the woman's stories of executives who treated her with contempt. They never saw a reason for her position until they needed information and discovered they could get it from her. The woman's experiences reminded Jo Ann some of her troubles at JAX just went with the territory.

As they shared anecdotes, Jo Ann understood better something Robert told her about big companies. "There's usually less than meets the eye in corporate life. Don't assume people are smart enough to create more than the simplest explanation for any behavior. Stuff we think has hidden meaning is often the result of people being busy, frazzled, or stupid."

The second conversation took a personal turn. An attractive black woman approached and introduced herself as Clarissa Lloyd, a lawyer with a mid-sized, Denver-based, gas exploration company. Her light brown skin, thin lips, high cheek bones, and narrow nose reminded Jo Ann of her daughters and of Kendra. Jo Ann admired her trim figure, presented in a clingy black skirt with a back slit and a low-neck, cream-colored blouse.

After small talk about the fact Tony lived and worked in Denver, Clarissa asked how she'd been accepted by white male colleagues.

"Until I started dating one, I might have said some unkind things," Jo Ann reported. "Now, I better understand them. I'm more tolerant. My boyfriend might say the same thing about black women executives. He knows more than he did a few months ago."

"You're dating a white man?" Clarissa asked. Jo Ann thought she seemed startled.

"I am."

"He works with you?"

"Robert's a consultant who retired from another company before joining us. Given his reputation in the Houston energy community and his influence with our CEO, people listen when he talks. He works on what he wants to work on and what the CEO assigns him, which might be anything."

"How do people in the company respond to the two of you?"

"We were a hot topic for six weeks, but people pay us less attention lately."

Clarissa pushed up her wire framed glasses. "What about the outside world?"

"I get occasional nasty comments. We were in a restaurant once, sitting near the cashier, and Robert left for the restroom. Three black guys paying their check asked why I wasn't with a brother. I ignored them."

"What about black girlfriends?"

"Two disowned me. One is okay with it, but won't challenge the others."

"You sound happy."

"I never expected this, but it beats the hell out of being

alone. Like I told my daughter, I'm 51 and I may not get many more chances."

Through a clenched jaw, Clarissa replied, "I wonder if that's what I have ahead."

"Are you dealing with the black man shortage?"

"I find black men. They won't commit. At 38, I'm not interested in guys who play around. My clock is ticking, if you know what I mean."

"I do," Jo Ann said.

Clarissa continued, "Two years ago I dated this neat black bank vice president -- Stanford MBA, good looks, great lover. I suggested we move in together. He said he had no reason for moving in with one woman when he could have three or four. I dropped him."

Jo Ann bit her lip. "I won't say you should or shouldn't date white men. Decide what you're comfortable with. My relationship works for me."

As she raised her eyebrows, Clarissa asked, "Will you marry him?"

"Who knows? I haven't thought past getting home Saturday so I can climb into bed with him."

Until 5:30 p.m. Thursday, Jo Ann hovered around the JAX booth on the exhibition floor, glad handing vendors, people from other companies, and convention staff. She wandered away a few times, reaching out to people Don Tiption suggested she contact. Finally, the crowd thinned and she left.

With the help of the hotel concierge, she located a shopping mall. A cab ride put her there at six o'clock. Having decided she'd buy only basic outfits for the remaining convention events and the upcoming weekend, she headed for a national chain department store.

On her way, she noticed an attractive lingerie shop. She decided she'd go there after buying her outfits; if it wasn't what it appeared she could return to the department store or look for a national chain like Victoria's Secret.

Jo Ann didn't spend hours trying on clothes. She thought through in advance what she wanted, looked carefully for that, and bought it if it fit.

For Friday's business meeting she picked out a blue suit she accentuated with a green and blue patterned blouse. For the closing dinner, she selected a dark, bare shouldered, knee-length cocktail dress. For the weekend she bought shorts, one pair khaki, the other white, and two polo shirts, one white and one metallic blue.

As she walked into the lingerie shop, Jo Ann reflected on the fact that in her years alone she shopped for intimates as a treat for herself, a personal indulgence that eased her loneliness. Now that she was with Robert, her lingerie had become a part of their togetherness. Pleasing him with it meant as much to her as rewarding herself.

She took care of Friday with a simple white bra and panties set for the day and flesh-toned panties and a black strapless bra for the evening. She bought a bright yellow bra and panties set for Saturday and a black push up bra and bikini panties for Sunday. At the hosiery rack, she picked out a pair of functional pantyhose for the day Friday, sheer pantyhose for the evening, and stockings for a special occasion with Robert.

Jo Ann took a cab back to the hotel, ate dinner, and dived into the briefing material for Friday's panel. She and Robert talked for 45 minutes before she went to bed, letting her fingers and fantasies about him induce an orgasm and, then, deep sleep.

Early Friday, Robert called and asked, "Did I catch you still getting ready?"

"Well, yes. I'm not dressed yet."

"You're not? Tell me about that."

"You caught me pulling up my pantyhose over my panties. That means, as you well know, I don't yet have on my bra."

"That sounds delicious."

"I realize this little discussion gives you a morning bonus, but I doubt it's why you called. What's up?"

"I didn't confirm the flight you're on and your exact arrival time tomorrow. We probably can't talk tonight. You're in bed early and I'm out late. We're signing the Jimmy Hundley deal and he's taking the investors out for a big dinner and a party. I won't get home until after midnight."

She gave him her flight number. "I arrive at 8:15 a.m., Terminal C at Bush. You're signing the deal?"

"Monday we got an agreement. We put the lawyers on a fast track and they have the documents ready."

"That's wonderful. This'll be good for you."

"I think that too. Now you should go. You still need to put on that bra."

Chapter 21

One cell phone waiting lot at Bush Intercontinental Airport once housed the car rental companies. Robert arrived there at 7:55 a.m. Saturday and opened the *Houston Chronicle*. His phone rang eight minutes later.

"We just landed." Jo Ann announced. Robert heard excitement and longing in her voice.

"What do you think, 15 minutes?" he asked.

"Yes. I didn't check luggage, so I'll be on the curb as soon as I can get off the plane, down the concourse, and out the door."

At the predicted time, she stood outside the terminal in her new khaki shorts and white polo shirt. She waved as Robert drove into the pick-up area. He popped the trunk and she tossed in her bag. He swung open the passenger door. She slipped into the seat and leaned over to kiss him.

"We can't linger," he said. "The parking security guys will go nuts."

"Where're we going?" she asked as he squeezed her hand. "Breakfast, I hope."

"My favorite breakfast place – The Egg and I. There's one on the Katy Freeway, on the way to Austin."

She gave him a hearty laugh. "I won't, as my mother always said, 'starve to death and die?'"

"We can't have that. I have plans for you. You'll need energy."

"Don't tempt me. Home isn't far from that restaurant. The game might have to wait."

"We have time before the game. We'll be in Austin by quarter to two. Game time is seven o'clock."

"Tell me about the dinner and the party. You signed the deal?"

"Yes, I'm excited. The party was great. I got a better sense of who's in this and what we're doing. I wish I'd done this sooner. I let go of some money, but I'll make it back soon."

"How many investors? How many projects?"

"Eight investors and, for now, 12 projects. I'm the second largest investor. Jimmy retains majority interest in each project. I have one-third interest in six projects, 40% in two others, 45% in two more, and 17 % in two. It's a little weird, but that worked best."

"Gas projects?"

"Yes, two in South America, the rest in the continental U.S."

"What are you doing management wise?"

"That's some of why Jimmy wanted me in this. I'm the one investor who was a corporate manager. My partners don't know much about running offices, managing people, or setting up systems. They're E & P guys."

"You'll open an office?"

"Jimmy found space not far from our house."

Robert gave Jo Ann more details as they drove on. His enthusiasm showed. She said she appreciated that he shared with her this turn in his life. She said she felt even better when he told her he'd introduce her to his new partners, so they'd understand her importance to him.

At the restaurant, he handed her a gift bag as they waited for seating. "This is for you."

She opened the bag and took out two shirts, one red, one orange. Once she looked at the front logos, she broke out laughing, then hugged him. "You're so thoughtful, getting me a New Mexico State shirt for tonight. You remembered that Tony played there."

"After you said you wouldn't get here until this morning, I knew we couldn't get clothes at your house and stay on schedule. So, I ordered these on line."

She held up the other shirt. "You got me a Texas shirt."

"That's for the rest of the year. Remember, I'm a season ticket holder."

Breakfast went quickly. Jo Ann filled Robert in on her time in Miami and they talked about that night's game. As they left the restaurant, she reached for his arm and whispered, "I'm so glad I'm home. I missed you so much."

∞∞∞

Robert spent Sunday night at Jo Ann's house because it was a few blocks from the golf course at which he was playing in a Labor Day tournament. After he left, Jo Ann took a call from Betty Martin that reminded her of the one unpleasant fact of her current life, the loss of her friendship with Tiffany and Kendra.

"I won't take long," Betty promised. "We're having a Labor Day cookout. I wondered if you'd give me the recipe for your beans and sausage dish. People like it so much."

Jo Ann's anger flashed. She took a deep breath. Don't be tacky about this, she thought. "I'll send it by e-mail shortly."

"I'd like having you there, but there'd be a scene."

"I imagine so," Jo Ann replied, reeling from not being invited, though she wouldn't have gone. "I can't imagine Kendra not getting in my face."

"I'm afraid of that."

"I can hear her asking, 'Where's your white boy lover?

Think the brothers and sisters will beat him up?' I don't need that."

"How're you doing? I miss you."

Jo Ann took a deep satisfied breath. "My life is wonderful. I think you saw that when you had lunch with us."

"I know," Betty said, "but I so loved our times together, the four of us. It's not the same without you."

"I didn't leave. I don't have as much time as I did, because every moment with Robert is precious. We could still do things together, but I'm not giving up Robert and I'm not taking abuse from Kendra and Tiffany about him."

"They won't change," Betty said with a sigh. "After our lunch, I told them they should meet him. 'He's still a white boy and she shouldn't be with him,' they said. Robert seems like a good man. He cherishes you."

"He does. That's making my life great, that and one other thing. He's terrific in bed. He has disapproved one myth."

"What's that?"

"That white men have equipment that doesn't measure up against black men and they don't know what to do with it. Robert's is very large, thank you, and he uses it quite well. When it's in me, I can't tell what color it is."

"Robert," Jo Ann asked, "what are you looking for under my dress?"

"For something, I want," he said, staring into her eyes in the skimpy light. "Based on what I'm finding, something you'd like giving me."

"What makes you say that?"

"It's uncovered. There's no gate at the entrance."

"You're referring, I assume, to me not wearing panties?"

"That, and the fact the further I go, the wider you spread your legs."

They sat in Robert's car in a dimly lit, half-full parking lot outside a trendy west Houston restaurant the Friday after the Austin trip and the day before the book club meeting Jo Ann anticipated so much. They'd driven there after seeing an early movie.

Jo Ann's new dress, bright green, low cut, and with a flared, pleated skirt, ended miles further up her thighs than anything she'd wear to work.

All evening, Robert found Jo Ann wanton and alluring. He first noticed that though nylons covered her legs, when he groped her butt, he didn't feel the tight, smoothness of a derriere covered by the top of pantyhose. Nor did he find the ridge of a panty line.

As Robert continued exploring beneath the skirt, he left Jo Ann's core for a moment and ran his fingers along her thigh. He touched skin and the strap of a garter belt he traced to a tethered stocking. When his journey ended at the top of her nylon, he leaned over and kissed her before returning his fingers to her center. She gasped a little and thrust her hips upwards.

They finally broke the kiss, but he left his fingers inside her. "We'd better stop," she said. "Let's eat. I can't take any more of this without having you inside me."

"Fair enough," he said, as she pulled his hand from under her skirt. "All things in time."

In the restaurant, between bites of her shrimp and of his steak, they held hands across a table. They left, his arm around her middle, his hand periodically dipping below her waist so he could feel bare flesh through her skirt.

"Be careful," she said as he swung the car out of the parking lot, one hand on the wheel and the other again pushing its way under her skirt. He toyed with the top of her stocking before sliding his fingers along her thigh.

"I got this," he said. "There are advantages to having the long arms that go with being 6-7."

She kept her eyes on him. "I couldn't concentrate on the road if I were driving and snaking my hand inside your slacks. You're making me crazy. Just get us home so I can have you in me."

His hand stayed under her dress all the way home. He alternated between rubbing naked thigh above her stockings and pushing his fingers into her center. She spread her legs, again easing his path. By the time they pulled into his driveway, a river flowed from her.

As Robert pressed the remote, opening the overhead garage door from the car, Jo Ann grabbed the passenger door handle. She opened it as soon as he stopped the car. She bounded out, then opened the inside door and waved him inside. "Hurry!" she exclaimed and grabbed his hand. She lead him into the kitchen.

Inside, the table beckoned. "There! Right there!" Jo Ann grasped the edge of the table and bent over it. With one hand, she reached behind and flipped up her skirt. "Get inside me! I can't wait. I want it now!"

In the stillness of the room, the sound of Robert's zipper marked their urgency. He unbuckled his belt. His slacks fell in a bundle around his ankles. He stepped out of them, and his loafers, as he moved behind her. He freed his erection from his briefs. An instant later she gasped when he pushed his rock hard flesh into her. For a long time, their moans, groans, and grunts filled the kitchen.

They ignored Rufus when he ambled under the table. With no prospect of food, the dog left after a few minutes. Few words passed between them. "Oh, Robert!" she managed between quickening breaths. "This is soooo good!" Her thigh muscles quivered.

He kept thrusting until her first orgasm shook them. He withdrew for an instant and took off his socks, allowing him better traction on the tile floor. Back inside her, he pounded her hard as her cries grew louder.

"Robert! Please go faster!"

Still, he said nothing. She bent over the table as far as she could. A lamp in an adjacent hallway illuminated the contrast between her dark butt and his pale thighs.

They built toward climax. "I'm cumming, Jo Ann! I'm going to shoot deep inside you. DEEP inside you!"

"Please, Robert, please! Please! Shoot inside me now! I need you. I need your seed!"

He could hold back no longer. He felt the semen begin its trip from deep in his middle.

"You're pulsing, Robert!" she screamed. "I feel it. Please give it to me, Robert! Fill me! Fill me!"

She climaxed as his fluid spilled into her. She slumped on the table. He didn't pull out, letting every drop seep into her.

He ran his hand over her smooth bare butt, visible in the light as her skirt remained flipped up on her back. He reached around her and grasped her hand. They remained connected. When he moved, she stopped him. "Stay! Just a little longer"

Finally, he withdrew. She stood up and turned around. They kissed, long and hard at first, then more tenderly. "I'm so glad," he said, "you didn't make us wait for the bedroom."

"I couldn't wait. I wanted you at that moment. Even better, we have a memory we'll always cherish. Nothing like this has ever happened for me."

"For me either," he said. "For me either."

Chapter 22

R obert believed his leaving JAX would end the remaining talk about him and Jo Ann. He also could push David Marks about her future. "There's one more thing we should talk about," Robert said after announcing his departure for a new venture.

"What's that?" the CEO asked, sitting on his corner couch across from a plush chair where Robert sat.

"Jo Ann Davis."

"I hear you are more than business colleagues."

"There's truth in those stories. That's one reason my leaving is a good thing. It allows you to do what you should do about her future here without people saying it's because of me."

The CEO asked in a soft tone, "What should I do with her?"

"Take her under your wing and see how far she can go."

Marks sat up. He didn't look like a man in his early 60s. His smooth, boyish face, stylishly cut hair with only hints of gray, and a trim, athletic build made him appear not yet 50. "How far is that?"

"I have ideas, but you should work through the specifics yourself. JAX is missing out. She has more leadership potential and can grasp big picture issues better than anybody I worked with here."

Marks rubbed his right hand across his shirt. "You aren't saying that because you sleep with her?"

"I'm not, though it's because we've become so close that I

know her potential. She's alone here. Nobody on your core team talks to her. Nobody understands what she can do because nobody knows her well. I now know."

Marks fiddled with a cuff link. "Maybe she hasn't worked hard enough at selling herself."

"People looking for up-and-comers have looked elsewhere when they should've looked at her."

"Assume you're right. What does this look like?"

Robert's eyes sparkled as he said, "Teach her corporate planning and general management, but not as your assistant. Give her authority and put her where she can learn from you and the others who run this place – Joe Sanders, Walt Corey, Karen Duffy, Tom Reese. She can hang with those people. Ultimately, she'll be better than any of them, if you give her a chance."

Marks shook his head slowly. "Most of them will feel threatened by her."

"Which is fine. Pushing some people out of their comfort zone would improve things."

"You've said that often. What's your plan?"

"Talk with Jo Ann. Ask her what works here and what doesn't. You'll be surprised at her insight."

"I'll bring her in for lunch in the boardroom, just the two of us."

"She has the horsepower, David. Trust me on this one."

∞∞∞

In mid-September Robert moved into high gear on the Hundley project. Jo Ann didn't complain. She'd encouraged his pursuit of the opportunity. The tennis matches, hikes in the woods, and leisurely evenings of reading and making

147

love dwindled from routine to special treat. Jo Ann's work life changed. A feather would have blown her over when David Marks called, extending an invitation to lunch in the boardroom.

She'd been there for a few meetings, but never for a private audience with the great man himself. Jo Ann assumed the lunch was Robert's doing, so she expected nothing from it. This likely amounted to a favor for an old friend. Still, she made sure she looked the part of an all-business, business woman by wearing a dark gray suit, conservative cream-colored blouse, and sheer hose along with black pumps.

Marks, in a blue suit, starched white shirt, and red tie, greeted her cheerfully. They sat in a space just off the main board meeting room with its mahogany paneling, mammoth conference table, and plush, high-backed chairs.

A waiter in a white jacket served a hot lunch of beef tenderloin, asparagus, and roasted potatoes. Jo Ann picked fresh fruit for dessert, noting she didn't "need more chocolate this week."

Marks pumped Jo Ann for information about her formative years, her family, and, gently, her romance with Robert. Marks professed relief Robert "finally found someone who makes him happy." He termed his friend's long stint alone after Darla's death "unhealthy."

"We have much to talk about," Marks began when they turned to business. "I assume you know why you're here."

"Only a guess, Mr. Marks," she allowed.

"Please, call me David."

"David."

"Robert thinks you're a star in the making. He says you only need my guidance on some things you don't know. Is he right?"

Jo Ann took a deep breath and looked directly at Marks. He

had a reputation for challenging his top lieutenants. She knew he wasn't looking for false modesty. "I believe I can contribute things I've not had the opportunity to contribute, if that's what you're asking."

"I'm asking what those things are."

For two hours, Jo Ann explained her view of JAX's strengths and weaknesses. The company carried out technical and operational tasks well, but struggled with people issues like employee satisfaction and mobility and was weak in strategic planning and forecasting.

Jo Ann pulled no punches; when Marks asked that she name names, she did. She said many departments lacked forward looking leadership and JAX lost talented young people because many saw limited opportunity for advancement.

The CEO became so engaged in their conversation he waved off his secretary when she appeared, reminding him of other scheduled meetings that afternoon. "Those things can wait," he told her. "I'm not sure this can."

The University of Texas engineering graduate and Stanford MBA pushed back on some of Jo Ann's criticisms. She acknowledged things she knew nothing about might explain some problems she saw, but stood her ground.

She pointed out cronyism in promotions, failures in anticipating industry trends and governmental actions, and low job satisfaction among middle managers who resented the good ol' boy chumminess rampant in the executive suite. Marks finally admitted Jo Ann's overall critique was "spot on."

"So, what do we do about this?" he asked. Before she could respond, he answered his own question.

"You must become immersed in how this company runs. For the time being, I'm promoting you to Senior Vice President. What happens next, we'll see. You report only to me. You and I should talk on a daily basis. You'll control our agenda. I'm holding you accountable for addressing the problems you've identified.

"You'll learn everything about everything that moves around here. Then you're going to help me run this place right. Eventually, I want a public profile that moves this company from backwater oil & gas producer to corporate force in the energy industry. I can't work on that now because I'm drowning in minutia.

"We'll announce your appointment immediately and start Monday. I'll expect you geared up and ready. You and I will meet Friday with others on the executive team on implementation details. Can you come in for lunch that day?"

"I'll be here," she said.

The Marks lunch produced training sessions and team meetings, reports for study, and new research projects. Jo Ann's promotion bumped her salary to "six figures starting with a crooked number" as she told Regina by phone one night. As Marks predicted, she sensed some in the executive suite resented her advancement.

Marks gave her perks suggesting he meant business. He assigned her an aide who would work on the nuts and bolts of her projects and authorized a personal assistant who functioned like a politician's "body man." Jo Ann hired a "body woman," 24 – year - old University of Miami graduate Rhonda Gonzalez. She kept her secretary, Janet Maxwell, a 56-year-old woman Jo Ann valued for her loyalty, competence, and judgment. Sitting in her cavernous new office, she rejoiced that she now captained a team.

∞ ∞ ∞

Jo Ann and Robert focused on work, though they took as much time as they could for each other. Both thought their love making became sweeter, though they did less of it. She marveled at how easily her orgasms came with him and at his staying power. Robert grew ever more enthralled with the unbridled joy she took in sex.

They expanded their repertoire as she enjoyed sitting astride him in the cowgirl position. Jo Ann never had a lover who liked her straddling him. Soon she cherished the sight of Robert lying on his back, his monstrous erection poised to enter her. The position gave him easier access to her breasts. She often leaned forward and brushed his chest with them. Her jet-black nipples and areole still mesmerized him.

Chapter 23

In mid-October, Jo Ann's mood turned sour, something Robert noticed and mentioned. Her energy waned and she lost her enthusiasm for their outdoor activities. She gladly changed her schedule when Connie Cross's nurse called and asked if she could come in early for her annual gynecological check-up.

Swinging her car into the parking lot at Connie's building in southwest Houston, Jo Ann flashed back to the September book club meeting, the last time she'd seen her doctor and friend.

The book was Jo Ann's selection, *Is Marriage for White People: How the African American Marriage Decline Affects Everyone*, by Stanford law professor Ralph Richard Banks. The other members peppered Jo Ann and Connie, the two black women in the club, with questions about the book's implications. As dinner and dessert settled and the wine flowed, the white members asked what they thought of Professor Banks's theory that black women could improve their marriage chances by dating white men.

"I'm not trying to be an example," Jo Ann said, nudging Robert on a couch in James and Della Bryant's family room. Earth tones and subtle paintings radiated a warm glow. "I looked for a black man, but I never found the right one. I'm happy with this man," Jo Ann said, clutching Robert's arm. "His color doesn't matter."

"I'm happy for Jo Ann," Connie said, sipping red wine and leaning back in her chair. Her sleek figure and regal bearing fit her educational and professional pedigree. She wore a pink silk dress, gold necklace, and matching earrings. "I've seen all sides of this. Between my own experience, those of my medical partners, and stories from patients, I have a good grasp of the professor's point. He's mostly right, but it's complex."

"Connie practices with four other women," Jo Ann explained. "One is white, one Hispanic, and the other two are black."

"The women in my practice group represent the marriage situations African-American women experience," Connie said. "I found my IBM. Unlike many men I dated in college and medical school, and that Professor Banks describes, he would commit. My partners haven't found theirs."

"IBM?" asked James Bryant. He sat beside his wife, Della, and across from Connie.

"Ideal Black Man," Connie replied to giggles and laughter. "He has what educated, upwardly mobile black women want — college degree, maybe a professional or graduate degree, good job, substantial income, and real career prospects."

"I get it," James responded, running a hand through his head of dark hair.

"Devin and I met after I moved to Houston for my residency," Connie continued. "He pursued me relentlessly. I was interested, but I let him know there weren't going to be three or four others."

"That's for damned sure!" her husband, Devin Allen, a trim, athletic man with brown skin and sharp facial features, said, laughing.

Connie resumed her story. "My partner, Cynthia Jones, is 43. She grew up in Wrightsville, Georgia, Herschel Walker's hometown. She did college at Georgia and medical school at Emory. She's a terrific doctor. She delivered my children. I trust her completely. But she's totally infected with the thou-shall-not-date-outside-the-race attitude Professor Banks describes."

Della Bryant perked up. "What does that mean for her?"

"Truth be told, Cynthia is miserable. She wants a husband and a family. The black guys she dates are hopelessly overmatched by her intellect, how well read she is, her overall dynamism. A white heart surgeon friend of mine told me he was interested, but she paid him no attention. I asked her why not. She said she couldn't take home a white boy."

Jo Ann broke in, "That –Don't Bring Home a White Boy-- is the title of another book I read on this subject, written by a black woman lawyer who married a white man. She goes through reasons black women hear and learn they shouldn't get involved with white men — the legacy of slavery, disloyalty to the race, even stereotypes about penis size."

"You mean that white men don't measure up, so to speak?" James Bryant asked with a smile.

"Yes," Jo Ann replied, giggling a little.

Devin spoke up. "I feel for Cynthia. We double dated with her and one of the black guys she was seeing, a retail clerk with no college. It was embarrassing. He couldn't begin to talk to her."

Connie scanned the room and said, "Cynthia believes what she believes. I doubt she'll change. It's different with my other African-American partner, Angela Timmons. She envies my marriage to Devin, adores our children, and desperately wants some of her own. Being in our business and not having children, if you want them, is hard."

"Tell us about Angela," Margie Scott requested.

Connie stretched her arms and picked up her wine glass. "She's 37, our youngest partner. She attended college and medical school at Kansas where she dated a black basketball player from St. Louis. Against the advice of everyone around him, after two seasons he left college for the NBA. No team drafted him. He played in Europe for a while, where he made some money, but spent it all. He got a tryout with the Atlanta Hawks. He stuck for a while but a knee injury ended his career."

"What happened with him and Angela?" asked Bonnie Walton, a plump woman with an engaging smile and whitening hair.

"They got married when she got out of medical school. They stayed married five years, and lived off her income. Despite her desire for children, she wouldn't have any with him because he wouldn't finish college."

Bonnie looked puzzled and asked, "Why not?"

"Said he didn't like school. He tried being a sports agent, but the guys and gals with law degrees and sports management degrees ran circles around him.

"Angela tired of his freeloading and divorced him. She dated several black men, but ran into the other thing the professor writes about – educated, desirable black men who won't commit because they have plenty of black and white women available and no reason for settling with one woman."

"What's Angela doing now?" Bonnie asked.

"She decided she'd date out. I expect she and Bruce Kendrick, the white hospital executive she's been seeing, will marry soon."

"Really interesting," Della Bryant said, refilling wine glasses. "I never knew any of this."

Jo Ann reached Connie's office and snapped out of her flashback. She signed in, sat down, and remembered how bad she felt. Irma Simpson's cancer battle flashed into her mind. The fact she'd started attending church with Robert might come in handy.

∞ ∞ ∞

Once Jo Ann went through the waiting room door, Connie's staff took the standard specimens and did a vaginal smear. The nurse asked the usual questions – most recent period – November last year, Jo Ann said – painful sex, discharges, etc. Connie arrived in the examination room and poked and prodded her insides. Jo Ann hoped for clues in Connie's expression but, with her feet in stirrups, she could barely see the doctor's face. "See you in a bit," Connie said as she finished her work and left the room, the nurse in tow.

A long interlude followed before the nurse returned and told Jo Ann she could get dressed, then step across the hall for a meeting in the doctor's office. That's strange, Jo Ann thought, her anxiety level rising. Usually her friend returned to the examination room, said things were fine, and sent her on her way.

In the doctor's office, Jo Ann asked, "Is there something wrong with me, Connie? You never have me come in here. Do I have cancer?" Again, Jo Ann thought of Irma Simpson and her description of feeling hit with a sledgehammer when given her diagnosis.

Connie took off her glasses and stuffed them into the pocket of her white lab coat. She pulled up a chair and slid it just across from Jo Ann. Connie sat down and looked directly at her friend and patient.

"That's what took so long. We ran the tests again, making sure of what we'd seen. Whether you consider that there's something wrong with you depends on how you look at it. You don't have cancer. You do have something growing inside you. You are seven to eight weeks pregnant."

Chapter 24

J o Ann buzzed Robert's mobile phone. Her text message said MEET ME. YOUR HOUSE 20 MINUTES. VERY IMPORTANT! Jo Ann considered finishing the message with MUST SEE YOU, but feared that might make him think she just wanted a nooner. "What's going on?" he asked when they talked.

"Get to your house ASAP. I'll tell you there." She hung up.

Jo Ann left Connie's office so stunned she didn't immediately focus on where she should go. After driving toward her office, she decided telling Robert came first. She beat him home by five minutes.

The moment Jo Ann hit the kitchen, she heard the flap on the dog door. Rufus appeared seconds later. "You aren't hungry, so don't look at me like that," Jo Ann said, staring at the pleading dog. "I fed you this morning!"

He acted as if he hadn't heard. His head remained cocked to one side and he let out his "I'm hungry" whimper.

"You get one treat, no more," Jo Ann said. She went into the laundry room and fished a treat from the box that sat on the shelf above the washer. Rufus, appearing satisfied with his efforts, gulped down the treat and slithered out the dog door.

Jo Ann walked back into the kitchen and gazed out onto the immaculately landscaped yard. Tall trees, trimmed hedges, cultivated flower beds and shrubs, and recently mowed grass created a green oasis.

She imagined a playground and swing set near the back fence. A lanky six-year old with light brown skin, hazel eyes, and frizzy hair climbed the steps of a slide and sped toward the ground, arms outstretched. To Jo Ann's surprise, the vision of the child warmed her inside.

The sound of Robert dropping his keys on the foyer table and his footsteps across the hallway tile pulled Jo Ann out of her vision. When she realized he'd reached the carpet just outside the kitchen she turned from the window, still not sure what she'd say. Tears streamed down her face. She remembered their relationship began when he found her crying.

Jo Ann feared that her tears terrified Robert. She imagined the grim news of Darla's cancer flashing before his eyes. Jo Ann rushed into his arms without saying anything. They held each other as tightly as she could remember, including for *The Kiss* in May.

Robert leaned back and looked into her face. "Please tell me. What is it?"

She hesitated another second, then said, "I'm pregnant." She wiped away a tear while holding him with her other arm.

He said nothing at first, but held her tighter. Finally, he spoke. "I love you."

"You're not angry with me?" she asked.

The pitch in his voice rose. "How could I be angry with you? What reason would I have?"

"I as much as told you I couldn't get pregnant. We never worried about it. We made love time after time, totally oblivious to the possibility I could get pregnant. I thought you might hate me for misleading you."

"I'm sure you told the truth as you knew it. We can talk about how this happened, but we're in this together. Nobody is blaming anybody. Nobody is getting mad at anybody. We love each other too much for that."

They broke their embrace and sat side by side at the kitchen table. Robert grasped her hand. He asked what happened on her doctor's visit.

"The nurse sent me to see Connie asked after my exam, which was unusual. I knew something was up. She said I'm seven or eight weeks pregnant, though physically I look further along. I told her I didn't see how I could be pregnant."

"You had sex with me. That's what happened," he said, grinning.

"I guess I did," Jo Ann replied, through a weak smile, at least acknowledging his try at humor. "Connie said she sees this from time to time. A menopausal woman thinks she's through having periods, stops using birth control, and turns up pregnant."

"I thought you were through having periods."

"You need a year – some doctors say two -- without one before you're safe. I had one last November, stopped, but apparently had one at the end of August."

Robert rubbed his eyelid. "You didn't know it?"

"In retrospect, I should have, but it was so short and so light it didn't register. It happened on the Washington trip."

"Really?"

"I remember sitting at Dulles Airport Monday night. I called Tony, hoping I could talk with Shonda, but she was out playing. I felt a twinge, a brief spasm. I didn't connect that and the wetness I later felt between my legs. I thought it was some random discharge. When I went to the bathroom, I didn't really look at what was there. I put a pad in my panties."

"You still didn't know?"

"The pad was lightly soiled when I undressed that night. I didn't notice anything after that. Connie thinks I ovulated ten days to two weeks later."

He sat quietly as he said, "There were plenty of chances

for you to get pregnant during that time. There were days I practically lived inside you."

"I was in heat. I couldn't get enough of you."

"I bet you got pregnant the Friday night before book club."

"The night I made you take me over this table?"

"Yes."

"You discovered I was naked under my new green dress."

"I knew that when I felt you up. You had on a garter belt and stockings, but nothing else. I fingered you all the way home."

"When we got here, I bent over this table, flipped up my dress, and begged that you put it in me. I couldn't wait until the bedroom."

He stood up, apparently not caring about his obvious erection. "I won't ask what we're going to do about this. We'll talk it to death. How do you feel, right now?"

She took a deep breath and looked out the window, at the place where the vision of the child on the playground appeared. Again, a warm feeling swept over her. "I can only say two things. One, I feel more love in my life than I ever have. Two, I'm sopping wet and I want you – now. Everything else can wait."

He took her hand and led her to the bedroom. They stayed there until well after the sun went down.

Chapter 25

The day after getting the pregnancy news, Jo Ann and Robert headed for Austin and that weekend's Kansas-Texas football game. Beforehand, she called her friend and fellow book club member, Margie Scott, the person who could give her advice based on experience. "Can we get together?" Jo Ann asked.

"I'm free all weekend," Margie replied. "What works?"

"The football game is Saturday night. Robert and some friends are playing golf in the morning."

"Where?"

"North of town. A place called Star Ranch."

"I live five minutes from there. What time?"

"They tee off at 8:15 a.m. There's a buffet breakfast that's part of the deal, so he should get there at seven o'clock."

"You and I can have a light breakfast at my house, talk all morning, then go somewhere for lunch. I'll get you back there by one thirty."

∞ ∞ ∞

Robert made the 160-mile drive from his house in west Houston to Austin 12 to 15 times a year for sporting events, golf, and business. He knew every twist and turn in the route.

As they moved into the I-10 traffic, he said, "From the second you told me about this, I wondered what being pregnant means for your health at 51 years old."

"I asked Connie about that and did some internet research. There are dangers."

He glanced over at her. "Like?"

"More complications for women my age. Connie thinks I'll do fine because I don't have risk factors going in like high blood pressure or diabetes. I'm not overweight. My body is in good shape."

"I appreciate knowing that. I've lost one life partner. That one was too many."

She looked at him from the passenger seat as they passed the outskirts of Houston and open space began appearing out his window. "You're so good to me," she said.

Robert lifted his chin. "I'm worried about it."

"With good care I can get through it. Connie will monitor me carefully. She said she'd see me about twice as often as she would a woman in her 20s or early 30s."

"Don't women your age more often have babies with genetic problems?"

"Yes. I'll need that awful testing."

He shifted in the driver seat. "The needle in the stomach? Talking about it makes me cringe."

"Connie will do amniocentesis. You're going with me." Her expression said he wasn't getting out of being there.

"Ouch!"

She pressed her fists to the side of her head. "There's one other thing."

"What?"

"I told you Connie said her physical examination suggested I'm further along than it appeared from calculating the likely conception date. That might mean I'm carrying twins."

His pulse raced. "You're kidding! Tell me you're kidding!"

"It's not uncommon in older women. It has to do with the nature of your eggs at this stage of life."

"What would twins mean for the physical burden on you?"

"Perhaps early bed rest. Twin pregnancies seldom reach term, even in younger women. One site said they result in four times more premature births than single pregnancies."

"What's your due date, assuming one baby?"

"Late May."

"You haven't had morning sickness. Is that why it never occurred to you that you might be pregnant?"

"I didn't have it with any of my kids."

"How do you feel now?"

"Still out of sorts, but knowing it's not cancer helps."

He parted his lips and bowed his head. "You worried about that too?"

"I was terrified. I saw how Irma Simpson suffered. Losing Darla still affects you. I didn't want you going through that again."

"My experience with Darla weighed on me when you said you felt bad but couldn't figure out why."

Miles rolled by and they talked about the childhoods of Bill, Al, and Sandra and Tony, Melissa, and Regina. As the sun set, the landscape changed. Rolling hills covered with scrub brush and short trees appeared when they turned northwest on to Texas 71.

Robert asked finally, "Should we be having children at our ages? I'll be over 80 when our kid gets out of high school."

She nodded, then added, "And I'll be 70."

"Isn't parenthood for younger people? Biologically, we can still conceive children, but we both know how much more there is to parenting than bringing a sperm and egg together.'"

She grinned and said, "There is, although that's a lot of fun."

He remained serious. "Is the "a" word off the table?"

"It's been on my mind. Connie says she never brings up abortion except to patients for whom pregnancy is a risk. At my age, by definition, I'm an at-risk patient."

"What did you say when she mentioned it?"

"I asked her how long it remains an option."

"And?"

"Twenty weeks under Texas law. Eight states and Washington, D.C. have no limit. Its 24 – 26 weeks a lot of places."

"What do you feel?"

"A pregnancy and a child are problems for us. There's my health, disruption of our life together, impact on my career and your business venture, and the bi-racial child issue. You're right about us being soccer mom and dad at 70 and 80. Do I take my walker and stand on the sidelines at pee-wee football games?"

Robert took a deep breath. "There's another side, though. I know much more about parenting now than last time. You do too, and you won't be alone."

"We'd be good at it."

"A child experiencing the caring we'd bring to being parents now, and feel what's between us, would grow up in the best circumstances."

Jo Ann looked at him. She put her hand on his thigh. He took one of his off the wheel and covered hers. Again, the car fell silent. Not another word passed between them until they reached Austin.

Chapter 26

Saturday morning Jo Ann embraced Robert when he stood up after tying his golf shoes while sitting on his back bumper in the Star Ranch Golf Club parking lot. A light, northerly breeze provided Austin's excuse for a nip in the air.

Jo Ann felt refreshed, livelier than in weeks. The recent sourness had melted away. Friday night they ate dinner, retired early, and slept like logs after an hour of gentle love making. She most relished Robert's ejaculation, confirming the connection between her pregnancy and his eruption into her.

Margie Scott drove up and leaned over as she stopped her car. They broke their embrace. "Let's get her out of here before things get out of control," Margie said. She laughed through the open window.

"I'm just saying good bye to my man." Jo Ann said.

Robert grabbed his clubs and slammed the trunk shut. "Hi, Margie," he said. "Take care of her, will you?"

"She's in good hands!" Margie replied.

"Hit 'em straight. Beats me what you see in this game, but since you love it so much, please do well."

"Is something up?" Margie asked as they left the parking lot. "You sounded distressed."

"Thursday, I found out I'm pregnant."

Margie's smile faded. She looked at Jo Ann, who was wearing red slacks, a white shell top, and a deep steel blue scarf around her neck. "I assume you hadn't planned on getting pregnant."

"I hadn't. Believe it or not, though, I feel joy I'm carrying Robert's child."

"What does he say?"

"He asked how hard the pregnancy will be at my age and about genetic problems. He said wonderful things about what loving parents we could make. He asked if this is too much at our ages. We'd be 70, 80 years old when our kid graduates high school. And, my ob-gyn thinks there's a chance I'm having twins."

They reached Margie's two-story brick home with a manicured lawn and a barking dog in the living room window. Inside, plush couches and paintings of open, green fields warmed Jo Ann. "Where's Kimberly?" she asked, referring to Margie's daughter.

"She spent the night with a neighborhood friend. I'll pick her up when I take you back. She can't miss Aunt Jo Ann."

They went into the kitchen. Margie moved gracefully as she fixed breakfast. She wore gray sweat pants and an orange University of Illinois sweatshirt. She had brown eyes, short, blonde hair, and a reddish pimple on her nose. A light touch of makeup put color into her cheeks. "Now, where were we?" she asked, setting out dishes.

"I should tell you the whole story of how Robert and I got together and why I turned up pregnant," Jo Ann said, as Margie sat down. Fifteen minutes later Jo Ann asked, "What do you think?"

"It's not what I think. It's what you feel."

"I'm very happy."

"What are you worried about?"

"How hard this could be – physically, emotionally, and practically."

"Is the physical part just being 51 and pregnant?"

"And being 65 and having a 13-year-old. I raised three children. It's hard work. I started in my 20s. This would be way different."

"What's the emotional issue?"

Jo Ann glanced at the wall clock. It said 8:18 a.m. "Suppose I have complications. Suppose I need a late term abortion because full term could kill me, but we've grown attached to the baby. I don't know if I can take that emotional trauma."

"Is that all?"

"There's raising a biracial child. I can handle black men at restaurants telling me I shouldn't be with Robert. I can even handle friends shunning me for being disloyal to the race by loving a white man. But what about a seven-year-old who gets asked at school, 'What are you?'"

"What's the practical problem?"

Jo Ann swallowed hard. "I got a wonderful promotion. I'm now a Senior Vice President at JAX, the CEO's right hand man. It's an intense job. Plus, Robert has a business opportunity that could make him millions."

Margie leaned back in the chair, then stood up. "I have a question."

"Yes?"

"Are you and Robert getting married?"

"We've never even talked about that. We've been living day-to-day and not worrying about the future. The pregnancy changes that, I suppose."

Margie looked out the window, then turned, and threw open her arms, inviting Jo Ann's embrace. They held each other tightly. "I know why you're here," Margie said as she stepped back. "You assumed my experience gives me special insight. We both got pregnant in middle age when we didn't plan on it, but that's where the similarity ends."

Jo Ann responded, "We talked about your fears, about how hard raising a child would be after all you'd been through with your son, about a baby interfering with your career. You considered abortion and adoption. It seems similar."

Margie frowned. "You have a loving partner. My man abandoned me. He blamed me for getting pregnant, when we both got careless. I doubt Robert thinks this is all your fault. He gets the impracticality. But, he loves you and he'll stick around. It's completely different."

"What about those things I listed?"

"You want the baby. That's in your voice, your face, your movements. This isn't about the pregnancy. It's about raising the child you and Robert created from your love for each other."

"You make it seem simple."

"It's not. Getting back in the kid-raising saddle is hard. But you have to trust your feelings. I sense what your feelings are and I think you can too."

Jo Ann took a deep breath. "What about the race thing?"

"That's hardly a reason for not having the baby. Biracial children may have special challenges, but your child will have a real advantage – loving, and wealthy, parents. The fact people say stupid things is just life."

They moved on and talked about mutual friends, the book club, and Margie's new love interest. After lunch at a nearby restaurant, Margie returned to Jo Ann's pregnancy. "I don't see what matters except how much you and Robert love each other. Seven years ago was an ordeal because I didn't have somebody who stayed with me. Having sex every night was fine, but when that came with a price, the child we conceived, he skipped out. Your man won't."

Jo Ann looked down. "I feared Robert would blame me

because I told him, in effect, I couldn't get pregnant anymore. He said we can't blame anybody."

"It's no more your mistake than his. He could have asked more about the details."

"I'm lucky, having a friend like you."

"You were there for me seven years ago. What little good I may have done for you today, you did ten times more for me then."

They embraced again in the restaurant parking lot. When they retrieved Kimberly, Jo Ann noticed her long frame, a model, perhaps, of what Robert's off spring might look like. Jo Ann mentally darkened Kimberly's skin and wondered if she saw a picture of the child she and Robert would bring into the world.

∞∞∞

Riding home Sunday afternoon, Jo Ann gave Robert the gist of her talk with Margie. As she finished, she brought up Margie's big question. "We've never talked about getting married. Should we?"

"Should we talk about it or should we do it?"

"Either, both."

"The 'm' word! What do you think?"

"We've been so focused on living day-to-day I never thought about it."

"I did once," he said.

"You did?"

"I assumed we would, eventually."

"We want to be together, don't we, whether we get married or not?"

"I want to be with you, married or not."

She said, "Since that Saturday when we first made love, I've wanted to be with you."

Robert stretched his arms against the steering wheel. They were still in the rolling hills on Texas 71. He looked over at Jo Ann and said, "If you got run over by a bus going home this afternoon, I'd be as devastated as I was when Darla died. I would have never believed that could happen, but that's how I feel."

Jo Ann reached over and took his hand. If she hadn't understood before that Margie was right about her wanting Robert's baby, any doubt melted at that moment.

Chapter 27

A few weeks after the Austin trip, the expectant parents began telling family members, friends, and business colleagues they didn't want finding out through the grapevine or only when it became obvious.

First, they took David Marks to lunch and told him Jo Ann would have all the support she needed so she could keep working at a high level through the pregnancy and afterwards. Marks put them at ease when he said Jo Ann's work had become so valuable he would babysit himself if needed so they could keep "The Project" going.

A week later, they compared notes on who they'd told, reactions, and who they hadn't told yet.

"Betty Martin was stoic," Jo Ann reported as they sat in a small café near Robert's house. "She asked how it happened and said she'd help in any way possible."

"What does she think Kendra and Tiffany will say?"

"She said Tiffany might call me and make sure I don't have an abortion. We both saw Kendra just getting meaner."

"Talk to your kids yet?" Robert asked, spreading his bread with butter.

Jo Ann sipped mineral water. Though Connie had approved an occasional glass of wine, she decided she'd stay off alcohol until their child was born and weaned. "Melissa and Regina, not Tony, not yet."

"What did your girls say?"

"Melissa was taken aback. She and I don't talk about

intimate things, mostly because she hasn't been around. She said she couldn't wait to see what I look like pregnant. She was too young to remember when I was pregnant with her sister.

"Regina approached it like you'd expect, as a lawyer sizing up options. I told her that while we didn't plan this, we've decided we want this baby. She will give me advice, but once I say what I want, that's it."

"What's the deal with Tony? Does he even know about us?"

"We haven't discussed the fact I'm in a relationship that includes sex."

Robert offered her an incredulous stare. "Why not?"

"He thinks sex outside marriage is against the teachings of the Bible. I didn't date right after the divorce but, once I started, he said I'd rot in hell because I slept with men without being married."

"He gave you a hard time?" Robert asked. Jo Ann could see his disbelief.

"If I spent a Friday night out, when I got home Saturday, Tony would come in from working out and complain about me not being there the night before. He said I was going against God's law."

Robert still looked dazed. "Getting pregnant out of wedlock, even at 51, is a terrible sin, right?"

"He'll see it that way. I don't like being estranged from him, which makes interacting with my granddaughter harder. Plus, I want our child to know Shonda. How're you doing?"

"I told my golf guys. Jerry was kind. That meeting at the club made you a real person. He asked how you're feeling and expressed concern about you getting through this. I was touched."

"What did the other two say?"

"Terry reacted like I thought he would. He said, whatever he and Joyce could do, they'd do. I want you to get to know them. Joyce was a great friend for Darla and she'll be for you too.

"Tommy was snide about it. 'Got your hook hung, huh, Robert?' he asked. 'I told you about chasing that black tail.' It was crass."

"What about Harry and Jeri Morris?"

"I figured we'd tell them together at our next tennis date. You can keep playing a little longer, can't you?"

She nodded and asked, "Did you tell Jimmy Hundley?"

He lightly stroked her forearms. "You know what he told me?"

"What?"

"He flashed this big grin and said, 'I could tell that morning at the hotel that you were head-over-heels in love with her. It was all over your face.' He said he and his wife had an unexpected pregnancy when she was 49, so he knows that it happens. They lost that baby. Even with three grown children, it hurt. He said he would pray for us and our child."

"That's really kind. What about your family?"

"First there's my brother, Tim."

"What's the deal with him?"

"He's a 61-year-old version of your son. It's not religion. He was raised as I was, in a forgiving spiritual environment. Tim has rigid notions of right and wrong. He can be harsh and judgmental."

"What'd he say?"

"He wondered if you tricked me so you can get at my money."

Jo Ann shook her head. "What about his wife?"

"Candace isn't like Tim. She puts up with his b.s. because he's a great provider and is kind to her and their children. She was alone for eight years after her first husband died in a car wreck when she was 22. Living with Tim's narrow mindedness is the price she pays for his good side."

"Does Tim care about race?"

"I told him two months ago I was seeing a black woman. This isn't about color."

Jo Ann fiddled with a button on her shirt. "What about your children?"

"I haven't told Sandy. I left her a voicemail message that we need to talk. I didn't say why. Bill was surprised, but offered his support. Marcia was elated at the prospect of a playmate for Tricia. Al said, 'I'm sure it was an accident Dad, but that's okay.' Then he put Deena on the phone."

"And?"

"She was more than gracious. She said, 'Every child is a blessing' and 'This is a gift from God.' She promised she'd come to Houston and help us. When I told her about the possibility of twins, she said that means we'll need even more support and she'll do all she can for us."

"How long have she and Al been married?"

"Eight years. They got married not long before Darla died."

Jo Ann blinked. "Do you know why they haven't had children?"

"No."

"Has either said anything about infertility?"

"Not that I remember. Why?"

"Deena, from all you've told me, seems like a woman who would've had children as soon as possible. She doesn't work outside the home, right?"

"No, and she doesn't seem career focused. She does substitute teaching to keep herself occupied."

Jo Ann noticed a troubled look on Robert's face. "What's bothering you? Something's on your mind."

"Sandy."

"Your daughter?"

He nodded. "My daughter."

"You haven't said much about her, but you're always talking about your boys."

"You and I have to talk about her. The pregnancy means we can't avoid it anymore."

"Avoid what?"

"You've coped with the attitudes of your former friends -- Kendra and Tiffany. They were good friends, but they're not family. Sandy is family."

Jo Ann's nostrils flared. "What're you talking about?"

"Sandy's not happy I'm with a black woman."

Jo Ann's voice deepened. "How do you know?"

"She said so."

"When?"

"In late summer. You were in Washington. I called Al, then Sandy. I was worried about Deena, as you know. That's seems okay, maybe better than okay. I never thought Sandy would be a problem. She is."

"What'd she say?"

"That black-white romances are 'weird.'"

"Anything else?"

"That people should date and marry their 'own kind', people from 'their tribe.'" Robert looked into Jo Ann's eyes and extended a hand across the table, touching her arm. Jo Ann grasped his hand for a second, but quickly let go.

He continued, "Please don't be angry with me. I was shocked when I heard that come out of her mouth."

Jo Ann took a sip of water. Sandy's attitude made her uncomfortable. It was the first time since she and

Robert started seeing each other she'd faced a white person's displeasure with their relationship. It made her think about Kendra and Tiffany. What was the difference between their attitudes and Sandy's? Was there one?

"I feel hurt and disappointed. It's not you saying those things. You told me you never thought much about race before you and I got involved. Maybe this is a consequence of that."

"That's what bothers me. I should have been a different parent."

"Does this mean she sees something wrong with being black – that black people are inferior?"

"We didn't talk about that. I was so shaken, I let it go."

"You said Darla had black women friends. Did Sandy know that? Did it mean anything to her?"

"I don't know. Some of those friendships started after Sandy left for college."

"What kind of relationship did Sandy and Darla have?"

"They drifted apart when Sandy was in high school. Darla did a poor job of hiding her disappointment that Sandy didn't measure up to her sons academically. Darla, if I haven't made clear to you, was a high-test-scores, high-grades, orange-bleeding University of Texas snob. That translated into her being especially unhappy about Sandy's college options and her ultimate choice."

"Central Missouri State?"

Robert nodded. "She had friends going there. Darla hoped one of her children would follow in her footsteps at Texas. She didn't begrudge the boys their opportunity at Stanford. Sandy couldn't get into Texas, much less Stanford, but Darla thought she could at least try for a major state university – maybe Georgia or Tennessee or Indiana, somewhere like that. Sandy wouldn't even apply."

Jo Ann hung her head. "Sandy thinks our being together is

'weird?'"

"She made a point, at the end of the conversation, of telling me she had a date with a white guy."

"That's mean."

"I'm embarrassed."

Jo Ann pointed her finger at him. "I will be upset with you about this only if you let it spoil things for us. You can't let Sandy dictate your life."

∞∞∞

Saturday morning, while Robert played golf, Jo Ann got up her nerve and called Tony. It had been a long time since she'd dreaded something as much. "How're you doing, Tony?" Jo Ann asked, pacing the floor of Robert's kitchen. Making the call from his house gave her a bad feeling.

"I'm okay. I've been busy," he said.

"I get it. My new job is hard, too."

"What's up?" he asked. "I'm glad to hear from you, but I have a meeting this morning, so I should get going before long."

Jo Ann took a deep breath. "There's something I should tell you. I've told your sisters and you should know about it, too."

"What?"

"I've had a new boyfriend for the last five months or so."

"I'm sure why you haven't told me. I assume you're sleeping with him and, since you didn't say you've gotten married, you know how I feel about that. Why tell me now?"

The disdain Jo Ann heard almost made her hang up. "There's more to it now, more than Robert and me being boyfriend/girlfriend. I'm about two months pregnant."

Jo Ann hadn't been sure what she should expect once she said those words. Pained silence? An outburst? The phone slammed in her ear?

She got something far worse - a stern, low voice spoken with chilling, controlled anger. "You're a slut, a common everyday slut. I'm ashamed you're my mother. I have nothing to say to you. Don't call me. Stay away from my daughter. As far as I'm concerned, you're just somebody who lives in Houston I happen to know." There was no goodbye.

∞∞∞

Jo Ann cried after the call, then pulled herself together long enough that she could clean the kitchen and feed Rufus. When Robert returned from playing golf, he found her at the kitchen table, crying her eyes out.

"You must've talked to Tony," he said after embracing her.

"He called me a slut," she whimpered. "He said he wants nothing to do with me. He told me to stay away from his daughter. I felt like a common criminal."

They sat down. "You knew it would be bad,"

"I didn't expect what I got."

"Did he make it about race?"

"We never got that far. After I said I'm pregnant, what hurt was how coldly he spoke. I've never felt such a chill from a family member. He could have been Kendra."

"I'm sorry. I wish I could make this better."

"What am I going to do? I'll never see my little Shonda again."

Robert reached for her hand and squeezed tight. "That won't happen. He'll get over this. At some point he'll want to see and get to know his sibling."

"What did I do wrong in raising him that makes him this way? His sisters aren't like this."

"Yours wasn't the only voice he heard. There are other people talking when he says these things."

They stood again and embraced. Jo Ann ignored the fact Robert hadn't cleaned up after golf. She led him to the bedroom. They stripped off their clothes, fell on the bed, and made love for the next hour before slipping into a deep sleep wrapped around each other.

Chapter 28

Despite the Tony trauma and Robert's unease about Sandy, the second Sunday in November began as delightful an eight weeks as Jo Ann had ever experienced. Only later did she understand it was the calm before several storms. What started that November Sunday and didn't end until early January was new for Jo Ann – the warm, holiday season embrace of family and friends.

She had forgotten – on purpose – what passed for holidays in her childhood. A holiday was just another day for survival. Memories of an overcrowded project apartment, absent parents, and grimy, violent streets generated pain, not cherished memories.

Holidays were nothing special in college. Once married, from the third or fourth year, Jo Ann's suspicions of James's infidelity cast long, dark shadows over holidays. Hints abounded – callers who hung up when she answered, hasty departures for "meetings," leaving town Thursdays for Saturday sporting events. She first ignored the signs, then denied to herself they meant what she knew they meant.

James's carelessness eventually gave him away. She found a woman's panties in his bag, a pair too small for her, still fighting the weight gain from her third pregnancy. From that moment, the marriage was over.

As a single mother, Jo Ann did what she could in creating a family life for her children. She had no extended family in Houston and, before she finished graduate school and started working again, little money for visiting relatives in Louisiana.

That November and December Jo Ann experienced something she never had before.

∞∞∞∞

Jackie McFadden called and said a friend had given him two tickets for a Houston Texans football game. Could he and Linda come for a visit? Notwithstanding plans for attending the Texas-Oklahoma State game in Austin that weekend, Robert eagerly said, "Yes."

"Call them back and say they should come Friday," Jo Ann said. "You take Jackie to Austin. I'll entertain Linda. Then they can go watch the Texans Sunday."

"That'll give Jackie and me time for the catching up we didn't do while I was in Little Rock. You can get acquainted with Linda."

∞∞∞∞

The McFaddens arrived on schedule. Jo Ann immediately liked Linda. Saturday they cruised through breakfast, a shopping trip, and a late lunch in the Rice Villages. Jo Ann soon wished Kendra and Tiffany could view her involvement with Robert as Linda did.

"You're so right for each other," Linda said at lunch, her face framed by wire-rimmed glasses and dangling, diamond shaped earrings. "I watched you make dinner last night. You knew each other's moves and seemingly could read each other's thoughts."

"I'm amazed at that too," Jo Ann said. "I've never connected with a man that way."

"How're you feeling about the pregnancy?" Linda asked,

bringing it up for the first time since Robert announced it at dinner Friday night.

"I'm over the shock now. I'm still not sure how we handle babies at this stage of life."

Linda's breath caught. "Babies?"

"My doctor says there's a chance I'm carrying twins."

Linda winced. "That'd be hard, wouldn't it?"

"It would, but if that's it, that's it. I feel okay now physically. Emotionally, I can't believe how at peace I am. This is a lot different than with my first set of children."

Linda leaned forward, listening intently. "Really?"

"James and I had our first child because we thought it was time. We had the second so we could give the first a playmate. The third was a pure and simple accident.

"I cherish each of them. They mean everything to me. But I never felt consumed with love for how they came about. Now, I feel the life I'm carrying is an extension of the love between Robert and me."

"What do your children think?"

"You mean about me being with Robert or me being pregnant?"

"Either. Both."

"The girls don't care about color. My oldest daughter can't wait until I'm big as a house. Her sister is cool with it. Tony has disowned me because he sees sex outside marriage as wrong."

"A religious thing?" Linda asked, sipping white wine.

"Yes."

"If he's really a man of God, he'll realize he's wrong. Otherwise, he'll just keep putting on a show about it until one of his sisters slaps some sense into him. You shouldn't worry about it."

Jo Ann raised her arms and opened her palms in relief. "That may be the best advice I've had."

"What does Robert's family think?"

"His boys and their wives have been positive. His daughter, apparently, is not on board with him being with me. She thinks interracial relationships are 'weird.'

"Robert's not sure what he should make of her attitude. He hasn't told her about the pregnancy. I suppose I'll see how they really feel when they're here for Christmas. His brother is a jerk, but Robert says it's not about race, he's just stupid about some things."

Linda offered a knowing look. "There's plenty of that in most families."

As the weekend raced by, Jo Ann grew sad about Jackie and Linda's departure. In a sliver of time, Linda became the black woman friend Jo Ann so craved but didn't have, the friend Betty could have been if she weren't so afraid of crossing Kendra and Tiffany.

Jo Ann fought back tears as Linda and Jackie got into their car Sunday. "Please come see me," Jo Ann pleaded when she and Linda embraced in Robert's driveway.

"Of course, and when you and the babies can travel, visit me in Little Rock."

"I will," Jo Ann whispered through tears.

∞∞∞

On Thanksgiving morning Jo Ann awakened, surprised Robert was already out of bed. She threw on shorts and an Austin College t-shirt. She was lacing up her shoes when he came in, sweating.

"I could've gone with you," she said, looking up at him, "I

can still run – slow, but I can still run."

"You were sleeping so peacefully."

"Please, wake me. Connie said I should exercise."

"Fair enough. I won't leave you behind again. But promise you won't whine about me waking you up."

"I don't whine," she said, sticking out her lip, feigning insult.

"Sure you don't," he laughed. He took her in his arms. "If we didn't have so much to do, you know what I'd do now."

"We have too much to do, no matter how much I'd love screwing your brains out."

Robert showered while Jo Ann started dinner. "I haven't cooked a big Thanksgiving dinner in ages," she said when he arrived in the kitchen, wearing shorts and a Stanford t-shirt.

"Why not?"

"James was always covering games, so we kept it simple. After the divorce, the kids did Thanksgiving with his family. Sometimes Tony was playing football. Usually, I made something quick and watched games by myself until I picked them up."

Robert opened the refrigerator and said, "We did what Terry and I are doing today. We had dinner early and headed for the Texas game. UT played A&M on Thanksgiving in those days. Having been in the Longhorn Band, Darla wouldn't dare miss the Thanksgiving Day game."

"I'm glad we seasoned the turkey last night," she said, watching him slide the bird into the oven. "What do you think, three and a half hours?"

"That's about right. It's 7:15a.m. now. Dinner is at noon. If we leave for the game by two o'clock, we should make it fine."

"I'm still surprised Betty and Charles are coming. I bet Tiffany and Kendra don't know that."

Robert stopped and sighed. "Are those two crazy? How long will they keep this up? Okay, they don't want anything to do with you because of me. But why ruin Betty's life too?"

"You just don't know Kendra. You like Betty, don't you?"

"I do. I know what her friendship means to you. I'm not unaware you need black friends. Since you've been with me, you spend your time with white people. I saw you bond with Linda McFadden."

With a furrowed brow, Jo Ann asked, "Did it show?"

"Yes, but so what? Loving me shouldn't mean giving up everything you've known. You need black friends, especially black women friends."

Jo Ann left the potatoes she'd been peeling and hugged him. "Thank you. You recognizing that makes me love you more, if that's possible."

She cut, chopped, and cooked vegetables and mixed a fruit medley of pineapple, various kinds of berries, and apple slices. He checked and rechecked the turkey and set the dining room table for eight. She filled water glasses and put three kinds of wine on a side table.

They took turns changing in the bedroom. Just before noon, the bell rang and Jo Ann opened the door. "Hanna!" Jo Ann exclaimed. Jo Ann now wore gray slacks and a white sweater. "You're the first one here. It's so good to see you!"

"Thanks for inviting me. It's been forever since I've had someone else cook Thanksgiving dinner. I couldn't miss it."

When Robert appeared, wearing a long-sleeved, orange Texas polo shirt and khaki slacks, Jo Ann introduced them. "This is Hanna Leslie. She was a friend of Irma Simpson, who knew Darla."

"It's nice to meet you, Hanna. Welcome to our home."

Jo Ann relished Robert's 'our home' reference. Though she still owned her house, she spent most of her time at his now.

It pleased her that he thought of and advertised his place as theirs.

Betty and Charles Martin arrived next, followed by Terry and Joyce Peters. Finally, Jon Weinstock, Robert's financial adviser and tennis buddy, appeared.

"I'll give the blessing," Robert announced as they gathered around the dinner table. "If you're comfortable doing so, please join hands.

"We have here today, several faith traditions. We honor them all. We say only this: Great Spirit, by whatever name, we thank You for the opportunity to come together on this day of thanks, amongst friends and family, to break bread, experience fellowship, and feel the warmth of human kindness. Grant us the compassion to support each other and the wisdom to do right in our lives and the lives of those we touch. Help us be better stewards of all that is given to us. Hear our prayer. Amen."

As Jo Ann slipped into her chair beside Robert, she held his hand and whispered, "That was beautiful. Maybe this religion thing isn't so bad after all." He kissed her and picked up carving knives, then addressed the group again.

"Today is special for Jo Ann and me. It's Thanksgiving, and something of a coming out party for us a couple. You all know a little of how we started seeing each other last spring. Some of you know that last month we discovered Jo Ann is pregnant. Even at our ages, we prepare for being parents. Though we didn't plan this, we're proud and happy because this pregnancy resulted from our love for each other."

Jo Ann shed a tear and Robert's voice cracked. He recovered and said, "I would introduce everybody, but since I don't know everyone equally well, you can introduce yourselves."

"I'm Jo Ann. Robert is right that we're happy about our news. We ask that you, our special friends, help us welcome our new addition, or additions, since we're told it's possible we're having twins." She grasped Robert's hand beneath the table and he squeezed back.

"I'm Jon Weinstock. I've known Robert for 20 years. I met Jo Ann a few months ago. I didn't know about the baby, or babies. Though I'm surprised, I'm happy, if you're happy. I know Terry and Joyce. I'm looking forward to knowing the rest of you. Friends of Robert are friends of mine."

"I'm Betty Martin. Jo Ann and I go back many years. Jo Ann told me about her pregnancy and I'll help her in getting through it as much as I can. Thank you both for inviting Charles and me. We're honored you asked that we share today with you."

"I'm Charles. I hang around with Betty." Laughter echoed around the table.

"I'm Joyce Peters. Terry hangs around with me. We knew Robert and Darla, as well as anybody. We're so happy Robert found Jo Ann. She's a delight, the best thing that could've happened to him." Jo Ann shed another tear.

"I'm Terry. Joyce said it all." More laughter erupted.

"I'm Hanna Leslie. Of those here, I know only Jo Ann, through a mutual friend, now deceased. I hope I can get to know the rest of you. The pregnancy is news to me. It will be a big challenge at this stage of your lives. Still, like Jon, I'm happy for you if you're happy, and thanks for including me today."

They passed around food and struck up conversations. Robert and Terry, facing a three-hour drive to Austin, skipped the wine, but nobody else did except Jo Ann. Things, therefore, became lively by the time they cleared the table. Hanna and Jon led the cleanup.

Once, when Hanna came out of the kitchen, she pulled Jo Ann aside and said, "If you were trying to fix me up, you succeeded. Jon asked me for my phone number."

"Did you give it to him?"

"I did. He's a handsome guy. I love his dark eyes. I like talking with him. He might be my type."

Finally, with everything put away, Robert took Jo Ann's hand and they walked together from the kitchen into the living room. "This has been wonderful," she whispered. "I feel embraced by everyone here."

"These people care about us. They'll be there for us through this pregnancy."

"I understand that now."

Jo Ann never let go of Robert's hand until he and Terry walked out the door. When she finally said good bye to Joyce, who left last, she couldn't remember feeling warmer inside.

Chapter 29

The week after Thanksgiving, Connie scheduled Jo Ann for an ultrasound examination. Robert tagged along. The technician helped her onto a table in a room full of complex-looking equipment, lifted her shirt, pushed down her slacks and panties, covered her middle with gel, and began running a wand over her.

Connie arrived, looked at the screen beside the examination table, and gasped. "Just like I thought!"

"What, Connie?" Jo Ann asked. Robert gripped her hand.

"There are two babies! You're having twins, my lady."

"How can you tell? All I see is wavy lines on a black background."

"As my dad always said, it's all in knowing how. That shows two little images, your twins. I can't tell the sex. We'll know that when we do genetic testing, but there are two babies in there."

"So now we know," Robert said as they left Connie's office.

"Let's talk later about what this means," Jo Ann said. "I need to process it, take it all in."

"Would you like lunch?"

Jo Ann suddenly drew in her breath and held it. "I'd like going home and making love."

"I'm real okay with that."

"Let me take a little detour so I can pick up my mail."

"Done," he said, turning the car toward her house.

In bed, he took her twice and, afterwards, they cuddled. Lying beside him, she noticed the bump in her belly. Later, Jo Ann sat up and rifled through the mail she'd left on the nightstand. A white envelope, with her name typed in large, capital letters and the street and city in smaller letters, caught her eye.

"What's this?" she asked out loud, slitting open the envelope.

Inside, she found one folded sheet of paper. Large type in the middle of the page said:

YOU'VE GONE TOO FAR.
YOU HAVE BEEN WARNED.

Jo Ann nudged a dozing Robert. "Look at this. What could it mean?"

"I don't know," he said, taking the paper. "Let me see the envelope."

She handed it to him. "Single stamp, no return address, mailed from zip code 78957. I'll look that up on my phone."

He beat her to it. "Smithville, Texas. You've been by it a zillion times. It's 45 miles from Austin on 71, halfway between Bastrop and LaGrange."

She cocked her head sideways. "I don't know anybody there."

"It probably was just mailed there. The sender could be from anywhere."

"What do they mean, 'You've gone too far?'"

"Who knows?"

Jo Ann drew back from him. "What should we do?"

"Nothing now. Let's see if anything else like this shows up. If something does, we'll call Jenny Dixon."

"Who's she?"

"Jennifer Dixon is a lawyer I know who's good at fixing things. This might be an accident. It might not have been intended for you."

Jo Ann went rigid as she sat up. "Something tells me it was. I have a bad feeling about this."

A few mornings after the ultra sound exam revealed the twins, Robert endured flying to Florida so he could meet with Sandy. He'd brooded for weeks about going and how he'd travel. He thought about driving, given how much he hated post-September 11 flying.

Robert once flew all over the world in his corporate jobs. He relished covering half a continent in a few hours. Now, he hated the loss of control that went with air travel. The airport indignities –practically getting undressed, being finger printed, seeing his aftershave lotion confiscated – he could sort of tolerate. Stories of flights being delayed and passengers sequestered for hours, however, made him want no part of flying. He especially feared that happening because a well-meaning, if clueless, traveler noticed a brown-skinned college professor working equations, mistook his scribblings for Arabic, and reported him as a terrorist.

The better part of two days for driving to Florida, some of one there, and most of two getting back, however, gave him enough pause he decided he'd grin and bear flying. Seeing Sandy was important, but being away from Jo Ann almost five days was too much.

He arrived in Orlando at 9:55 a.m. on a Tuesday, rented a car, and drove to Ocala, a town of almost 60,000, 80 miles northwest. A year after graduating from college, Sandy moved there, with the husband she never should have married, when he got a job managing an auto parts store. Florida grew on her and, after the divorce, she decided she'd stay there.

When Robert called, Sandy said his visit wouldn't change anything, but she finally told him, "I can't just blow you off, Dad, even though I want to. You deserve better than that from me."

Sandy took six months after the divorce in finding a good job and Robert floated her most of that time. He knew that generosity helped buy him today's audience. They agreed they'd meet at a Chili's near the apartment she shared with a female co-worker. Robert pulled into the parking lot and noticed Sandy's five-year old Honda Civic, a combination wedding/college graduation present, already there.

In the lobby, she offered no embrace and not much of a handshake. "Hi, Dad. You're on time."

Robert seethed inside, but remained calm. "Flight was a few minutes early and I had no trouble getting over here. I even remembered the way to the restaurant from the last time I was here."

As the hostess seated them, Robert studied his daughter. Sandy had Darla's round face, not his angular features. Her hair resembled Darla's darkish blonde, not his sandy brown. She had blue eyes, like all his children, and of course she was tall, nearly six-feet, two-inches. He wondered if she resented being that tall, if she thought it unbecoming a woman. Since giving up basketball and volleyball, she probably found that height of little use.

They exchanged small talk before Sandy said, "You're disappointed I'm not happy about your girlfriend. I've told you why. I wish you'd accept my feelings and go on. I don't live in Houston. You don't live here. Sometimes things happen in families that keep people apart. Maybe this is just one of them."

"I'm still your father, and you're still my daughter. I'm not writing you out of my life. There are holidays, family events. More important, help me understand why you feel this way. Is there something else going on here?"

She sat up and looked at him across the table. "There was a time I didn't want you with anyone. I couldn't see how you could do that to Mom. I'm over that now. I went through my divorce. I understand loneliness. No, this isn't about that. I just see this as strange."

Robert stroked his throat and grimaced. "What does that mean?"

"I can't say it any differently."

"Is that because even you understand it doesn't make sense? A person's color makes no difference in their capacity for love or their worthiness for being loved."

She waved a hand in front of her face. "That sounds good, but is it really what you want? Have you just convinced yourself that's the politically correct thing you should say? When I was growing up you never said anything like that. You never said anything about race."

"I regret that now, and not just because you and I are having this problem. I regret it because it kept our lives from being richer, fuller, more in tune with the world as it really is. We stayed, as you say, with our own tribe and never saw what kind of great big, diverse world there is out there."

She plucked at her blue blouse, which she wore above white slacks. "What's so great about hanging out with a black person? A lot of them don't even like white people."

"That's true. It's no different than what I'm saying about the way you feel. I don't like that either. Jo Ann has black friends who've disowned her because they don't like her being with me."

"They think it's weird, too?"

"They see black women as having an obligation toward black men. Having studied this now, I understand that. I don't agree with it, but I understand it."

"How'd you come to that?"

"I spent several days in Little Rock with an old basketball teammate, a black guy who runs a recreation center there. He gave me a crash course on the history of race in America. I understand a lot I didn't before, especially about how blacks feel they must stick together since whites have so mistreated them."

"Being Black 101?"

He stared at her with cold, flinty eyes. "That's not fair. I knew nothing about many events that shape how black people see the world. In understanding Jo Ann, I had to know about that. My teammate helped me see that not everybody sees the world through the rose colored glasses I have most of my life."

"Romance is different. And you got her pregnant!"

"So you know? How?"

"I have my sources. How did that happen?"

"It was an accident. Jo Ann thought she was past fertility and she wasn't. It's that simple."

"Why are you having it?"

"Why are we having them? She's carrying twins. We're having them because we want them."

"Twins! Oh, my God, Dad. That's disgusting."

"Did you really mean that? We're talking about your siblings."

"I'm sorry. I'm just having trouble with the whole idea. You're almost 64 years old."

"Life throws curve balls. I'm not much for saying that God has a plan and all that. There is something about this that seems like it was meant to happen. I love Jo Ann and she loves me. That love gave us these children. We're not casting them away because it's inconvenient."

Diving into their taco salads helped relieve the tension. Half-way through the meal, Sandy thawed a bit. "I'm not a hateful person. I wasn't prepared for how this hit me. I can't be part of it right now. I see how you feel, and I'm not oblivious to that. I'll try to understand it and maybe, eventually, I can accept it. How's that?"

"If it's all I can get, I'll take it."

"I know how much you hate flying, so the fact you flew down here tells me it's important to you."

He lowered his voice. "Are you coming home for Christmas? You can meet Jo Ann and her children, at least her daughters. Her son is on the outs with her about this, but for a different reason than yours."

"Oh?"

"He thinks sex outside marriage is wrong, period."

Sandy chuckled a moment, then turned serious again. "I'm not coming home for Christmas. I can't pretend. Being there and acting like I think this is okay when I don't would disrespect you and her family."

Robert couldn't hide his sadness. "This'll be the first time, ever, you and I and your brothers haven't been together at Christmas. I appreciate your concern for Jo Ann's feelings. Maybe you'll change your mind."

"I don't think so. I thought about Christmas before you came down here. I knew it would come up. Just let me be about this, okay? Who knows about the future?"

They finished up lunch talking about old times, particularly how Bill and Al tormented Sandy as a young child, yet became her teen age protectors. She took Robert by her office and introduced him to her staff and her bosses at the non-profit community action agency where she supervised a drug rehab program.

Before he left she gave him a modest hug and promised she'd call more often. He flew home thinking he hadn't achieved much, but he hadn't achieved nothing either. For now, that would have do.

∞∞∞

Three days before Christmas, Jo Ann received another envelope, identical to the first except the message:

YOU'RE GOING TO REGRET WHAT YOU DID.
IF YOU'D LET THINGS BE, WHAT'S GOING TO
HAPPEN WOULDN'T HAVE HAD TO HAPPEN.
THAT'S LIFE!

Jo Ann dialed Robert. "I got another one." She read it to him.

"Stay put. I'll be right over."

When he arrived, he looked at the letter and the envelope. "We'd better call Jenny. I'll try setting up something with her tomorrow."

"I have a big day. See if you can make it early morning or late afternoon so I can keep my meeting with David."

∞∞∞

The next morning, Jo Ann and Robert sat beside each other in a booth at Toast 'N Jam. Jenny Dixon arrived, carrying a briefcase and an umbrella.

"It's going to rain today, isn't it?" Robert asked. "I forgot all about that."

"We'll all need umbrellas, they claim," Jenny said, sitting across from them.

"Why do you look so familiar?" Jo Ann asked. "I could swear I've seen you before, but I know we've never met."

"We haven't met," Jenny replied. "People say I look like Teri Polo, the actress who played Helen Santos in the TV series *The West Wing*."

"You do! Regina and I watched that all the time."

"Regina is Jo Ann's nerd daughter," Robert explained. "She was about 15 years old at the time."

A waitress took their orders and Jenny asked, "What are these odd ball letters you're getting?"

Jo Ann handed Jenny the letters and envelopes. She read them and looked up at Jo Ann from across the table. "Who're your enemies?"

"I didn't know I had any, at least not any who'd do something like this."

"Now you know," Jenny said, pulling a yellow pad from her briefcase. "Let's make a list. And we can't leave anybody out."

Chapter 30

Bill, Marcia, and Tricia flew in the afternoon of the day Robert and Jo Ann met with Jenny Dixon. Al and Deena arrived that evening. Sandy's absence hung over the house like a looming family catastrophe. Robert and Jo Ann both knew they couldn't avoid talking about it at some point.

Jo Ann worked half the next day and spent the afternoon Christmas shopping with Deena. Jenny told Jo Ann she shouldn't go anywhere alone for a while and Jo Ann wanted time with Deena anyway.

Deena didn't fit the picture Robert painted of her. Jo Ann didn't see a looks-obsessed, sorority girl clothes horse. For shopping, she wore a touch of mascara, but no lipstick. Her white dress was functional, not gaudy, and her legs were bare.

She also wasn't a political animal spewing right wing venom. To Jo Ann, Deena appeared a polite, reserved, almost sad, young woman with something from her past gnawing at her. Jo Ann knew three hours of shopping wouldn't build enough trust for her to get the whole story but, when they stopped for a snack, Jo Ann tried peeling back the veneer. "What do you do every day, Deena?"

"Volunteer work, substitute teaching, things involving kids," she replied, munching on a chicken wrap.

"Why those things?"

"I love kids, young children especially, so I sub in the elementary schools. Second and third graders are great."

"Do you and Al have plans for kids?" Jo Ann hoped, and

feared, the question struck a nerve.

Deena whispered, "I'd like that someday."

Jo Ann said nothing as she sized up Deena's answer. There was a story there.

Deena asked, "So it's twins?" Robert had announced that the night before.

"My doctor always suspected it. An ultrasound confirmed it."

"I'll help in any way I can. I'm so proud you're having the babies. What will you need?"

"I'm worried about what happens after they're born. One baby is a lot of work, not to mention two. I bet I'm in no shape for doing much of anything, given what Connie says about how hard this could be physically, even without complications. How long can you stay?"

"As long as you need."

"My daughter, Melissa, says she'll move back here and help. Having you both would be great."

"We can work together." Deena smiled, reached across the table, and grasped Jo Ann's hand. In that grasp, Jo Ann felt support and pain.

∞∞∞

Two issues simmered below the holiday landscape surface - the letters and Sandy's absence. That concern bubbled to the top just before the family piled into cars for the Christmas Eve service at First Congregational Church.

Jo Ann and Robert stood in the kitchen, dressed and ready, when Deena walked in. She fidgeted with an earring. She'd put on her church clothes, a blue suit, white blouse, and sheer hose. "I guess I shouldn't ask since nobody has said anything.

Why's Sandy not here?"

Robert looked at Jo Ann and felt his heart sink. Jo Ann returned his look and shrugged her shoulders. She put down the glass of water she'd been drinking. "You tell her, Robert," Jo Ann said. "There's no point in keeping it a secret. Talking about it won't hurt my feelings any more than they already are."

A puzzled look appeared on Deena's face as she said, "I knew there was a story. Sandy hasn't missed being here for Christmas since I've been in the family. What does that have to do with you, Jo Ann?"

"Everything," Jo Ann replied. Robert heard anger in her voice. "Explain it, Robert."

He sighed. "Sandy is not pleased that my new partner is black."

Deena looked over at Jo Ann, now standing at the table. "I never would have thought that," Deena said. "I never saw anything in her that would have made me believe she'd think that way. I can't say we ever talked about it, so who knows?"

"She thinks interracial romances are 'weird' and people should stick to their own kind in matters of the heart," Robert responded.

"She said that?" Deena asked, straightening her skirt, and shuffling back a step.

Robert didn't hesitate. "She first told me that on the phone. I went to Florida in hopes of understanding it better. She couldn't – or wouldn't – say much else."

"There must have been more than that," Deena said.

"There wasn't."

"Have any idea why not?"

"Not really. It seems like a personal feeling that's not well thought out. I haven't convinced her she should look at it differently – and I've said all the stuff about color not mattering to me and love being color blind."

"Why wouldn't she come for Christmas?" Deena asked.

"She said pretending it was okay would make things worse, that being here would disrespect Jo Ann's family."

"Think she'll change?"

"I don't know. I hope so."

Deena looked at Jo Ann. "What are you feeling?"

"I can't do anything about it, so I've told Robert I only care that we not let it come between us. It hurts, because I assume Sandy thinks my being black makes me inferior, not good enough for her father."

Deena stepped across the room and embraced Jo Ann. "The rest of us – Al and I, Bill and Marcia, already love you. We love you, first, because Robert loves you. But I love you, because you're a special person. I'm glad you're in my life. I'm sure Sandy's feelings are painful for you, but it's not how the rest of us feel."

As the embrace continued, Jo Ann began crying. Deena held her tighter. Finally, Jo Ann lifted her head from Deena's shoulder and mouthed a barely audible, "Thank you."

Rufus trotted into the room, followed by Bill, Marcia, Tricia, and Al. Jo Ann wiped her tears on her sleeve and excused herself. Robert looked at the new arrivals, touched his index finger to his lips, and whispered, "We'll tell you about it later. She'll be okay."

∞∞∞

Melissa and Regina flew in Christmas Eve. They showed up at Robert's house early Christmas morning loaded with gifts. The present opening and dinner went smoothly enough that

Robert, despite Sandy's absence, and Tony's, declared the first Hart-Davis family Christmas a success.

During clean-up, Jo Ann pulled Robert aside, reached up, and patted him on the shoulder, "You're handling Sandy's absence well. I was put out with you last night, but I'm proud of you for how you're dealing with it. You could have taken it out on me. I'm the reason she's not here."

He took her hand for a moment. "It's not your fault. I wish she was here, but we can't let whatever's going on with her interfere with making a family for the twins you're carrying."

∞∞∞

Robert's sons and their families left the Friday after Christmas, as did Regina. Jo Ann worked short days Monday and Tuesday of the next week, using the afternoons for shopping with Melissa.

"The clerks think we're getting baby stuff for me," Melissa said as they left one store with bags of infant clothes.

"If they looked, they'd see I have the baby bump," Jo Ann laughed.

"How're you feeling?"

"I'm fine now. I don't know what carrying these two around will be like by May, if I get there."

"Think they'll be premature?"

"It happens a lot with twins."

"I still can't believe I'll have new sisters or brothers."

"I've had to get used to that idea, too."

"You really love Robert, don't you?"

"Like I've never loved a man before."

"It shows. You seem so happy around him. He seems that

way with you."

"That's why this is okay," she said, rubbing her bump.

∞∞∞

Robert and Jo Ann spent New Year's weekend at a resort in the Texas hill country. He played golf with friends from Austin, while she swam in the heated indoor pool and read two books, Bianca Sloane's mystery novel *Sweet Little Lies* and *The Warmth of Other Suns* by Isabel Wilkerson, the story of the 20th Century black migration out of the South.

On the way home, Robert brought up the letters. "Something will tell us soon what this is about."

"The other shoe will surely drop," Jo Ann replied, looking at him after gazing out the car window.

"The holidays were nice, weren't they?" Robert asked.

"More than nice," she replied. "Your boys and their families embraced me. Sandy's absence was hard for you, but you didn't go nuts about it. I got time with Melissa and Regina. Thanksgiving with our friends was great. Only having Tony's family here could have made it better. I wonder if Tony will ever forgive me."

"Give him time."

"I miss my granddaughter -- and my son."

Part 4
CRISES

Chapter 31

The holiday glow faded with the New Year and Jo Ann's return to work. Plans for appointing a new Exploration and Production vice president landed her in an intense corporate struggle. The threatening letters remained on her mind. She worried Sandy's estrangement – and the reason for it – could affect her life with Robert. And, she began feeling the effects of being pregnant with twins at age 51.

The E & P appointment tested David Marks's resolve about changing JAX's culture and Jo Ann's role in that. Normally, Joe Sanders, the senior executive in charge of E & P, would have promoted his favorite underling, perhaps with input from Executive Vice President Walt Corey. Now, Marks wanted control of the appointment. He accepted Jo Ann's contention that JAX's good ol' boy promotion practices hurt the company. Thinking no one would push back against doing things differently, however, was naive.

Jo Ann needed allies. She decided she'd try enlisting Karen Duffy, JAX's general counsel, in the cause of change. A tall, lean woman with short hair, a beak-like nose, and a sharp chin, Duffy had been the company's chief lawyer for eight years. At 47, she enjoyed a reputation for both open mindedness and aggressive corporate infighting.

"This appointment goes beyond one job," Jo Ann said, during a meeting in Karen's spacious office, decorated with her Stanford law degree, bar license, and photos from her UCLA volleyball days.

Jo Ann sat on a couch across from her and heard wariness.

"I'm curious why you want me in this," Karen said. "You have David's ear. Why worry what I think?"

"You also have David's ear and the ears of others," Jo Ann reminded her. "This is about how we do things."

"Fair enough. What can I tell you?"

"How we get this done without gallons of blood on the floor."

"Why would there be blood on the floor?"

"This is a test case. Certain people have their guy for the job – Ben Martin. He's part of the in crowd. If they get him through, to them, nothing has changed."

"What's wrong with Martin? He seems okay."

Jo Ann leaned forward. She raised her voice and jabbed her forefingers through the air, the rest of both hands curled into fists. "That's just it. He's okay, status quo. Promoting him says succeeding at JAX means going along, buddying up, and cruising through. Creativity and innovation don't matter."

"You can't beat somebody with nobody," Karen responded. "Is there a qualified candidate who's different?" Jo Ann noticed Karen's dark blue slacks and white blouse. Jo Ann couldn't remember her ever wearing a dress or skirt.

"Yes, a woman."

"That'll go over great with the E & P crowd."

"Probably like some people thought a woman would go over as general counsel." Jo Ann wasn't sure how Karen would take the remark or the laugh that went with it.

Karen flashed her teeth for an instant. "Point taken," she said. "I should look at this. What do you want from me?"

"Meet with the candidate, Kelly Matthews. If you like her, get behind her. She has a petroleum engineering degree from Texas and law school at LSU. She worked for the Energy Department and the Texas Railroad Commission. Then she did

E & P work at Exxon and spent two years with a small service company."

Karen sat up before she responded. "That's good, someone with that background might shake things up around here."

"Will you meet with her? My assistant, Rhonda Gonzalez, can set it up."

"I'll meet with her. If I like her, I'll consider jumping in with you."

Jo Ann got up and Karen stood as well. As Jo Ann edged toward the door, with a hint of a smile, Karen asked, "So it's true?"

"What's true?"

"That you're pregnant. I'd heard the rumors, but now I see for myself."

Jo Ann didn't know Karen well, so she had no idea how she should take this directness. She responded evenly and briefly. "Yes, I am."

"I hear Robert Hart's the father."

"He is." Jo Ann hoped her terse answers would discourage more questions, but Karen plowed ahead.

"Are you getting married?"

"Eventually, I think, but we've got too much else on our plates right now."

"How will you keep up with all this you're taking on in the company and have a baby at what, 51-52?"

This is a test, Jo Ann thought. Despite David Marks's supportive attitude, others in the JAX hierarchy might not be so kind. "I'll have lots of help. We've thought this through."

"I'm not saying you can't do it. I'm surprised you'd try."

"Robert and I didn't plan on having babies, but now that we are, we'll do what's necessary."

"Babies?"

"I'm carrying twins."

"Really?" Karen asked, leaning on the desk and adjusting her wire framed glasses as Jo Ann nodded. "I'm sorry if I seem skeptical. I don't doubt you. But being in the job you're in now is hard, as this E & P business shows. I hope you're up to it."

"I'm up to it, Karen. Thanks for your concern."

∞∞∞

Back in her office, Jo Ann found a phone message from Jenny Dixon. That put a knot in her stomach. She'd only call about the letters.

"Any news?" Jo Ann asked when Jenny answered.

"No, but I have a question."

"Yes?"

"I need total honesty."

Jo Ann felt ill at ease, afraid of what might be coming. "Okay, what?"

"What skeletons do you have rattling around in your closet?"

Jenny's question sent a chill down Jo Ann's back. "Skeletons?"

"Things from prior lives you aren't proud of – drugs, scrapes with the law, boyfriends buried in shallow graves."

"Gee--"

"Think about what you confided in somebody who was a friend, but isn't anymore."

Images of Kendra and Tiffany flashed into Jo Ann's mind, but still she said, "I've lived a mundane life. Can I think about it?"

"Please do. Get back to me. Good bye."

As she put down the phone, Jo Ann thought of a 'skeleton' that, to her, wasn't much, but to Tiffany would matter a lot. She sat at her desk and stared ahead for a moment. Yes, Tiffany would care about this, but Kendra would make it a big deal.

At four o'clock, Jo Ann grabbed her purse, walked out of her office, and told Rhonda she was leaving for the day.

"What's going on?" Rhonda asked, looking up from her desk with a frown. The dark-haired, brown-skinned woman whose parents arrived in the United States from Mexico a year before she was born had become essential to Jo Ann's work. She scheduled meetings, shielded her from people grabbing for face time, and provided a sounding board Jo Ann hadn't expected from a 24-year-old. "Except during the holidays, you haven't left this early in ages. Are you okay?"

"Carrying twins around could be getting to me. That and all that's going on around here."

Rhonda's eyes narrowed. "You're caught up in this E & P thing, aren't you? You hardly worked on anything else today."

"It could be important in changing JAX's culture."

"What will happen?"

Jo Ann stood beside Rhonda's desk, fiddling with her keys. "I hope the people I've asked will take a good look at Kelly Matthews, decide she's the right person, and help get her hired."

"Who'd you talk with?"

"Karen Duffy and Tom Reese."

Rhonda stood up. "What'd they say?"

"They'll meet with Kelly. Karen said if she liked her she'd consider getting behind her. Tom was noncommittal, but claimed he understood why we should consider an outsider. Oh, you need to set up a meeting with Kelly for Karen."

"Yeah, I'll arrange it."

"It's not just that she's an outsider. She's got the right background and personal qualities we need."

"What happens if she doesn't get the job?"

Jo Ann edged toward the door. "This isn't the last battle. I've told David that. This could be like a football team that's been down for a long time and is figuring out success. Sometimes you lose close games before you win a big one."

Chapter 32

J o Ann first thought she would go home and share with Robert her suspicions about who was behind the letters. Then she remembered he'd taken a day trip with his investor group for a look at gas properties in East Texas and wouldn't get home until after midnight. There was, however, someone else to whom she could float her theories. She dialed Hanna Leslie's number.

"How's the pregnant lady?" Hanna asked cheerfully.

"The pregnant lady is tired."

"It's only a few more months. Twin pregnancies often don't reach term."

Jo Ann shifted in her chair. "A long few months, I bet."

"How were the rest of the holidays? I still cherish Thanksgiving. It was so much fun."

The family scenes flashed through Jo Ann's mind. "Christmas was great. I met Robert's sons and their families, and I spent time with my daughters." She left out Sandy's absence, her estrangement from Tony, and the fact this had been her first Christmas without seeing her granddaughter. She changed the subject. "By the way, have you seen Jon, Jon Weinstock?"

"I have! He called in early December and we went out for drinks. He's neat. We're still sizing up each other, but so far, so good."

"I have something sensitive to talk with you about. Could we get together soon."

"How about lunch tomorrow?"

"I'll meet you at that place in The Woodlands where we went last summer. Jo's I think it is."

Feeling reassured by Hanna's warmth, Jo Ann decided she wouldn't tell Robert her suspicions.

∞ ∞ ∞

To Jo Ann, Hannah looked younger than at Thanksgiving. Her face was thinner and the lines less prominent. They talked about the letters and who and what Jo Ann thought might be behind them. Hannah found her theory "amusing," adding, "I can't imagine worrying about that these days. Nobody I hang out with would get upset about that."

"You live in a different world than the people I think are behind these letters. With one of them, I might as well have shot up a school. I'm not sure which she'd think was worse."

∞ ∞ ∞

Later that day another chapter in the E & P saga unfolded. David Marks asked that Jo Ann meet him at the office that night. He said, "Things are coming to a head."

While Jo Ann waited for David, her mobile phone rang. It was Connie Cross.

"I'm sorry I couldn't call you back today," she said. "I had several deliveries and a heavy patient load. Are you okay?"

"I'm tired, but nothing hurts. My fatigue may be from how busy I am. I'll lie around this weekend."

"Good."

"I didn't call about me."

"Oh?"

"What causes infertility?"

Connie laughed. "That isn't a problem you have."

Jo Ann chuckled. "This is about my maybe one-of-these-days daughter-in-law, the wife of Robert's younger son."

"Lots of things cause infertility. About one-third of the time it's the man's problem, about one-third of the time it's the woman's, and the other one-third either it's a combination or we can't tell. You think this is the wife's problem?"

"I get that feeling. Deena and I aren't close enough yet so she'd tell me all her story, but I sense pain."

"I should ask if she and her husband meet the definition of infertility."

"Which is?"

"One year of unprotected intercourse without conception."

"I'd bet a lot of money that's the case."

"If she has the problem, it could result from a pelvic infection or endometriosis. Sometimes pelvic surgeries lead to scar tissue or damage to the fallopian tubes. There might be a blockage there."

The words 'pelvic surgeries' gave Jo Ann an idea. "Do abortions cause infertility?"

"That's controversial," Connie replied. "Studies suggest maybe, but the research is conflicting and inconclusive. Politics gets into it. Pro-lifers say yes, pro-choice people say no. The medical evidence doesn't satisfactorily answer the question for me."

"But it's possible?"

"It's unlikely, but one study suggested that with surgical abortions, fetal bone can get left in the uterus, causing infertility. A post-procedure infection could happen. That isn't a problem with adequate temperature monitoring after the abortion. I've never had a case like that, but if a woman had an abortion and didn't have good aftercare, she could develop an infection that might cause infertility."

"Can you treat it?"

"If it's scar tissue, ovarian cysts, blocked fallopian tubes, or endometriosis, laparoscopic surgery usually works. First, you need an ultrasound or x-ray to find the exact problem."

"That's helpful. I may have a new patient for you."

Twenty minutes after the Connie Cross call, David Marks summoned Jo Ann to his office. His troubled look struck her. His collar was open, his red tie loosened. For once, she noticed hairs out of place.

"I never would have imagined this E & P thing would cause such an uproar," he said. He sat behind his desk, not on one of the couches as usual when they talked.

Jo Ann sat down in a high-backed chair in front of the desk. She smoothed down her beige dress. Her growing middle made crossing her legs at the knees awkward, so she crossed her ankles and pointed her knees toward the side of the chair. "Change is hard. What's happened?"

"Joe Sanders and Walt Corey say they'll quit if I don't give Ben Martin this job."

Jo Ann dropped her head. "Would they go through with it?"

"I don't know about Walt. Joe will. He's adamant."

"He says what?"

"Oh, it was nasty."

Jo Ann made sure she laughed. "It was about me, right."

David grinned. "How'd you know?"

"He can't win on the merits. His man doesn't measure up. So, he claims I'm leading you astray. It's like my lawyer daughter says. When you have the facts on your side, argue the facts. When you have the law, argue the law. When you have neither, change the subject."

"I'll remember that," he said, forcing another smile. "That's what he's doing."

Her eyes scanned the room. She noticed a golf course photo of David with long time JAX executives. In the picture, he stood between Joe Sanders and Walt Corey. "Are you afraid of losing him?"

"Between you, me, and the gatepost, yes."

Jo Ann now looked directly at the CEO. This might be a test for how strong she'd stand. She wasn't backing down. "Why? Because he's been here forever or because he does his job so well that you – we—can't do without him? What if he left?"

David hesitated. "I'm not sure."

Jo Ann stayed on offense. "You asked that I help you change this company. We aren't going to be what we can be without change. In four months, we've taken baby steps, snipped at the edges. Now, we have a chance at something big, something serious."

"This is big," he said. "They've made sure of that."

"You can give Sanders what he wants and we can fight another day. We can't put this off forever. Eventually, you must pick a side. Either you want change or you don't. If you pick change, somebody won't like it. Joe won't be the last person who threatens they'll leave over something like this.

"Ignore the fact he insulted me. I'll keep pushing until you kick me out the door. I signed on for helping you make this place special. I'll see that through."

David looked up at her. His face remained anguished, but lightened a bit. "Robert was right about you. He said you see big picture stuff better than anybody here."

"I appreciate that, but this isn't about me." She stood up, walked behind the chair, and leaned on it. "This is about the soul of this company. It's about your leadership."

"What if they leave? That's a big hole."

Jo Ann looked straight at Marks. "If that happens, so be it. They're not the only fish in the sea."

"That a tough thing to say."

She set her jaw and tightened her fists at her side. "No skin off my nose. I don't need this job anymore. Robert will be very wealthy pretty soon. Headhunters will be after me once the babies are born. But, helping you do this would give me a sense of accomplishment I've never had before. That would be, as they said in the old MasterCard commercial, 'priceless.'"

"If I make them hire Kelly and we have a palace revolt, how do I handle that?"

Jo Ann paced the room. "Don't make it a big deal. Announce Kelly's appointment as you'd announce any other major appointment. If somebody leaves, accept their resignation and thank them for their service to JAX.

"Stay out of the rumor mill and ignore social media. Let it be known, quietly, you didn't back down, you did this because you thought it best for the company. Run the traps with the board before the announcement so they know in advance of any pressure they get."

David sat back in his chair. He seemed, to Jo Ann, more at ease. "I'll think about it overnight. Tomorrow is Friday. Let's talk in the morning."

Jo Ann thought about pushing harder, but decided she'd back off. David needed a breather. Before she said more, he changed the subject. "How're you doing with the babies?"

She moved toward his desk from the window where she'd been standing. "I'm okay. Thanks for asking."

"I worry about you," he said. "You've been working so hard on this E & P hire, plus all the other stuff I've given you or you've dived into on your own. How're you keeping up?"

She backed away from his desk and started toward the door. "Rhonda's great. She keeps me organized. Robert's a terrific partner. I am tired. I admit that."

He stood up. "No matter what I decide about this E & P thing, please keep doing what you're doing."

∞∞∞

When Jo Ann walked out of the building that night, she decided she'd forget her job for a while. Her mind turned to the letters and telling Robert who she thought was behind them.

She realized she'd put off telling him for reasons other than how busy they'd both been. How he might react still sent waves of fear through her. They hadn't talked about such things. And, it was just a theory. She might be totally off base.

Getting into the car, she thought of someone else she could share her suspicions with. She reached for her phone. "Betty? Are you there?"

"I'm here, Jo Ann. I dozed off, I guess. What time is it?"

"A little after nine. Is this too late? Could we talk for a few minutes?"

"What's on your mind? I haven't heard from you in a while. Are you okay?"

"I'm fine. I am tired. I've been working hard. We have a big issue going on in the company. It's consumed me since getting back from the holidays."

"Are the babies okay?"

"My last checkup was good."

"When do you have another one?"

"Early next week. Because of my age and the fact I'm carrying twins, Connie sees me more often than most patients at this stage."

Jo Ann pulled into the parking lot of a well-lit strip center. She locked the car doors and left the engine running. "I need to ask you something."

"What?"

"Do you remember one night when you and Tiffany and Kendra and I sat around talking and confessed things we'd done that were risqué or wild?"

After a short pause Betty said, "I sort of remember that. You and Kendra drank a lot of wine that night. Why do you ask?"

"I'll tell you in a minute. But first, do you remember what I confessed to?"

"Not really. That was a long time ago."

Jo Ann scanned the parking lot. "Do you remember me talking about somebody who left town and about Irma Simpson, my friend who died of cancer?"

"Oh, yeah! I do! That threw everybody for a loop. None of us could imagine doing that. Why does that matter now?"

"Kendra and Tiffany might be planning on blackmailing me with that."

"How?"

"I don't know."

"What makes you think that?"

Jo Ann told her about the letters. "I can't think of anybody else who'd send them. Our lawyer asked that I think about what I might have done I'm not proud of and who I might have told about it, especially someone who now sees me as an enemy. Kendra and Tiffany sure qualify on that score."

Chapter 33

Friday came and went without David Marks making a decision on the E & P job. He got pulled into another crisis involving a regulatory matter. He sent Jo Ann a text as he boarded the company jet for Washington, saying they'd resolve the E & P problem next week.

Her plan for lying around and not thinking about JAX worked most of the weekend. Robert's regular golf round and a Saturday afternoon meeting with his investor group made easier putting off telling him her theory about the letters. They ate out Saturday evening and she didn't risk spoiling the mood.

Sunday night, as she relaxed with a book while Robert puttered in his home office, her phone rang. Karen Duffy's name flashed. "Hi, Karen," Jo Ann answered. "How are you?"

"I'm great. I hope you don't mind me calling this evening."

"Not at all. What's up?"

"I met with Kelly Matthews today. This thing is about to blow up. I got wind Saturday that Joe Sanders, perhaps with Walt Corey's help, is organizing a revolt if Ben Martin doesn't get the job. I figured I'd better meet Kelly before it really hits the fan. I arranged lunch with her today. We talked for three hours. She's impressive. You were dead on right about her. I'm not sure hiring her for this job is the right thing right now, but she's exactly what JAX needs."

"She should get the job."

"She should get a job at JAX," Karen countered. "Maybe not

this one."

"Because Joe and the boys want a crony?"

"Among other things."

"Such as?"

"The E & P job might not be where she can do the most good or where she can best help us get where we should go."

Jo Ann appreciated that Karen seemed to have signed on for the big picture goal of changing the JAX culture, but where was she headed? "I'm not sure I follow you. She's right for E & P vice president. Shuttling her off to some made up spot, if that's what you have in mind, doesn't make the point very well."

"Ordinarily, I'd agree, but this E & P vice presidency is now a symbol for both sides in what's become a battle for the soul of the company. Putting her there would make a huge statement, but might set her up for failure, given the opposition. I have an idea that could make this come out right."

Jo Ann felt her chest tighten. "What?"

"In our first meeting about this, you asked me how we could get this done without gallons of blood on the floor, right?"

Jo Ann got up from her overstuffed chair and paced. "I said that."

"Your instincts about that were correct. Forcing this down Joe Sanders's throat will produce exactly that result. He's planning on playing the board card. He's buddies with several directors and he's asking that they pressure David so he gives in on this. David doesn't need that and neither do you."

Jo Ann decided she wouldn't argue, at least not at the moment. "Okay. What's your plan?"

"Kelly can work for me. She's a lawyer, you know. She worked in the counsel's office at the Energy Department. I'll make her Associate General Counsel. Notice I said Associate General Counsel, not Assistant General Counsel. She wouldn't be just another lawyer handling contracts or a litigation docket. She'd be my right hand man. It'll require moving money and people around, but I'll make it work."

Jo Ann stopped pacing and looked out the window into the dark. "Sounds good, but how does it help change the culture?'

"I told David we should dust off the reorganization plan we considered two years ago. That plan puts four major divisions, including E & P, under a senior vice president for corporate development. I know somebody for that, by the way, who'd support our objectives."

"You do?"

"Over time, he could help root out the cronyism. Joe Sanders would report to him. Joe won't stomach that long. He'll retire. He and Walt aren't far away. Maybe we can entice them out early. Let Joe have this moment. He wins this battle, but we win the war.

"In the meantime, Kelly comes in and learns the company. I give her legal responsibility for E & P. Soon, she takes over that section and other things too. It's a long term strategy, but it could get us where we want to go."

Jo Ann ran a hand over her face. "I should understand this better before I say what I think."

"That's fine. I like that about you. You don't shoot from the hip. You think things through. You're very good in evaluating people. Kelly is first class. Find us a few more like her and we'll get this place in shape."

∞∞∞

As Jo Ann dressed for work Monday, David Marks called. "When will you be in?" he asked.

"Twenty, thirty minutes."

"Come straight to my office. I talked with Karen. Her idea is wonderful. What do you think?"

"I like it. I'm at a disadvantage because I don't know anything about this reorganization plan, especially who we'd hire as senior vice president for corporate development."

"You'll like who Karen and I have in mind for that. I'll fill you in when you get here. Give Robert my best." He hung up before she could respond.

Robert walked into the bedroom as she put down the phone. "Who was that?" he asked, shedding his running shoes.

"David," Jo Ann said, as she buttoned her shirt. During the weekend she decided she'd relax her office dress code. She'd wear maternity pants to work, a concession to the awkwardness of skirts and dresses. The time had also come for substituting loose fitting tops and shirts for her stylish blouses. She decided she'd send her pantyhose on vacation, and wear knee highs, socks, or nothing.

"What'd he want this early?" Robert asked.

"He wants me in his office as soon as I get there. Karen Duffy has an idea for solving this E & P vice presidency crisis."

"What's the idea?" he asked.

"An old reorganization plan that puts E & P under a new senior vice president, a plan I know nothing about."

Robert frowned. "That came up while I was there. If Karen thinks it would work, I'd try it."

"If it works, maybe a small win for me."

He took her into his arms, grasping her shoulders and cradling her head into his chest. After a long embrace, he stepped back and smiled down at her. "This makes me want you," he said. "We have time, don't we?"

"I have to leave. David is waiting for me. Tonight?"

He touched his forefinger to her lips and whispered,

"Tonight."

∞∞∞

Between the garage and her office, Jo Ann made a call. She was sent to voice mail. "This is Jo Ann," she said when Deena didn't answer. "I've been thinking about you. It's time I took you up on your offer. Want to help with getting the nursery ready? Let's talk about when you can come down here. I'll take off from work. I enjoyed our time at Christmas. Let me hear from you."

∞∞∞

When Jo Ann walked into David Marks's office, Karen Duffy, wearing a green blouse, gray slacks, and open toed shoes, stood by him at his desk. David handed Jo Ann an envelope addressed to her and marked "HIGHLY CONFIDENTIAL."

David began, "This is the reorganization plan. The name of the candidate for senior vice president for development is in there, along with his resume. Let me know if anything else we have working conflicts with this. Assuming you don't find a major flaw, we're going with it."

Karen, now sitting on one of David's couches, said to Jo Ann, "After you've looked at it, let's visit. Are you free for lunch today?"

"I'll check with Rhonda and let you know."

David moved behind his desk. "The two of you will have the heavy lifting on this," he said. "Jo Ann, you have some catching up to do."

Karen stood up and announced, "One of our outside lawyers is arguing a major appeal this week and we're meeting on it in 15 minutes. Jo Ann, call me about lunch."

After Karen left, David, still standing behind his desk, said, "Don't feel bad about this. We're not doing exactly what you wanted, but what we're accomplishing wouldn't have happened without you."

Jo Ann nodded crisply. "You think not?"

Marks returned the nod and said, "I know that. Karen is convinced you're right about Kelly Matthews. She's way better than Ben Martin. You found Kelly. You pulled the right levers in trying to get her hired. You performed the job I asked that you perform. The problem is, we aren't organized for change. This plan may help get us closer."

"What made you finally look at it this way?"

"Your getting Karen involved. This really isn't her area, but you understood where she fits in the company. Her input contributed to development of a long-term strategy for change. That's better than a pitched battle over one job."

"I learned a lot from this."

"You taught me as much. We'll make this work."

Jo Ann walked out of David's office. She thought about hugging him in the final moments of their meeting, but his position behind the desk made that awkward. There'll be other times, she realized, plenty of other times.

Chapter 34

After Jo Ann read the reorganization plan and talked with Karen, she told David she saw no reason they shouldn't proceed. He said he'd announce Ben Martin's appointment and the hiring of Kelly Matthews the next day and she and Karen should start working on the reorganization project.

Jo Ann thought she could catch her breath the next few days. A few days became two, with her first troublesome pregnancy checkup the next day. As she finished dressing, Connie arrived in the exam room with a pained look.

"I see things I don't like," she said. "Your blood pressure is up for the first time. I detect ever-so-slight signs of dilation in your cervix, as if you're going into labor. It's way too early, of course, for that. What I see might not mean anything. It's slight, but it's there."

Jo Ann sat down in a hard, plastic chair. "What do we do?"

"Take precautions," Connie replied. "Come back in a week. If these trends continue, we may have to put you to bed. We need to get you through another eight to ten weeks."

"Are you worried?"

Connie slipped her hands into the pockets of her lab coat, then withdrew them. "Concerned, but not worried, not yet."

"That's okay, I guess."

The doctor twisted the wedding ring on her left hand. "Reduce your work time. Four to six hours a day max. Off your feet as much as possible. And, drink eight to ten glasses of water a day."

Jo Ann sighed. "I guess I'll live in the bathroom."

"I'll give you some things that will help with fetal development – corticosteroids for lung function and folic acid, which reduces the chance of birth defects. You're already on magnesium sulfate, for lessening the chance of cerebral palsy.

"One other thing. No sex! You and Robert are done until after they're here. Your pelvic area will get fragile soon. A thrusting penis won't help."

Jo Ann laughed. "Robert sensed this coming. After we made love night before last, he said he hoped this wasn't the last time."

"It was for a while," Connie said, but she didn't laugh.

Driving home, Jo Ann flashed back to that last lovemaking. She left work early. They saw a movie and ate dinner at a neighborhood Italian place. Robert suggested a stroll through a nearby mall. At toy stores, they reflected on how toy buying now might differ from a quarter century ago.

As they walked, hand-in-hand, Jo Ann's desire built. She felt herself getting wet. Robert's firm grasp told her where things were headed.

In his kitchen, she wrapped her arms around his waist. He hugged her, less tightly than she wanted, but she appreciated that he didn't squeeze too hard. They kissed, at first gently, then intensely.

She remembered it was in this room they believed they conceived their twins, when he took her bent over the kitchen table. She looked around. "I want you on the table!"

She moved around him, her back to that table. She started

shedding clothes. In the subdued light of a hallway lamp, the contrast between his paleness and her dark skin, partially covered by white lingerie, fueled her desire.

All his clothes reached the floor. He unsnapped her bra and it fell away as she leaned against the table. Standing between her legs, he said, "Your body has changed."

"My breasts are huge and tender." She ran one hand over her nipples and stroked his erection with the other.

He rubbed her protruding belly. "I hadn't realized how much bigger you've gotten, just in the last few weeks. I hear you're having two babies."

"You got that right."

He laughed. "No more bikinis and hipsters for you. These qualify as granny panties."

She put a finger to his lips. "Stop talking. I need you, now!"

She lay back on the table, her feet just on the edge, her legs spread open. She lifted her hips and he took off the panties. She guided him into her and gasped.

He moved in her with a gentle rhythm. She began writhing, ignoring the table's hard, wooden surface. Their moans and cries filled the house. Jo Ann felt herself nearing an orgasm.

A thought crossed her mind. With children around for the next however many years, this might be the last time they made love like this, in this room, maybe ever. The thought triggered the orgasm.

Robert didn't stop when she climaxed. He pushed harder. Jo Ann felt herself hurtling toward another orgasm. When she sensed him nearing his finish, she spread her legs wider, hoping she could draw him in deeper. She felt him pulse and knew he was ejaculating. She thought of their first lovemaking after discovering the pregnancy. She remembered her joy at receiving his sperm – the sperm that put their twins inside her. Those feelings, and his final thrusts, pushed her over the edge again.

∞∞∞

As Jo Ann turned into Robert's driveway, her mind returned to the present and Connie's Rules. She put the car in the garage and walked into the kitchen. Inside Robert stood at the island, chopping vegetables, Rufus at his feet. He saw the look on her face and rushed to her. They embraced, for a long time. Finally, she said, "This will be hard, very hard."

Chapter 35

After the new year began, the new company absorbed Robert's time and energy. He raced to get its critical systems in place. As February neared, he told himself he hadn't been as present for Jo Ann as he'd promised.

So, on a Thursday afternoon in late January, he left his office at 4:30 p.m. and went home so he could make them dinner. They'd been out two nights before, leading to a memorable 20 minutes on the kitchen table. Tonight, he'd show her he could make life nice when they stayed home.

Robert knew she'd had a doctor's appointment that day. Her checkups had been good, so her distressed look when she walked into the kitchen startled him. They embraced and she mumbled something about how hard this would be.

"Connie sees problems," Jo Ann said. "She's laid down rules. You won't like some of them."

"We can't fuck anymore?"

"You guessed the other night it'd come to that soon."

He spread his arms, palms turned out. "We're lucky we got this far. You're nearing five months and bigger than I would've thought by now. I assume things will get sensitive down there soon."

"Connie used the word 'fragile.'"

He resumed chopping vegetables, but she stopped him and they embraced again. "I'm going to miss making love with you," she said. "Since we've been together, I haven't gone without you for more than a few days. This could be months."

He wiped a tear from her face. "It's okay. We must take care of our twins. Once they're here and you've healed, we'll make better love than ever."

∞ ∞ ∞

In bed they settled for cuddling and conversation. She told him about her elevated blood pressure and partially dilated cervix. She described the medications and the rules on water and work.

"How worried is Connie?" he asked, curling an arm under her breasts.

"She says she's concerned. Not worried. I took comfort in that."

"I've never been around a difficult pregnancy, so I have no clue. Darla's were easy."

"Mine were a breeze, except for weight gain."

He frowned. "Are you worried?"

He threw his leg over her as she said, "I trust Connie. If she's not worried, I'm not."

"What'll be the fallout from cutting back at work? Things have been crazy."

"Having the E & P thing finished is good, but David says we're going ahead with the reorganization. Karen and I are in charge."

"That's good."

"But if I'm not around, who knows what happens?"

He looked into her eyes. "Pretend you're traveling on business. Let Rhonda do your leg work. Keep the phone close by. Use e-mail and don't let anybody think you're not paying attention, even if you aren't in the building."

She focused her gaze on him. "Can I make that work?"

"In one of my jobs, I ran a whole division while out of the country for three weeks at a stretch. If people think you're the boss, you're the boss."

"I have David's trust, but I made enemies in the E & P fight. Those people will work at undermining me."

"I could've told you that," he said, stroking her hip. "This job is a great opportunity, but some people won't like what you're doing. Some especially won't like who's doing it. You're turning their world upside down. They wouldn't like anybody who was orchestrating that. Add that it's a black woman doing it and you have a recipe for an explosion."

She turned over and looked into his eyes through soft light from a bathroom lamp. "Can we stay away from each other for three or four months while I'm pregnant and for that long or longer after the babies are born?"

She threw back the covers, exposing her swelling abdomen. As it had when they made love on the kitchen table, the contrast between his whiteness and her dark skin, now glistening with baby oil, stirred her desire. Tonight, she tamped it down.

He spoke softly. "I look at us and I still can't believe this. And I couldn't be happier. That's what's amazing."

"This should make us crazy," she agreed. "A fifty-year old black woman and a sixty-year old white guy, taking on parenthood. Lying here in bed with you, seeing our nakedness, and looking at the life growing inside me, I'm overwhelmed with joy."

"I feel that. I can't describe it."

"Let's make a deal," she said, lifting her arms and wrapping them around his neck. "Let's never miss a chance for saying, for showing, what we mean to each other and what the children we've conceived mean to us. Can we do that?"

"I can."

They kissed and locked their arms around each other. But for Connie's Rules, she'd have climbed onto him and eased his erection into her. Instead, she turned over, her back to him, as he pulled the covers over them. He wrapped an arm around her again, below her breasts and above her bulging abdomen. They fell asleep.

∞∞∞

Jo Ann's next checkup produced no new concerns. Still, she got a refresher course on Connie's Rules. "Stay off your feet, drink lots of water, and no sex," the doctor warned. "It's good that we got through another week, but we have a long way to go.

After that visit, Jo Ann stopped at her house, checked the mail and grabbed more clothes. It wasn't until she sat at Robert's kitchen table she saw and opened the envelope.

THOUGHT WE FORGOT YOU, RIGHT?
WE HAVEN'T.
TIME IS RUNNING OUT.
YOU'LL HEAR FROM US AGAIN SOON.
YOU SHOULD PAY ATTENTION.

Jo Ann dialed Jenny Dixon's number. As she waited, her mind settled on the fact she still hadn't told Robert her suspicions. This letter made her even more certain about who sent the letters and increased her anxiety about telling him her theory.

"Hello, Jo Ann. This is Jenny."

"I got another letter."

"What's it say?"

Jo Ann read it, and added, "This came from the same place, Smithville, Texas. It has the same typeface."

"This one says 'we.' That could mean something."

"I was thinking that too, that we're dealing with two people."

"Maybe, maybe not. That might be the royal we, somebody who just talks like that. It could be somebody who hopes we believe there are two – or three – people when there's only one."

"I see that," Jo Ann said, gulping water. She'd gotten a little behind on Connie's Rules.

"Did you think of any skeletons or people you told about them?"

Jo Ann dreaded the question. Despite talking about her ideas with Betty and Hanna, she wasn't ready for sharing them with Jenny. Telling Jenny, meant telling Robert. "I haven't nailed that down," she said. "I'm thinking about it, but I'm not sure." Her answer wasn't an outright lie, but it wasn't the truth either.

"Whoever is doing this may soon show their hand," Jenny said. "We should get out front, go on offense rather than sit here, waiting for the other shoe to drop."

Jo Ann sensed the lawyer's frustration. Her half-truth likely wasn't the first a client had ever told Jenny.

Chapter 36

Jo Ann didn't tell Robert about getting another letter or talking with Jenny Dixon. A call from Memphis gave her an excuse for more delay.

Deena said, "I'm sorry I took so long in getting back with you. I've been teaching every day the last few weeks. I didn't know when I could get away. I now know. I'll come down and help with the nursery."

"That's wonderful. When can you get here?"

"I have a flight arriving at Bush at three thirty Friday afternoon. I'll rent a car, so you don't have to pick me up."

"How long can you stay?"

"I told Al ten days. Is that enough?"

"Yes. I'm looking forward to this. We have a lot to talk about."

On the day Deena arrived, Jo Ann left work at 11:45 a.m. After a light lunch and a nap, she spent the rest of the afternoon making lists of things needed for the nursery. She reminded herself she should get two of everything which, in many cases, meant getting four or eight of everything.

Deena called at four thirty, saying she was on the way from the airport, over an hour's drive in afternoon traffic. She pulled into the driveway at a quarter to six. Jo Ann greeted her outside. Rufus tagged along, seeking at least a pat on the head.

"You're huge!" Deena said. When their embrace ended and Jo Ann grabbed her roller bag, Deena reached down and petted the dog. "Hello Rufus. Jo Ann, there sure isn't any doubt you're having twins!"

"Carrying them around is hard work."

They went inside and sat in the family room. As Rufus took a spot at her feet, Jo Ann studied Deena, struck as at Christmas by her simple appearance. She wore a plain, knee length blue dress, no jewelry save her wedding rings, flat, open toed shoes, and her hair in a ponytail. Bare legs and light make up emphasized informality.

From the kitchen Jo Ann retrieved two glasses filled with ice, a pitcher of water, and dishes of carrots, broccoli, and celery sticks. "I can munch on vegetables," she explained. "No junk food and I must drink eight to ten glasses of water a day."

"You're familiar with the bathroom?" Deena asked.

"At home, I don't notice it as much. I'm self-conscious about it at work."

"What's happening, overall?"

Jo Ann chewed on celery. "I'm spending four to six hours a day at the office and otherwise working here. That's helped a lot. I'm not as tired."

"What does your doctor say?"

"Check-up this week was good. Connie got concerned last week when my blood pressure spiked and she thought I was trying to go into labor. Things have settled down."

"How often do you go to the doctor?"

"Every ten days, unless she wants to see me more often because something happens, like last week."

Jo Ann went back to the kitchen for more ice. When she returned, Deena stood staring out the window. Rufus remained beside Jo Ann's chair.

"I wondered if you'd be offended by what I was thinking," Deena said.

"Try me and see."

"You asked for it, so don't get mad."

Jo Ann chuckled. "I won't get mad."

Deena blurted, "How'd you get pregnant? Aren't you too old?"

Jo Ann's chuckle turned into a full throated laugh. Finally, she said, "And I thought you were going to complain about my deodorant."

"I'd have told you that a long time ago."

The tension in the room broke. Jo Ann understood how much she liked this young woman. "I'll tell you the story, if you promise you won't tell Robert I told you."

"I'd have no reason for telling him."

Jo Ann lifted her chin and bit her lip. "He thinks the details make two mature, well-educated, professionally savvy people look like horny teenagers who didn't know where babies come from."

For an instant, Deena's face told Jo Ann she'd struck a nerve. Deena recovered and asked, "What do you tell people? I'm sure nobody thinks you planned this."

"We just say it happened and we're happy because our babies are a product of our love for each other. That's true, but it leaves out the details."

"Which are?"

"Robert and I met last May," Jo Ann said, making a quote gesture with her hands around the word met. "We'd known that the other worked at JAX – even been in a few meetings together, but that's all.

"On the Friday before Memorial Day – May 24, a date burned

236

into my memory – Robert found me crying in my office. Right now, why isn't important. A week and a day later, we were in a hotel room, making the best, most intense, most passionate, love I'd ever known.

"We talked about disease and pregnancy beforehand. I told Robert I hadn't had a period in months." She made another quote gesture. "I said we're good to go."

"That sounds reasonable," Deena said, chin in her hand, leaning forward on the couch. "What happened?"

"I misunderstood the biology."

"How so?"

"I didn't know until after I got pregnant a menopausal woman needs a year, maybe two, without a period before having unprotected sex. I hadn't had one since November. That's not a year and it's certainly not two."

"You later had one?"

"I did, though I didn't know it."

Deena flinched and raised an eyebrow, as if in disbelief. "How'd you not know?"

"Because of how light it was. That happens with some women going through menopause. I was in Washington, at Dulles Airport waiting for a flight to North Carolina to see Regina. I noticed a twinge and slight wetness between my legs. I thought it was a random discharge. The idea of a period didn't cross my mind."

"Then what happened?"

"The company sent me to a convention in Miami. When I got back, Connie figures I ovulated. It's like I was in heat. I couldn't get enough of Robert. He thinks I got pregnant one night when we couldn't wait to get to our bedroom and did it over the kitchen table." Jo Ann giggled, but Deena stayed silent.

"That could happen to anybody." Deena said, finally. "I bet a lot of women don't know either the one-year rule, certainly not the two-year rule."

"Now you'll know when you get there."

Deena's face went blank. "That's a long way off."

Jo Ann let the room grow quiet. She almost pressed for the story she knew lurked behind Deena's sad expression, but decided she'd leave that for another day. She hoped revelation of her own intimate secrets would let Deena know she could share hers.

∞∞∞

During Deena's visit, Jo Ann spent only a couple of hours in the office most days and sometimes she didn't go at all. She stayed on the phone with Karen Duffy about the reorganization project. The major task was roping in Gary Betters, the prime candidate for senior vice president who'd oversee the corporate development section the plan created.

Jo Ann went in early one day for her first meeting with him. She'd read his resume and Rhonda's research about him. The resume told a compelling story – Purdue engineering degree, Northwestern MBA, 20 years of important positions in energy companies, culminating in a major company vice presidency.

He served as Assistant Energy Secretary in the first Obama administration. After Obama's first term, Betters joined his current consulting firm. The resume didn't tell the one thing that likely made Karen see Jo Ann as essential in recruiting Betters. When he walked into her office, Jo Ann thought she'd never seen a blacker man.

She stood up. "Mr. Betters, I'm Jo Ann Davis."

"I've heard a great deal about you. You're held in high esteem both by Karen Duffy and my friend, David Marks."

"As are you, Mr. Betters." Jo Ann didn't invite him to call her by her first name. Something already made her uneasy about Betters and she decided she'd keep her distance for the time being.

She offered him a chair. Six feet tall and with a physique obviously honed in a gym, he looked the part of a confident, middle-aged business executive. His dark suit, blue dress shirt, red tie, immaculately shined shoes, and a touch of gray hair gave him a professional, mature presence.

"Can I get you something to drink?" she asked.

He spoke deliberately, with practiced caution. "I'll pass. I'm aware your time is limited, so we should make the most of it."

"I appreciate that. As you can see, I'm in the midst of a pregnancy. I work a lot from home, so I'm in the office only a short time each day."

"What can I tell you about myself? I have many questions about JAX. I understand you have been here a number of years, so I'm sure you can give me an interesting perspective."

They talked for two hours, then Jo Ann called Karen Duffy.

"Can we visit? I spent my morning with Gary Betters."

"He's Impressive, huh?" Jo Ann felt a grin on Karen's face through the phone.

A pause followed, creating an uneasy silence. "He is, but let's talk, okay?"

"You have reservations?"

"I don't know what I have. I'm on my way to your office."

∞ ∞ ∞

Karen's secretary waved Jo Ann in and closed the door. Jo Ann sat on the couch and again noticed the volleyball pictures.

Despite how close they'd become as business associates, aside from Karen's questions about the pregnancy, they never talked about their personal lives.

Karen didn't look up from the papers on her desk. "So you have doubts?"

"I'm not sure. My instincts about Betters aren't great."

"Tell me."

Jo Ann felt a quiver in her stomach. She sensed being on edge. "I'm having trouble putting a finger on it. On paper he has it all. We may not find a stronger looking resume."

Karen had moved to the couch across from Jo Ann. "We sure won't in a black candidate. David thinks we should do better on that score."

"I think we should do better on that score. Except for Jason Hanson and me, the executive suite in this place is as lily-white as a KKK rally. Still, something makes me uneasy about Betters."

Karen cocked her head to the side and rocked back in her chair. "Can you get a little concrete?"

In a strained, tense voice, Jo Ann said, "I'll give you one substantive thing and one intuition thing."

"What's the substantive thing?"

"Except his entry level job at Exxon, years ago, he has no experience in production or finance. It appears he got pushed into what I'd call soft areas – marketing, governmental liaison, etc. His job at the Energy Department was legislative affairs."

"Why do you say pushed?"

"I've seen black executives and managers steered to such jobs. After a few years, Betters only did marketing, public relations, and governmental stuff. He wasn't in E & P, despite being a trained engineer. He knows nothing about finance."

Karen cleared her throat. "What's the intuition thing?"

"What he didn't know about us. He knew nothing of our history except what's public. Hadn't talked with anyone about our culture, our problems, or successes."

"Anything else you noticed?"

"For somebody who's done as much governmental relations work as he has, he seemed stiff. Communicating with him wasn't easy. I found him odd. By the way, how does he know David?"

"Politics. David was one of the few oil company CEOs who supported Obama."

"I'd feel better if they knew each other through business, which gives me an idea. I'll ask Robert about him."

"Think Robert knows him?"

"Robert never did the kind of work Betters did, so I wouldn't expect they crossed paths. But, Robert knows everybody who's anybody in this industry. I'm sure he knows people who know Betters from business, not politics."

Chapter 37

Worrying about Betters was exactly what Jo Ann didn't want as February sped by. She'd hoped for a respite from business problems. Karen took some of the burden off by promising she'd handle the reorganization project until Jo Ann finished the nursery.

Jo Ann and Deena neared completion of their work and Deena prepared for going home. When Jo Ann got a positive checkup on February 17, Deena said she'd leave the next day and stand by for a return on a moment's notice.

"I've so much enjoyed being here," Deena said as they put away baby clothes. "I wish I could've talked with my mother like I can with you. She was about your age now when I was a teenager."

"Is your mother still alive?" Jo Ann asked, as they headed for the kitchen and lunch.

Deena shook her head. "She died seven years ago of a heart attack. I barely knew her after high school. She took no interest in me while I was in college. She didn't like my friends, especially my black friends. I wish she could see me now."

"Did she detest all black people?"

"She mimicked my father, who really was a racist."

Jo Ann opened the refrigerator door and took out a package of turkey slices. "Robert feared you wouldn't accept us because of my color."

"Al told me that. Robert doesn't understand my political leanings don't mean I'm racist. I hope I've shown you that."

Jo Ann nodded as she spread mayonnaise on bread. "Have you always seen politics as you do now?"

Deena put plates and glasses on the table. "I didn't care about politics until college. I realized how wrong abortion is, so I started listening to people trying to stop it. What many of them say about race, and other things, I don't believe. Stopping abortion is so important I put up with it. Maybe that's not right."

Jo Ann treaded carefully. "Did something happen that made you feel as you do about abortion?"

Deena hesitated. Jo Ann sensed there was something she wanted to say, but couldn't. Finally, Deena sighed and said, "Let's just say I got a better understanding of the issue."

Jo Ann considered pressing for more, but decided the trust wasn't quite there. Patience would one day yield the story. "It's a hard issue," Jo Ann said as they sat down to sandwiches, carrot sticks, grapes, and glasses of water.

Now, Jo Ann saw pleading in Deena's eyes. "Tell me you didn't consider that."

"Robert and I really didn't, but it wasn't because of religion or the politics of abortion. I don't believe abortion is wrong and Robert doesn't either. But, from the instant we found out I was pregnant, we were overwhelmed by the fact these children came from the love between us. Because of that feeling, despite our ages, we decided we'd have them."

"Were you worried about them being biracial?"

"I thought about that, but a friend reminded me that, biracial or not, our children will have huge advantages in life because of the loving home they will grow up in, the skill Robert and I now have as parents, and we're well off. Abortion wasn't much of a possibility.

"If we'd been poor, if my health was bad, if a lot of other things were different, we might have decided differently." Jo

Ann looked for signs of disapproval from Deena. She couldn't be sure what she saw in that plain, expressionless face.

"I'm just glad you're having the babies. I don't care what keeps people from having abortions. I just want them not to."

They ate in silence as Jo Ann pondered what she'd heard. She felt surer than ever Deena carried around a secret she wanted to reveal, but wasn't yet convinced she could confide in Jo Ann.

∞ ∞ ∞

Melissa arrived three days after Deena's departure. Jo Ann, still not ready to share with Robert her theory about the letters, thought Melissa could do some snooping that might confirm her intuition. "You know Kendra and Tiffany," Jo Ann told her. "Do you think they're capable of blackmail?"

"I don't know. Why?"

They sat at Jo Ann's kitchen table after digging out long stored household items now needed so Melissa could reclaim her room. "I got threatening, anonymous letters in the mail," Jo Ann replied. "Robert hired a lawyer named Jenny Dixon to help us. She thinks whoever is behind this might try to use something from my past against me."

Melissa wore jeans and a KU sweatshirt. She sipped water from a plastic tumbler. "What do Tiffany and Kendra know that they could use against you and why would they do that?"

Jo Ann answered the last part of the question. "I haven't told you about this, but Regina knows. Tiffany and Kendra won't speak to me because Robert is white. They're adamant. They believe I'm a traitor to the race. Now that I'm pregnant, I suppose they have even more reason for being disgusted with me. Betty told me they said whatever bad happens to me is just fine."

Melissa jerked her head back. "That's sick."

"That's how they feel."

Still looking dazed, Melissa asked, "How can I can help?"

"Check with your friends, especially ones whose parents know them. See if they're talking about Robert and me. Maybe one let something slip that'll give us a clue or help confirm it's really them sending the letters."

"Who do you have in mind?"

"Tricia Scott's mother knows Tiffany well. Donnie Young's father knows Kendra. You might think of others."

"Kenny Snell ran track with me in high school. His mother and Tiffany are close. I'll call him."

"It's just a wild idea. We're looking for any possible clue. I hate believing this about them, but I can't think of anybody else who'd do it."

"What about people at work? I bet some of them don't like that you got the job you have or that you're with Robert."

"Some people at JAX aren't happy with what I'm doing, but the letters started before the stuff happened they got so mad about."

Melissa crossed her arms over her chest and raised her eyebrows. "What could Tiffany and Kendra have on you?"

"It's not much in today's world, but Tiffany would see it as a real sin and Kendra is mean enough she'd mastermind some kind of plot."

Melissa's exasperation showed. "What, Mom?"

Jo Ann told her. At the end, Melissa said simply, "Oh."

Chapter 38

As March neared, Robert grew concerned about Jo Ann's condition. Despite being at home at least half of most days, she looked tired, anxious, and bloated. She moved haltingly. Small tasks required a major effort.

"You're going too fast," he said as they lay in bed together, his arm in its familiar spot between her breasts and her expanded middle.

"I'm trying to slow down," she replied. "You know how little time I spend at the office now. I take only a few meetings. I've finished shopping for baby clothes. The nursery is done. You get groceries. I hope we can finish this reorganization thing in a few weeks. Then I can relax."

Robert shook his head. "After that, there'll be a public relations fiasco David wants fixed, followed by an environmental crisis that needs solving, then something else. You must let go."

She tugged at her ear. "You can help finish the reorganization project. When Karen and I have it under control, I'll come home."

"What can I do?"

She told him about the Gary Betters problem.

"You're right," he said. "I don't know him. I first heard of him when he was nominated for Assistant Secretary of Energy. I've got contacts in the companies where he's worked. I'll see what I can find. Once I do, you can take it easier. You won't take it easy, so I'll settle for easier."

Before she fell asleep, Jo Ann thought about Deena and the letters. Jo Ann regretted she didn't probe for reasons Deena had no children. At each opportunity, she sensed the time wasn't right. Something troubled Deena. Jo Ann felt sure it was about the fact she'd been married to Al Hart for eight years, adored and wanted children, but hadn't had any.

Otherwise, Deena's fixation on her pregnancy made no sense. Jo Ann could understand her offer of help, but wasn't there more? She needed a special reason for upending her life over a pregnancy caused by a father-in-law she hadn't been especially close to. This was about her issues.

She felt guilty about not telling Robert who she thought was behind the letters and why. She feared telling him would create disappointment and anger. She imagined he'd press her on why she'd never told him about six years ago. Hadn't they promised they wouldn't keep secrets from each other? Would he say she'd misled him about who she really was? Would he say she was a fraud?

∞ ∞ ∞

Robert went with Jo Ann for her March 3 checkup. It was the first one of her final trimester and he hoped he could learn what he should expect in the home stretch.

Connie, wearing her white lab coat as always, stood behind her desk. Robert and Jo Ann sat, holding hands, in chairs across from her. "Your babies are okay," she said. "I now see on ultrasound what the genetic testing showed. One is a boy and one a girl. Neither is in distress. That's the good news."

"There's bad news?" Robert asked.

Connie sat down. "There is, but it's nothing we can't manage."

"What Connie?" Jo Ann asked, tightly gripping Robert's hand.

"I see early signs of preeclampsia."

Robert's throat went dry. "What's that?" he asked.

"I know what it is," Jo Ann spoke up, squirming in her chair. "I researched it. There's a lot about it in the books I bought. It often starts after 20 weeks. The mother's blood vessels can constrict, which may reduce blood flow to vital organs and the uterus, harming the babies."

"That's right," Connie said. "I see symptoms – elevated blood pressure, swelling in your face, feet, and ankles. There's a trace of protein in your urine."

Robert felt a knot in his gut. He asked, "Is this something that's a real threat, to Jo Ann or to the babies?"

Connie remained calm. "It can be, but when it shows up about this time, we usually can control it."

"What do we do?" Jo Ann asked.

"Many doctors would put you on bed rest. I don't think it's necessary now, and there's uncertainty about how well that works. Some doctors prescribe it because that's always been prescribed. Without exercise, it can do more harm than good.

"Keep doing what you've been doing – reduced work schedule, staying off your feet, lots of water. I'll give you a blood pressure medication. Come in every week from now until delivery. It goes without saying that if you see or feel anything unusual, such as vaginal bleeding or a discharge, get in here or go to the hospital fast if something happens at an odd hour."

As Connie spoke, Robert understood why Jo Ann so trusted

her. She took control, stated her instructions clearly, and showed no sign of panic. He squeezed Jo Ann's hand, signaling that Connie's soliloquy had reassured him.

Connie continued, looking at Jo Ann. "Your cervix is holding steady, so you aren't starting labor. That was a false alarm. Maybe we can get you past 33 weeks. If so, you'll be in good shape, though I'd bet we should do a Cesarean section."

"What? I had vaginal deliveries with my other kids."

"You were 25-30 years old. Those were single pregnancies. Delivering twins vaginally at this age could stress your heart and tear up your pelvic area making your recovery longer than with surgery. The way this pregnancy is stretching your uterus, you may not have strong enough contractions for a vaginal delivery. I often do C-sections on younger women carrying twins. Let's cross that bridge when we come to it, okay? Now, let me write you that prescription."

Jo Ann returned to JAX for a short time that day. Rhonda said things were quiet and suggested she go home. As Jo Ann left, her mobile phone rang.

"Mom, this is Melissa. Can you talk?"

"Let me get to the car. I'll call you back in ten minutes."

Jo Ann left the garage, weaved through traffic, and parked in a department store lot. She thought of how distant she had been from Melissa when compared to her close relationship with Regina.

Unlike her younger daughter, whom she called "Baby," Jo Ann didn't have a pet name for Melissa. Melissa hadn't been around much since leaving for college over seven years ago. Volunteering that she would help with the babies surprised Jo Ann and meant a new connection opportunity.

"I didn't find out much," Melissa said when she answered. "I heard one thing that might interest you."

Jo Ann's heart raced. "What?"

"Kenny Snell's mother knows Tiffany. He heard Tiffany and his mother talking about somebody getting a big surprise. Tiffany was laughing about it, but his mother's jaw dropped and she put her hand over her mouth as if it shocked her. They went quiet when they realized Kenny was in the room."

"Did he hear anything else?"

"No."

"When?"

"Yesterday."

"Was it just Tiffany and Kenny's mother?"

"Yes."

"What did you tell him about why you were asking?"

"That my mother was once good friends with Tiffany and we wondered if Tiffany ever told anyone why she thought the friendship soured."

"Did he say anything else?"

"No. He said they were certainly talking about somebody Tiffany was on the outs with."

Jo Ann's muscles tightened all over. "Tiffany and Kendra are behind this. I know it."

"That's bad, Mom. I had white boyfriends in Europe. What's the big deal?"

"This is painful for some black women."

"What happened with the doctor today? How're my little brother and sister?"

"Connie says they're fine."

Chapter 39

Jo Ann's potential development of preeclampsia told Robert he should get more involved in her day-to-day care. He dug out her books and studied the condition. He learned it sometimes precedes HELLP Syndrome, a disturbing possibility, since that involves a breakdown of red blood cells, elevated liver enzymes, and low platelet count, which can inhibit blood clotting.

He worked more from home so he could help keep Jo Ann away from the office. He reminded her she should handle things that came up by phone or e-mail.

One day, as they ate lunch, she said, "I never would have believed it. This morning I made 13 phone calls, exchanged e-mails with 11 people, and finished two reports. I wouldn't have gotten half that done if I'd gone in."

"You'd have had to put on work clothes, navigate the traffic and, between the parking garage and your office, fight off three people who claimed they needed just a few minutes."

"Working from home makes getting through the pregnancy easier, but what happens when the babies get here, and I go back, especially before they're weaned?"

"You're planning on breast feeding?"

"That's better for kids."

"I've read the books and it's better. I never paid any attention when Darla and I were having kids. I left it all to her. I wasn't involved."

When Jo Ann returned from refilling her water glass she

leaned down and kissed him. "You're involved now. We said we'd be better this time. You're doing your part."

∞∞∞

March and early April crawled along. Jo Ann grew concerned about her size. By her April 14 checkup, she'd gained 40 of the 45 pounds Connie said was an acceptable gain for the entire pregnancy. Though she hadn't developed full-blown preeclampsia, her blood pressure stayed stubbornly high and puffiness remained in her ankles and feet.

"I'm putting you to bed," Connie said. "I want you off your feet. You can walk around periodically. I'll give you a booklet with exercises, because you're bumping up against the weight gain target. No office, no cooking and cleaning, no grocery shopping, no mall trips, no going out for dinner. If you've got family help coming, it's time they showed up. Have somebody drive you here for checkups."

"I expected this. I haven't felt good the last two weeks. I'm tired. I have a hard time getting around because of the swelling. But, it's April," Jo Ann said. "That was the target, wasn't it?"

"It was, but we have another one."

"We do?"

"You're about 32 weeks now. Let's see if we can reach 36-37 weeks, mid-May. That's best. I'm sending you to an ultrasound specialist who should give us a better sense of when we should take them, which I've tentatively decided I should do. We'll start looking at their position in the womb and make a final decision."

"You know what would be funny?"

"What?"

"If they were born May 24."

Connie looked puzzled. "That's probably a stretch. What's special about that date?"

"Robert and I met that day last year."

The doctor wriggled her eyebrows. "I thought you knew each other from working the same place."

"May 24 started us on the road to all this. He found me crying in my office and reached out to me that day."

Connie nodded. "If you get that far, you should have two healthy – and large – babies."

∞∞∞∞

Robert dropped Jo Ann at the doctor and picked her up after the appointment. He wasn't surprised Connie clipped her wings. "I knew this was coming," he said in the parking lot. "The books say this usually happens with twin pregnancies, sometimes to women your age with just one baby. You avoided it a long time."

"Deena and I got the nursery done, the changes we needed at home are finished, and Melissa is set up at my house. We're as ready as we're going to be."

"Where are you with work?"

"I can read and make calls. Rhonda can bring me a folder of stuff every day."

Robert chewed his lip. "I know, but can you keep from getting emotionally involved in the upstairs – downstairs politics that creates tension and makes you crazy?"

"If you'll get your traps run on Betters, I can get that behind me."

"Betters is a tough nut. The people I've called — friends,

folks I trust and have done favors for — won't talk about him. It's like I've brought up a long-buried, toxic family secret.

"The guy I really want to talk with has been out of the country the last six weeks. He's back in early May. We go way back. If there's anything worth knowing about Betters, Jack Prince will tell me."

She looked at him after staring out the window. "David wants the reorganization done soon, as Karen and I do. We've got everything done except having someone for that senior vice president spot. Unless I have more to go on than I do now, I can't stand in the way, though I sense Betters would be a mistake."

"Hold it off for two weeks."

"I think I can do that, even from home."

∞∞∞

Later that day, Jo Ann called Deena and asked when she could come back.

"Now," she replied. "I'll drive down so I have my car. I might fly home a few times, but otherwise I'll be there, as long as you need me."

"You don't know how much this means. With you and Melissa helping, we'll get through this."

"You're doing me a favor. I'll be there by dinner time day after tomorrow."

"We've got a place for you and things for you to do."

∞∞∞

Soon after Jo Ann talked with Deena, Melissa called. Jo Ann

started telling her about the doctor visit and her expectations for the next few weeks. Before she could get that out, Melissa said she had news.

"You do?" Jo Ann asked.

"You remember me saying Kenny Snell overheard his mother's conversation with Tiffany?"

"I wish he'd heard more."

"Later he did. It sounds like you were right."

"What's the deal?"

Melissa took a deep breath. "Kenny said he heard his mother and Tiffany talking again yesterday. This time Tiffany mentioned somebody named Tony."

Jo Ann rubbed the back of her neck. "Tony?"

"Yes, Tony. Kenny said Tiffany told his mother, 'Tony will fix her.'"

Jo Ann stood at a window, admiring the budding shrubs and trees in Robert's yard. When Melissa mentioned the name Tony, Jo Ann sat down, her back to the window, and looked around the room. Her eye fell on the only two photos she'd put in this space – a present from Hanna Leslie of Jo Ann and Robert fixing Thanksgiving dinner and an old picture of her with the children at one of Tony's high school football games.

Melissa and Regina, bundled in coats, stood beside and partially in front of their mother and brother. The photo highlighted Tony, in full football gear, with Jo Ann dressed in Tony's school colors. Sweat covered his forehead and he still wore his game day eye black. Tiffany took the picture following a playoff game Tony's team won, aided by tackles he made that stopped the opponent's potentially game winning drive.

At that instant Jo Ann believed she knew exactly what Tiffany and Kendra were up to. She had to stop them if she was to ever again have a relationship with her first born and with her only grandchild.

"Was Kenny sure Tiffany said, 'Tony will fix her'?" Jo Ann asked.

"He said he heard them clearly."

"What did his friend's mother say?"

"According to Kenny, Tiffany did most of the talking." Melissa paused. "Is this about my brother?"

"I'm confident this is about your brother. Didn't he start attending Tiffany's church?"

"He attended Mount Zion until he got a car. Then he started going to Antioch. Did he ever tell you why?"

"He said he could feel the spirit better there. I thought there was a girl at Antioch he was after, but he denied it."

"And that's Tiffany's church, right?"

"Tiffany has attended Antioch Baptist Church for as long as I can remember."

Part 5
ANOTHER WEEK
IN MAY

Chapter 40

At Jo Ann's May 12 checkup, Connie expressed concerns. "You're showing early signs of HEELP Syndrome. It's not serious, but I see troubling things in your blood work. The babies should come out soon."

Robert attended this exam. He asked, "What's more important, full term pregnancy or dealing with these conditions she may have?"

"They're not mutually exclusive. In some ways, the longer they stay in the womb, the better. But I won't take chances just so they stay a few days longer. I've got targets for her blood work, what we see on ultrasound, and how she's tolerating the situation. Those things will determine when we take them."

Jo Ann looked at Robert and extended her hand. He took it and squeezed. "I trust Connie," she said.

"I do too," he said. "I just want to know what we're dealing with."

"I'm glad he's here, asking questions," Connie said. "It means he cares."

"Thank you, Doctor," Robert said. "I just want to know that she's okay."

Connie smiled and, at the exam door, turned back to them. "I love having intelligent patients who ask questions. I adore fathers who show they care for their women and their children. You two are the kind of people who make me glad I do what I do."

∞ ∞ ∞

Just after they started for home that day, Jo Ann began opening the mail she'd picked up at her house before the appointment. Wedged between the electric bill and a credit card solicitation she saw an envelope, addressed and postmarked like the others. Her heart raced. She squirmed, keeping the seat belt from pulling too tight across her swollen belly. She looked over at Robert, his attention fixed on the road.

She said nothing as she opened the envelope. The other shoe had dropped.

NOW WE'RE GOING TO TELL YOU WHAT WE WANT.

IF YOU DON'T WANT US TALKING TO YOUR MAN

IN DENVER, FOLLOW OUR INSTRUCTIONS.

YOU KNOW WHAT WE'LL TELL HIM.

DON'T PLAY DUMB AND DON'T BE STUPID!

The one paragraph at the bottom of the page read:

ONCE YOUR HALF-BREED BASTARDS ARE BORN, LEAVE TOWN. WE DON'T CARE WHERE YOU GO, JUST LEAVE AND DON'T COME BACK.
NOT FOR HOLIDAYS. NOT FOR FAMILY VISITS. NOT FOR CLASS REUNIONS. NOT FOR BUSINESS. NOT FOR ANYTHING. NOT EVER. IF WE FIND OUT YOU'RE BACK IN THIS TOWN – AND WE'LL BE WATCHING -- THE DEAL IS OFF.
IF YOU GO AWAY AND STAY AWAY, THIS WILL REMAIN BETWEEN YOU AND US. DON'T MESS WITH US. WE'RE

SERIOUS AS A HEART ATTACK. YOU HAVE 30 DAYS
AFTER THE BIRTH OF YOUR HALF-BREED BASTARDS TO
GET GONE.
LOOK AT THE SECOND PAGE AND SEE IF WE MEAN
BUSINESS!!!
T.B K.W

Jo Ann flipped the page. What she read confirmed her
suspicions. This was about Tony and it was about six years
ago. That second page was a copy of a printed document.

THE PLEDGE

I, Anthony James Davis hereby take THE PLEDGE.

Before God, I promise I will not knowingly associate with any person, male or female, who claims to be "GAY" or any similar label for a queer person.

I promise I will not knowingly associate with any person who has had homosexual relations and who has not come forward and repented and publicly confessed his or her sin in a House of the Lord and agreed they will undergo rehabilitation as ordered, defined, and required by that church. I will not permit any member of my family or any child of mine to knowingly associate with such persons.

Signed   Dated: April 14, 2013 Houston, Texas

Anthony James Davis

Without looking up, Jo Ann said, "Robert, we'd better go back to Connie's office. I'm going to faint." The letter fell to her feet. Robert never saw it. He grabbed his phone with one hand and called Connie's office and, with the other, wheeled the car into a U-turn. At the doctor's building, two members of her staff waited in the circle driveway. Robert helped them wrestle Jo Ann into a wheelchair. Her eyes stayed closed. She moaned, but never said an intelligible word.

Chapter 41

"**W**hat happened, Robert?" Connie asked as one of her nurses, a plump, dark-skinned black woman with braided hair and dressed in green hospital scrubs and pink running shoes, wheeled Jo Ann into the fifth floor office suite.

"I'm not sure," he replied. "She was reading her mail and said we should come back here. The next thing I knew she was out. I turned the car around and called your office."

In the exam room, Robert heard one nurse say, "Her blood pressure is way up, doctor."

Robert saw only calm on Connie's face as she checked the reading herself. She turned toward him. "She's in some distress. Let us have some time with her. Go back to the reception area. I'll let you know where we are shortly."

"Will she be okay?"

"I'll let you know," Connie said as the nurse closed the door.

Weeks later, Robert wondered why he didn't go back to the car and find what Jo Ann had been reading. It was probably better that he hadn't. The way things unfolded, she could tell him the story in her own words, give him her explanation. Finding the letter, before the explanation, would only have produced fear, loathing, and anger, things neither of them needed.

While Connie and her staff attended Jo Ann, Robert paced, first in the reception area, then in the elevator lobby outside the office suite. He decided he'd call in reinforcements.

Though a bond had been developing between Jo Ann and

Deena, he thought that when Jo Ann woke up, she might first need her daughter. He called Melissa. "It's Robert," he told her. "Your mother fainted and is at the doctor's office. I'm here, waiting for word from Dr. Cross on what's what."

Robert heard a gasp over the phone. "Is she okay? Are my brother and sister okay?" Melissa asked.

"I don't know. We'd just left the doctor's office after her appointment. She was looking at her mail when she said she was fainting. I got her back here as fast as I could."

"Where is she now?" Melissa's voice rose.

"With the doctor. They kicked me out."

"I'll be right there. I'm five minutes from your house. I'll stop and get Deena. She'll want to be there."

Melissa and Deena arrived at the doctor's office in half an hour. Robert studied them as they left the elevator. Melissa's lithe track athlete's body would impress anyone. She wore khaki shorts that accentuated her long, muscular legs and narrow waist. He saw no fat on her. Her breasts, covered by a red USA Track & Field polo shirt and smaller than her mother's before the pregnancy, complemented her trim physique.

Deena, five years older, didn't have the superbly trained athlete's body of the young black woman she followed out of the elevator. She was two inches taller, but the lack of definition in her arms and legs stood out against Melissa's toned limbs. It was her face, though, that Robert noticed that afternoon. Though he'd been around Deena for years, for the first time, he saw the sadness there Jo Ann described. He agreed Deena carried around a secret, a burden of some kind. He wondered if Al had seen it.

Deena spoke first. "Do we know any more?" she asked,

walking toward Robert.

"No. I've been pacing, waiting for something from Connie."

"How long have they been working on her?" Melissa asked.

"Since I called you, 30 minutes ago," Robert replied.

"Let's sit in the waiting room," Deena said. She wore red shorts, a white shirt, and sandals.

"Thanks for coming," Robert told a nodding Deena.

A few minutes after they sat down, the nurse in the green scrubs and pink shoes appeared in a doorway and said, "Mr. Hart, Dr. Cross would like to see you."

"Can Deena and Melissa come with me? Melissa is Jo Ann's daughter. Deena is my daughter-in-law."

"They can come."

The nurse led them down a hallway. Outside a patient room, Connie Cross, in her white lab coat as usual, talked with a thin, black woman with a stethoscope around her neck. She wore dark slacks, a light top, and a broad, green headband in her curly black hair.

"Robert, this is my partner, Dr. Cynthia Jones," Connie said as they arrived. Robert recalled Connie's telling of the Cynthia Jones story at the September book club meeting. "I've asked that she help me with Jo Ann's pregnancy. She has lots of experience with deliveries in older women. Doctor Jones, this is Robert Hart, the father of Jo Ann's twins."

"How is she?" Robert asked, shaking hands with Cynthia Jones, but looking at Connie.

"Yeah, we want to know," Melissa said.

"She's okay, Melissa," Connie responded. "She's alert, though she might fall asleep any minute. She's as comfortable as somebody can be under the circumstances."

"Doctor Jones, this is Jo Ann's daughter. She's also a patient of mine, at least for checkups. No babies yet, right Melissa?"

"Won't be for a while," Melissa said, her jaw set. "What's going on with Mom and with my brother and sister?" Robert put an arm around Melissa's shoulder and squeezed.

"I can't say why your mother fainted," Connie said, scratching below her ear. "Her blood pressure is now going down. Otherwise, her vital signs are what they were when I saw her earlier today. Something that happened between when she was here and when she fainted could have caused this. Any clues, Robert?"

"She was looking at her mail and said she felt faint."

Cynthia Jones spoke up for the first time. "We'll admit her to the hospital overnight. A woman her age, carrying twins, near term, who has this kind of episode, needs close observation."

"Can we see her?" Deena asked, stepping from behind Robert into the middle of the group.

"Oh, I'm sorry," Robert said. "Doctor Connie Cross, Doctor Cynthia Jones, this is Deena Hart, my daughter-in-law. She's here from Memphis helping us."

"I'm pleased to meet you," Connie said. "Jo Ann told me how you've helped her. Being here is kind of you. She appreciates what you've done. Yes, please go in."

Connie pushed open the exam room door. Robert, Deena, and Melissa followed the doctors. Another nurse, a short, Mexican-American woman with black hair, brown skin, and a face marred by several scars, stood beside Jo Ann, lying on the examination table. A blue sheet covered her neck to toe and her clothes lay in a pile on a chair. Her eyes scanned the room.

"Are you okay?" Melissa asked. "How do you feel?"

"Woozy," Jo Ann replied. "I'll be okay." She looked at Robert, standing next to Deena. She extended her hand and he grasped it.

"What happened, Mom?"

By now, Jo Ann understood the events in the car and that she couldn't fully answer Melissa's question in this crowd. "I'm not sure. I felt faint. Robert must have gotten me here as fast as he could."

"Take it easy, my love," he said. "Now you have two doctors taking care of you," he added, glancing at Cynthia Jones.

"That's right," Connie said. "I've asked that my partner, Dr. Cynthia Jones, help me with your care. As you know, I think she's the best."

Cynthia Jones nodded and looked at Jo Ann. "We're admitting you to Memorial Hermann so we can keep close tabs on you and the babies for the next 48 to 72 hours. Connie – Dr. Cross – and I will decide soon when we should take them."

"Who can drive her there?" Connie asked. "If no one can we can arrange an Ambulance."

Jo Ann wondered if Robert had seen the letter she was reading when she fainted. He probably had, but maybe not. Keeping control of when she told him the whole story, assuming he didn't already know it, meant acting fast.

The sheet fell away, revealing a white, pinstriped hospital gown. "Melissa you and Deena should take me to the hospital. Robert needs to get some work finished so he can be available if these guys take the babies in the next day or two. Would one of you get my bag out of Robert's car? I've been keeping one packed just in case. It's on the back seat. Bring me that mail I left in the front seat."

Jo Ann looked at Robert. If he understood the motive behind her directions, neither his expression nor words gave him away. "That's fine," he said, turning to Deena and handing her a parking ticket. "Ask the valet guys for my car. I'll stay here while you and Melissa get those things. Jo Ann and I could use a few minutes alone."

"I'll see you tonight, Jo Ann," Connie said. "After you're in the hospital."

Chapter 42

T hinking Jo Ann's hospital stay might last a while, Robert stopped at home for clothes and toiletries before going to his office. After an hour reviewing drilling and production reports his mobile phone rang. "This is Robert."

"Hey, Robert, it's Jack Prince," came the voice on the other end. "Sorry I took so long getting back with you. It seems I've been in the Middle East for ages."

Robert's face brightened. Maybe now he could help Jo Ann get the Betters problem behind her. "How the hell are you, man?"

"I'm good. The message I got said you wanted to talk to me about Gary Betters. What's up with that?"

"My old JAX crowd is looking at bringing him in as part of a reorganization. I said I knew people who might have worked with him. I called you."

Silence came from the other end of the phone. Finally, Prince said, "This is hard, Robert. You and I go way back. Talking about Gary Betters is something I do as little of as possible."

"I've heard that before. You can imagine who I've asked."

"The usual suspects?"

"Of course."

Prince's strained, tense voice announced his wariness. "I can point you to where the bodies are buried. But I can't be the guy with the shovel. That must be someone else."

Robert stood up. He marveled at how Jo Ann had sensed

Betters had baggage JAX didn't need. "What's the bottom line?"

"Tell your friends they should find another way."

"Where are the bodies," Robert asked.

"Texas Railroad Commission records on major on-shore finds in the early 1990s, plus missing EPA reports. A *Houston Chronicle* reporter named Terrance Peters is looking into this. I won't say more. Maybe I don't need to."

"I know what you mean." The Gary Betters talk was over.

"Hey, Robert," Prince said, "I heard a story about you while I was overseas. Tell me if it's true."

"Business or personal?"

"I know the business stuff. You and Jimmy Hundley and your buddies are kicking ass and taking names on gas projects in the U. S. and South America. I wasn't asking about that."

"I have a new personal life. After all these years alone, I have a girlfriend."

"I heard she's part of the darker nation and she's pregnant."

"True."

"I could give a rat's ass what color she is. As for her being pregnant, you're a hell of a man for getting that done at your age. More power to you, sir."

∞∞∞

Checking into Memorial Hermann Hospital took over an hour. When Jo Ann got settled, Deena headed off for dinner, leaving Melissa and her mother alone. Afternoon sun filtered into the room. Melissa closed the curtains. "I know why you fainted," she said.

"You found the letter?"

Melissa's chin and lip trembled. "It was on the floor in the front of Robert's car. I read it. It's awful. How could they do this to you? To our family?"

"I told you this is personal for some black women. These two have just taken it to an extreme."

"What're you going to do?" Melissa asked, from the window.

"I don't know."

"There's one thing you must do, and soon."

"Tell Robert?"

"Yes."

"You're right." Jo Ann felt a weight lift from her shoulders. Sharing this with her daughter made the world seem less like it was closing in on her. "How did you know I hadn't told him?"

"First, that I had to get the mail and your bag. If he knew, you wouldn't have cared who got your things. Second, it appeared the letter hadn't been touched. If he'd found it and read it, he wouldn't have left it on the floor."

"I knew he could have seen it, but I also thought he might not have in the rush to get me into the doctor's office."

"Why haven't you told him?"

Melissa's look of disbelief startled Jo Ann. "I was scared."

"Scared of what?"

"That he'd feel I wasn't honest with him."

Melissa stared at her mother. "Why would he think that?"

"I didn't tell him about six years ago."

"Why would you have to tell him about that?"

"I told him everything else."

"I've only been around you and Robert a little, but I can see how much he loves you. He won't hold against you something that happened years before he started seeing you. If he's like you say he is, he'll want the details. He'll find it funny, maybe even titillating."

Melissa laughed and Jo Ann smiled as she asked, "You think so?"

"Men like Robert, who get sex, who relish it, are curious about that kind of thing. What he'll be mad about is you carrying this around for who knows how long without telling him. When did you suspect Kendra and Tiffany were up to something?"

"Three, four months ago. but I kept finding an excuse for not telling him."

"Big mistake."

"But what do we do about the threat behind the letters? Kendra and Tiffany will tell Tony. Tony will do what they hope he'll do – cut me off from himself and Shonda. If he'd call me a slut because I had sex without being married, how farfetched is thinking he'd abandon me because of my other indiscretion?"

"Not much. I know one thing."

"What?"

Furrowing her brow, Melissa said, "We need the smartest person in our family helping on this."

"Regina?"

"Regina."

∞ ∞ ∞

When Deena returned, she and Melissa agreed they'd take turns staying with Jo Ann through the night, even though the patient said it wasn't necessary.

"Robert will be here soon," she said. "He'll also say he

271

should stay with me. You all should go home. The next few days might make everybody tired."

"Let's wait until Robert gets here before deciding," Melissa said. "I'm going out and make some calls. I'll be back in a half hour—45 minutes."

After talking with Melissa, Jo Ann felt refreshed. Enlisting Regina's help with the Kendra/Tiffany problem encouraged her. The prospect of telling Robert what they were up to relieved her of the burden of keeping it secret. She also decided she should now poke Deena and see if her instincts about her situation had been right.

Jo Ann looked at Deena, sitting in a chair near the window, reading a magazine. "Could you come over here? Let's talk for a few minutes."

"Sure, what's up?" She dropped the magazine and stood by the bed. Jo Ann turned on her side toward Deena.

"There's something I've been thinking about for a while. I might be all wet. Robert keeps saying I have good instincts about people, and I should trust them. So, I'll do that and ask you a personal question."

A puzzled look spread over Deena's face. She ran her tongue along her top lip. She rubbed her palms together, entwined her fingers, and dropped her arms in front of her. Her shoulders tensed. "What do you want to ask?"

"Is the reason you haven't had children yet that you're infertile, or think you are?" Jo Ann looked at Deena. There, she thought. I asked her. What does she do now?

At first, Deena's face went blank. Jo Ann couldn't read it. She said nothing. For a second, Jo Ann feared Deena would bolt from the room. Then she saw the first hint of a tear forming in Deena's right eye. That one fell. Then there was another. Then there were many. Finally, there was a flood. Jo Ann reached for Deena's hand. She leaned down and hugged Jo Ann. For long minutes, they embraced. Still, no words passed between them. Deena's tears flowed. Jo Ann couldn't hold out any longer. She cried with her.

Deena finally broke their embrace. "How did you know?"

Jo Ann pressed the button to raise the bed and reached for Deena. They embraced again before Deena stepped back.

Jo Ann said, "I saw how much you care about children. You told me about your teaching, your community work. I saw you reading children's books. I saw my pregnancy draw you in. You put your life on hold while helping me. I knew there was a story there."

Deena grimaced and dipped her chin. "I've never told anyone."

"Not even Al?"

"Not even Al."

"How did you kept it from him?"

"I lied about not wanting children 'right now.'" She made a quote gesture. "I said it's not quite time, so we kept using birth control. If he brings it up, I tell him I need a little longer."

"How long have you known?"

"After we'd been married three years, we stopped using birth control for a year. Nothing happened. I suspected I had a problem. I told Al I wasn't sure I was ready for kids, after all. I went back on birth control."

"Why did you think you had a problem?"

Deena hesitated. Finally she said, "Because of what I did as a teenager."

"Which was?" Jo Ann knew what was coming. Before she got her answer, another flood of Deena's tears fell, these more intense than those before. Then, Deena regained her composure. The tears stopped and she blew her nose into a tissue Jo Ann handed her.

"I had an abortion," she said flatly. The emotion drained out of her. Jo Ann heard resignation, almost hopelessness.

Jo Ann's anger flared. "Stop, Deena!"

"What?" Deena asked the puzzled look on her face returned.

"How do you know having an abortion made you infertile?"

"Everybody knows that."

Jo Ann balled up her fists and slammed them into the bed. "Everybody does not know that! I talked with Connie. I told her my fear something was bothering you, you were carrying around something painful from your past. I suspected this was it. She told me there's a lot of doubt in the medical world about whether abortions cause infertility. Has any doctor ever told you that's what caused your problem?"

"No."

"Then how do you know?"

Deena spoke in a weakened voice. "I've read that they do."

"What have you read?"

The younger woman shook her head, then fixed her gaze on Jo Ann. "Publications by people I work with on stopping abortions."

Jo Ann opened her mouth, but closed it before saying anything. She buzzed the nurse's station.

"Who're you calling?" Deena asked.

"Hold on."

The intercom crackled. "May I help you, Ms. Davis?"

"When is Doctor Cross coming next?"

"About six thirty on her evening rounds. Is anything wrong?"

"No. Thank you."

Jo Ann turned to Deena and pointed at the chair. "Stay until Connie gets here. We'll talk. And it will be about more than me and these two," she said, rubbing her enlarged middle.

Chapter 43

Melissa returned to Jo Ann's room before Connie Cross got there. She had news for her mother. "Regina arrives tomorrow. Her judge told her she could stay as long as needed."

"Did she have any ideas?"

"She said she might."

"Good, very good."

"Is the doctor seeing you tonight?"

"She should be here soon, about six thirty."

"How're you feeling, Mom?"

"I'm okay. I want this over though."

Melissa and Deena left when Connie Cross showed up for Jo Ann's examination. The doctor reported, "No change from earlier. We'll do another ultrasound tomorrow and check where they are in the womb. Your daughter was head down on the last one."

"What's next?" Jo Ann asked.

"We could keep you a few more days. We could send you home, though I doubt that. We could decide we should take them, which is most likely."

"Can I talk to you about something else?"

"Sure, though I have another patient to see."

"This is about Deena, Robert's daughter-in-law. I have more of the story. I'd hope you can talk with her."

"Let me go see that patient and I'll come back. What's the bottom line?"

"She thinks she's infertile because she had an abortion. No doctor has ever told her that and she's never had treatment."

"I should talk with her. Give me 15 minutes."

"Thank you. I see the pain this has caused her. If you can help her, I'd be forever grateful."

$$\infty \infty \infty$$

Robert called Jo Ann after the doctor left. "How're you doing?" he asked.

"I'm good. I slept this afternoon. Connie came by this evening."

"And?"

"They're doing an ultrasound tomorrow and will decide what happens next."

"I'll stay with you tonight."

"Don't do that. I want everybody at home and sleeping in their own beds. I'm fine here. There'll be plenty of time for that later."

"I'll come see you for a while."

"That's good. We should talk."

"We should?"

"Yes." Jo Ann looked at the wall clock. It said 6:55 p.m.

"Come about eight o'clock. We can talk for an hour and you can go home and rest. Tomorrow might be a big day."

Connie Cross returned to Jo Ann's room at 7:05 p.m. Jo Ann asked that Melissa give Deena time alone with the doctor. Connie closed the door. Deena stood beside the bed, with Connie at the foot. Jo Ann reached for Deena's hand and squeezed.

"Deena," Connie began, "Jo Ann has told me some of your story. She wants to help because she cares. I've known her a long time, as a friend and as a patient. She feels deeply about her family. I can already tell you're family to her. Thank whatever God you worship you have her in your life. If I can help, I will. What's important to her is important to me."

Jo Ann gripped Deena's hand harder.

"You were pregnant once?" Connie asked.

In Deena's face, Jo Ann saw less hurt than earlier, as if just having this out eased her burden. "I was 17, about to start my senior year in high school. We were like lots of teenagers. We couldn't stay away from each other. His name was DeShawn. DeShawn Bryant."

A shiver shot down Jo Ann's spine. A first name like DeShawn meant one thing. She remembered Deena's characterization of her father.

"We were in love," Deena continued. Though her voice was strong and calm now, Jo Ann imagined how frightened and alone she must have felt at the time. "I've never forgotten him. It probably wouldn't have worked out for us and I love Al dearly, but I've never forgotten DeShawn. He was caring, gentle, and real smart. We both knew we should use protection. We did except once, when we were so hot for each other, we got careless. I turned up pregnant."

Jo Ann thought of that Friday night when she bent over the

kitchen table, flipped up her dress, and begged that Robert take her. She remembered how Deena's face dropped when told Robert thought the details of how she probably got pregnant made them seem like horny, sex crazed teenagers.

"You had an abortion?" Connie asked.

"I couldn't let my parents know I'd gotten pregnant. They would've killed both of us. My father would've gone crazy if he knew I was seeing DeShawn, if he knew I even spoke to him."

Jo Ann listened. Telling the story was as important for Deena as any medical advice Connie could give her. Telling the story lifted the weight she'd carried for years.

"A friend's mother took me to Memphis," Deena continued. "It wasn't painful. I had a little cramping on the way back, but I got through it okay. The emotional part bothered me, but I never had any physical symptoms."

"Did you see a doctor for follow-up?"

"I couldn't in my little town. In college, I got check-ups at the student health center. Nobody ever said anything was wrong."

"Were you sexually active in college?"

"Yes, but I was careful. I took the pill at first, but I got scared about side effects and AIDS, so I made the guys use condoms. I met Al. We got married after two years."

"What did you do then?"

"We used a diaphragm for three years. Then we decided we wanted a baby, so we stopped using anything. Nothing happened. I believed I had a problem. I told Al I wasn't sure I was ready for kids. I got an implant. We've used that ever since."

"That's been how long?"

"Four years."

"And you've told him the same story?"

"Yes."

"What made you think you were infertile because of the abortion?"

"I read it."

"Where?"

"In books and pamphlets I got from people I work with on stopping abortions."

Jo Ann saw Connie struggling with what she should say about those publications. She needed Deena's trust. Attacking something sacred to her wouldn't help.

"What made you get involved in stopping abortions," Connie said.

"I felt guilty. We could have raised our baby if I hadn't been afraid of confronting my parents – really my father's - racism. I took our baby's life because I was a coward."

Jo Ann looked at Connie and realized she didn't know.

"Your father's racism?" Connie asked.

"DeShawn, my baby's father, was black. My dad hated black people. If he'd known I had sex with DeShawn, I believe he would've gotten a gun and shot us. He hated I had to go to school with black kids."

Connie nodded her head. "You didn't feel the guilt immediately?"

"Not seriously until college when I met this girl who'd also had an abortion in high school. She convinced me God would forgive us only if we dedicated our lives to saving babies from what we'd done to ours.

"I started attending anti-abortion rallies and demonstrating at clinics, not that there were many clinics in Mississippi. We went to Memphis a time or two. It was weird demonstrating in front of the clinic where I had my abortion. I was terrified somebody who worked there would remember me and call me out in front of my friends. I couldn't not go. I was part of the movement."

Stepping toward Deena at the side of the bed, Connie asked, "And you haven't been examined by a doctor to find out what might be wrong?"

Deena shook her head. "I've been afraid of what I'd find out and of how awful that would make me feel. Not knowing was better than knowing something bad."

Connie put her hand on Deena's shoulder. "You aren't the first person who's thought that."

"That's for damned sure," Jo Ann said, laughing. She felt the air flow back into the room.

"Tell you what," Connie said as the mood lightened. "Let me examine you while you're here. I'll see what's really going on and tell you your options. I will keep all your secrets. Fair enough?"

"Fair enough, doctor. Thank you."

Jo Ann released her grip on Deena's hand. "Thank you, Connie. Thank you so much." As the doctor left, Deena and Jo Ann embraced, holding each other for dear life.

Chapter 44

When Robert walked into Jo Ann's room at 8:05 p.m. calm spread over her. She'd long dreaded this moment, the angst building as she contemplated revealing her one remaining secret to the person she loved more than any in her life. Until earlier that day, the thought of telling him tied up her stomach and left her wishing she could withdraw into a shell on a beach somewhere.

Talking with Melissa and Deena changed Jo Ann's outlook. Telling her daughter lifted the burden of carrying the story around alone, and of not having told Robert, as this monumental moment in their lives – the birth of their twins – approached.

Melissa's admonition that she must tell him reminded her of what she already knew – leaving him in the dark was worse than whatever anger he threw at her once she spoke. It was unfair. He should know what she knew.

The story of Deena's pregnancy and fears her abortion caused infertility made Jo Ann feel she'd been selfish in not telling Robert she knew about the letters. Maybe keeping quiet about her pregnancy and the abortion had been best for Deena, since she knew the hatred her parents would direct at her because a black man fathered her baby. Not telling Al, however, potentially jeopardized their marriage. Deena's fears weren't worth that and her own weren't worth endangering her life with Robert.

Jo Ann took a deep breath. "Hi," she said as he neared her bed.

"Are you okay?" he asked. He leaned down and kissed her, then took her hand. "Is something up? Is there news?"

"No. But something is up. I have things to tell you."

Robert's face went blank. "You do?"

"I know what's behind the letters. I know who sent them."

"You know? Since when?"

"I thought I knew in January/February. Recently, I saw clues that my suspicions were correct. Today, I got confirmation."

Robert wrinkled his brow. "Let's start at the beginning. You believed you knew months ago? You didn't say anything."

"I didn't really know. If I told you what I suspected, I'd have had to tell you why I suspected it. I didn't want to tell you that."

"What did you think I'd do if you told me why you suspected it?"

Her heart raced. "I feared you'd think I was depraved, that I was weak, that I was stupid."

He smiled a little smile before he turned serious. "I doubt I'd have thought any of those things, but tell me and let me decide what I think."

She took another deep breath, squeezed his hand and motioned him to a chair near the bed. "You should sit down for this. Do you remember when I told you I'd been involved with only a few men since my divorce?"

"Of course."

"I didn't tell you about having an affair with a woman."

Robert said nothing for a long moment. Jo Ann looked for hints in his face. She saw none. She considered asking him to say something, anything. She kept staring into his blue eyes. Still, nothing told her anything of his thoughts or feelings.

Later – several times- she asked him how long that silence

lasted. He never had an answer. Eventually, she stopped asking that question and asked how long the loud laugh that finally broke the silence lasted.

"You're laughing at me, Robert! You're laughing at me! Why are you laughing at me?"

Every time he opened his mouth to say something, he laughed again. She rubbed her cheeks with her fists and asked again, with more exasperation, "Why are you laughing at me?"

Finally, he said, "Because you're so silly! You thought I'd think those things because you slept with some woman who knows how many years ago?"

"I didn't know what you'd say once you heard the details. Even if you didn't disapprove because I slept with a woman, I feared you'd think I was just a stupid, weak little girl who got used."

"Tell me the details."

Jo Ann gathered herself again. "It was six years ago. I was depressed about my man troubles. A woman friend invited me to a party. I didn't know anybody there. She introduced me around.

"I met was a woman who wasn't with anybody. She looked early 40s. It turned out she was older than me. Most of the women at this party were taken – a few by men, many by other women. That should have been my clue."

"Probably should have," he said, leaning forward and cracking a smile. "Go on."

"Her name was Clara. Clara Gibson. She was 52 at the time, to my 46. She was attractive enough. Light brown skin, short hair, not butch. She was round without being fat. She had well-padded places but, with her clothes on, she was just a middle aged woman who wasn't thin anymore."

He tilted his head to the side. "What happened?"

"She was super nice from the first hello. I thought she was

just being friendly. I was so lonely. I wasn't getting anywhere with men. I just wanted interaction with another person.

"Looking back, I realized she had it all planned. She was slick. We talked a while. She didn't lay a finger on me that night. I never suspected anything. I figured out later even how she dressed was part of her act. She wore loose-fitting slacks and a high-necked top. Nothing hinted this was about sex."

"It didn't stay that way?"

"It didn't. A few days later, she called me. We met for drinks a few times and just talked about work, places we'd been, people we knew. It stayed that way for a month."

"It changed?"

"She invited me to her apartment for sleepovers, first with other women present, then it was just the two of us. The next thing was she wanted to give me a massage. Then she asked me to give her one."

His eyes widened. "Did you get naked for that?"

Jo Ann smiled. Maybe Melissa had been right. Perhaps this would titillate him. "Not to begin with. She made a point of telling me I could keep my panties and bra on if I wanted. She took hers off, of course –"

"Of course."

"—saying she got more out of the massage if she undressed completely."

"What was next?"

"Because she was so good at giving massages, one night I fell asleep on her bed after she did mine. When I woke up, she was cuddled up next to me. She felt so warm, like she was protecting me. I let her kiss me. She unsnapped my bra and started nibbling on my nipples."

"Like us?"

"Nothing like us. It was what I needed then. I let her take

off my panties and she went down on me. As you know, I hadn't had much oral sex. It was good because I needed touch, intimacy, orgasms that came from being with somebody."

"Did she ask that you return the favor?"

"In time. I got decent at it. She said I was good."

He grinned. "I bet you were."

"This fascinates you doesn't it?"

"A little."

"Have you ever talked to a woman about gay sex?"

"No."

"So this is new for you?"

"Yes."

"It doesn't disgust you?"

"No."

She looked at him, still annoyed he'd laughed at her. "It went on for six months."

He lifted his eyebrows and asked, "It ended at some point?"

"She demanded I move in with her, that we come out as a couple. She wanted to go to gay bars."

"And you didn't?"

Jo Ann crossed her arms over her chest. "I'm not gay, Robert."

"Did she think you were?"

"For a while, I acted like it. The longer it went on, the more I realized I wasn't gay. I was just lonely."

He sat back in the chair. "What did you do?"

"I told my friend, Irma Simpson."

"What'd she say?"

"If it didn't feel right, end it."

"And you did?"

"Yes."

His expression turned serious. "That wasn't pretty?"

"It was awful. Clara left town. She said being here without me was too painful. She tried making me feel like I was the worst person ever. She even threatened she'd --"

"Commit suicide?"

"Yes," Jo Ann replied, nodding.

"How'd that make you feel?"

"Like it was supposed to – guilty."

"Why?"

"I didn't say I didn't like her. I just didn't want to be her lover. She didn't have the right equipment."

He returned her grin. "You're about as far from being gay as anyone I know. I could have told you that before you started."

"You weren't around."

"So what's this got to do with the letters?"

Jo Ann sat up and paused a moment. "In January, Jenny asked me if I'd ever confessed anything to somebody who was a friend once, but had become an enemy. That's exactly what had happened."

A puzzled look came over his face. "Huh?"

"One night a few years ago, Kendra, Tiffany, Betty, and I were sitting around, talking. Tiffany asked what the wildest thing was each of us had ever done. I'd had too much to drink. I told them about this."

He shook his head. "That was a mistake."

"It seemed like a good idea at the time. I realized Kendra and Tiffany were enemies now and might be behind the letters. Melissa talked with friends whose parents know Tiffany. One of them overheard Tiffany saying she and Kendra would fix me."

Robert tapped his heal on the floor. "Fix you how?"

"That wasn't clear until today. There was another letter in the mail I opened before I fainted. Kendra and Tiffany finally revealed themselves by initialing this letter. They enclosed a pledge my son, Tony, signed that promised he would have nothing to do with anyone who was gay or who'd had gay sex."

"What?" Robert asked with disbelief she'd never heard from him.

"I think, now, I saw him sign it. When he, Kristin, and Shonda came home in April for my birthday last year, as they were leaving, we were out in my front yard. I saw Tiffany slip Tony something which he signed on the hood of his car. The thing they sent me was dated about that time."

Robert stood up, walked to the bed, and took Jo Ann's hand. "What did they threaten they'd do?"

"They said that after the twins – they called them half-breed bastards – are born, I must leave town or they'll tell Tony about my lesbian affair. You know what Tony will do. He's disowned me because you and I had sex without being married and I got pregnant. He'll comply with that pledge he signed."

Robert looked into her eyes. "I want to be mad at you for not telling me about this. I am mad about it. That was stupid. We can talk about that later. First, we must figure out what we do about this."

"Melissa called Regina and she's coming in tomorrow to help."

"I'll have Jenny stop by. The more smart people we have on this, the better."

Chapter 45

Robert enjoyed morning runs in Memorial Park, a short drive from his house. When he awoke at 5:30 a.m., before pulling on a t-shirt and running shorts, he sent Terry Peters and Jon Weinstock a text:

PARK THIS AM?

Terry responded two minutes later:

MEET YOU THERE AT 6:30

A minute later, Jon replied:

NO RUN TODAY. BREAKFAST IHOP 7:30?

Robert told Terry:

I'M THERE

To Jon, he responded:

DEAL

∞ ∞ ∞

Glimpses of the Galleria area skyline pulled Robert east along I-10 before he turned south onto the I-610 Loop and headed into Memorial park. An orange glow tinted the clear sky, announcing a spectacular, cloudless day.

He parked near the tennis center, got out, and savored the moment before stretching. The still air felt fresh. Houston's famous humidity hadn't arrived yet. Across the street, green soccer and softball fields beckoned, newly mowed and manicured. A few runners pounded the path, their shoes crunching the finely graveled surface.

"Hey, Robert," a voice called from behind.

He turned. The morning light made his friend's eyes seem bluer than usual. Robert noticed the tiny black mole on his right temple, the only imperfection in an otherwise flawless face. "Terry! Thanks for coming on short notice. I didn't know if you'd be up."

"Joyce asked last night if I'd heard from you. I said I hadn't for over a week. When I got up, there was your text."

They eased onto the path, behind a short, blonde woman who looked about 30 and her running companion, a tall man with a ruddy complexion, dark hair, and an easy gait. Both wore Northwestern University shorts, t-shirts, and headbands.

"No doubt about what team they're for," Terry whispered.

"Not much," Robert said.

They picked up the pace. "What's going on with Jo Ann and the twins?"

"It's any day now, C-section."

"How's she handling it?"

"There are a few complications. She is 52 years old. It's the other shit she – we—are dealing with that's a pain."

"Other shit?"

"Other shit, which you won't believe."

"Try me," Terry said, as three young women passed them.

"A few months ago, Jo Ann started getting anonymous letters in plain envelopes, post marked in a little Texas town, with cryptic, veiled threats. I was amused at first, but they kept coming. I hired Jenny Dixon to advise us."

Terry raised an arm and waved a finger. "She's good, a fellow Columbia Law School graduate you know. One of my litigation partners has had cases with and against her and raves about her."

Robert continued, "Unbeknownst to me, Jenny asked Jo Ann that she think about what skeletons she had she might have told somebody about who was once a friend, but was now an enemy."

"Okay."

"Jo Ann has two women friends, ex-friends, who are livid she's with me, a white man. They say that makes her a traitor to the black race."

They fell into an easy running rhythm. "Do black people think that way?"

"Apparently, some do. Jo Ann remembered she had confessed something to these two a few years ago."

They overtook the couple in the Northwestern gear. "What'd she confess? Murder? Belonging to the Mafia?" Terry chuckled as they turned west, onto the part of the trail that ran along Memorial Drive. Traffic heading east into downtown sped by.

"That she had a lesbian affair six years ago."

"So? Lots of women try that. Jo Ann isn't gay. Must have been an experiment."

In a sharp tone, Robert said, "That's all it was. She was frustrated and lonely, not having any luck with men. The woman seduced her, plain and simple. The novelty wore off. Jo Ann isn't gay so she ended it. The woman took it so hard she threatened suicide before moving away."

"What difference does that make to the two women who are mad at her about you?"

They plodded along. "Jo Ann's son, Tony, hates gay people. He signed a formal pledge he and his family will have nothing to do with anybody who claims they're gay or who's had gay sex. These two women say they'll tell Tony about Jo Ann's affair if she doesn't leave town after our twins are born. Jo Ann is convinced Tony will live up to his pledge and cut her off from both him and his daughter, her only grandchild."

"You are fucking kidding! What makes Jo Ann think her son will go along with such crap?"

"Tony is serious about this anti-gay stuff, all morality stuff. When Jo Ann told him about the pregnancy, he called her a slut because she and I aren't married. If he'll do that, why wouldn't he cut her off over something else he thinks is a sin?"

"This is a religion thing?"

"It is."

Between breaths, Terry asked, "You say he signed a 'pledge?' What's that about?"

"He and one of these women attend a stridently anti-gay church. They held a contest for who could get the most signatures on these pledges. He lives in Denver. When he was home last spring, Jo Ann saw him signing something one of these women gave him."

"Has she actually seen it?"

The path turned back toward the tennis center. It was getting warmer, as the first hint of the day's humidity crept into the air. Robert and Terry now sweated and breathed harder. "The last letter, which included their demand that Jo Ann leave town, showed up yesterday with the signed pledge attached. It bothered Jo Ann so much she fainted. That's why her doctor put her in the hospital last night."

Terry let out a quick, disgusted snort. "She's not – you're not –caving in on this?"

"No, but can you imagine if somebody gave you that choice – undo your life with your new significant other and your new babies or never see your grandchild until she grows up and understands how stupid her parent has been, maybe has to defy the parent at some point?"

"Isn't this against the law?"

"I called Jenny last night after Jo Ann told me about it. I was highly pissed Jo Ann didn't tell me she's suspected this for a while. I cut her some slack. She didn't know. She was just guessing until she got the letter yesterday.

"Jenny says there's probably no crime a prosecutor would be interested in. There's no demand for money. She didn't think a civil suit would accomplish much either."

"That's right. Even a real estate lawyer should see that."

They neared the end of the 2.9-mile loop. As they eased up, Terry asked, "What're you doing about this?"

"Hell if I know," Robert said when he stopped. "First, I want Jo Ann to get through having our twins with all three of them healthy. I'll worry about this other shit after that."

Robert pulled on sweats after he and Terry finished running and drove west on I-10. He met Jon Weinstock at an IHOP. Robert asked that he look at rebalancing his portfolio, reflecting developments in his new business. They also discussed revising his will so he provided for Jo Ann and the twins. Jon said he'd coordinate with one of Jenny Dixon's partners in getting that done.

As they wound up breakfast Jon, wearing a yellow, button down dress shirt sans tie, a blue blazer, and gray slacks, asked, "How're you really feeling about having these babies? I'm amazed you seem so calm. This is a big change for somebody your age. Aren't you freaked out?"

Robert pushed aside his plate and took the last gulp of his orange juice. "Jo Ann and I talk about that all the time. She looked at me one night and said something like, 'This is amazing. Here we are a black woman in her 50s and a white guy in his 60s having twins together. But I'm deliriously happy.' I feel the same way."

Jon peered over wire framed glasses sitting low on his big nose. "You're a better man than me. I'd go crazy."

"She's given me a new lease on life. That's why I'm not bummed."

"I saw that at Thanksgiving. I never thought I'd see you that way again."

"I never thought I'd be that way again."

"Did you ever feel you were betraying Darla?"

"I was so afraid of that before Jo Ann came along. I got cold feet if I thought about being with a woman. You know me. I love to fuck. Darla and I had a great sex life until she got sick. After she died, if I looked at a woman on the street or in a store and thought about what was under her dress, about her breasts and thighs, I slapped my own hand for even thinking about going after her.

"With Jo Ann, it was different. From that first night when we met accidentally, then went out and ate together, I could see myself with her. There was no guilt. I called her the next day and invited her to a ball game. When I laid eyes on her again, I wanted her."

"What about the pregnancy? Doesn't that feel weird?"

"Yeah, I dread changing diapers the next few years. I assume it'll be strange having little kids in my 70s and teenagers in my 80s, if I live that long. Because I'm with Jo Ann, I'm pumped about having them. What came from what's between us can only be good."

"You're a hell of a man, Robert. I'm in awe of you."

"Just be happy for me I found her. Most of us don't get one love that makes us so happy. I got two."

Jon paid the check. As they walked to their cars, the morning heated up under a brightening sun and increasing humidity. Robert said, "We talked about me. Are you getting anywhere with Jo Ann's friend, Hannah?"

A cat-swallowed-the-canary smile spread over Jon's face. "There's a reason I couldn't go running with you. She and I weren't done with our morning work."

"You're as old as I am."

"There's one difference."

"What?"

"I had my tubes tied."

Chapter 46

"Don't come until afternoon," Jo Ann told Robert when he called after breakfast with Jon. "They're doing tests this morning."

"How're you feeling?" he asked.

In a bubbly voice, Jo Ann replied, "I'm good. Our talk last night helped."

"Are you okay physically?"

"I'm tired but that started in January."

"It's almost over. I'd go with tomorrow for when Connie takes them. How does May 14 sound for birthday parties?"

"I hoped for May 24."

"The day we started seeing each other?"

She let out a satisfied sigh. "You remembered too?"

"How could I forget?"

"May 14 is fine. I just want them healthy."

When the hospital staff returned Jo Ann to her room at 12:30 p.m., she found three young women there, not two. "Regina! I'm so glad you're here, Baby! You won't be my youngest child much longer."

"You're huge, Mom!" Regina shouted, backing away after they embraced. "How do you get around?"

Deena laughed. "She waddles."

Wearing a red skirt, white blouse, and gold necklace, Regina looked relaxed despite flying halfway across the country that morning. The Houston humidity hadn't yet taken its toll on her curly hair. Her smooth, light brown skin glowed and her eyes sparkled. She spoke with purpose. "Melissa brought me up to speed on what Kendra and Tiffany are doing. We need a game plan."

"I laid it out for Deena on the way to the airport," Melissa said. "She may also have some ideas." Today Melissa wore black slacks, a tan knit top, and dark flats.

"Let's approach this logically," Regina said. "I'm sure, Mom, you're not leaving town, but the price of staying shouldn't be losing your relationship with Shonda."

"Or with Tony," Deena said.

"He already said he wants nothing to do with me because Robert and I have sex and aren't married," Jo Ann reminded them.

Regina paced the floor, then stopped. "He won't stick with that. Seeing his new siblings will cure him. There are people in that church who've had children out of wedlock. He doesn't shun them all.

"The gay thing is different. I'd guess Tony takes seriously this pledge he signed. People in that church will chastise him if he violates it. I've heard Tony say awful things about gay people and gay sex." Regina looked directly at her mother. "On the merits, Mom, he thinks you've committed a horrible sin."

This girl thinks, talks, and acts like a lawyer, Jo Ann thought. She looked down, then up into Regina's unwavering gaze and said, "In his eyes, I have. Must I pay for it like this?"

"Mom didn't do anything wrong," Melissa said. "She was lonely, that's all. Tony shouldn't have signed that paper. It's mean and cruel."

"It is," Regina responded. "That's the field we're playing on and we deal with Tony as he is, not as we wish he was."

Jo Ann leaned back, listening. Regina was being true to her nature and to her training – cool, analytical, in control, realistic. They needed that now, but Jo Ann still could have wrung her neck.

∞∞∞

A few minutes past one o'clock, Robert arrived in Jo Ann's room, Jenny Dixon in tow. Between Jenny and Regina, we sure have the legal talent we need, Jo Ann thought. She hoped the giant egos around her wouldn't crash into each other too often.

"We need to solve this problem, people," Regina said, standing at the partially closed door. "We'll likely have babies we're dealing with in a day or two. Mom could be in a daze."

"That's right," Robert said, standing beside Jo Ann's bed. "I brought Jenny. Regina, you're here. I'm all ears."

"Is there any chance we do nothing and this goes away?" Deena asked, standing beside the window.

Jo Ann shook her head. "Maybe with rational people. We're not dealing with rational people. I'm certain of how serious they are."

Robert expressed his skepticism with a jutting chin and a wrinkled nose. "Why're you so sure? Maybe this is a bluff, a ruse to have fun at our expense."

"A clue in yesterday's letter tells me that's not the case," Jo Ann explained. "Only I would have gotten it." Pointing at Melissa, she asked, "Do you have the letter?"

Melissa dug it out of her bag. "Here."

Jo Ann ran her finger over the page. "They wrote 'Don't mess with us. We're serious as a heart attack.' Kendra and

Tiffany recognize I know Kendra only uses that expression when she really means something. This isn't a bluff."

"So," Jenny said, "we focus on Tony." She wore her blonde hair up, a black dress, heels, and dark hose. "Can we get Tony to not comply with their request, in effect, violating the pledge?"

"Which means," Robert said, as he stroked Jo Ann's forehead, "we have to tell him about the affair and convince him to break the pledge."

"Correct," Regina said. "Who could get him to do that?"

"Nobody here has that kind of influence with him," Melissa observed. "You'd be asking him to go against his church. He's not doing that because I ask him."

"He's certainly not doing it for me," Jo Ann said.

Regina said, "One person not here might have a chance." She dragged a forefinger across her lips. "It'd take some doing and we'd have to do what Jenny and Robert suggested – tell Tony what Kendra and Tiffany are threatening to tell him on pain of him cutting Mom off from his family."

The group turned in unison to Regina. "Who?"

Regina smiled. "When I was a smart alec little kid, if asked that question in a situation like this, I'd say 'That's for me to know and you to find out.'"

Melissa and Deena chuckled, but Robert, Jo Ann, and Jenny remained silent. Regina's effort at breaking the tension had only partly succeeded.

"Okay," she said. "I'll tell you. It shouldn't surprise Melissa. I bet Deena understands once she has the facts. Her parents divorced, so she knows something about this. The one person who might have a chance at convincing Tony he should stop this madness is Dad."

"James?" Jo Ann blurted out. "Why him?"

"It's simple," Melissa said, her eyes widening. "Regina's

right. I should have thought of it myself. The fact she did and I didn't is why she made those high grades in school, not me.

"Tony thinks Dad has never, ever, done anything wrong. He believes the divorce was Mom's fault, when Regina and I know the opposite is true. Because Dad quotes the Bible so much, Tony thinks his father lived up to the church stuff, the thou-shall-nots."

Regina picked up where her sister left off. "If Dad confesses his sin, Tony might realize he should forgive Mom for hers. Tony might understand the world isn't as black and white as he believes. If he sees Dad did wrong and it didn't make him an evil person, that he's still been a good father, there's a chance he'll decide whatever Mom did, he should forgive."

Robert scratched his head and asked, "Tony doesn't know about his father's infidelity?" He looked at Jo Ann. "You even told me about finding another woman's panties in his suitcase."

"I couldn't ever find a reason for telling Tony that wasn't just being mean," Jo Ann said. "I told the girls, long after they grew up, because it was important they understand men cheat and they'd have disappointments. I wanted them prepared for that. I didn't do it until I felt telling them wouldn't destroy their relationship with James. There never was a right time or a right reason for telling Tony."

"Are you sure he hasn't told Tony himself?" Jenny asked.

"He hasn't," Melissa said. "Last year, Dad came to see me run at nationals. Mom had told me about Dad's cheating and how it led to the divorce. I asked Dad if it was true. He admitted it. During the conversation, he said he'd never told Tony."

"How does this work?" Robert asked. "Do Regina and Melissa ask James that he talk with Tony?"

Regina laid out her plan. "I suggest I get on a plane and visit Dad. I'll ask that he call Tony and suggest that Tony meet us all here. Melissa should go to Denver and work on getting Tony to come back here with her."

"What should I use for ammunition in getting him to do that?" Melissa asked, a deep furrow in her brow.

"I have an idea. We'll talk about it on the way to the airport."

Jenny said, "For this to work, both James and Tony have to do things they may not want to do."

"No guarantees, Jenny," Regina said. "When you take on a hard case, you promise your client your best effort, no more. I don't see any good alternatives."

Robert scanned the room. "I agree with that. It may be this or nothing."

When the meeting broke up, everybody moved fast. Jo Ann called Rhonda Gonzalez and told her she should keep Regina and Melissa supplied with plane tickets, hotel rooms, and rental cars. "Have American Express Card, will travel," she said as she hung up.

Regina called her father and told him he shouldn't worry about why she was headed his way, just meet her for breakfast Wednesday at their favorite Baltimore restaurant.

Deena drove Melissa to Jo Ann's house so she could pack. When they returned, Melissa reported her talk with Tony had been difficult, but he would see her. Melissa didn't volunteer what reason she'd given him for her trip and nobody asked.

"We should get going," Melissa said. "We leave from Hobby in three hours and within five minutes of each other. Let's hope this works."

Regina picked up her briefcase. "It'll work. Mom will have two healthy babies. She'll have a good relationship with Tony and Shonda. I'm always optimistic."

Deena, who'd been waiting in the hall, stuck her head in and said she was ready. Robert embraced Melissa and Regina. As he released Regina, he looked back at their mother, lying on the bed, smiling through tears. "God speed, Regina," Robert said. "God speed, Melissa."

Chapter 47

"**I** wish I could be on one of those planes," Jo Ann told Robert after everyone cleared out.

"Which one?"

"Either. Both. Melissa and Regina are brave for taking this on. This could get ugly. I'd like being nearby, so I could let them know I'll be okay, even if it doesn't work. I have them. I have you. We'll have our twins. That may be it."

"Don't resign yourself yet to a life without your son and grandchild."

"Tony believes this anti-gay stuff. He'll think what I did is unpardonable. He might not want anything to do with me, even if he hadn't signed that damn pledge."

"Without that this might not be such a big deal. There'd be no public proclamation he'd be going back on, nothing he's violating in the eyes of his tribe."

She'd been sitting up and now let her head fall back. "I hope you never believed I'd leave over this."

"I didn't, but I'd go with you. They didn't say you had to leave me, just leave town."

"And leave behind your business, your opportunity of a life time? I couldn't do that to you."

"You and our children mean more to me than any amount of money I could ever make. If you decided you were moving to Elephant Breath, Alaska, I'd move with you."

She laughed, and then she couldn't stop laughing. Then she cried. They hugged. Soon she fell asleep.

∞∞∞

At 6:30 p.m. that Tuesday, Dr. Connie Cross and Dr. Cynthia Jones arrived in Jo Ann's room and told her they'd decided a birthdate. "We're taking them day after tomorrow- "

"Thursday, May 15?" Robert asked. He stood at the window.

Doctor Jones said, "We thought about tomorrow, but we'd like a full day of preparation for surgery. Neither she nor the babies are in distress. We can wait one more day."

"Can you make another day?" Connie asked, looking at Jo Ann. "How're you feeling?"

"I was hoping for tomorrow. I'm tired and my body feels abused. If Thursday's best, I'm okay with it. What time?"

"Seven a.m.," Connie said. "By mid-morning, you'll be a new mother."

"I'll be a new father," Robert said. "I'd have never thought it, but it's here."

"Tomorrow, the nurses will tell you everything you should expect," Connie told them. "Robert, are you planning on being in the delivery room?"

Connie's question startled him. "Can I? I came up back in the day when fathers waited in the parking lot. If I can be there, I want to be there."

"Since it's a C-section," she responded, "there are limits on where you can be, where you have to stand, things like that." She wrote something in a notebook. "I'll have the nurses give you literature on the delivery room. You should watch internet videos of C-sections."

"Okay."

Connie looked at them. "Of all my patients, I thought the two of you would most want to be together for this."

Robert had moved beside the bed. He held Jo Ann's hand tightly. Together they said to the doctors, "We do!"

∞ ∞ ∞

That evening, Robert read and puttered around the hospital room while Jo Ann slept. When she awoke, he decided he should address one more issue before things got crazy the next day. "You were right about Gary Betters," he told her.

A grin spread across her face. "I was? What did you find out?"

"He'll likely be indicted by a federal grand jury within a few weeks. Jack Prince put me on to a *Houston Chronicle* reporter who told me he's breaking a story later this week about how Betters and his cronies falsified drilling records and misled the EPA and state agencies about environmental violations. JAX should stay as far away from him as possible."

"I should tell David and Karen ---"

"I did."

"You did?"

"I talked with the reporter today. Jenny confirmed the story with a source she has in the U.S. Attorney's Office in Austin where they're running the investigation.

"I called Karen and gave her details, many of which I won't bother you with now. I asked if she objected to me calling David. She didn't. I told him you recognized Betters might be a problem. I gave him the news because you have other fish to fry."

"What'd he say?"

Robert felt warmth spreading through his body. "That he needs you back at work. You're the best eyes and ears he has. I said I knew that, but you're having our children before he can have you back. He said if that's the best deal he can get, he'll take it."

"When did this happen, the violations and falsified records?"

"Mid '90s."

A puzzled look crossed her face. "Why didn't someone find this when Betters was nominated for Assistant Energy Secretary?"

"He had lots of help hiding it. Others are going down with him. The conspiracy involved 15 to 20 people. That's why unraveling it took so long."

"I had a hunch based on one interview."

"That's why you're remarkable. You see things most people don't."

Chapter 48

Wednesday, the nurses descended on Jo Ann's room. They ran tests and presented instructions for Thursday. Robert came and went.

Connie's office called, telling Jo Ann of an unexpected hole in the doctor's schedule, so Deena could come in for an exam that morning. While Robert was down the hall, Jo Ann enlisted Betty Martin, who'd stopped by, for driving Deena there since she didn't know the way from the hospital.

When Deena returned, Robert was at lunch. Jo Ann saw a different woman walk into the room, drop her purse in a chair, lean against the wall beside the window, and look directly at her.

"Give me good news," Jo Ann said, her voice tinged with hope and fear.

At first, Deena said nothing, her arms crossed. She wore a crisp white blouse over a knee length blue skirt and had combed out her hair. Diamond-shaped earrings dangled from her ears. Finally, she broke into a smile. "There is good news. If everything goes as it should, you'll have saved my life. I can never, ever thank you enough."

"Can you have a baby?"

Deena bit her lip. "I think so. I need a surgical procedure they can do on an outpatient basis. Connie suggested doing it right after you have your twins. I can't be out of commission long."

"Don't worry about me. You get this taken care of."

"It's important I help you. I said I would, and I will."

Jo Ann fixed her gaze on Deena. "What did Connie find?"

"I have pelvic inflammation that could have resulted from who knows what. She sees it in women who haven't had abortions."

Jo Ann beckoned Deena with her right hand. "Come here."

Deena walked to the bed. Jo Ann took her hand and said, "I'm so happy for you. Have you told Al?"

"Not yet."

"He doesn't know about any of this?"

Deena shook her head. "What should I tell him? I've been living a lie."

"There are reasons you shouldn't tell him. You could have the procedure, say you're now ready for children, and the odds are he'll never know the difference. Aren't the only people who know about this you, me, and Connie?"

Deena nodded. "You didn't tell Robert?"

"I didn't. That's why I had Betty take you to Connie's office. She had no reason for knowing why you were going there. Robert would have asked. I would've had to make up something or tell him the truth, which I preferred not doing without your permission."

Deena asked, "You think I shouldn't tell Al?"

"I didn't say that. I said you could not tell him if that's what you decide. Whether you should is another matter. Not telling Robert my suspicions about Kendra and Tiffany and what they were planning was a mistake. I was afraid of telling him about the affair."

"What were you so afraid of about that?"

"Shame about how I let the woman manipulate me."

"If you told Robert, you were afraid he'd think, what?"

"That I was weak and stupid for letting such a thing happen."

"What did he say when you finally told him?"

"That he was upset only because I kept my secret. I know now we must trust each other completely."

Deena frowned. "And the lesson for me is?"

"Only you can know that. You understand what your life with Al is like, I don't. All I can say is that when I told Robert, a weight lifted. I no longer carried that burden around by myself."

∞∞∞∞

By four o'clock, Robert and Jo Ann had received the hospital briefings and read the material on C-sections. Robert called two friends from one of his old companies who'd been in the delivery room when their wives gave birth. He also watched four internet videos of C-sections, including two of twins.

"We're ready," he told Jo Ann, as he closed the curtains, shutting out the afternoon sun. "Connie comes by one last time, at six thirty?"

"Yes. Hanna Leslie will be here at five o'clock. Joyce Peters and Jeri Morris are coming a half hour later so they can wish me luck. I told Jeri she didn't need her tennis racket today."

Robert sat down. "Jackie and Linda McFadden are praying for us. Linda said she'd come down whenever you want her to, especially if you need help after you get home."

"Connie says I may be here five days."

"We've got you covered. I'm here, Deena's here, and Betty Martin reminded me that anything we need, we should just call. She said you shouldn't worry about Tiffany and Kendra interfering. She won't let them keep her from helping you."

Jo Ann smiled broadly. "We have great friends, don't we?"

"I told you they'd help us get through this."

He noticed a sad expression overtake her face. "I know what you're thinking," he said. "They'll call when they have something to tell us. You have remarkable daughters. They're different, but they're both remarkable. And they both love you fiercely."

"You really can read me, can't you? I've been thinking about them all day. I wonder what's going on. I thought we'd have heard something by now."

He winced. "They're asking a lot. Jenny may have been right. Neither James nor Tony may do what we want them to."

"I can accept that. If that's what happens, that's what happens. It's a long shot."

"The fat lady hasn't sung yet, to coin a phrase. The game's not over, until it's over, to coin another one."

She laughed. "You're on a roll aren't you?"

"You can't spend as much of your life playing sports and watching sports as I have without picking up a few clichés -- might as well use them when it's semi-appropriate."

When Jo Ann's visitors stopped by that afternoon Robert remained only for brief hellos. He left and called his sons, thanking Al for Deena's presence and telling Bill how Marcia's tender counsel had put him at ease about Jo Ann at the beginning of their relationship. He resisted inquiries about names for their siblings, saying he and Jo Ann had decided, but their lips were sealed until after the birth. He promised he'd call, with names, when the babies arrived.

Robert felt trepidation about calling Sandy, but decided he

should. He'd talked to her only twice since his December trip. She'd been cordial, but non-committal. He hadn't pushed her about changing her stance and called only so he could let her know how important she still was in his life.

As he stepped outside, she answered her phone. He noted a more engaged tone. "Hi, Dad. I'm glad you called. I've wondered what was going on."

"Oh?" He hoped he didn't sound too optimistic.

"It's getting close to time for birth of the twins, isn't it?"

Was it a good sign that she said 'the twins' and not 'your twins?' "That's why I'm calling. Jo Ann's doctors plan on taking them tomorrow."

"A boy and a girl, right Dad?"

"Yeah, how'd you know?"

"I have my sources."

He paused in his pacing. "I'll let you leave it at that, if you want."

"I do. Have you picked out names?"

"We have, but there's an embargo until after the birth. Your brothers pestered me and I wouldn't tell them. Jo Ann and I promised each other."

"Fair enough. You'll call after they're born, okay?"

He wondered about what felt like a change in her attitude, but decided he wouldn't push his luck. The acknowledgement of interest was more than he'd expected. "I will, as soon as they're here. Hey, they're letting me in the delivery room. How neat is that?"

"You couldn't do that with any of us, could you?"

"They wouldn't let fathers anywhere near delivery rooms in those days. I would have been scared to death. I'm not sure I'd have done it, even if they'd told me I could."

As he walked back into the hospital, Robert wondered

about Sandy's source. Bill? Al? Deena? Somebody outside the family? She was close to Terry and Joyce's daughter, Mindy. It didn't matter, Robert thought as he got into the elevator. This conversation had been a lot better than all the others he'd had with Sandy in the last eight months.

∞ ∞ ∞

Jo Ann told Robert and Deena they should go home for the night instead of staying at the hospital as they'd wanted. Just before they left, Deena's phone buzzed.

"Melissa sent a text." Deena reported. "It says 'Progress being made. Regina in Florida. In holding pattern here. Good luck with babies. Forgot to ask names. They are?' That's all she said."

"Florida!" Robert and Jo Ann exclaimed together.

"What's that about?" Robert asked.

"I asked her that," Deena said. A few seconds passed. "She says, 'Will let you know. Names?'"

"There's an embargo on names until after the birth," Robert said.

Deena's fingers flew on the phone keyboard. "I'll tell her that. I wondered that myself."

"To quote someone we know," Jo Ann said, "'that's for us to know and everyone else to find out.'"

Chapter 49

Robert couldn't sleep past 4:30 a.m. Thursday. After dressing in khakis, a blue polo shirt, and running shoes, he headed for the kitchen, expecting he'd find it dark. It wasn't. Deena sat at the table, drinking orange juice, and dressed in a white Ole Miss polo shirt and blue shorts. Rufus held his usual spot under the table.

"Comfort is the order of the day," he said, looking at her running shoes.

"It is," she agreed. "You couldn't sleep either?"

"Of course not?"

"We should take two cars in case I have airport pick up duty."

"Good idea."

Deena nodded her head slowly. "What do you think is going on? That message from Melissa wasn't much. And what's with Florida? Why would Regina go there? I thought her father lived in Baltimore."

A blank expression covered Robert's face and he clasped his hands together. "He does and I'll tell you what I told Jo Ann last night. Guessing about this will drive us nuts, which is not what we need today."

∞∞∞

Robert arrived at the hospital a few minutes before six o'clock.

In Jo Ann's room he found two nurses already there, taking her vital signs.

"She's doing fine," one of them said, a pencil-thin blonde woman with blue eyes and wire famed glasses. "Everything looks good now." Like her colleague, a taller, larger black woman with curly hair, she wore green hospital garb and light-colored running shoes.

Robert leaned over and kissed Jo Ann. She said nothing at first, but squeezed his hand. "I'm here," he told her. "I'm not leaving you until this is done. Are you okay?"

"A little woozy but, overall, I'm fine. These two must want out. They're beating on me."

"Won't be long," the blonde nurse said. "Doctor Cross and Dr. Jones are really good. We love working with them."

"Will you two be in the delivery room?" Robert asked.

"Both of us," the black woman replied. "We'll monitor her vital signs while the doctors do the incision and take out the babies."

"Are there nurses for the babies?" Jo Ann asked.

"Two," the blonde woman said. "We use two nurses for the mother and one for each baby."

"There's a cast of thousands for twins," Robert said. "Two obstetricians, the anesthesiologist, a pediatrician, all the nurses. Each baby gets their own warmer."

"You read all that yesterday?" Jo Ann asked.

"I did. I'm up to date."

At 6:30 a.m., another hospital worker appeared with Robert's scrubs and told him he should get them on if he wanted to

walk along with Jo Ann as the transport team wheeled her to the delivery room. He stepped into the bathroom, pulled on the pants and shirt, and put the booties on over his shoes. He left the mask dangling around his neck and threw the gown over his shoulder.

When he came out and grabbed his camera off a table, Jo Ann said, "I hadn't seen that."

"I bought it day before yesterday. I got a crash course from the guy at the camera store on using it. I should get great pictures. We can see them instantly since its digital."

"You aren't taking a video?"

"I'll use my phone for that," he replied, pulling it out of his pocket.

"Just don't get in the way."

Robert scanned the room and fidgeted with the camera and the phone. "Fathers stay in a narrow space. But I'll be beside you, right around your shoulders and head."

He hung the camera around his neck and put the phone back in his pocket. He took her hand, rubbing each of her fingers. The transport team arrived. "Show time," said one of them, a thirtyish black man with a shaved head. He and a younger looking white man with long hair and a goatee wheeled the bed into the hallway.

After an elevator ride and going through double door after double door, they reached a room with a big open space. Next came a little patient room with light blue walls where the attendants parked Jo Ann and told them to wait. Robert paced until Connie Cross, wearing green scrubs, and the taller nurse walked through the door.

"Good morning, Jo Ann, Robert," Connie said. "This is it. Are you ready?"

"I think so," Jo Ann replied. "I'm ready to get them here."

Cynthia Jones arrived, along with a strapping, big boned

man with brown hair and a deep tan. He wore blue scrubs and held a little package in his hand.

"Jo Ann, Robert," Connie said, "meet Dr. Rex Milford. He doles out the anesthesia. Cynthia and I will perform the surgery and deliver your twins. Once Dr. Raddish, your pediatrician, gets here, we'll start. Any questions?"

Robert looked at Jo Ann and shrugged. She smiled back, but stayed silent. His watch read 7:13 a.m. He wanted this over, but he also hoped he could savor every moment.

∞ ∞ ∞

Doctor Janet Raddish didn't arrive until 7:35 a.m. Robert sensed Jo Ann getting restless, but she seemed relieved when a new transport team wheeled her out of the holding room and into the operating and delivery area. The doctors weren't there yet – Robert assumed they were scrubbing as he'd been told to do when he got there.

Both nurses who'd been in Jo Ann's room took places beside the operating table. Two slim, middle-aged women, one Latino, the other white, sat in chairs in the corner of the room. They must be the pediatric nurses, Robert thought.

Six people, in a perfectly coordinated exercise, aligned Jo Ann's bed and the operating table and shifted her from one to the other. Robert saw her wince once, but she showed no other sign of discomfort.

The nurses directed him to a spot right of her shoulders. A huge blue sheet went up just below her breasts. Even at six-feet, seven-inches tall, Robert couldn't see much. He felt a twinge of irritation at having his view blocked but remembered the old adage about being careful what he wished for.

The nurses began connecting Jo Ann to the medical

equipment. As screens flashed to life and beeping sounds filled the room, Robert soon figured out that one machine monitored her heart rate and another kept track of her blood pressure. Recalling a news story about a woman dying in childbirth when her blood pressure spiraled out of control, Robert vowed he'd keep an eye on that screen.

Jo Ann would remain awake during the births. The anesthetic deadened her middle. She wouldn't feel being cut or the babies being taken out except, they'd been told, for "a little pressure" from time to time. Robert wanted to talk to her, but he vowed he wouldn't interfere with the communication between the medical people.

The doctors arrived and began work. Assured by Dr. Milford that the correct anesthetic had been administered and by the black nurse that Jo Ann's middle had been properly scrubbed, Dr. Jones started an incision.

Robert, of course, couldn't see the result of her work, since the sheet blocked his view. He also couldn't see much of the doctor's face, covered as it was by her surgical mask. As he watched her upper body movements, as much as he'd liked seeing more, Robert gave silent thanks he couldn't see Dr. Jones slicing open Jo Ann's flesh. Moths must feel this way about flames, he thought.

As Cynthia Jones finished the incision, Robert noticed Connie standing to her left. She stayed still, eyes intently following her partner's work. She was waiting, he thought, for a cue that would put her in action. In a moment, he saw and heard it.

"There!" Dr. Jones exclaimed, moving a step to her right.

"I've got her. It's the girl," Connie said, reaching her hands forward and taking the spot where the other doctor stood seconds before. The calm in Connie's voice astounded and reassured Robert.

"She's not small," Dr. Jones said.

Robert, for whatever reason, at that moment looked at the blood pressure monitor. It appeared different than the last time he checked it. The high pitched voice of the blonde nurse told him he'd seen something important. "B. P. is up, 176 over 90, Dr. Cross," she said.

"Thank you," Connie replied.

Robert pursed his lips. He didn't say anything, though he thought about asking what the blood pressure reading meant. He looked down at Jo Ann. She seemed uncomfortable. The smile he'd seen before the cutting began had vanished, replaced by grimaces. She groaned. 'A little pressure?' he wondered, shaking his head.

They'd been told that, given positioning seen on ultrasound, their daughter would arrive first. Suddenly Robert heard crying, wailing really, of a baby very unhappy about being removed from a comfortable place. He'd been focused on the beeps of the medical equipment and the talk between the doctors and nurses. Had he not noticed the crying or did it just start? He wasn't sure, but he heard it now, the first sounds from Jasmine Marie Hart.

Robert tried staying focused on his picture taking. He snapped shots of each member of the medical team and took Jo Ann's picture many times, recording every change in her expression. Periodically, he exchanged the still camera for the video feature on his phone, hanging the still camera around his neck while using the phone. Despite the importance of the pictures, he found himself wanting to watch, to just take in the experience of seeing the children to whom he'd given life coming into the world.

"How's her b. p.?" Dr. Jones asked. Her attention seemed focused on Connie's effort at pulling Jasmine out of Jo Ann's uterus. She was now apparently poised for cutting the umbilical cord that sustained her in the womb.

"It's 180 over 90," said the blonde nurse.

"That's high," Dr. Jones said, shaking her head.

Jo Ann grimaced again. A louder cry filled the room, this one a shriek that provoked what Robert thought was a smile from Dr. Jones behind her mask. Then, Connie was holding their daughter and looking at him. He checked his watch – 8:44 a.m. "Forty-four." His old basketball number.

"There you are, Robert," Connie said. "She's long. She might win that basketball championship you missed. Now, let's get her brother out."

One of the pediatric nurses took Jasmine and put her on a table for cleaning. The wailing continued as Robert used the telephoto lens in taking long shots from across the room. The nurse finished her work and headed off to an adjacent area. The pediatrician followed. Robert whispered in Jo Ann's ear, "She's beautiful. Just like we knew she'd be."

For the first time since they arrived in the delivery room, Jo Ann's emotions overtook her. She shed tears. He found a tissue in his pocket and wiped her face. "I'm so happy," she said.

Connie continued working inside Jo Ann's body, trying to get their son into the light. The nurse monitoring blood pressure spoke up again. "Another spike. She's 192 over 95."

Connie's said only, "Thank you."

Robert heard crying again, this time at a lower volume. For some reason he noticed the antiseptic smell of the room. He tried keeping his eyes focused on the doctors, but he couldn't help looking at the blood pressure monitor. He still had trouble sorting out the numbers, but he didn't miss the nurse's eyes fixed there.

"I have him," Connie said. Her matter-of-fact tone reminded Robert of early space flights and the cryptic exchanges between astronauts and ground controllers. "How's she doing, Cindy?"

"Heart rate is up a little, b.p. steady," replied the blonde nurse.

"I just need one more -- there he is, he's coming out. Stand by."

Robert Stanley Hart, Jr. was no match for his sister in weight, length, or voice. As Connie pulled the boy from his mother, Robert snapped pictures of him. His watch read 9:03 a.m. He leaned down and said "Our son is here.

Jo Ann shed more tears. "What does he look like?"

"Like us, my love. Like us."

As Connie handed Bobby to the second pediatric nurse, the pediatrician arrived back in the room with Jasmine, letting Jo Ann see her. The second nurse performed the cleaning ritual on Bobby, Robert took more pictures, and exhaustion seemed to set in for Jo Ann as soon as they brought him back for her to see. Robert sensed she was done for the day.

The doctors had one more chore before sewing her up – tying Jo Ann's tubes. She told Connie the day before Robert wasn't leaving the operating room without being sure that got done.

∞∞∞

The transport team returned Jo Ann to her room at 2:30 p.m. She spent over four hours in recovery, given how her blood pressure spiked during surgery. She hadn't been back in the room more than an hour before she experienced pain in her incision area. The nurses said much of that resulted from air getting inside her body during the births.

She slept fitfully that afternoon and not much that night. Robert and Deena stayed close, sharing the jobs of comforting Jo Ann, making calls and sending friends and family members texts and e-mails. They gave everyone the same message. "Their names are Jasmine and Robert, Jr., a/k/a Bobby. They're good. No, they're great! Jo Ann is fine, recovering, but fine. We'll let you know when you can see them."

Chapter 50

Fatigue hammered Robert by noon Friday. He asked that Deena watch Jo Ann while he crashed at home. On his way out, near the elevator, Regina appeared. He embraced her. "You're back!" She wore Tuesday's red skirt, but today a blue top, white headband, and the gold necklace completed her outfit.

"I took an Uber from the airport. I'm sorry I didn't stay in touch. It's a long story."

He nodded. "There was a story here, too."

The hugged again, looked at each other, and laughed. "I know," she said. "Deena sent texts, including pictures of Jasmine and Bobby. They're beautiful! They look like you, and like Mom!"

"So, where do we start?"

"Let's talk in the waiting area. You look tired."

"I'm awake now that you're here."

They walked to green leather couches near the nurses's station and sat across from each other.

"I was going to see Mom. How is she?" Regina asked.

"She's okay. She's asleep. She had a rough night after a difficult day yesterday. This wasn't easy."

Regina clutched her chest. "Was she ever in danger?"

"Connie would say no. I heard anxiety in her other doctor's voice when her blood pressure spiked."

Regina threw her shoulders back. "What was being in the

delivery room like?"

"Like nothing else. I took gobs of pictures with my still camera and a video with my phone. Let's get everybody together in a few days and I'll narrate. What happened on your trip?"

"I'll give you the bottom line. Others should tell the details."

Robert's heart beat faster. "What's the bottom line?"

Regina smiled broadly. "Tiffany and Kendra won't be sending Mom any more threating letters."

Robert let out a huge sigh. "Jo Ann says you're the most awesome person in the world, but how did you pull that off?"

"I set things in motion. Other people did the heavy lifting."

Robert relaxed. "I'll walk you to the nursery so you can see your sister and brother, if you'll let me take you to lunch and tell me about the trip."

"Fair enough. Melissa and Dad will be here soon."

That news startled Robert. "Your father is coming here?"

"To see Mom and the twins. He wants to see his children's siblings. Tony will be here tomorrow."

"He will?"

"He will."

∞∞∞

"How do you tell them apart?" Regina asked as she gazed through the nursery window. "The names on their carts just say 'Hart.' I can't tell Jasmine from Bobby."

Robert put his arm around her. "Your sister is bigger. She weighed almost two pounds more – 6lb,14oz to Bobby's 5lb,1oz. Jasmine's two inches longer."

Regina leaned against him, his arm still around her shoulder. "I'm sorry if my jaw keeps dropping. They're awesome." He heard a catch in her throat. "I can't believe I have a new sister and a new brother at this stage of my life." Robert noticed Regina had some of Jo Ann's mannerisms, like scratching beneath her left ear with her right ring finger. "You know what's strange?"

"What?"

"I saw birth pictures of Melissa and me. We were as light as they are. Our dad is black."

"Jo Ann told me black babies are sometimes very light at birth, but get darker as time goes on. I don't know what color they'll be when they grow up, probably a combination of your mother and me."

"I don't care if that's their color. I hope that's what they are as people – a combination of you and Mom."

After five more minutes of staring at Jasmine and Bobby, Robert sensed others nearby. "Melissa!" he said, turning around. "You're back, too!" He reached out and they embraced. The features on the face of the man standing behind her said he was her father. He wore a blue print, long-sleeved shirt, dark slacks, and brown, slip-on loafers.

So, Robert thought, this is James Davis, the man Jo Ann left that led to the loneliness that led her to me. He was handsome. He still had thick, dark, wavy hair. His facial features seemed gentle - brown eyes covered by generous lashes and eyebrows, a smallish nose, and thin lips. His skin tone fell somewhere between brown and light brown. As a former basketball player, Robert was good at estimating height. He pegged James at six-feet, one-inch.

"Dad, this is Robert Hart," Melissa said, as they ended their hug. "He's Mom's boyfriend and the father of my sister and brother, Jasmine and Bobby."

"I'm pleased to meet you, Robert," James said, extending a hand. "Congratulations on the twins. You must be very proud."

"I am, thank you. I'm pleased to meet you," Robert said. He stepped away from the nursery window. "You two should look. Regina and I have gawked enough."

∞ ∞ ∞

In Jo Ann's room, they found her awake and talking with Deena. Greetings, introductions, and congratulations took ten minutes before Jo Ann called a halt. "Before I feed the babies, tell me what happened. Despite constantly wondering and worrying while you were gone, I did everything I could that would keep my mind here. Then, the surgery and last night's pain wore me out. I'm okay now. Let's have it."

Regina said, "I'll tell you, Mom, what I told Robert – the bottom line. You won't get any more threatening letters from Tiffany and Kendra. I doubt you ever hear from them again.

"Because it was Dad who knew what we should do about this and he did the most important thing, which was confront Tiffany, I'll let him tell the story."

Robert moved next to the bed and took Jo Ann's hand. Deena asked if she should leave. Jo Ann and Melissa said, in unison, "Stay!"

James spoke. "When Regina and I had breakfast Wednesday morning, this was news to me. One of the girls — I think Melissa – told me months ago, Jo Ann, you had a new boyfriend, but she didn't mention the pregnancy. That was a shock."

Jo Ann beckoned Robert to lean down to her. She kissed him.

James continued, "She told me about Tiffany and her friend blackmailing you. I said Tiffany is the last person who can blackmail somebody about morality."

Regina stopped him. "What you did, was quote some Bible verse I can't remember the number of."

"John 8:7," James said.

" 'Let he who is without sin, cast the first stone'," Robert said, his mouth dropping open and his brain spinning at the idea of where this might be going.

"That's the one," James said, pointing at Robert, but looking at Jo Ann. "You found a good man. A man who knows the scripture is alright in my book."

He paused. "I told Regina I knew Tiffany had one secret she might not like people in that church knowing. I said I'd reveal it if it took that to keep her from going to Tony about Jo Ann's walk on the wild side."

"What's the secret?" Jo Ann and Robert asked, together.

James smiled. "Should I tell them, Regina? You could tell them."

"You do it. You have, as lawyers say, firsthand knowledge."

"This may be hard for you, Jo Ann, but Tiffany and I had an affair – while you and I were married. She was a regular. We carried on for years before you and I split. She went on trips with me. She was the woman you found out about."

Jo Ann's mouth fell open. "Those were Tiffany's panties I found in your bag?"

"They were."

"This is weird," Robert said.

"The big deal was that Tiffany confided in me another affair she had after she and I stopped sleeping together. Tiffany has a love child from that affair. Her daughter's father is the minister of the church that's so eager to pass judgment on you,

Jo Ann – the Reverend J. C. Patterson!"

Jo Ann looked up at Robert, at Deena sitting by the window, at her daughters leaning on the wall, and, finally, at James standing at the foot of the bed. "Tiffany has a daughter? By the minister of the church that would condemn me? I can't believe it."

"Believe it, Mom," Regina said. "I have a newspaper announcement of the birth and her picture. She's definitely Tiffany's."

Deena spoke up. "So, Regina finds out about this at breakfast on Wednesday. What happened then?"

James answered, "Lawyer that she is, Regina felt we'd need proof beyond my say so. That's why she headed for Florida Wednesday afternoon."

Regina interjected, "I thought Tiffany might deny the story and Kendra would believe her. We needed evidence confirming the kid's existence and her parentage.

"I first went to Jacksonville, to the Florida vital statistics office. I couldn't get the birth certificate, but I found a registry that showed Tiffany Ellen Boyd gave birth to a daughter named Ariel Ann Robinson – Robinson is her sister's married name -- on March 16, 2000, in Ft. Lauderdale, so she's 14 now."

James said, "I had an idea of where she lived. A buddy at a newspaper in Ft. Lauderdale said he could help find her. I gave him the information I had about Tiffany's sister. He and Regina traced the location."

Regina picked up on her trip. "I flew to Ft. Lauderdale Thursday morning and contacted Dad's friend. He'd already found an old newspaper listing of births in March 2000 that included Tiffany and her daughter. Thursday afternoon, we drove out to where we thought she lived and watched her get off the school bus. It wasn't hard to see Tiffany in her face. I got pictures."

Regina looked at Jo Ann. "That's why you have purchase of a camera and telephoto lens on your credit card bill."

James resumed telling the story. "Tiffany disappeared in 1999. She was 37 – 38 years old, had a good job, strong ties to the community and the church, and lots of friends. Nobody would say where she was.

"My reporter's instincts told me that didn't just happen. I kept calling her and she finally answered. She confessed she was in Ft. Lauderdale with her sister. She told me how Patterson seduced her, used her for a year, then threatened her if she wouldn't have an abortion or leave town."

Jo Ann shook her head and shifted in the bed. "Tiffany hates abortion. She wouldn't do that."

"How did the preacher threaten her?" Deena asked.

"He has a goon squad if you can believe that," James replied. "Young toughs under his spell, guys who could at least make Tiffany think they'd rough her up. She feared for her safety.

"I visited Tiffany once. I was covering a game in Miami. She was seven months along and distraught. She'd wanted a child, but not like this. I think the reason Tiffany let herself go, physically, was because of how the pregnancy and giving up her baby affected her."

He turned to Jo Ann. "You didn't know Tiffany when she was attractive. Three years ago she sent me a picture of her with you and two other women. I guess one is Kendra. I was shocked, first, that Tiffany had become friends with my ex-wife and second, she'd let herself go to seed. I barely recognized her."

"Why didn't she keep the baby and raise her herself?" Jo Ann asked, looking puzzled. "I know single women who've done that."

James replied, "Two people made that impossible, Patterson and Tiffany's sister, Tai, who gave her refuge during the pregnancy. Tiffany couldn't stay in Houston because Patterson wanted her gone. He didn't want the child anywhere near his church or people in the church. He was afraid if the daughter was born in or lived in Houston, somebody would find out."

Jo Ann shook her head. "Why didn't Tiffany stay in Florida and raise her daughter there herself?"

"Her sister wanted the daughter as her own or Tiffany could get out of her house. There Tiffany was pregnant, no job, no money. She couldn't go back to Houston and she couldn't stay in Florida unless she played by her sister's rules. She was manipulated by Patterson, whose only interest was in keeping secret the fact he'd knocked her up, and by her childless sister who wanted a kid of her own as the price for giving Tiffany a port in the storm."

"Wouldn't the little girl find out who her mother really was?" Deena asked from near the door.

"They told her her mother died giving birth to her. I assume the sister's name isn't on her birth certificate, but that story would explain why not. Until she figures out what happened, she'll believe her aunt raised her because her mother died. Tiffany hasn't seen her since birth. It's like she gave her up for adoption."

"That was cruel of the sister," Jo Ann said, shaking her head. "I almost feel sorry for Tiffany, but then I think about what she tried to do to Robert and me."

"I don't know Kendra," James said, "but I'd guess she hatched this plot. Tiffany is a follower who went along, never thinking you'd find out about her secret and fight back."

"I wouldn't have, if it weren't for you and our daughters. I could be angry about you cheating with Tiffany but, I didn't know her then and, well, after what you've done for us, I can't be mad at you."

Deena spoke up again. "James, Regina said you confronted

Tiffany. When was that and what happened?"

"Once Regina got the documents and the pictures, we had to put the story in front of Tiffany. I called her and said I'd be in Houston on business and I wanted to say hello. I asked that she have breakfast with me this morning. I flew to Houston last night – another ding on your credit card, Jo Ann"

"My pleasure," Jo Ann said, through a grin.

"I told her my daughters knew she was blackmailing their mother. She denied it at first, but Regina had given me a copy of the letter with Tiffany's initials and the so-called pledge attached. She had no answer for that and fessed up.

"I told her that if she went through with it, everything I knew about her, and Ariel, and Patterson was coming out, with documents and pictures. This was a little bit of a bluff, but I told her, Jo Ann, that you'd sue and force her to get a DNA test, which would show who Ariel's parents are."

"I don't know if we could get that done, legally," Regina said. "But the threat was good strategy."

"She started crying," James said. "After a while she went outside to make a call. She came back and said she'd told Kendra they had to drop it. I got her assurance Kendra wouldn't try doing something on her own because, if she did, my lips weren't sealed.

"She told me I shouldn't worry about Kendra, and I believe that. Tiffany can't have this get out, not with Patterson's name involved. No matter how much Kendra still may want to go on, she can't without Tiffany and Tiffany is done."

"Thank you, James," Jo Ann said. "You're a good man."

Robert looked at Regina. "Wow! You were busy. Melissa, what was going on in Colorado? You must have told Tony something."

"Regina gave me an idea. I spent Wednesday leaning on him about how mean he'd been to Mom about the pregnancy.

Eventually, I played the last card I had. I told him how dangerous the birth might be for Mom. He backed down some. I asked that he call Mom Wednesday night, but he said he needed to pray on it overnight. When he called Thursday morning, they'd taken Mom to ---"

Jo Ann's wide-eyed expression stopped Melissa cold. "I haven't looked at my phone since before they took me in. I have messages from Tony?"

"Many. After Deena told us Thursday afternoon you and the twins were okay, he quit calling and decided he'd come down here. He and Kristin and Shonda are flying in tomorrow."

Deena asked, "What about the idea of James shaming Tony into forgiving Jo Ann for her affair six years ago?"

Melissa responded, "Regina called me Wednesday morning while she and Dad ate breakfast. That idea became Plan B once we found out about Tiffany's love child. I focused on getting Tony to stop condemning Mom about the pregnancy."

"That might have worked," James said. "This was easier."

"Tony doesn't know what Tiffany and Kendra were up to?" Robert asked.

"And won't," Melissa said. "That's between the people in this room."

"Our lips are sealed, right everybody?" Regina asked, scanning the scene of nodding heads.

Denna spoke up again. "Jo Ann, Robert, there's one last thing you should know. Sandy will be here tomorrow."

"She will?" the new parents asked.

"I've been talking to her for months, updating her on the pregnancy, and telling her how much you two mean to each other. I listened to her about the race deal. Her feelings came from not ever knowing anybody black and from her fears about Robert being with anybody at all after Darla died.

"When I called her with names she said she's cool now with you two being together. Jo Ann, she says the first thing she'll do is apologize to you."

"I'll accept her apology," Jo Ann said, "if she first apologizes to Robert."

"She'll do that," Deena said, moving over and squeezing Robert's hand. "She knows she must repair her relationship with her father."

"I bet it was you, Deena, who helped her see that," Jo Ann said.

"I did what I could."

Robert released Deena's hand. "We're done here."

"You and I aren't," Jo Ann said. "I need your help in feeding the babies, which it's almost time for. We have a wedding to plan. It might be a ways away, but there will be one."

Robert looked into her eyes and grasped her hand. "Yes, there will, Ms. Davis. Yes, there will."

The room broke into applause.

Epilogue

Houston Chronicle

May 22, 2016

ENERGY POWERS WED

By Jane Phillips Markel, *Chronicle* Society Editor, and P. C. Lofton, *Chronicle* Business Reporter

The elite of the Houston energy industry gathered Saturday afternoon at First Congregational Church for the marriage of two energy powerhouses, one of them reportedly in line to become the first African-American leader of a publicly traded U.S. oil and gas exploration company.

JAX Oil Company Executive Vice President Jo Ann Davis married her longtime boyfriend, Robert Hart, in a ceremony attended by over 200 people, many of them executives of Houston energy companies.

Industry insiders expect Ms. Davis will succeed David Marks as JAX's Chief Executive Officer when he becomes Chairman of the Board at the end of this year. She would become the first American-born black CEO of a public oil and gas producer in the United States (a Nigerian man heads up another publicly traded Houston-based energy company) and one of only a handful of women ever to lead a U.S. energy company.

Sources inside and outside JAX say Marks, who walked the 54-year old Ms. Davis down the aisle Saturday, has for more than two years been grooming her as his successor. Ms. Davis was the featured speaker at JAX's annual stockholder's meeting in March.

Mr. Hart, 66, is a founding partner and President of HH & J, Inc., a leading independent gas producer with significant holdings in the U.S. and South America. He worked in executive positions at four other large oil and gas companies during a 39-year career before retiring in 2011. Prior to joining the investor group that started HH & J in 2013, he worked as a consultant at JAX, where he met Ms. Davis.

The Reverend Jennifer Lang, pastor of First Congregational, officiated the double ring ceremony in which the wedding party wore business attire. Ms. Davis accentuated her gray suit and cream-colored blouse with gold earrings and off-white pearls. She carried a single red rose.

Margie Scott of Austin, a longtime friend and former JAX colleague, served as Ms. Davis's maid of honor. Her other two attendants were Betty Martin of Houston and Deena Hart of Memphis, the wife of Mr. Hart's son, Al.

Mr. Hart's best man was Jackie McFadden of Little Rock, Arkansas, a basketball teammate at Drury College in Missouri in the 1970s. Terry Peters, a Houston attorney, and Jon Weinstock, a Houston investment professional, served as his other two attendants.

The couple's two-year-old twins, Jasmine and Robert Jr., participated in the wedding ceremony as flower girl and ring bearer, respectively, supervised by Ms. Davis's adult children, Tony Davis of Denver, Melissa Davis of Lawrence, Kansas, *and Regina Davis of Winston-Salem, North Carolina, and Mr. Hart's adult children, sons Bill Hart of Cleveland, Ohio and Al Hart of Memphis, Tennessee and daughter, Sandra Hart of Ocala, Florida.*

After a vacation in Bermuda, the couple will return to their home in the Memorial area of Houston.

Bonus content

see the following pages for bonus content the opening chapters of A Love for the Ages: A Novel by I G Cummings

2024

Available now through Amazon

A Love for the Ages

A Novel

by I. G. Cummings

Chapter 1

September 2016

On a hot, cloudless early September Friday, Minnie Donaldson told nursing goodbye. She gathered her gift bags and offered her Lutheran Memorial Hospital colleagues' thanks for her retirement party. Minnie felt a slight pang of regret as she got off the elevator and walked through the bright, modern lobby, but it was minute. She wasn't sad she wouldn't pass this way again soon, maybe not ever.

Her co-workers presented her with decks of cards, DVDs of movies and television shows, golf-related items, books, board games, and a tea pot, Minnie's affinity for tea being widely known around the hospital. Nobody bought clothes. Some joked that she owned more outfits in more styles than the rest of the nursing staff combined.

With the DVDs, Minnie could catch up on her favorite British television shows like Death in Paradise, Doc Martin, and Lewis, along with a full set of one of the few American shows she'd give the time of day, The West Wing.

She had plans for the evening. At least she thought she did. A little voice told her she shouldn't get her hopes up, but she felt giddy over the prospect of a retirement night dinner with her husband, then maybe, just maybe, a night in bed with him. She'd planned her wardrobe from the skin out.

Brutal sun and the 80 percent Dallas humidity struck Minnie hard as she navigated the revolving doors. Her brown skin glistened even before she reached her car. She'd lived in north Texas or southeast Oklahoma all her life and hated July, August, and September more each year. Would retirement make them bearable? One can only hope, she thought as she started the car.

Turning out of the parking lot, doubts about the evening seeped into her head. At the wheel of her late-model Lexus, Minnie acknowledged her loneliness. She would never have believed she'd feel this way after 31 years of marriage, not with the financial security she had, not with three grown, successful children.

But, here she was, starved for affection, starved for sex, and uncertain of where this life was taking her. Despite some doubts, she'd decided shedding work would help. So, she retired at 54. For an instant, she asked if she'd made a mistake. Would she come crawling back to this place, to the people she'd left, bored out of her mind, unfulfilled, and searching for a port in a storm worse than the one she'd braved the last few years?

Her husband, Bradley, was, pure and simple, preoccupied with his business. Hardly anything mattered except the company's fast-food restaurants and real estate holdings. They brought in more money than she and Bradley would ever spend. What was the point? Making their children and grandchildren rich?

Still, when she turned onto the freeway from the street that adjoined the hospital, she smiled. She previewed the evening she hoped lay ahead. Surely, she could command his attention on the occasion of her retirement. Surely, Bradley would agree they should try rekindling their old magic. Surely, he would hold her hand at dinner, take her home, and ravish her. Surely, this night would turn things around.

At home, Minnie surveyed their too-big house. Two people didn't need six bedrooms or five thousand square feet. Bradley, however, showed no more interest in downsizing than she expected he'd have in her new DVDs, books, and games.

Minnie shook her head as she placed the bags in the corner of the first-floor bedroom she sometimes used as a hideaway. She'd sort things out later. Right now, she could think only of the coming night and the hope it offered for the future. She looked at her watch. It said 5:45 p.m. She should get ready. She expected Bradley home in 45 minutes.

Having stripped, Minnie caught a glimpse of herself in the full-length bedroom mirror. She noted the toned, muscular arms and legs and narrow waist she worked so hard at keeping. Her 34B breasts didn't sag. Gray streaks hadn't invaded her jet black hair. A modest nose and thin lips made up part of a calm, put together look. Not an unattractive picture, she said to herself, not unattractive at all.

In the shower, she let the warm water flow over her. Body wash produced a rich, white lather she worked into her brown skin with a long handled, bristled brush. Rinsing off left her feeling fresh and new. When she stepped out of the shower onto a plush green rug, she grabbed a thick white towel and wrapped herself in its softness. Minnie spent the next few minutes drying every inch of her body. Now came dressing and make up. She'd planned both down to the last detail. A glance at the black dress hanging on the closet door ramped up her hopes for tonight. On the bed, she'd laid out a black lace bra, a matching half-slip, and the evening's treat – seamed nylon stockings and black garter panties.

During Minnie's college years, her older sister, Mildred, taught her about panties with attached garters. They let her wear stockings rather than pantyhose yet avoid a cumbersome garter belt. Bare thigh between the stocking tops and the panties always helped pull Bradley into her clutches. Please, God, let tonight be no different.

Minnie slipped the bra around her middle, fastened the back clasp, then rotated it into place, pulling the straps over her shoulders. She stepped into the panties, rolled each stocking up a leg, and fastened six garters. An instant later, she'd pulled on the slip, worked the dress over her head, then smoothed it down. Another look in the mirror told her that if a 54-year-old woman could radiate sex, she did.

Her watch lay on the table in the dressing area just outside the bedroom. It now read 6:22 p.m. She put it on and sat down at her make-up table. Before she could apply the foundation, her cell phone, lying on the dresser, rang. A sick feeling raced through her middle. She scurried into the bedroom and answered on the fourth ring. "Hello."

The deep voice on the other end boomed, "Hey. It's me. I won't be there for another hour, maybe an hour and a half. What's going on?"

Minnie sat on the bed, stunned. "What's going on? What do you mean, what's going on?"

"Just what I asked. What's new?"

He doesn't remember! She said nothing for a few seconds, grappling for what words could possibly meet the moment.

"You still there, Minnie? What's the problem?"

She grunted. "What's the problem? You must be kidding. What's the damn problem? You can do better than that, Bradley Donaldson."

"Minnie, don't go off on me. What's wrong with you?"

Her voice rose almost to a shriek. "You don't remember what today is, do you? What tonight is?"

Now he yelled at her. "What the hell are you talking about?"

Minnie stopped and took a breath. She wasn't doing this. "If you don't know what's going on, if you don't know what today is, I sure won't tell you. I'm not doing your work for you. Good bye!"

Minnie threw the phone down on the bed. For a second she sat in disbelief, her makeup unfinished. This could not be happening.

Forty-eight hours after Minnie's bitter disappointment that Bradley didn't remember her retirement, she found herself in a little restaurant in suburban Detroit sitting across the table from her longtime lawyer friend, Connie Wilson. After half an hour of crying Friday night, Minnie called Connie and asked what would happen if she showed up on her doorstep for the weekend.

"Oh, at least three rounds of golf and four or five bottles of wine," Connie had replied.

She found a 10:35 p.m. flight to Detroit. Minnie traded the garter panties, seamed stockings, cocktail dress, and stilettos for an everyday cotton hipster, white half-socks, khaki shorts, a green polo, and running shoes.

With the time zone change it was 3:10 a.m. when her head hit a pillow at an airport hotel, but she happily crawled out of bed four hours later for the start of a two-day golf adventure in central and northern Michigan. Frank Withers, a former Air Force pilot, retired heart surgeon, and one-time medical colleague of Connie's wife, Gretchen Downs, made things easy by flying them around in his twin engine plane.

Chapter 2

Minnie arrived home Monday glowing from 54 holes of golf, enthralling company, and the sense of freedom that went with a day of no work. Bradley wasn't there. She found a note asking if she could "spare a few moments" Tuesday morning before he left for the office.

Still seething about Friday, she wrinkled her nose, wondering what he wanted. Minnie slept in the spare bedroom and didn't notice when Bradley arrived home Monday night. She rose at 6:30 a.m. Tuesday, threw on shorts and a t-shirt, and headed for the kitchen.

She saw him at the island in the spacious, remodeled room, pouring coffee. Bradley Donaldson stood six-feet-three inches tall and weighed over 240 pounds. His bulging belly annoyed Minnie. She silently berated him for not exercising and for his fried food habit. The fact he often ate late at night didn't help.

In their brightly lit kitchen, his coal black skin stood out against the stainless steel appliances and cream colored wallpaper. He still had black, closely cropped, tightly curled hair. As she watched him, Minnie remembered when she thought Bradley Donaldson the most graceful, handsome man in the world. Now, he looked tired, awkward, and ill at ease.

He turned to her. "You're up, I see. What're you doing today?"

She clenched her jaw, annoyed by the question. "I'm retired, something you obviously didn't remember Friday. I'm not sure I'm doing anything. Why?"

He ignored the Friday reference. "You could help me with some things at the office."

She bit her tongue and balled up her fists. "I'm not doing that."

"Not doing that? What's that about?"

"I've been working at the hospital all these years. You've gotten along fine without me. I'm retired."

"You could help me get a handle on changes we're making in our inventory control system."

She crossed her arms. "Somebody has done inventory control all this time. Why do you need me now?"

"It's our family business and I – "

"You think you can save money by having the wife provide free labor, right?" Minnie asked him through a tight frown. "No thanks. I earned my retirement and I'm taking it. Hire somebody who can get a handle on inventory control. I have other fish to fry." She walked out.For the next four weeks, Minnie and Bradley said little to each other except "good morning." They never said "good night" because they never retired at the same time and never slept together. Bradley arrived home from work at about 7:45 p.m., gorged himself on burgers and fries, watched Sports Center on ESPN or a Dallas Mavericks basketball game, then fell into bed about 10:30 p.m.

Minnie read or watched recorded episodes of British TV shows. More nights than not, she pulled out her vibrator and gave herself the orgasm that brought sleep.

During the day, she ran and worked out, practiced her golf game, or played rounds by herself or with this or that friend. Before or after golf, she took in movies, sometimes alone, sometimes with others. Plays and concerts occupied her an evening or two each week.

One night in October, as Minnie put on her makeup before heading off for another play, she looked up and saw Bradley in the mirror, standing in the doorway between her dressing area and the bedroom. "Did you want something?" she asked as she powdered her nose.

"Do you have any idea what you're doing? You're aimless."

"That's the point," she said, unscrewing the cap on a bottle of eyeliner and shaking her head. "I'm retired."

"I barely know what you do with yourself."

"I'm sure you don't. You have no interest in anything about me if it doesn't involve making you money."

"Making us money."

She continued applying eyeliner. "You don't need my help. I know the bottom line. I see tax returns. I read financial statements. The company's doing fine."

"It's not just money." Finally, as she turned toward him, she shook her head. "You could've fooled me. That's all you talk about."

"It's the principle of the thing. We should help each other."

She tilted her head and sneered at him. "We're not a struggling young couple, Bradley. We're mature people who set our course a long time ago. You ran the business. I worked as a nurse and raised the kids. Both are over for me. I want a different life."

343

"But, Minnie...."

"Now, if you'll excuse me, I'm out of here. Don't wait up."

She turned back to the mirror, checked her makeup and hair one last time, then closed her compact and dropped it and a tube of lipstick into her purse. She rose from the table, grabbed her bag and keys, and walked past him. Perfunctory pecks on the cheek or ritual brushing of lips ended a while ago.

Before she reached the kitchen, she thought of something she'd seen while driving home that afternoon. She returned to the bedroom, where Bradley stood by the closet door, unbuttoning his shirt. "Didn't I see you heading east on Northwest Highway today? And didn't you have a kid with you?"

He averted her gaze. She noticed his chin quiver. "Wasn't me," he said. "Must have been somebody with a car like mine."

Her eyes widened. "I know your car." "Lots of blue cars in Dallas."

Minnie wrinkled her brow. "Sure looked like your car. And why would you be going that way? That's the opposite direction from the office."

He blew out a series of short breaths, as if trying to control himself. "It wasn't me."

Minnie looked at her watch. She should go. Something wasn't right, but pursuing this seemed pointless. Friends and a supposedly enthralling play beckoned. She turned and walked toward the garage. As Minnie opened the overhead door with the remote on the car visor, her cell phone rang.

"Carol? Carol Robbins?"

"Hello, Minnie. Did I catch you at a bad time?"

"I'm heading for a night of theater with friends."

Minnie started the car's engine, but didn't back out of the garage.

"This won't take but a second. I'm inviting you for a round of golf at my club next week. Are you up for that?"

Minnie blew out a long breath and grinned in the darkness.

"You know my answer. When?"

"I thought Wednesday, the 19th. Let's play early and have lunch there."

Minnie widened her grin. "Sounds like a great treat."

"Your retirement present. See if your friend Cynthia McFadden can play. I'll find somebody else and we'll make it a foursome. If the weather keeps cooling off, we'll get caddies and walk. I know how much you like that."

"Sounds wonderful. I'm seeing Cynthia tonight."

"We'll have a memorable day."

Carol Robbins was about the wealthiest person Minnie knew, yet maybe the fairest. The suggestion she include Cynthia McFadden demonstrated that. Most white women Minnie played golf with would never have asked that she bring a black friend. Private club invitations usually meant a one-black-at-a-time rule. Aside from adoring the Jackson Creek course, Minnie relished the invitation because Carol let her bring her own guest and didn't care if that person was black.

The game Minnie cherished remained mostly white, especially among women her age. Despite a rich history in amateur golf, black female participation in the sport remained flat. Barely a handful of her black women friends played and only a few of those played well enough that she enjoyed playing with them.

Word got around that Minnie Donaldson played golf especially well, so black women's social clubs introducing younger members to the game asked her for advice and instruction. That was well and good, but when Minnie played for personal enjoyment, she had little patience with sprayed and topped drives, flubbed chips, and five tries at getting out of a bunker. Yes, she was a golf snob.

She found Dallas-area tournaments for black social and charity groups frustrating. In individual women's events, she always won her age group, often with a better score than many younger players. Eight years ago she began playing against men in tournaments, from their tees. It wasn't uncommon that she finished ahead of male players 10 years younger. Even if they out-drove her by 30-35 yards, as many did, her deadly short game and deft putting stroke often let her finish among the leaders and once or twice the winner.

Minnie thought for a second about Bradley. What had she expected when she retired? As the years rolled by, the more paranoid he got. He reacted defensively or became confrontational when she tried engaging him about his attitudes. He stopped taking vacations and became hyper-vigilant about everything in the business. It was as if something bad would happen if he wasn't there all the time.

Perhaps memories of the 2008 recession fed his insecurities. In fact, though, Bradley made that downturn work for him. He acquired fast food restaurants in suburban areas and small towns near Dallas at bargain prices, refurbished them, and hired better managers. Now they thrived and turbocharged the company's bottom line.

Minnie wasn't interested in getting involved in the business. She needed time for herself before taking on a divorce fight or working at repairing the marriage. If she gave in now, for a while, Bradley would express his gratitude by doing things she thought he should do anyway – share her activities, show affection, maybe even get interested in sex again. She feared, though, he'd quickly resume his old ways.

As she wheeled her car into the theater parking lot, she pressed her lips together, more determined than ever she'd live her own life. Bradley wasn't getting control over her.

The striking, unflappable Cynthia McFadden waited out front. Little flustered the tall, light-brown skinned woman with curly hair. Tonight, she wore a green pantsuit and a beige blouse revealing a hint of cleavage. The wife of a wealthy black lawyer, she'd retired last year at 60 after a 38-year career in real estate sales. For a time, she'd been the top selling black residential real estate agent in Dallas.

"You're the first one here, Cynthia," Minnie said.

"I have a modest proposal I'll give you before the others arrive."

She tilted her head to the side. "A modest proposal?"

"You and I have a golf invitation at Jackson Creek Country Club next Wednesday." Cynthia's face beamed.

"I'm in!"

"What about checking your calendar?"

"So I can play golf at Jackson Creek, whatever I have I'll reschedule."

"It's a date," Minnie said, noticing the approach of the three other women attending the play with them.

"I'll call you with details."

"Deal," Cynthia said and turned to greet that group.

W ednesday, October 19, 2016, dawned clear and pleasant for mid-October in Dallas. Minnie had slept in the spare bedroom, so she only heard Bradley leave at 5:30 a.m. While retrieving the Dallas Morning News from the driveway, she glimpsed his taillights when he turned the corner on the next block.

Getting to Jackson Creek in morning traffic took 45 minutes. She looked at her watch and targeted six o'clock for departure. After a light breakfast, she brushed her teeth and dressed. Minnie preferred shorts for golf, but she'd play today in a skort that ended mid-thigh. A skort let her comply with Jackson Creek's preference that "ladies" wear skirts, yet eliminate worry about someone gawking at her panties as she lined up putts or retrieved a ball from a cup.

Today, she slipped into a blue skort that included matching shorts beneath the skirt, covered her black sports bra with a bright yellow polo shirt, and topped her head with a red straw hat. The hat wasn't part of her standard golf uniform either. She usually played in a baseball cap or a visor, but the Jackson Creek membership frowned on baseball caps and visors for women, so she wore a narrow-brimmed straw hat.

It wasn't Magnolia Lane at Augusta National, but the tree-lined entrance at Jackson Creek gave the place the feel of old money, haughtiness, and racial exclusion. Minnie had seen and played at her share of such places, in tournaments and as guests of white women friends. She often felt conflicted. Sometimes she experienced tightness in her chest upon arrival. Was she betraying other black people and the cause of equality by indulging herself at such places? When she made it about the golf, her reservations receded.

She'd tried, without success, to get Bradley to join a private club near their home. Though they could afford it, he saw private club memberships as a waste. He could pay the freight at any daily fee course in town. That was enough for him. Minnie, however, liked the idea of a place she could regularly play, practice, eat, work out, and socialize. A private club membership would make life easier for her, but Bradley wouldn't hear of it.

Because she'd played Jackson Creek with Carol four or five times, she had less trouble putting aside her misgivings today. She wondered how Cynthia, a Jackson Creek rookie, would react to the Old South feel of the place. That feel appeared immediately, from the moment a guest entered the grounds. The servants – valets, caddies, maids, maintenance people, food service workers – were mostly black or brown. They wore black and white uniforms that fit a 1950s movie.

Carol said the club began hiring white attendants only five years ago. Some members objected, almost as much as they'd objected when the club relaxed its rules against black, brown, and Jewish members a few years before. That happened because members who held or sought public office and couldn't remain in racially discriminatory clubs threatened, they'd leave and take a big group with them.

This club had one thing Minnie wasn't uneasy about – a spectacular golf course unlike any other in Dallas-Fort Worth. Minnie had seen and played great courses around the world – Pebble Beach and Torey Pines in California, Medina in Chicago, Pumpkin Ridge in Oregon, Bethpage Black in New York, and golf's holy grail, the Old Course at St. Andrews. She'd attended the Masters at Augusta National, a U.S. Open at Wingfoot, and a Women's British Open at Royal Birkdale. Not one had anything on Jackson Creek. Whatever her misgivings about the club's culture, Minnie decided she could deal with the unease in exchange for playing, every once in a while, as good a golf course as existed.

Jackson Creek did what great courses do – reward good shots and penalize bad ones. It included no tricks that massaged the designer's ego. "Tweener" holes that played as long par fours, but were really par fives, didn't muck up the scorecard. Bunkers served a real function, like protecting otherwise easy pin placements. Water hazards and swampy areas created forced carries that generated justifiable tension, not agony. Elevation changes made holes more attractive, not more difficult.

At the pro shop counter, Minnie saw Carol standing behind three men.

347

She always first noticed Carol's raven hair, thin waist, and broad shoulders. Three inches shorter than Minnie, she wore a green skort topped with a white polo and a brown straw hat.

Minnie looked at her watch. It said 6:59 a.m.

"I knew I couldn't beat you here, Carol, though I tried."

Her host turned and they embraced.

"I planned on being here half an hour ago," Carol said when she stepped back. "It's so good to see you. I've been looking forward to this. We should have a great time."

"I know we will. Who's our fourth?"

"Ginger Goodman. She called and said she'd be here by a quarter after seven. And Cynthia?"

"I spoke with her on the way. Said she wasn't far behind me."

"Great."

"Tell me about Ginger." They reached the front of the line at that instant, interrupting the conversation. From behind the counter, a 50-something man wearing a smile on his weather-beaten face and the obligatory white Jackson Creek polo shirt, greeted them.

"Good morning, Mrs. Robbins," he said, brushing aside his sandy hair. "I take it all your group isn't here yet?"

"They're not, David, but I'll tell you who they are so you can check them in now."

"That's fine, Mrs. Robbins. You can meet them outside and go straight to the range. Your caddies will meet you there. Tell me their names and I'll let outside reception know they're coming."

"Cynthia McFadden and Ginger Goodman. They're not together, but both should arrive any moment."

"I know Mrs. Goodman. I believe she's played here with you. Ms. McFadden will be with us for the first time, right?"

"Yes. Thanks for whatever the staff can do that makes her feel welcome."

"My pleasure," he said when he handed her a receipt. Minnie knew not to offer to pay for anything, though she'd make sure she generously tipped her caddie – perhaps $150 to $300 if he performed well. Cynthia had played at enough private clubs that she knew the drill, but Minnie wasn't sure if she understood just how rich the blood was at Jackson Creek. She made a mental note to give Cynthia a heads up before the round ended.

Carol and Minnie walked out the door together and stood at the front of the elegant, ornate clubhouse complete with massive white columns and bronze statues of horses. While waiting for their playing companions,

Carol said, "Our fourth is Ginger Goodman, a charity board colleague. She played at LSU in the late 1980s, so she's a little younger than we are. She's very good, though she doesn't shoot below par very often these days. She doesn't play or practice enough. She'll shoot 75-76 today."

"You've played with Cynthia haven't you?" Minnie asked. "I played with the two of you in a tournament at Bear Creek, that great daily fee course near DFW airport. She was good that day."

Minnie scanned a Jackson Creek scorecard. "She should shoot in the low 80s on this course. You and I are about the same, just like we're the same age. How should we pair up?"

Carol turned and grinned. "You and I are not the same. I never beat you. You won by three strokes the last time we played."

"You have the advantage of local knowledge."

"We played here."

Minnie laughed. "I guess we did."

"I'll play with Cynthia. Otherwise, somebody will say it's a color thing."

"Yeah, Cynthia and I probably shouldn't be partners."

Minnie often told people playing golf beat anything else she could have been doing at a given time except sex. Never had that been more true than that October Wednesday. Visions of the hours between their 7:55 a.m. start and the 12:07 p.m. finish stuck with her for years, blotting out other memories of 10/19/2016.

Above all, there was how she played, a three under par round of 69, fueling the two up win she and Ginger took over Carol and Cynthia. She couldn't forget the way the course, the cloudless sky, low 70s temperatures, less than 20 percent humidity, and calm winds embraced her. There was the easy camaraderie among the four of them – laughter, jokes, gentle putdowns, encouragement.

As she told Cynthia near the end of the round, "I couldn't have written the story of today any better if I were Ernest Hemingway."

Nothing eventful happened on the first two holes except Minnie's 15-foot par-saving putt that halved No.2, leaving the match tied.

Ginger exclaimed in a loud voice, "I won the partner picking contest!"

"You wait," Carol said as they ambled toward No.3.

"I did okay. I've seen Cynthia play."

That hole presented a greater challenge than the first two. "I have more trouble making a birdie on this hole than any other on the course," Carol said.

Minnie looked at her playing companions as she took the tee.

"It's really simple," she said. She took an easy breath and relaxed her shoulders. She went through her pre-shot routine, beginning with a practice swing behind the ball while she looked down the fairway. Once she addressed the ball, there was one more practice swing before she fired away. Her Titlist Pro V1 flew high and long, bending left with an ever-so-slight draw. It landed in the fairway, shy of the deep rough, 240 yards out from the tee.

She turned and looked at her three playing companions again. "See, I told you it was simple."

"You're full of it," Cynthia said through a frown. "This'll be a long day if we have to put up with that the whole round."

Ginger, Cynthia, and Carol placed their shorter drives on the 470 yard, par five hole on the right side of the fairway, leaving more difficult second shots than Minnie's. Her angle took out of play an array of deep bunkers 75 yards from the green. A perfectly struck second shot rolled to within 20 yards of the putting surface.

"Ten years ago, I might have reached this green in two," Minnie lamented as she walked beside Carol and took the club for her next shot from her caddie, a young black man with dark skin, white teeth, and a toothpick in his mouth. He wore the Jackson Creek caddie's uniform – black shorts, white polo shirt, ivory-colored caddie's apron, and green cap.

"Ten years ago that shot might have gone anywhere," Carol replied. "I played with you in those days. You hit it farther, but you are vastly more accurate and more consistent now."

"Lessons and practice have benefits," Minnie said with a sly smile. She deftly swung through her chip shot, sending the ball past the edge of the green. It stopped a foot from the pin.

"Somebody made a birdie on this hole," Ginger said, the putt having been conceded.

"Might be my partner."

"Might be," Minnie said, high-fiving Ginger when they walked off the green.

With Minnie's birdie on No.3, her team took a one up lead in the match. They moved two up on No. 5, a 140-yard par three with a forced carry over a pond.

Minnie carded her second birdie of the day, when she coaxed in an eight-foot downhill putt that died at the hole and barely fell.

The lead grew to three-up on the 361-yard par four No.8 when Ginger rolled in a chip from 15 feet off the green that eliminated the effect of Minnie's only bogey of the day. Cynthia had her moment on No.9, a long par four Minnie thought she'd birdied herself when her sweetly struck approach shot landed six feet from the pin and stopped. But she missed the putt and Cynthia drained a 25-footer for a birdie. That left Robbins-

McFadden only two down at the turn.

"Want anything from the grill?" Carol asked as they walked past the clubhouse toward the back nine. "Drinks? A snack?"

Everyone shook their heads. "I'll pass," Minnie said. "There are lots of things I love about this golf course. Having cold drinking water on every hole sure is one of them."

"I'll second that," Ginger said, gulping from the tumbler she filled on the last hole.

"What's next, Carol?" Cynthia asked. She would hit first because of the birdie she made on No.9.

"Might be my favorite hole on the course. They have the tee up today, meaning it's only 325 yards. It might play like 275. It's downhill, so you can get a good roll and have no more than a sand wedge into the green. There's a creek just right of the green and a deep bunker left, so hit that wedge straight. The green slopes front to back. Ideally, hit the approach shot past the pin so you have a putt back up the hill. It's a short hole, but it's not easy."

"Show us the way, Cynthia," Minnie said, for the moment caring more about her friend's success than the effect of the upcoming shot on the match. She watched as Cynthia hit her best drive of the day, a towering shot that landed on the downslope and didn't stop until it reached the bottom of the hill.

Minnie grinned and ran over to Cynthia, still eyeing where the ball rested, perhaps 50 yards from the green. Minnie held up her hand, inviting a high five.

"I'm not supposed to do that, since you're on the other team, but that was spectacular. Well done, my friend."

Carol, Minnie, and Ginger matched Cynthia's effort.

"I guess it's game on," Carol said as they headed down the fairway.

All of them put their second shots within birdie range, but only Carol made her putt. Ginger, who hit her shot closest, groaned when her five-footer lipped out. That kept Donaldson– Goodman from halving the hole. They sat one up as they moved to No.11.

"I hate this hole," Carol said, pushing her tee into the ground.

"I thought you hated the third hole," Minnie replied. She folded her arms over her chest.

"That's the hole on which I have more trouble making a birdie. I like that hole. I just don't play it well. I dislike this hole."

"It is diabolical," Ginger said. She smoothed out wrinkles in her blue polo shirt. "I made seven the last time I played here."

"You guys are scaring me," Cynthia said, tightly gripping her driver and scanning the 346 yards that lay ahead. "It doesn't look so bad."

"That's because you haven't seen the green," Minnie replied. "Just wait."

As they reached their drives, the reasons for Carol's disdain became obvious. Deep, unforgiving bunkers surrounded the left side and center of a kidney-shaped green that sloped right to left. Those bunkers suggested going right, though an approach shot hit in that direction but short, would leave a dangerous chip the most skilled players could have trouble stopping.

Minnie, who outdrove the others by 15 yards, said with a straight face, "I have a solution for the problems on this hole."

"What?" Carol asked with a smirk, as she took a practice swing.

"Just watch."

With a six iron, Minnie ran through her pre-shot routine. Her free and easy swing propelled her ball over the bunkers and onto the green, where it stopped six feet from the pin. "Just hit the green," she said. "If you hit the green, there's no problem."

Cynthia's smirk would have filled a good-sized room. "I hate you."

"So do I," Carol said, tilting her head away.

"I don't," laughed Ginger. "She's my partner."

They didn't know it at the time, but that shot, which set up Minnie's birdie, her third of the day, turned the match to Donaldson – Goodman for good. That put them two up with seven holes remaining.

Minnie played the next four holes cautiously, helping protect her team's two-hole lead. She didn't fire at difficult pin placements but instead dumped the ball into the middle of greens and two-putted for pars. That worked until No.16 when Carol holed another birdie chip, suddenly leaving the outcome in doubt. The teams halved the next hole when Minnie's long birdie try, carrying a touch too much speed, lipped out.

As they climbed stairs to an elevated tee, Carol said, "You're one up and if we win the next hole, we'd halve the match. The last hole means something."

"It often does when we play," Minnie told her. "You usually save some magic for this one."

"I do love this hole," Minnie acknowledged.

"What do you like about it?" Cynthia asked. She stood beside Minnie as Carol talked with her caddie.

Minnie's face, shielded by her hat, lit up. "If you don't hit a long, straight drive and a solid approach shot, you won't hit the green in regulation. The deep rough on the right in the landing area makes me think about leaving the driver in the bag. If you keep the ball in the fairway, drive it past that bad rough, and hit the approach shot well, there's lots of reward, because the green is flat and you can make a birdie here. I like holes like that. Hit a bad shot, pay for it. Hit a good shot, get rewarded."

Carol held the honor because of her birdie on No.16. She hit a long, low drive down the left side of the fairway, which produced a good chance of reaching the green on her next shot. Cynthia's shorter drive likely left Carol on her own in trying to tie up the match. Minnie drove past Carol, but by only five yards. Ginger pushed her shot into the right rough. The match became a contest between Carol and Minnie.

"Poetic justice, I guess," Carol said.

"Something like that," Minnie replied, as she surveyed her approach shot.

Carol, because she was away, hit first. Her shot with a fairway metal soared high and landed in the middle of the green, but didn't release. It ended up 20 feet from the flag. She had a birdie chance, but only a chance.

Minnie continued looking over her shot. She checked her GPS watch. It said 161 yards to the hole, but only 138 to the front of the green. "How does this pin placement work?" she asked her caddie while rubbing her chin. "That doesn't look like 161 yards."

"Trust the number, Miss Minnie," he said. "Most people, men and women, make that mistake on this hole. That pin is farther back than it looks. That's all of whatever you hit 160 yards."

"I'll take your word for it, my man."

Minnie grabbed a hybrid club from the caddie, lined up the shot, and let it fly. The ball landed past the middle of the green and rolled toward the flag. Initially, neither Minnie nor her caddie could see exactly how close she'd gotten, but both soon knew the shot left her with a putt their opponents would concede. Minnie turned and received the caddie's high five. Out of the corner of her eye, she saw Carol, standing next to Cynthia, shake her head.

"So much for that," they said in unison.

Sitting in the Jackson Creek grill, lunch behind them, Minnie turned to Carol, as a warm feeling spread through her body. "Thank you for one of the best days of my life. I can't imagine a better time."

"You're so welcome. And thanks for bringing Cynthia."

Cynthia flashed a huge smile. "Thank you. This was wonderful. And thanks for being a great partner. Didn't you shoot even par – 72?"

"I did. Thank you. Your 83 is very respectable on this course for someone who'd never played it before." She stopped. "Minnie and I often shop a little after our round."

"We sure do," Minnie said, nodding and remembering the backpack she'd brought.

"Like to join us?" Carol asked. "I can't," Cynthia said as she rose from the table. "Tomorrow is our 33rd wedding anniversary. My husband's taking me to dinner tonight because he has a business trip tomorrow. I should get home and get pretty, at least as pretty as I can these days."

Carol turned to Ginger. "How about you?"

"I'll pass. I have a family party tonight celebrating my son's promotion."

"You told me about that. Please congratulate Donnie for me. Thanks again for playing. What'd you end up with?"

"I shot 76, which for me these days is good. I'm pleased."

She looked at Minnie. "Thanks to my partner, I have a great memory of winning our match, two up."

As Ginger and Cynthia left, Carol turned to Minnie.

"Looks like it's just us." Minnie followed Carol home and, after a hot shower in her guest bathroom, changed clothes. They spent the afternoon cruising stores and rehashing the round.

As day became night, Carol suggested dinner at a jazz club near their shopping haunts. Drinks, food, and live music led inevitably to Carol's gentle, but persistent probing about Minnie's marital situation.

"Things aren't better than the last time we talked," Minnie said between sips of white wine. "Actually, they're worse. Since I'm retired, Bradley wants my help in his office."

"What's that about?"

With a shake of her head, Minnie responded, "Controlling me. He's afraid I'll do what I want, not what he wants."

"Will you just put up with it?"

Minnie told Carol of her belief that after a year of relaxing and indulging herself she could better decide between ditching Bradley and working at repairing the marriage.

"I'm just not up for a fight right now," she said with a sigh. They took in one more set by the band and called it a night.

Standing by their cars, they embraced.

Minnie teared up for a nanosecond, then said, "Thank you, Carol. Today meant so much to me."

"After tonight, I understand why."

Getting home took Minnie 40 minutes. She pulled into the garage and closed the overhead door with the remote. Her dashboard clock read 9:53 p.m. In the kitchen, she retrieved a glass of water from the refrigerator ice maker, then walked to the master bedroom.

Bradley wasn't there. The bed, made up by the housekeeper during the day, appeared untouched. He's in his game room, she thought, and briefly considered just getting ready for bed herself and not worrying about him. No, that's needlessly rude, she decided. I should say hello.

Nearing the game room, Minnie heard the ESPN Sports Center theme music coming from the television set inside. She opened the door on a room lighted only by the glow of the TV set. She looked toward the recliner where she expected she'd see her husband. He wasn't there.

She flipped a light switch. Her eyes adjusted and dropped to the floor.

There, Minnie Donaldson saw something she knew well. Death

—

Available now on Amazon Books and wherever good books are sold.

Acknowledgement

As with all my work, a lot of people have helped with Weeks in May over a long period of time. I begin, as always, with my readers:

* Steve Carow
* Vicki Carow
* Mary Donohoe
* Phil Donohoe
* Susan Hammond
* Steve Harr
* Hallie Moore
* Mary Jo O'Neal
* Hope Walker

Each offered something that improved the end product.
The remaining shortcomings fall on me.

Others who deserve recognition for big and small contributions:

* Kelly Hooper and Raven Cole, manuscript cleanup.
* Karyl Paige, proofreader extraordinaire.
* Karen Soane, assisted to publish book into digital and paperback format using Kindle Direct Publishing.
* Shaun Wiley, my daughter, who has forgotten more about this enterprise than I'll ever know and shared some of what she knows with me.

About The Author

I G Cummings

Author I G Cummings is based in Houston, Texas and besides writing, enjoys reading, sports, and learning about the world.

I G Cummings writes novels and short stories about relationships. These works involve people who look to their inner feelings and put aside superficial differences in the quest for love.

Other books by J G Cummings

A Love for the Ages: A Novel

Minnie Donaldson and John Dawson couldn't be right for each other, could they? She's middle–aged and black. He's young and white. A Love for the Ages tells the story of how Minnie found with John what she thought she'd lost forever – the joy of giving and receiving love, companionship, and genuine affection. Before a serious accident brought them together, Minnie had endured a decaying marriage, death of a spouse, and discovery of her late husband's plan for betraying her and two of their children. Minnie and John's story shows what's possible when people open their hearts, trust their inner feelings, and ignore what's on the outside.

That's Different: A Novel

Jennifer and Gavin McCain, after thirty plus years of marriage, divorced for many of the same reasons hundreds of thousands of other Americans divorce each year -- neglect, infidelity, out growing each other, etc. Both Jennifer and Gavin wound up with new, much younger partners. While the age gap between Gavin and his new girlfriend and Jennifer and her new beau may have been identical, the reaction of the three adult McCain children wasn't. That's Different is about what can happen in a family when one parent's new relationship gets viewed one way and the other parent's new relationship receives an entirely different look. Age gap relationships happen in America. Sometimes the man is older, the woman younger. Sometimes the woman is older, the man younger. As That's Different shows, which is which can be a big deal, a very big deal.

Find on Amazon website

Check out these other Authors

Bianca Sloane

The author of KILLING ME SOFTLY (previously published as Live and Let Die), chosen as "Thriller of the Month" by e-Thriller.com and a 2013 Top Read by OOSA Book Club, SWEET LITTLE LIES, EVERY BREATH YOU TAKE and the forthcoming, LIVE TO TELL. When she's not writing, she can be found reading, traveling, watching movies, cooking or answering questionnaires. She is a member of Sisters in Crime and Crime Writers of Color. When she's not writing, she's watching Bravo TV, Investigation Discovery, reading or cooking. Sloane resides in Chicago.
www.biancasloane.com

Rusty Rhoad

During the last decade of a 32-year career as a chemical engineer, Rusty began writing novels over lunch. And now safely out of the grip of the complexity of the military-industrial rat race, he continues to write. "I turned to the legend of King Arthur, a lifelong obsession of mine. "Why Arthur? I'm not sure I can explain if you don't already have at least a touch of the fever. A bastard fated to become king by both the tutelage and the meddling of a mage/druid, an honest man doomed by a totally unconscious act of incest. Betrayed by his wife and best friend for reasons we can speculate on but can't articulate for certain. And yet despite it all, Arthur sets the standard of heroism and dignity." All of Rhoad's novels except for his latest, *Kaffka, the Holy Grail, and a Woman Who Reads: The Quests of Sir Kay,* are set in contemporary times.
www.rustyrhoad.com

Susan Hammond

None of my earlier writing prepared me for the rush of telling a story—the one that's in my head and wants to be told. My fondest wish is that readers will laugh and cry and sigh, maybe even think "what if..." My writing "career" began in third grade when I wrote a story about a pioneer family and decided I'd grow up to be a novelist. The journey to those bright lights took off (Not!) when I was tapped to write the junior high gossip column for our local newspaper. Over the years, I wrote instructional materials for accountants, exploration geophysicists, and airline pilots. One gig included writing a newsletter on raising dairy goats. (Somebody had to write it!) Returning to my small town newspaper roots, I wrote a humor column on living with teenagers. And believe me, there was never a shortage of material.
www.susanhammondwrites.com

Reviews of Weeks in May

An Uncommon Love - Reviewed in the United States on March 21, 2024
Review Verified Purchase (Amazon)

Reviewed by: CLorraine

I G Cummings gives us a gentle love story that shows that love knows no barriers. Minnie has lived a full life and is retiring as the story starts. She is hoping that in retirement she will be able to get closer to her husband. They have been married for a number of years with grown children....their marriage is splintered in all aspects. Minnie does not know the extent of this alienation until her husband passes unexpectedly. The rest of the story focuses on the aftermath of his passing and her subsequent encounter with a younger love interest. John and Minnie meet when he is injured in an accident. They become friends and gradually find that they have so much more in common. But how will the world, their friends and families view their marked differences? Their love story was told in a very uncommon way and the author's leisurely tone was enjoyable. However, I would have appreciated a bit more closure in the ending.

Deft handling of age and race obstacles Reviewed in the United States on March 12, 2024 Review Verified Purchase (Amazon)

Reviewed by: LT-STAHLER

A rock solid, well-written romance between an older black woman and a young white lawyer. Characters are well-crafted, likeable, believable. The tension caused by the difference in their ages (which, of course would be no problem if it were an older man and a younger woman) and race is a powerful driver for the arc of the novel. Found myself picking it up at every opportunity and finished in a couple of days. Ready for the next one.